DIRTY MIRROR

JUSTICE KEEPERS SAGA BOOK VI

R. S. PENNEY

Published 2021 by Next Chapter

Cover art by Cover Mint

Edited by Jourdan Vian and Gregg Chambers

Back cover texture by David M. Schrader, used under license
from Shutterstock.com

PROLOGUE

(Four months ago)

The city was a mess.

Ever since those cybernetic monstrosities started showing up, everything had gone straight to hell. People ran to the furthest corners of Long Island; creatures out of some B-movie roamed the streets, and the cops were too busy dealing with the sci-fi freak show to worry about small-time dealers like Nate. That meant the business was good!

Most of Queens had been evacuated a few days ago, but the folks who had stayed behind would still need their fix. Lots of opportunities for an enterprising young man to make a quick buck, assuming you had clients who actually paid what they owed you.

He threw Sheila up against the wall.

She slammed into the house's gray aluminum siding with a groan, thin ringlets of platinum blonde hair falling over her face. "Stop, stop!" she protested, raising both hands defensively. "I don't have it."

Nate clicked his tongue.

A tall, skinny string-bean of a man in beige pants and a denim vest with frayed arm holes, he pointed the knife at Sheila. “Not the answer I was looking for,” he said. “You've been stiffing me for months.”

His pasty-white, hollow-cheeked face was marked by acne, and his brown hair was kept short in a mushroom cut. “Last month at Jimmy's party,” he said. “Two weeks ago at McGinty's. Over and over, it's the same thing with you.”

Sheila closed her eyes, head hanging. A lock of white hair fell over one eye. “Okay, okay,” she said. “Look, I can get you eighty.”

“Which doesn't mean shit when you bought two hundred bucks worth of coke.” He pressed the knife-blade to her cheek, and she winced at the touch of steel. “Did you think I was gonna run just because this city's burning?”

Gunfire in the distance punctuated his question.

He squeezed Sheila's face with his free hand, thumb and fingers digging into her cheeks. “Don't listen to that,” he said, turning her head toward the noise. “You focus on me. I want my god damn money, Sheila.”

“I don't have it.”

“Well, that's a shame.”

He dug the knife into Sheila's cheek and cut a thin line from the corner of her mouth to her ear. She squealed at the pain, thrashing against the wall. Ordinarily, that would have made him try to silence her, but there was no one around to care. Unless you counted those weird silver-eyed freaks. Still, those guys seemed more eager to kill cops than men like Nate.

“Pretty little whore like you,” Nate said. “Stupid, go-nowhere high school dropout. Really, your only shot at some kind of future is to open your legs for the right guy. Looks are your bread and butter, honey. And I'm gonna take 'em from you.”

He bared his teeth like a snarling animal, shaking his head in disgust. "This time, it's just one little cut," he said. "Next time, it's a bigger one. Then I start breaking fingers. *Then* I start gouging eyes."

"Okay! Okay!"

Nate grabbed a fistful of her hair and flung her to the ground. She landed sprawled out on her side in the space between two houses, sobbing and shaking with every breath. "Get me my fucking money," he said. "I don't wanna-"

Turning his back on her, Nate marched out of the alley with the knife clutched in one hand, growling under his breath. "Stupid bitch," he whispered. "When are people gonna learn that nothing's free."

He'd made it to the foot of the driveway when something caught his attention. Out of the corner of his eye, he saw something so bizarre that he had to pause and look just to make sure he wasn't going crazy.

At the end of this quiet suburban street was an intersection, and on the far side of that intersection, a ten-story apartment building rose up to tower over the houses there. His eyes weren't perfect, but they didn't lie.

A woman and a man locked in a tight grapple fell off the roof of that building and tumbled toward the street below. The woman pulled herself free, and then suddenly, she was yanked back toward the rooftop like she was caught on some invisible fishing line.

The man, however, dropped like a stone to land in the street, shattering his legs on impact and screaming like a banshee. He was just sitting there in the middle of the road, crying. Damn it, the guy should have been dead.

Opportunities, opportunities.

Creeping closer with the knife in hand, Nate smiled down at himself. "Idiot," he said, shaking his head. "You fight one of those space cops, and you should expect to get your ass dumped off a building."

Of course, Keepers had a rep for not wanting to kill, but it was war out there. He'd always been the kind of guy who knew when to make exceptions. Why should the Justice Keepers be any different?

He made it to the intersection, pausing to watch the wounded man. The guy didn't seem to be aware of Nate's presence. He was too focused on his broken legs and probably the internal bleeding.

Nate crouched behind a mailbox, taking stock of the situation. Just when he thought the guy was weak enough to make easy pickings, something caught his attention. So he waited. Smart men knew when to wait.

The woman came around the side of the building, hobbling as if she had just run one of those five-mile marathons. She was tall, kind of hot in that brown trench coat, but her hair was too short. It wasn't so different from his own haircut: boyishly short and parted in the middle. He hated short hair on girls.

The woman stepped into the street, doubled over and gasping for breath. "You just don't know when to die, do you?" she asked, shaking her head. "Some people just stick around long past the point when you want them to leave."

The wounded man looked up at her, blinking. "I thought I was done for," he said, wheezing with laughter. "Leave it to a Keeper to save her worst enemy."

Keepers were idiots.

The woman pulled her pistol.

"What are you doing?"

She thrust her arm out and pointed the gun right at the wounded man's forehead, cocking her head to one side. "Sorry, friend," she said. "There are already too many evil pieces of shit like you in the world."

Nate felt his eyebrows rise.

Maybe Keepers *weren't* so dumb.

"But you can't!"

The gun buzzed as it went off, and the man's head jerked backward. Blood and gore splattered on the road before he fell backward to stare up at the sky with dead eyes.

The woman stood over him for a very long moment, maybe trying to decide what she would do with his body. Nate could see the calculation in her eyes. She was thinking about the pros and cons.

The woman turned around, holstering her pistol and walking away.

He waited a good two minutes for her to get out of sight; Keepers were stupid, but not so stupid that they would ignore him while he went fishing through a dead man's pockets for a wallet or some stray cash.

When she was gone, Nate ran out into the street and dropped to his knees next to the corpse. He started pawing over the guy's pants, looking for anything that might be of value. Some people would be squeamish at the thought of doing that. Some people were too stupid to live.

He took the dead man's hand, lifting it so he could get a look at the guy's vest, and when he did, something that felt like an electric jolt went through his body. Nate wanted to let go, but he couldn't.

The corpse's skin began to glow, white light exploding from every pore. Was this guy some kind of angel? Nate had never believed in such things, but nothing else could glow like that.

The halo transferred, spreading over Nate's hand and then up his arm, a creeping wave of light that made his skin tingle. It flowed over his face and made him throw his head back, screaming as something sank into his flesh.

Suddenly, it felt as though he had run one of those five-k marathons himself. His every muscle felt watery, and he wanted to curl up in a ball and sleep. First, he had to get out of the street.

Crawling on all fours, he made it to the sidewalk and then he collapsed there. It was only then that Nate realized he wasn't alone. Something else was with him.

And it was powerful.

(Three Months Ago)

Admiral Telixa Ethran stepped onto the ship's bridge.

In her fine gray uniform with red epaulettes on the shoulders, she was very imposing despite being barely five feet tall. Her thin, dark-skinned face was framed by a short bob of black hair. "Report."

The bridge was a simple room with a large, empty chair in the middle and people at computer stations along the wall. The screen along the front wall displayed a large, bluish star that seemed to pulse, sending waves of light into the blackness of space.

Lieutenant Janis – a tall man in a gray uniform who stood with his back turned at one of the starboard-side stations – stiffened at the sound of her voice. "The Class 2 Gate is active and broadcasting."

Crossing her arms with a grunt, Telixa stepped forward to stand behind her chair. Her mouth twisted as she studied the screen. "Let's see it," she said. "You do know the old saying, don't you?"

Janis twisted partway around to look over his shoulder. He was handsome enough, with pale skin and short brown hair. "Ma'am?" he asked, raising an eyebrow. "Just what old saying would that be?"

Telixa smiled, bowing her head to stare down at herself. "When the Overseers give you a present," she said, tapping the back of the Captain's Chair. "Make damn sure that it isn't going to explode."

"I don't believe that *is* an old saying, ma'am."

"I'm sure I heard it somewhere."

In truth, she had made it up right there on the spot, but it was good to be the sort of captain who was always referencing old sayings that supposedly came from the military commanders of past generations. That fact was no less true now that she was an admiral. "Put the Gate on the screen, Mr. Janis," she said. "Let's get a good look at the thing."

The image on the screen shifted, zooming in to give a close-up of something that looked very much like a diamond of sleek, shiny metal with blue sunlight glinting off its surface. Just looking at the damn thing made her feel a sense of awe. "The Gate is over five kilometers long," Janis said.

Pressing her lips into a tight frown, Telixa narrowed her eyes. "And we're sure that it can send a ship across the galaxy?" she asked in a flat tone that consistently made her subordinates hop. "We've tested it?"

Janis spun to face her, standing by his station with his hands clasped in front of himself. "We sent a probe through this morning," he said. "The probe's telemetry said it reached a system designated on our charts as S475AD. What little we know of that side of the galaxy has the system in a neutral area between Leyrian and Antauran space."

Telixa stepped around her chair.

Dropping into it with a sigh, she crossed one leg over the other and gripped the armrests for all she was worth. "Well then," she murmured. "It seems that the Overseers have granted us the ability to travel across the galaxy."

Squeezing her eyes shut, Telixa sucked in a deep breath. "Signal the fleet captains immediately," she said, leaning back in her chair. "I want twenty ships stationed in this system within ten days. The Gate is to be guarded at all times against possible Leyrian incursions."

"Yes, ma'am."

That was only the beginning, of course. In too many wars, she who struck first also struck last, and war was all too likely now that the Leyrians had the ability to encroach on Ragnosian territory. A defensive posture was inadequate. If her people wanted to prevent any violations of their borders, it would be necessary to establish a foothold on the far side of the galaxy, to keep the other major powers in this galaxy off balance.

"Open a channel to the Assembly of Generals," Telixa said. "And put it through to my office. We have much to discuss."

(Present Day)

Sunlight through stained-glass windows broke into streams of bright colours that fell upon wooden pews on either side of an aisle that ran through the church. Those pews were filled with people, young and old, who sat with their heads down.

At the altar, an older man in a simple pair of gray pants and a blue shirt with a high collar that almost touched his chin looked out at his flock. He was copper-skinned with a thick gray beard and a receding hairline. "Thus do I walk in the light of the Companion," he said. "For he walks at my side in all things..."

Brinton listened to the sermon.

A younger man in black pants and a matching shirt, he stood at the side of the dais with his arms folded. He was tall and slim, and he wore his blonde hair cut short, as was proper for an acolyte of the faith. Watching the reverent speak always left him feeling a little...hollow inside. The man was just so pompous.

Reverend Vanorel spread his arms wide as if he intended to

soar over the crowd as proof of some divine miracle. "The Companion is with me in all things," he said. "And thus I do not fear."

Brinton shut his eyes tight, sucking in a deep breath. *Yes, Reverend, you've made your point,* he thought, shaking his head. *Honestly, if these sermons of yours went on any longer, half the congregation would fall asleep.*

It was an unholy thought, one unworthy of an acolyte, but he didn't chastise himself for having it. He had given up trying to purge his mind of impure thoughts after the first month of enduring this...nonsense. The Companion loved all his children and wished to be a force for good in their lives. He was utterly uninterested in the endless praise that so many devotees of the faith insisted on giving.

"Our service today is ended," the Reverend said. "Go forth in the light of the Holy Companion and be well."

Finally...

The congregation rose from their pews and immediately began talking quietly with one another. In seconds, the church was filled with the soft buzz of several dozen voices speaking at a low volume.

Brinton started through the crowd.

"Where are you going?"

He grimaced at the sound of Reverend Vanorel's shrill voice, pressing a palm to his forehead. "I wish to greet members of the congregation," he explained. "There are some I did not see before the start of the service."

When he turned, Haran Vanorel stood at the altar with his hands clasped behind himself, his chest puffed up as if he intended to begin yet another sermon. "Your duty is to begin cleaning up."

A blush singed Brinton's cheeks, and he bowed his head to the other man. "A duty I cannot perform to completion until the church is empty," he replied. "What harm is there in letting me say my hellos."

He hoped the other man didn't notice his apprehension. It wouldn't do to allow the good reverend to begin suspecting that Brinton might have ulterior motives.

Vanorel's face twisted so fiercely you might have thought he'd been slapped. "Your attitude is unbecoming, Brinton," he said in clipped tones. "We will discuss this again in my office, after you have completed your duties."

"Yes, Reverend..."

Brinton hurried along.

With a sigh, he retrieved one of several tablets from a small wooden table at the side of the room and powered it up to access the home menu. Then, quietly, when no one was watching, he ran an app that he himself had coded several days ago and loaded onto each of these devices. It ran in the background, displaying no visible effect.

Then he brought up a page that listed information on the next church retreat along with pictures of a forest of pine trees under beautiful snow-capped mountains. Time to go to work.

The man he was looking for was tall with a bit of a belly, dark of skin and gray of hair and dressed in a fine suit jacket over a light sweater. Miles Tarso was smiling and nodding as he spoke to an older woman in a blue dress. After patting him on the arm, the lady turned and made her way out of the room.

Brinton approached cautiously.

Mr. Tarso turned his head and blinked when he noticed him. "Acolyte Seral!" he said in pleasant tones. "How are you?"

Shutting his eyes, Brinton nodded to the man. "Quite well, Mr. Tarso," he replied, moving closer. "I wanted to ask about your work on the vertical farm system. I couldn't help but overhear your discussions in the lobby earlier."

Mr. Tarso smiled politely. "Yes, well, it *is* quite a bit of work," he replied. "I'm overseeing the installation of new upgrades to the automated drones, upgrades that should improve efficiency."

"Really? That must be challenging."

"More time consuming than anything else."

"Still, I imagine there would be some stress."

The other man nodded slowly. "A bit." His voice was gruffer now, as if the question brought to mind things he would rather not think about. "The City Planning Commission is always looking over my shoulder."

"Yes, I thought I heard you say as much." This would require some delicacy, but if Brinton managed his performance, he would look like yet another devoted follower of the faith trying to console a wayward member of his flock. "The church is planning a retreat next month to the Adalean Mountains. An opportunity for reflection and meditation and restoration of the soul."

"Ha ha," Tarso said. "I'm afraid I'm much too busy."

"Yes, I imagined as much," Brinton said, casually offering the tablet despite the other man's objections. "However, Reverend Vanorel would be most distressed if I didn't at least persuade you to look over the details."

Miles Tarso accepted the tablet with a soft sigh of frustration and began swiping his finger across the screen, scrolling through photos of the church's mountain retreat. Little did he know that as he shuffled through those old pictures, the tablet's biometric scanner was recording his fingerprints thanks to the app Brinton had coded.

Hacking was not about writing a piece of code that would unravel encryption so dense it would require more time than the heat death of the universe to crack; no, hacking was about exploiting the weak point in every security system. The human factor.

Mr. Tarso grimaced, then shook his head. "No, I'm sorry," he said, thrusting the tablet at Brinton. "I'm not interested."

Grinning with a quiet chuckle, Brinton bowed his head to the other man. “Much as I expected,” he said, taking the tablet. “But I appreciate your indulgence nonetheless. The reverend does care for his flock.”

“Thank you, Acolyte,” Tarso said, turning away.

When he was gone, Brinton brought up the app he had programmed, a dark purple background where bright orange fingerprints appeared on the screen. Excellent. Now, he would have access to the vertical farm's security systems.

PART I

1

Sunlight through an open window illuminated a bedroom with light blue walls and a dome-like ceiling. Her furniture was made of a white synthetic polymer that she could not pronounce, as was the frame around her mirror. You couldn't exactly bring an entire bedroom set across the galaxy.

Melissa was curled up on her side with her back to the window, the covers clutched to her chest. "Mmmph..." she groaned, blinking sleep out of her eyes. "Already? I was so sure morning was still a few hours away."

She sat up.

Pressing the heels of her hands to her eyes, she smoothed long dark hair away from her face. Normally, she was quite happy to go to bed early and wake up feeling chipper, but the paper she had been writing had kept her up all damn night.

Swinging her legs over the side of the bed, Melissa stood up and stretched her arms over her head. "Lovely," she mumbled, making her way over to the mirror. "Now I get to feel like I'm half asleep all day."

Her reflection was haggard, with dark circles under her eyes and black hair that was now tangled and messy. They had told her that Keeper training would be difficult, but she had never imagined that she would feel tired all the time.

Well...Maybe not *all* the time. Carrying a Nassai did have its advantages, and her symbiont was slowly but surely coming to grips with the passing of its former host. She hissed as memories of Jena flooded into her mind.

Melissa closed her eyes, tears leaking from them to run over her cheeks. "We are going to be just fine," she whispered, leaning over the dresser. "Day by day, it gets a little easier, doesn't it, Nala?"

The symbiont reacted with disgust to a name it really didn't want. During the few conversations they had shared, Melissa had learned that her Nassai was open to the idea of having a name, but she seemed to reject everything Melissa came up with. It was hard not to think of the symbiont as female despite the fact that Nassai had no gender.

Outside her bedroom door, she found a small hallway bordered by a white railing that overlooked the first floor; she could already hear her father down in the kitchen. He had taken to making breakfast every morning.

Claire's bedroom door swung open and the girl stepped out in pajama bottoms and a pink t-shirt. Before anyone could say a word, she charged through the narrow corridor for the bathroom and crashed into Melissa's stomach.

Melissa winced, grunting from the impact. "Really?" she asked, shaking her head. "You can't wait *ten* minutes for me to shower and get out the door? God help me, Claire! You're gonna drive me nuts."

Her younger sister stood in the narrow hallway with her arms folded, craning her neck to stare into Melissa's eyes. "I have school," she said in a flat voice. "*Some* of us do have to follow a schedule."

As if Melissa didn't! For some reason, Claire didn't seem to understand that having classes at different times each day of the week did not mean that Melissa's schedule just magically adapted to suit her needs. Or maybe it was because her sister was ten now and nearing that age when kids became whiny.

Claire pushed past her, into the bathroom.

"What's going on up there?" Harry shouted.

Gripping the railing with both hands, Melissa leaned over to answer her father. "Oh, nothing!" she called out. "Your youngest daughter just insists on having the manners of a drunken sailor on shore leave!"

The stairs led down to an open area where a white couch sat in the light that came in through the living room window. Blue walls were decorated with pictures of gorgeous landscapes, and the glass coffee table supported a vase of yellow tulips.

She went to the back of the house where her father was cooking breakfast.

The white-tiled kitchen was much larger than the one they'd had in their old house. White cupboards made a ring around a room with an oven and a fridge that looked both different from what she would have expected and also similar enough that she had been able to identify them at first glance.

Melissa sat down at the table and watched her father at the stove. Harry stood with his back turned, fussing with something that was probably a pot of oat meal. "So, did you finish that paper?"

Melissa yawned so hard her face hurt, then covered her gaping mouth with her fist. "Yeah," she mumbled. "A couple hours passed midnight. Who would have thought that the philosophy of law would be so complex?"

Her father chuckled.

Aside from a few cosmetic differences, it looked like just another ordinary kitchen in an ordinary home. Not the set of a science fiction movie. Melissa hadn't known exactly what to picture on the long flight to Leyria, but she had imagined something a lot like the Jetsons. Of course, there was one thing that stood out.

A six-foot tall robot made of a flexible gray plastic stood silently next to the pantry. Its face had human features with a small bump for a nose and a speaker for a mouth. And two long eyes.

Those eyes began to glow with deep blue light as soon as it recognized the sound of her voice. "Good morning, Melissa," the robot said in cheerful tones. "Would you like me to prepare you a light breakfast?"

She looked to her father at the stove.

Harry stiffened at the sound of the robot's voice but carried on with what he was doing, refusing to so much as glance in her direction. "No, thank you, Michael," Melissa said. "I think Dad has that covered."

"Michael..." The robot seemed to be pondering its new name. "Shall I respond to that from now on?"

"Yes," Melissa said.

"No!" Harry insisted.

Setting her elbow on the table's surface, Melissa rested her chin in the palm of her hand. "It's just a robot," she said, her eyebrows rising. "It's not going to mean the end of life as we know it."

Her father stood with hands braced on the counter, head hanging as he let out a soft sigh. "I know that," he muttered. "But there's already so little for me to do that...At what point does technology make a man obsolete?"

Closing her eyes, Melissa tilted her head back. She took a deep breath of her own and let it out slowly. "It doesn't make you obsolete, Dad," she began. "You could just as easily say the same thing about a washing machine."

Grabbing a pot in one hand and stirring his concoction with a wooden spoon, Harry whirled around and shuffled over to her. "So I'm told." He emptied half the oatmeal into a bowl he had left in front of her.

"Are you sure this is about Michael?"

"Stop calling it that."

"This unit will now answer to 'Michael.' " the robot said, stepping proudly forward as if it expected someone to pin a medal on its chest. Hell, the damn thing was practically smiling; she had never noticed the slight curve of its mouth speaker.

Michael wasn't sapient, of course – not a true AI like Ven. It was merely one of the many appliances controlled by the house's main computer. A convenience to make life a little easier, to cook meals and perform light cleaning duties. Why her father despised it so much was beyond her.

There was a slight whirring noise as the robot stepped forward and turned its head to fix those glowing blue eyes on Harry. "Mr. Carlson," it began. "I have been informed that this week's grocery delivery will take place at the standard time. You have made no special orders this week."

With an open mouth, Harry tossed his head back to blink at the ceiling. "Grocery deliveries," he muttered under his breath. "Do the people of this planet do *anything* for themselves anymore?"

" 'Damn that new-fangled SnapChat!' " Melissa barked, quoting one of her earliest memories. " 'These kids today use technology for the stupidest things!' "

"Shouldn't you be on your way to class?"

"I will be," Melissa said. "Once Claire lets me take a shower."

One wall of the classroom was actually a large window that looked out on a round garden in the middle of a green field. Six curved desk – shaped like horseshoes – were scattered throughout the room, all positioned to face a wide, open area in the middle of the gray tiled floor.

Dressed in gray pants and a black t-shirt with a silver pattern on the cuff of each sleeve, Melissa strode through the door. Her dark hair was pulled back in a bun with two sticks forming an *x* through it.

Instantly, her eyes found a gorgeous young man who sat turned so that she saw him in profile. Tall and slim with bronze skin and thick dark hair, Aiden Tenalo seemed to be focused on something on the wall.

Melissa closed her eyes, breathing deeply to calm herself. "Don't make an idiot of yourself," she whispered, shaking her head. "He's just an ordinary guy. Like every other guy you've ever met."

Aiden smiled up at her, his dark eyes glittering in the warm light. "Hey!" he exclaimed. "I was hoping I'd get a chance to talk to you before class got going. Did you finish the assignment?"

Crossing her arms with a heavy sigh, Melissa shook her head. "I did," she said with a shrug. "But analyzing the theories of Toralus Bendai kept me awake well past my usual bed time."

"It was that hard?"

She tilted one of the horseshoe-shaped slabs of plastic up so she could drop into the cushy chair, then pulled it back down over herself to form a desk. "I was trying to find a fresh take," she said, swiveling to face Aiden.

He sat with his elbows on the desk, his chin resting on laced fingers. "I'm sure you came up with something," he said, his eyebrows climbing. "After all that effort, you must have rewritten the book on law."

She was about to answer when a man in black pants and a matching shirt cut in the Leyrian style came striding through the door. Wil Asten, their teacher, was a shorter but well-muscled man with Asian features. From what Melissa had heard, he had grown up on Salus Prime and then moved to Leyria to become a Keeper.

Wil shut his eyes, grunting in displeasure. "Let's get started," he said, stepping into the empty space in the middle of the room. "In our last session, we reviewed the work of Toralus Bendai; I trust your papers have been submitted."

Melissa raised her hand.

The teacher froze in place when he caught sight of it, turning his head to glare at her. "Ms. Carlson," he said, arching a thick dark eyebrow. "I thought that we were going to curb your tendency to interrupt the lecture."

Those words sent a wave of heat burning through her face. If there was one thing Wil despised, it was interruptions. The man would sigh with frustration every time she raised her hand and then provide the most sparse of answers. From what she had heard, he was an amazing Keeper, but he wasn't much of a teacher. "I wanted to ask about the undercurrent of Legal positivism in Bendai's work."

"Something I'm more than happy to discuss with you after class," Wil snapped. "For the moment, let's resume."

A hologram appeared before him, depicting a man in a gray suit that might have come out of the 1800s. Except it didn't. The cut of his beige shirt was different, with a high collar that almost touched his chin.

Toralus Bendai was one of those stately men with dark bronze skin and a fringe of white hair around the back of his head. His face seemed to be fixed in an eternal frown. "Bendai believed that the law is an extension of 'natural morals' that evolved to allow us to function as a social unit," Wil began. "As such, he saw adherence to the law as one of the principle virtues of any decent human being."

Unclipping the metal disk from her gauntlet, Melissa set it down on the surface of her desk. Tiny nanobots emerged from it, linking together to form a small keyboard right in front of her.

The holographic projector displayed a blank white screen

with a blinking cursor, and she began to type, filling out notes. *This,* she realized, *is going to be a very long day.*

Daisies sprouted from a bed of soil, white petals fanning out around a yellow disk that seemed to drink up the sun. He dug in the dirt with his trowel, making a small trench into which he poured water.

Harry was on his knees in the grass, next to the flowerbed, muttering softly as he inspected his work. "Not bad," he muttered, wiping sweat off his brow with the back of his hand. "At least they're growing."

The damnable robots that "kept this house in order" would maintain his yard if he allowed it, but he wanted to do a few things himself. That, he realized, was a big part of his problem. Since coming to this world, he'd had so little to do and so much free time that he wasn't entirely sure what to do with himself.

The small house was off to his left with its domed roof collecting sunlight that it fed into the city's power grid. Behind it, a green lawn stretched across the length of his backyard to the very edge of a small patch of woodland.

Baring his teeth, Harry squeezed his eyes shut. He rubbed his forehead again. " 'A man's worth is in his work,' " he mumbled, quoting his father. "So what exactly are you worth now, Detective Carlson?"

"Talking to yourself?"

He looked up to see a young woman in blue jeans and a white t-shirt with thin laces over its V-neck coming around the side of the house. Anna wore a pair of sunglasses with large dark lenses that glinted in the sunlight. Her hair was tied back in a ponytail, but she had dyed it to a pale blue.

"Trying to do something productive."

Anna paused ten feet away from him, planting fists on her hips and standing over him like a disapproving drill sergeant.

"Have you never learned how to relax, Harry?" she asked in disapproving tones.

He felt his mouth tighten, then shook his head in dismay. "I've had just about all the relaxation I can handle," he said, getting to his feet. "Three months of reading and going to shows and taking care of the girls."

"And you're looking for something to do?"

"I don't know *what* to do."

"What do you want to do?"

Harry slipped his hands into his back pockets, then spun around to face the house. He marched over to the wall and let out a breath. "That's just it!" he said. "I don't know! Back home, there was always something that needed doing."

Cocking her head to one side, Anna watched him through those dark lenses. "Well, there *is* the task force," she offered. "I know things have been quiet lately, but you could always focus on that."

"I attend the weekly meetings." After three months, the hunt for Grecken Slade's lackeys had pretty much come to a standstill. There was no sign of the woman that Anna had fought in Tennessee, or of the one Jena had encountered in New York. Arin was safely tucked away in a holding cell.

It seemed Jena had dealt their little cabal a crippling blow when she killed Slade. On top of that, patrol ships had seen no evidence of an incursion from the Ragnosians. More and more, it was starting to seem as if this task force had no purpose. Not that he minded; if the horror of Grecken Slade's treachery was truly over, then he would gladly put up with a little boredom.

His heart sank.

Thinking of Jena always had that effect.

Harry turned around to lean against the wall with his arms folded, looking down at himself. "So, what about you?" he asked in a gruff voice. "How is that leave of absence going for you?"

She turned her face away from him, staring intently at the fence. "Don't ask," she muttered under her breath. Something had happened between her and Jack, and neither one would discuss it.

Harry had used a little careful prodding with each of them – a good Detective had many ways to get information out of a suspect – but neither one was forthcoming, and it was the sort of thing that a friend just left alone. Sometimes people just had to figure out their issues on their own.

"Came for a little company then?" Harry asked.

"I thought we could have coffee."

He felt his lips curl into a small smile, then bowed his head to her. "I'd like that," he said, nodding. "Come on. I've got some in the kitchen."

Once inside, Anna took a seat at his table, in the same chair that Melissa had used just a few hours earlier. The dirty dish that had once contained oatmeal was still sitting there in the open, and Harry suppressed a moment of annoyance. His eldest should know enough to put it in the dishwasher.

The kids were getting lazy now that they had a robot to pick up after them, which was one reason why he insisted that the damn thing remain in standby mode. No doubt it was waiting for his groceries to arrive or something along those lines.

Anna slouched in the chair, tossing her head back to stare up at the ceiling. "So, Melissa tells me you hate your new appliances," she said. "I would've thought you'd appreciate the extra help."

"I got by just fine for almost forty years," Harry grumbled, making no effort to hide his irritation. "I really don't need that mechanical monstrosity to do my chores for me."

The coffee dispenser on his counter filled one cup with piping-hot dark liquid. "I made decaf for you," Harry said, adding milk and a spoonful of sugar. Anna had a sweet tooth. "I know Seth isn't a fan of the stimulants."

"You know me so well."

He turned, carrying a cup to the table where Anna sat with her hands folded behind her head. It was strange to see her with blue hair; he'd always thought that she had looked nice as a blonde, but then she'd gone with cherry-red, and now this. Needless to say, he wasn't exactly a fan of unnatural hair colour. But it really wasn't his place to criticize. He had learned that much in his old age.

He set the cup down in front of her.

Then he took the chair on her right, stretching his feet under the table. "So, what *really* brings you by?" he asked. "And don't tell me you just wanted a good cup of coffee. Detective skills, remember?"

"I was thinking you and the girls might join me for a trip to Ryloth City," she said. "The granite monuments there are gorgeous. If you're going to live on this planet, you really should see the sights."

"Feeling starved for company, hmm?"

She blinked at him.

"Detective skills."

Anna gingerly lifted her cup in both hands, brought it to her lips and slurped as she took a sip. "I haven't lived on Leyria in almost five years," she said. "Most of my friends from that time have moved off world."

Hunching over the table with a grunt, Harry shook his head. "I think you know that's not true," he muttered, trying to keep the frustration out of his voice. "Your best friend lives in this very city."

The flash of grief that twisted Anna's features told him that he shouldn't have said that. "I can't..." she murmured and then went silent for almost half a minute. "I can't talk to Jack right now."

"Well, then I graciously accept your offer," Harry replied. Inwardly, he chastised himself for trying to get involved in what was obviously a very personal matter. He had no business trying to coax Anna and Jack into making up. "I'm sure the girls would be happy to visit Ryloth on their next free day."

Funny how things that had seemed so permanent just a few months ago had fallen apart. Jack and Anna's friendship was a fixed point in his life, a cornerstone of his reality. No longer, it seemed.

Worse yet, he didn't think anything could do Jena in. Bitter laughter almost passed through his lips when he realized that that was probably still true. The only thing in this universe that could kill Jena was Jena herself. The world *was* changing.

He just wasn't sure that it was changing for the better.

2

"Take me through it again."

This holding cell in Justice Keeper Headquarters had lights that would simulate natural sunlight. Ordinarily, prisoners would get a window, but these cells weren't meant to hold anyone indefinitely; so many of the amenities that were supposed to help a prisoner on their path to rehabilitation weren't available.

But what could you do when the prisoner in question was a Justice Keeper? Or had been at least. Only Keepers really knew how to contain other Keepers. That was the logic Larani had used when she insisted on allowing Calissa Narim to serve at least part of her sentence here. Jack wasn't sure he agreed, but it *did* give him the chance to get some very important answers.

The woman who sat with her elbows on the small, round table, her face hidden in her hands, wore sweat pants and a tank-top. "We've been through this," she moaned. "I serve the Inzari because they are gods."

In gray jeans and a simple black polo shirt, Jack stood by the wall with his arms folded, shaking his head. "Would you like to call your lawyer, Calissa?" he asked. "We can arrange that for you; maybe, if you give us some intel that we can use, we might be able to reduce your sentence."

When she looked up, strands of dark hair fell over her flushed face, and she blinked at him. "There is no deal you could offer," she said. "I tell you everything freely because I have no need to hide."

"Great. Start talking."

"There is nothing more to tell!"

"Why did Slade want you to kill Ben?"

"I didn't ask."

Chewing on his lip, Jack shut his eyes and nodded. "You didn't ask," he mumbled. "So, let me get this straight: the guy orders you to blow your cover and risk jail time just to kill one LIS agent, and you didn't want to know why?"

He paced a circle around her table.

Calissa turned her head to keep her green eyes fixed upon him, eyes that threatened to peel strips off his hide. "It wasn't my place to ask," she answered. "Slade told me what was expected of me, and I did it."

"You were a Keeper once."

"Your point?"

"Keepers aren't exactly known for being good little soldiers." Jack came up behind her, then leaned over to bring his lips to her ear. "So, what would make an anarchist like you decide to go on an obey-a-thon?"

"Slade is my lord and saviour."

Frustration made him want to beat his head against the wall. This was getting him nowhere. What little he had learned from Ben suggested that Calissa had been much the same way with him – taunting, mocking, hinting at some reckoning to come and constantly reaffirming her devotion to His Royal Douchebag.

He strode past Calissa, back to the wall.

Closing his eyes, Jack tilted his head back and took a deep

breath through his nose. “Let's try something else,” he said. “There have to be other Keepers working as moles for Slade and his minions. Who are they?”

In his mind's eye, the woman just sat there with hands on her table, staring into her own lap. “I don't know any names,” she said. “We're told only what we need to know in case we're captured.”

“How very NSA of you.”

“I'm sorry?”

Jack rounded on her.

“Look,” he said, “you can't expect me to believe that you know absolutely nothing about the inner workings of your own secret society. Someone had to deliver the message to kill Ben. Who was it? How did you verify your orders? How do you communicate with the other members of your cell?”

Calissa stood.

It was hard not to assume a fighting stance – this woman *was* a Justice Keeper after all – but Jack managed to maintain his composure. That thin metal collar around her neck would prevent her from using any of her Bending talents. A part of him was sickened by the thought of employing a slaver's collar, but what else could you do against somebody who carried a symbiont?

The woman just folded her hands behind herself and kept her eyes on the floor. “You haven't given me any reason to cooperate,” she said. “If I'm going to risk a reprisal by Slade or his people, well...”

“You're serving two consecutive life sentences.”

“Yes...”

“Maybe I could talk to the Sector Attorney.”

Turning on her heel, Calissa marched to the cell's back wall. For a little while, she just stayed there without saying anything. “No,” she replied at last. “There is nothing that you can offer me.”

"You sure?" Jack said. "I make a *mean* apple pie."

"You don't understand the Inzari," Calissa muttered. "Their power is absolute. They have shown me their majesty and glory."

Jack yawned and then covered his mouth with his fist, groaning softly. "I'm sorry," he said. "Lengthy sob stories in the genre of 'I'm so evil – ask me how' always put me to sleep. Any chance you could record that one for me? Been having some *nasty* insomnia these last few weeks."

Calissa turned back to the wall, refusing to look at him. "You don't understand," she said. "But you will...Leave me be."

"Not how it works, lady," Jack said. "You're on my time. This conversation is over when I decide I've gotten something useful out of it. Now, if you want to make with the answers, I'd be eternally...less contemptuous."

Calissa returned to her chair.

Stretching her legs out and folding her hands behind her head, she smiled up at the ceiling. "I've been a Keeper longer than you," she said. "I know what to expect. You will stand there and make noises about lessening my sentence or granting me privileges, but you won't actually do anything to me."

Jack flinched, turning his face away from her.

"So, unless you're willing to start torturing me," Calissa went on. "I suggest you be on your way. Because I'm not telling you anything else."

Steam rose from a cup of mint tea where Larani's dim reflection rippled in the dark liquid, thin trails of vapor wafting upward. She always drank mint tea when she needed to soothe away her anxieties, and since taking over as head of the Justice Keepers, she had been drinking it more and more.

The back wall of her office was one long floor-to-ceiling window that looked out upon two glittering buildings on the other side of the street. Through the space between them, she could see the trees of Aletha Park.

Larani sat in her comfortable desk chair with her legs stretched out and crossed at the ankle, lifting the cup to her lips. The tea was good, not too sweet. She couldn't figure out why people insisted on dumping sugar into it.

A door opened behind her.

Larani closed her eyes, pressing the back of her head to her chair. She let out a soft sigh. "I take it you spoke with Calissa Narin," she said. "And furthermore, I'm guessing that your conversation was less than fruitful."

She swiveled around.

Her office was a simple room of dark gray floor tiles and blue walls the colour of a twilight sky. Paintings done in soft pastels depicted a forest, and there was a couch along the wall, though she never used it.

The young man who stood before her was tall and lean, dressed in Earth fashions and wearing one of those cautious stares. Had she felt any interest in men, she supposed that Jack would be handsome enough with his firm jawline and dark brown hair that had a practiced messiness. "You could say that."

Lifting her chin, Larani studied the young man for a moment. "And what did my former agent tell you?" she asked, raising one dark eyebrow. "More promises about what Slade will do when his plans come to fruition?"

"Not so much," Jack answered, approaching the desk. "It was the usual display of rehearsed bravado until I told her that Slade's been dead for four months now."

"And then?"

"And then I left her to stew."

As she watched her reflection in the cup, Larani couldn't help but wonder whether it might have been wiser to press the advantage then and there. Assuming that Jack was indeed correct and that Calissa was expecting a rescue, pressing her for information right after her hopes had been dashed might have been more fruitful.

Giving her time to "stew," as the young man put it, would only give her opportunity to consider her options. Panic was the enemy of anyone who wanted to keep a secret, but Larani kept that opinion to herself. She had requested Jack for a reason, and that meant trusting his instincts.

Pressing his lips into a thin line, Jack held her gaze. "I think we might be on a wild goose chase." What a curious expression! "We've been going through personnel files for months, and we haven't found any double agents."

Tapping her lips with one finger, Larani shut her eyes. "Perhaps you're right," she said, wheeling her chair back from the desk. "But Cal Breslan and then Calissa Narin? It seems as though Slade didn't lack for accomplices."

"True."

Larani stood up with a sigh, bracing her hands on the desk and leaning over it. "Let us not forget Slade's ability to plant a virus in Station One's computer." Thinking about that day still left her feeling uneasy. "I highly doubt he would be able to do such a thing without assistance."

"What makes you think Keepers assisted him?"

"What makes you think they didn't?"

The young man's jaw worked as he tried to form a response, but then he sniffed and rubbed his eyes with the back of his hand. "Most Keepers aren't computer programmers," he said. "Even if they were, we'd have to investigate the ones who were working on Earth when the stations were being built."

A point in his favour.

She was beginning to notice that Jack had a habit of drawing her into one of these hypothetical arguments. His mind spun intricate webs of theories and propositions, and he voiced them all without ever feeling the urge to stand on ceremony. He never asked permission to share his opinions. It was both refreshing and occasionally irritating.

But then, the man had had Jena's ear for months.

"What do you suggest?"

Jack crossed his arms and looked down at himself, heaving out a deep breath. "I don't know," he said, taking one shaky step forward. "I don't want to ignore a potential threat as big as this, but..."

"But you don't want to start questioning Keepers?"

He stiffened.

"Is your honour so prickly?" Larani demanded. "A year ago, you were more than eager to hold our feet to the fire, and now you're afraid to implicate your colleagues? It's quite the juxtaposition."

Jack wrinkled his nose as though he smelled something awful, then shook his head in contempt. "It's got nothing to do with honour," he insisted. "This can't become a witch hunt, or we're no better than the worst dirty cop."

Licking her lips nervously, Larani hung her head. "You showed no such restraint in your efforts to prosecute Cal Breslan." Quite the opposite, as she recalled it. The young man in front of her had been a thorn in everyone's side. "Is it only authority figures who receive your scorn and mistrust?"

To her surprise, Jack looked up to study her with blue eyes that seemed to burn with righteous fury. "Authority figures have a tendency to misuse their power," he said. "Therefore, they deserve a little extra scrutiny."

"And you apply this standard to yourself?"

"Absolutely."

How intriguing.

She turned around to find herself face to face with her own faint reflection in the window pane. The skyscrapers in the distance drew the eye, sunlight glinting off of their windows. "I believe I see the problem," Larani began. "I've given you authority, and you are afraid that by using it, you become the very thing you fear most."

Spatial awareness allowed her to perceive Jack shifting his weight from one foot to the other, anxiously contemplating her words. Yes, she *had* found the mark with that last observation. Jack Hunter mistrusted authority figures.

In most people, that was a prejudice reserved for *others* – most people believed that they themselves were capable of using authority wisely – but Jack distrusted authority as a *concept*. He didn't think anyone should have it! Least of all himself! "Over the last few months, we have compiled a list of Keepers who have exhibited unexplained behaviour. I want you to begin questioning them."

Her lips curled into a small smile, and she nodded to her own reflection. "Think of it as a check on power," she said. "Keepers have an extraordinary amount of it. Your job is to give them a little extra scrutiny."

"Yes, ma'am."

"And, Jack," she said. "Good luck."

The vertical farm was somewhat intimidating up close: a twenty-story skyscraper with a tip that seemed to touch the star-filled sky. Each floor was used to grow a different crop through hydroponic and aeroponic technologies, all perfectly managed by a series of robots and complex computer algorithms.

There were forty-two others just like it on the outskirts of Denabria. Food was sent to individual distribution centres by mag-lev trains that ran through underground tunnels. There, it was sorted, some produce going directly into grocery deliveries, some sent to refineries where it was used to make cereals, canned soups or any number of products. Over the centuries, Leyria had created a well-oiled economy that saw to everyone's needs with a minimum amount of human labour.

That was why Brinton had to destroy it.

The farm stood alone in the middle of a grassy field, on the other side of a chain-link fence. Not exactly high security, but then who would attack a farm when access to food was a given for every citizen?

Brinton stood just outside the gate in black pants and a matching sweater with the hood pulled up to hide his face, a suitcase in one hand. "The Companion watches over me," he murmured, stepping forward.

Rolling up his sleeve, he tapped at his multi-tool and ran an app that he had coded after stealing Miles Tarso's fingerprints. Tiny nanobots emerged from the metal disk on his gauntlet, a swarm of them that crawled over his fist and onto his thumb.

They molded together to form a fingerprint that was not his own. Something that looked very much like sand coating his thumb. Advanced biometric scanners would be able to tell that it wasn't organic material, but he had done his research, and he knew that the security systems of this farm were somewhat out of date.

Again, who would attack a farm?

He strode up to the scanner next to the gate.

Pressing his thumb to its surface, he watched as a scan line ran up and down. There was a slight beep, and then a picture of Miles Tarso appeared on the screen along with the words "Access Granted."

The gate slid open.

Brinton went inside, carrying the bomb with him.

Bright lights in the ceiling illuminated a train car where seats with green cushions were positioned on either side of an aisle. At the moment, most were empty with only a few passengers sitting quietly.

In the window, tall buildings streaked by under a starry sky with a purple crescent moon. They were leaving the downtown core, heading for the residential sections of the city. Melissa was amazed by how smooth the ride felt. Mag-lev trains were a wonderful form of transit, one that her own world should embrace with open arms.

Aiden was gorgeous, sitting across from her with his hands on his knees, smiling into his own lap. "So, your friend just... beamed Slade's memories into your mind?" he asked. "Every last scrap he pulled from that monster?"

Grinning with a burst of soft laughter, Melissa shut her eyes. "Something like that," she said, nodding to him. "It was all fragmented, a bunch of images and sensations with no real coherence at first."

"What was that like?"

She tossed her head back, rolling her eyes. "Not fun," she admitted, slouching in her seat. "But I was able to piece it all together after a few days, and then I knew what Slade was planning."

It was clear that her story was having some effect on Aiden. He had told her before that he had read up on the Keepers, studied the case files that were made available to the public. But reading about all the crazy things this life could throw at you was one thing; actually *living* it was quite another, and even by Justice Keepers standards, Melissa's life was complicated. Aiden was starting to figure that out.

He sat forward with his elbows on his thighs, his chin resting on laced fingers. "It's quite the story," he murmured. "But I thought you were going to tell me about how you Bonded your symbiont."

"I'm getting to that."

"You mean the telepath thing was part of it?"

Covering her mouth with two fingers, Melissa trembled as she laughed. "Are you *going* to let me finish the story?" she teased. "Or do you want me to just give you all the spoilers up front?"

"Spoilers?"

"An Earth concept."

He looked up at her with those smoldering dark eyes, and suddenly she was having a hard time putting her thoughts in order. "Tell the story," he said. "I promise no further interruptions from this-"

He cut off when they both noticed a sudden flash in the window. Something that looked very much like a huge fireball rising into the sky. It was miles away – she could tell that much – but for her to see it, the explosion must have been very large. "I think," Melissa said, "that I had better call Director Andalon."

3

A pair of double doors slid apart, revealing a train platform under the light of a few tall lamps, and Melissa bolted through. Even in the dark of night, she could see the plume of smoke rising up to the sky, dark clouds briefly obscuring the purple moon. The vertical farm had been thoroughly destroyed.

She turned.

Aiden exited the train behind her, stepping out into a cool spring night. "Bleakness take me," he said, looking around. "Who would blow up a farm? There is nothing to be gained by that."

Melissa smiled, bowing her head to him. "That's what we're here to find out," she said, brushing a lock of hair off her cheek. "Come on. Director Andalon told us to meet him at the crime scene."

She ran down the steps from the raised platform, taking them two by two. Very few people used this particular train station – for the most part, only people who worked on the farm's systems came this far out of the city – but there was certainly a lot of activity tonight. A whole lot of it.

A simple concrete walkway ran through a field of grass to a

chain-link fence that surrounded the farm. Beyond that, she could see that what had once been a tall building was now a tower of rubble belching flames into the night and casting smoke into the air. The explosive force necessary to take out something that big...

Police officers in gray uniforms stood in a line with their backs turned, each one watching as the building burned. "That's where we start," Melissa grumbled. "Come on. We should get a status report."

She broke into a sprint.

One of the officers spun around to stand before her with his arms crossed, blocking her way. A tall man with broad shoulders and white skin, he looked her up and down and then snorted. "Go home, kid," he said. "You're trespassing."

Melissa lifted her forearm to expose her multi-tool, and the holographic projector displayed an image of her badge, complete with her picture and everything. "I'm with the Justice Keepers," she said. "So is my friend."

"You're a cadet," the cop shot back.

"She's with me."

At the sound of a firm, decisive voice, Melissa turned to find Jon Andalon coming up the walkway. The new head of their team – it still pained her to remember that Jena was gone – wore simple beige pants and a black sweater under an even darker jacket.

Jon had a handsome face with a firm jaw, skin even darker than her father's and hair that he kept short and neat. "Officer," he said, nodding to the other man. "Cadet Carlson is part of my investigation."

"If you say so."

Melissa made a vexed noise and then hoped that nobody noticed. The cops didn't feel the need to make Jon display *his* badge. She might have chalked it up to the fact that he was a known quantity at this point, but the man had spent nearly a year working out on Belos Colony – this wasn't the first time he had taken over for Jena – and the cops here didn't know him from Adam. Or...Whoever the Leyrian equivalent of Adam was.

Melissa was suddenly hit with a wave of emotion that wasn't her own. Too many thoughts of Jena made her symbiont ache. She forced those feelings out of her mind. It would not do to lose her composure in front of these men.

"Follow me," Jon said.

He pushed through the crowd of cops without so much as an apology and made his way to the open gate in the fence. The officer who had greeted her gave her a dirty look that would make any high school queen bee proud.

Craning her neck, Melissa squinted at him. "Something I can do for you?" she asked, shaking her head. "Or would you prefer to get out of my way and actually let me do my damn job?"

He snorted but moved aside.

Melissa ran to catch up with Jon.

In her mind's eye, Aiden was a silhouette only two steps behind her, looking back over his shoulder at the cops as if he couldn't believe they had tolerated Melissa's sass. Maybe he couldn't believe that she had mouthed off like that – to be honest, Melissa did not really believe it either; some of Jena must be rubbing off on her – but then Aiden had not grown up on Earth.

Cops back home were often sexist jerks who refused to believe that a woman could do this job. On top of that, there were...other issues. She was half white, but her colouring was dark enough that most people just assumed she was black. And even in Canada, cops often failed to treat black people with respect.

She ran.

Jon was down on one knee, scanning the gate with his multi-tool. "No signs of any forced entry," he said when she got within a few feet of him. "It looks as if our perp used a valid ID to get in."

Crossing her arms, Melissa looked down at him. "Okay," she said with a shrug of her shoulders. "Wouldn't that narrow the pool of suspects to people who work on the farm's systems?"

"Possibly."

Aiden stepped forward with hands in his jacket pockets, shaking his head. "It's just as possible that somebody hacked the systems," he said, and Melissa felt a brief moment of chagrin.

Jon looked over his shoulder with a sour expression, then nodded to the young man. "Exactly," he said. "I want you both to inspect the fence for any other possible signs of a breach, then report back to me."

It felt like a dismissal, but what else could she do? Even among the Keepers, there was a certain amount of "start at the bottom and work your way up." Maybe if she hadn't made such a dumb comment.

Her Nassai seemed to disagree, and if anyone knew better, it would be the symbiont who had spent over twenty years with Jena Morane. It was hard to tell from the emotions alone, but she was fairly certain that the symbiont did *not* consider her observation to be dumb. A flare of happy emotions told her she was correct.

Scanning the fence with her multi-tool took some time – there were no visible signs of a break in, and she picked up nothing out of the ordinary – but after ten minutes or so, she made her way back to the gate.

Jon had gone through and now stood in the road that led up to the building's front entrance, watching the wreckage with fists on his hips. "Cadets," he said without looking. "Have you found anything?"

Closing her eyes, Melissa shook her head in dismay. "No signs of a break in," she answered. "So, we're back to our original assessment. Either someone who worked here did this, or the system was hacked."

As she stepped up beside Jon, she saw a cluster of men in women in bright orange Hazmat gear just a short ways ahead. No one wanted to get close to the burning building, not when there was a chance that rubble might fall.

Fire-suppression bots floated around the building like a swarm of bees, spraying the upper levels with water, but the flames were still going strong in some places. "So, what's our next move," Melissa asked.

Director Andalon sucked on his lip as he watched the building, his face bathed in the orange glow of firelight. "For now, there's not much we can do," he said. "Once we know it's safe, a CSI team will investigate the wreckage and determine what caused the explosion. We'll go forward from there."

"Is there any chance this was an accident?"

"The probability is extremely low."

"So, a bomb then," Melissa said. "Well, that's just lovely."

Aiden came up on her other side, craning his neck to stare at the building. The look on his face...It was clear that he was still wondering what could possess someone to do a thing like this.

Maybe growing up on Earth had twisted her perspective, but Melissa had no trouble believing that someone would do something like this. People were always finding reasons to do something violent and stupid. "Orders, sir?" Melissa asked.

"Well, for now, you're coming with me."

"Where, sir?"

The man shot a glance over his shoulder, his lips curling into a thin smile. "Where do you think, Cadet?" he asked. "We have to make a preliminary report on what we have discovered here. We're going to see Larani Tal."

A large desk with a surface of SmartGlass sat in the middle

of an office with blue walls and potted plants in every corner. The paintings of forests and gardens hung up in places that drew the eye gave one a sense of ease and contentment. This wasn't at all like the drab, gray office Melissa remembered from Station One; that was just a room Larani used as a workspace when she visited Earth. *This* was her real home.

The head of the Justice Keepers stood with her back turned, hands clasped behind herself as she stared out the window at tall buildings with lights in their windows. "Did you learn anything?" she asked without turning.

Jon frowned, then bowed his head to her. "I'm afraid not, ma'am," he said in tones that made his frustration evident. "The farm has been destroyed; fire suppression teams are still working to put out the flames."

Melissa wanted to say something about the fact that they had discovered no sign of forced entry, but she was a cadet. This meeting was for professionals, and she was lucky to even be standing here. Best to keep her mouth shut and let the adults do the talking. At least for now.

The doors opened behind her to allow Jack to come striding into the room in jeans and a polo shirt. "Bloody hell," he grumbled, shaking his head. "Just when I thought that maybe things would start to quiet down."

"Sorry to get you out of bed, Agent Hunter," Jon said.

"Oh, that's fine. I was just cuddling up with my insomnia."

"Well, you-" Melissa began.

She cut off when Larani Tal spun around to face them with an expression so hard it could smash diamonds. "Can we focus on the topic at hand, please?" she asked in a cool, crisp voice.

Crossing his arms, Jack lifted his chin to study her. "So, what's the damage?" he asked, eyebrows rising. "How severe will the food shortage be now that one of the farms is out of commission?"

Breathing through her open mouth, Larani shook her head.

"No shortage at all," she said. "The Food Distribution Network was designed to have redundancies. We could lose one-third of the farms and still operate at normal output levels."

"Even if Denabria's food systems were severely damaged," Jon added, "we could still import food from other cities."

"Then this is likely a political statement."

A statement? Melissa wondered. *A statement meant to say what, exactly?* If this was some idiot's idea of terrorism, then whoever had planted that bomb was doing a piss-poor job of it. She was young, but she could see that much. The city would go on as if nothing had changed.

She was half ready to give voice to her thoughts when Larani essentially said the same thing. That irked her, but the other woman *was* head of the Justice Keepers. It was hardly fair to complain when your leader took the lead.

Jon stepped forward so that she was forced to stare at the back of his head. "At the moment," he began. "I'm half tempted to leave this in the hands of local police. It could be nothing more than some angry malcontent committing arson."

Turning her face up to the ceiling, Larani narrowed her eyes. "No, I don't think so," she said, shaking her head. "Perhaps recent events have made me paranoid, but I cannot help but wonder why anyone would target a farm."

Jack nodded to that.

A heavy sigh exploded from Larani as she dropped into her chair, setting one elbow on the armrest and leaning her cheek against the palm of her hand. "The Justice Keepers will handle this case," she said firmly. "Anybody who attacks a population's food supply has a motive. We're going to figure out what that is."

Melissa found herself in agreement, even knowing that Larani might be making a mountain out of a molehill. Jurisdiction on Leyria was somewhat prickly; she had learned as much from her studies. Theoretically, the Keepers could reserve the right to investigate any case that fell under the purview of any other branch of law-enforcement.

However, once the Keepers took something under their jurisdiction, it was theirs to deal with, no matter how small the case turned out to be. Other cops weren't exactly fond of the idea of having a case dumped in their laps again if it was deemed to no longer be a threat to planetary security.

Jon turned his back on the desk, frowning down at the floor. "Very well then," he said, taking a few steps across the length of the office. "I'm quite happy to rededicate my team's efforts; we've had little luck in the search for Slade's minions."

"That's not necessary," Larani said. "There are many people to whom I could assign this case; I want you to continue your search for Slade."

Jon looked up, and his eyes flicked open, focusing on Melissa like a pair of lasers. "We can't do much as it stands right now," he said. "All leads have gone cold. And this would give Ms. Carlson a chance to get some field experience."

"If you insist," Larani said. "But I am reassigning this case should one of Slade's former lieutenants surface."

A scowl twisted Jack's face, and he shook his head. "You can't go at this alone," he said, stepping forward. "Anna's still on leave, and you'll need more than one experienced Keeper in the mix. I volun-"

"No!" Larani's voice cracked like a whip.

She leaned back in her chair with arms folded, frowning at him. "You have duties of your own, Agent Hunter," she said. "I'm quite certain that Director Andalon will find whatever support he needs."

Melissa shut her eyes, trembling as she worked up the nerve to speak. "We could ask my father," she suggested, marching over to the desk. "Jena always trusted him. And there's Ben Loranai."

Larani looked up to study her for a moment, then nodded

her approval. "I suppose that would work." She stood up with a sigh. "Very well. The matter is settled. You're all dismissed."

They filed out of the room, and Melissa felt the tension in her chest drain away to be replaced with a sense of pride. She had contributed. She had overcome her self-doubt enough to be a part of the meeting, to speak to the others as an equal. And the head of the Keepers had treated her as an equal. It was a big step forward!

Now all she had to do was solve a case of arson.

Lifting a small, rectangular device about the size of his thumb, Brinton pressed a button, and nanobots extended from it. They emerged from a tiny slot, linking together to form a key that he slid into the lock of his own front door. It wasn't just the shape of the key that mattered.

These nanobots would send an electrical signal that would be read by the house's main computer, a signal that changed with each use. It was a safeguard against a multi-tool's ability to fabricate almost any shape – including that of keys – with nanobots. Only he could get into his own house.

When he pushed the door open, lights came on, revealing a narrow front hallway with a white tiled floor. A hallway that opened into a kitchen at the other end. He'd more than half expected to find police waiting for him here after having planted the explosives in the vertical farm. But he was alone.

Brinton forced out a deep breath, then reached up to run fingers through his hair. "You had to do it," he whispered. "Decadence, sin, vice...Someone has to take a stand!"

He stepped inside and shut the door.

Off to his left, an open doorway in the corridor led into his living room, and he saw, from the corner of his eye, someone sitting on his couch. Brinton almost jumped, but he quickly recognized Jarl.

Tall and handsome in a pair of gray pants and a black

turtleneck sweater, Jarl had a striking face of brown skin. His head was completely shaved without a single follicle of hair. "I see you completed your task."

It took a moment for Brinton to calm himself. He was beginning to regret giving the other man a key to his house.

Brinton closed his eyes, bowing his head to the man. "I did," he said, stepping into the living room. "And you'll be pleased to know that I was careful. There were no people in the farm when the bomb went off."

Jarl lifted a glass of whiskey up in front of his face, studying the amber liquid with a curious expression. "Well, that's a good thing," he replied without much enthusiasm. "I do hope you've prepared the necessary sacrifices."

"Sacrifices."

"Our people have become weak, Brinton. You yourself have seen it. This life we live where all our needs are provided for has made us soft. The threat of starvation, the threat of pain. These are the things that keep a man sharp."

Brinton knew he was correct about that. The texts of Layat spoke of hardship and its role in forging humankind into the people the Companion wanted them to be. A life where a home, clothing, food and water were just a given was a life in which people were doomed to stagnate.

And with the Ragnosians coming, his people needed to be harder. They couldn't afford to be coddled anymore. "Sacrifices," Brinton said. Was he really speaking openly about terrorism? "*If* it's necessary. Only if."

The other man leaned back against the couch cushions, directing a lazy smile up at the ceiling. "Of course," he said. "No one wants any unnecessary deaths, but we won't go on trying to keep people alive anymore."

Brinton stiffened.

"From now on," Jarl went on. "If a man can't take care of

himself, then he falls by the wayside. It's the only way to be strong."

He was right, though Brinton hated having to admit it.

"Don't worry," Jarl said. "We've made a good beginning, and soon, we'll move on to the next step."

4

From her perch near the edge of a cliff some two hundred feet high, Anna saw the city of Vesala stretched out before her. The outer buildings of the agricultural sector were nearest, tall cylinders with windows on every floor. She could even see some of the crops under banks of fluorescent lights.

The city was almost circular – almost – with mag-lev train tubes extending from the centre like spokes on a wheel, running through sections of glittering skyscrapers and lush green parks with ponds that sparkled. It was quite the view, and she was more than a little daunted by the task of trying to capture it.

The bristles of her paintbrush left a trail of blue across the canvas. She'd managed to create a fuzzy representation of the city as viewed from this cliff. Close enough, but it would be hard to make out individual buildings if you looked too closely.

Chewing on her lip, Anna nodded to herself. “It'll have to do,” she muttered, a lock of blue hair falling over her eye. She tossed her head back to send it flying away. “It's the best I can manage, at least.”

Seth offered encouragement.

Painting took her mind off things that she would rather not think about, and right then, there were a lot of things that she would rather not think about. Her heart still ached as if an iron hand was squeezing it to the point of bursting.

She missed Bradley.

His face popped into her mind frequently – usually at the most inconvenient time – and she often had to struggle to focus on what she was doing instead of just melting into a lump of sadness. It was new for her. She'd had boyfriends before, and breaking up was always painful, but those relationships hadn't been quite so...deep.

Worst of all, on some level, she *knew* she had made the right decision. Or, at least, she did *most* of the time. But knowing that did little to ease her pain. And there were too many moments when the grief made her think she was an idiot.

Anna closed her eyes, tears streaming over her cheeks. "Not now," she whispered, shaking her head. "I really don't need another bout of break-up blues to ruin yet another fine afternoon."

Her heart seemed to disagree.

In her mind's eye, she saw the silhouette of a car drive up the narrow road behind her and settle to a stop near the trail that led to the cliff's edge. Since she hadn't ordered a cab to come take her home, it could only mean that someone else was coming out here to enjoy the view. Likely some couple.

The car's door swung open, and a woman emerged. At least, Anna thought it was a woman; at this distance, it was hard for Seth to make out anything beyond a vague human shape. She didn't mind sharing her spot.

Anna winced, scraping a knuckle across her forehead, brushing blue bangs aside. "Just don't expect me to be sociable," she muttered under her breath. "This girl is in need of some serious alone time."

The silhouette of the woman came toward her, and she felt

a spike of alarm when she recognized the newcomer as her mother. "I thought I'd find you out here. You never could resist a good view."

Dropping the paint brush, Anna turned around.

Dressed in black pants and a white blouse with short sleeves, Sierin Elana stood in a field of green grass with her blonde hair left loose. "You should have been a painter. You have a natural talent."

"What are you doing here, Mom?"

"I came to see my daughter."

"I see you several hours a day, every day," Anna said. "It's one of the many perks of living together."

Sierin crossed her arms and started forward with her head down. "True," she said with a curt nod. "But when your daughter moves back in with you despite the fact that she could have a home in any city simply by asking for it..."

Anna felt her mouth twist, then turned her head so that her mother wouldn't see. "I'm fine, Mom," she muttered in the mildest tones she could manage. "Taking a leave of absence is quite normal. I just need-"

"To do something productive." Once again, that judgy tone from Sierin made her want to growl in frustration. Her mother was the sort of woman who thought that she knew what was best for everyone. "It's a lovely painting. Have you considered submitting it to any galleries for review?"

Spinning around to face the cliff with arms folded, Anna heaved out a breath. This was not what she needed right now. "I just painted it for fun," she said. "I'm not looking to go professional."

"Why not, Leana?"

"I have a career already," Anna snapped. "A career I happen to love. And we've been over this many times now."

The other woman strode forward until she was standing right in front of the easel Anna had set up. This close, it was possible to sense her facial expressions with spatial awareness, and she did seem impressed. “It really is quite good, Leana... And if you love that career of yours so much, why aren't you doing it?”

A sigh escaped her as she considered the answer to that question. She had been on leave for nearly a month now, trying to give herself time to sort things out. At first, she had been following up leads off-world, living in a shuttle while she hunted down Isara or any of Slade's other goons. Sadly, she had come up empty.

It was a big galaxy.

But the best thing about being off-world most of the time? There was no chance of her running into Jack. She felt awful thinking such things, but she really did not want to see him right then. Her feelings were already muddled enough without adding even more confusion to the mix.

However, when it became clear that they *weren't* going to find Slade's people, and that the task force was essentially spinning its wheels, she decided the time had come to focus on her own life.

“Is it that Earth boyfriend of yours?”

Anna looked over her shoulder.

Her mother wore a small smile as she stared down at her own feet. “Please, Leana. I've known you long enough to know the look.” This would probably be a good time to bring the conversation to an abrupt halt, but Sierin just kept right on talking. “That sulky expression you get as you stare wistfully through the window.”

Anna stared wistfully over the edge of the cliff, watching the city with its gleaming buildings. Would it be so bad if she jumped? “Mom, I really don't want to talk about this with you.”

“You broke up with him?”

“Yes.”

“Well, that was wise.”

Rage flared up, and she had to resist the urge to kick the easel over the edge of the cliff. The absolute last thing Anna wanted to hear from her mother was a list of reasons why breaking a good man's heart had been "wise." And she missed him. Bleakness take her, the best thing anyone could say about her love life was nothing at all. But Sierin kept right on talking.

"He was an Earther, Leana."

Red-faced, Anna forced her eyes shut. "Oh good," she said. "I really didn't have enough useless prejudice today."

"They're a primitive culture, Leana: a culture fraught with hatred, bigotry and any number of backward beliefs."

"But also the ability to detect irony!" Anna shot back. "Our people seem to have lost that one."

"All I'm saying-"

Anna spun to face her mother with her hands raised defensively, backing away from the other woman. "Look," she began, "if it's all the same to you, I'd rather not hear the speech about how it was never gonna work."

A momentary grimace was Sierin's only reaction, but she covered it quickly. "Very well," she breathed out, her voice dripping with exasperation. "But if you're going to set aside your duties as a Keeper, then at least do something productive."

Craning her neck to make eye-contact, Anna raised a thin eyebrow. "You're the one who wanted me to be a painter," she said, gesturing to the canvas. "That's not productive enough for you?"

"I suppose," Sierin muttered. "Will you be joining me for supper?"

"Yeah...Looks like I will."

Harry opened his eyes to find deep-blue twilight in his bedroom window. Clearly, dawn had come, but while his daily routine wouldn't have him up and about for another hour, he knew perfectly well that he wasn't going to get any more sleep. He was feeling restless, agitated.

Harry sat up.

Scrubbing two hands over his face, he pressed the heels to his eyelids and rubbed away the sleep. "Damn it!" he muttered, getting to his feet. "A grown-ass adult needs to feel useful if he wants a good night's rest."

He pulled a blue robe around himself, knotting the belt, and made his way over to the window. "Face it, Harry," he told himself. "Going to Leyria was just a nice way of being put out to pasture."

Outside, his backyard was gloomy in the early-morning light, but he could make out the flowerbeds in neat little rows and the line of elm trees at the edge of his property. It *was* a nice home, really. He just hadn't planned on retirement for another twenty years at least. There were still good years ahead of him!

But what use was a washed-up old city cop in a world full of Keepers and terrorists with nanotechnology and who knows what other god-forsaken surprises these people had hidden up their sleeves. He-

The distinctive sound of the front door opening made him freeze.

"Melissa," he said, spinning around and making his way to the door. "If the damn girl was out all night with her friends, there will be hell to pay."

His bedroom door was across from the head of the stairs, and he quickly descended to find the silhouette of his daughter standing in the foyer, still dressed in the clothes she had worn yesterday. "You were out all night?"

Melissa looked up at him, blinking as if surprised to find that he was awake. "It's not what you think," she assured him. "One of the vertical farms was destroyed; I had to go with Director Andalon to inspect the crime scene."

Well...His daughter was getting her first taste of the odd hours that went with a job in law enforcement. He supposed that was a good thing. In the last few months, they had called her in the evening or on her free days to job-shadow someone on this case or that case. "What did you find?"

Harry rounded the foot of the stairs and paced through the narrow hallway to the kitchen at the back of the house. It was still chilly on these spring mornings, and he was regretful over leaving one of the windows open.

"It was arson," Melissa said. "A bomb."

Harry sat down at the table, resting an elbow on its surface and burying his face in his hand. "Ugh..." he grumbled. "Why would anybody want to blow up a farm? There is nothing to be gained from it."

"That's what we're trying to figure out." His daughter went to the sink, turned on the water and began washing her hands. It was too dark to see her face, but he suspected that she was frowning. "You'd have to do a whole lot more to compromise the city's food systems; so even if this is an act of terrorism, it's kind of an incompetent one."

"Maybe this is just the start of something." That left him feeling rather uneasy. The reason they had come to Leyria was so that Melissa could do her training in a safe place; Earth was a focal point of craziness as people came from all over the galaxy to see the birthplace of humanity and run amok with their advanced technology. Here, things would be calm. Or, at least, they should have been!

He wasn't sure he liked the thought of his untrained daughter working an arson case, but then there was no safe way to be a Justice Keeper, and she carried a symbiont now. Jena's symbiont. Christ! Just how much did the Nassai share with their hosts? There were things he had told Jena that he would rather Melissa not know.

"What would you do?"

He looked up to find his daughter standing on the opposite side of the table with her hands folded on the back of a chair, staring at him in the dim light. "Where would you go from here?"

Was his daughter asking for advice? More importantly, was it messed up that he was so thrilled by the prospect of being useful?

Scratching his chin with three fingers, Harry squinted down at the table's surface. "That's a tough one," he muttered. "I suppose I would wait for the lab report, determine the composition of the bomb and see if that told me where it came from."

Melissa slid her chair back and dropped into it, lacing her fingers on the table. "I figured as much," she said, leaning forward. "But I keep thinking that there should be *something* else I can do."

"Much of law enforcement is waiting."

"Good thing I'm patient. I just..."

Harry slouched in his chair with his arms folded, tossing his head back. "You want to make a good impression with your bosses," he said. "And you're afraid that sitting on your hands makes you look lazy."

A smile blossomed on his daughter's face – he could see it as the room brightened – and she lowered her eyes. "You know me so well," she mumbled. "But dig deep, Dad. Is there anything else you could do?"

"You could canvass the area."

"Hmm?"

"Talk to people who may have seen something. The vertical farms are right on the city limits – so it's not very likely that anyone was around – but it's worth a shot. This job involves a lot of throwing things at the wall to see what sticks."

Tilting her head to one side, Melissa smiled. "Do you want to come with me?" she asked, raising an eyebrow. "Maybe help me learn some interview skills."

He chuckled. "Are you asking me to be your partner?"

"Sure! Why not?" Melissa stood up, clapping her hands. "Father-daughter crime fighting team. You could even have your own catchphrase like 'I'm too old for this shit!' "

After a moment, she froze. "Okay, I promise to leave the pop-culture references to Jack from now, and-" Her mouth snapped shut when her multi-tool chirped, cutting her off in mid-sentence. Melissa tapped the screen.

"Check the news," Jon Andalon's voice came through the speaker.

Putting on her sternest expression, Melissa looked up to stare across the room at the wall behind Harry. "Computer," she said. "Denabrian local news."

Harry twisted in his seat to watch the thin sheet of Smart-Glass on the wall light up with the image of a newsroom. A hard-faced woman with an olive complexion and eyes that tried to bore right through you sat behind the desk with her hands folded primly on its surface. "Once again," she began, "this video from a group claiming responsibility for the destruction of Vertical Farm 17 came in just this morning."

The image shifted to the silhouette of a hooded man against a gray backdrop. "Yes, it's true," he said in a slimy voice, nodding to the camera. "We destroyed the farm for the greater good of all Leyria. You will all come to know us as the Sons of Savard, and when this era of crisis is over, history will look back on us as your saviours.

"The blood of all Leyrians has thinned. We have constructed a society that coddles the weak, allowing those who would otherwise have fallen behind to slow the rest of us down. We can no longer tolerate such weakness."

The man leaned in closer to the camera, but only the barest outline of his face was visible. "From this point onward," he said, "those who cannot fend for themselves will be left behind. We restore a culture of traditional values, a culture prepared to face the threat of Ragnosian incursions into our space.

"You think we are joking," he went on. "But I can promise you that we are deadly serious. The farm was just the beginning. More will follow. Those who foolishly choose to put themselves between us and our goals will be extinguished. You have been warned."

The news anchor reappeared.

"Off!" Melissa barked.

She stood at the end of the table with her arms crossed, her head drooping in what looked like fatigue. "Well, at least we know their motives," she rasped. "So, Dad, can I count on your help?"

Sucking on his lower lip, Harry closed his eyes. He nodded once to her. "Yeah," he said. "Yeah, you can."

5

Tiny raindrops poured from an overcast sky, falling between the skyscrapers of Ta Arrelas, sliding across the windowpanes in thin streams on their inexorable journey to the sidewalk. People shuffled about on that sidewalk, many in raincoats with their hoods up, shielding their faces from the rain.

Jack emerged from a subway terminal.

Craning his neck to stare at a building, he squinted as the rain pelted his face. “As usual,” he muttered. “You come completely unprepared! Well, at least you're consistent.”

He stood on the sidewalk in black pants and a t-shirt under a soaked denim jacket, his hair soaking wet and cold. In Denabria, it was warm and sunny! So, he had dressed for warm and sunny weather, and it never even occurred to him to check Link to find out if things were different in Ta Arrelas.

The building he wanted had a revolving door in its glass facade, and he could see into the lobby. Of course, he couldn't *sense* anything inside the lobby. To Summer, that window may as well have been a slab of concrete. People milled about inside, some in the high-collared shirts of Leyrian formal attire.

He went in.

Stepping away from the revolving door, Jack shook his head. "Just call me Captain Disorganized," he said, moving deeper into the lobby. "With the amazing power to come stumbling into every meeting five minutes late."

The lobby was huge with two lines of marble columns that stretched from floor to ceiling. On the far side of the room, a bank of elevators stood with their doors shut. From what he had heard, there was a medical clinic on the top floor.

A hologram appeared before him: a woman in a black skirt and a matching blouse who wore her dark hair pulled back in a clip. "Good afternoon, sir," she said, nodding to him. "May I be of assistance."

With a small smile, Jack bowed his head to the hologram. "I'm looking for the local Keeper office," he said. "I have an appointment with Operative Thon Elias."

"Certainly," the hologram replied. "Twelfth floor."

He moved across the lobby in time to see a set of double doors slide apart to reveal a small elevator car inside. Then he was riding upward. It was still a little odd, thinking of Keepers as people who worked in office buildings. And Leyrian cities had far fewer of those than Earth cities did.

Corporations didn't exist on Leyria as they did on Earth; for one thing, the Leyrian people had abandoned the use of currency-economics centuries ago. Most people didn't have "jobs" so much as they had "projects." A person trained in software development might join a team to create a new application, and when that task was done, maybe the team would stay together. Or maybe not.

Some people had multiple projects on the go; Anna's mother was both a school teacher and the lead designer for the Vesala Art Centre's garden. Of course, certain jobs still required official training. Doctors still went to med-school, engineers still pursued degrees in their field, but life was a lot more flexible, and the urban planning of Leyrian cities reflected that.

The doors slid apart to reveal a hallway with blue walls and SmartGlass windows that looked into conference rooms or small offices. Many were empty, but then Keepers seldom spent time in their offices.

Jack stepped out of the elevator.

He closed his eyes, ignoring the fat drop of water sliding over his forehead, then nodded to himself. "No time like the present," he murmured. "Besides, *nothing* is more intimidating than the disheveled bum look."

Jack started up the hallway, noting the presence of a short woman in a black skirt and white blouse who leaned against the wall with her arms folded. It was the pink hair that drew his attention. She wore it in a pixie cut. Was this woman a Keeper? If so, what was she doing just standing around?

A door on his left looked into a small office with gray walls and a rectangular desk of SmartGlass. The man who sat in the chair – turned so that Jack saw his profile – was a little shorter than average height, but very handsome in a pair of black pants and a white shirt that he wore untucked under a black jacket.

His thin face was pale, with rosy cheeks, and his blonde hair was combed back. "I take it you're Special Agent Hunter," he said without looking. "Can I get you anything? A cup of tea? Or maybe a towel?"

Jack crossed his arms and stood in the doorway with his head down. "No, thanks," he said with a shrug. "I just came to conduct an interview; so, let's get this over with, and you can be on your way."

The other man's face twisted into a grimace, and he shook his head. "I'm afraid we'll have to postpone," he said. "I just got a call about a case I'm working on. I was planning to leave in ten minutes."

"I think your case can wait."

Thon Elias swiveled to face Jack with his hands folded over his chest, leaning back. "Really, *Special Agent* Hunter?" he asked. “And who exactly gave you the authority to order me around?”

Grinning down at the floor, Jack shut his eyes tight. “Why, Larani Tal, of course,” he said, stepping into the office. “Maybe you're not picking up on the subtext here, but my investigation? Little bigger than your investigation.”

“All right,” Elias replied, gesturing to the wall behind Jack. “Why don't we use the conference room? I prefer to have a little more space.”

A large table in the shape of an oval took up most of the space in a room with blue walls. Gray daylight came in through a floor-to-ceiling window that looked out upon the city. Rather than a forest of skyscrapers – simple towers of varying height – Ta Arrelas had elegant, curved buildings with fields of lush green grass and trees on their rooftops.

Jack dropped into a chair, reclining and directing a smile up at the ceiling. “Well then,” he began. “Let's start by reviewing some basic details, shall we? How long have you been a Keeper?”

The other man paced a slow circuit around the table, dragging his fingertips along the top of each chair. “Eleven years,” he answered. “I Bonded my symbiont on the third day Barlan, 741.”

“Who was head of the Keepers at that time?”

Thon Elias froze near the table's rounded tip, clasping his hands together behind his back and heaving out a deep breath. “Tiana Zadul,” he answered. “What precisely are you getting at, Agent Hunter?”

Biting his lower lip, Jack looked down at himself. The moisture on his brow was noticeable, and it wasn't all water. “After completing your training, you were assigned to a team in Kenthera Province.”

“Yes.”

“A team led by Grecken Slade.”

The other man stiffened and shot a glance over his shoulder. His eyes could have set ice on fire. "So that's what this is about," Elias muttered. "You're thinking maybe I never stopped working for my old boss."

"What *do* you think of Slade?"

Rich, boisterous laughter erupted from Elias, and he threw his head back like a drunken sailor at his favourite tavern. "What do I think of Slade?" he mocked. "The man had all the humor of a glacier."

Elias sat down gracefully.

He leaned forward, setting his elbows on the table's surface, and resting his chin on the heels of his hands. "Slade was a prig," he went on. "Puffed up with a pompous, self-righteous attitude, acting like some feudal lord. I'm not surprised he went insane."

"So, you didn't like him much."

"I didn't *have* to like him," Elias shot back. "I was an agent; he was my supervising officer. I did what he told me to do."

Not the resounding declaration of revulsion Jack was looking for – he was really hoping this guy was clean – but not a firm statement of support either. The idea that you didn't have to like somebody to do as you were told had never sat well with Jack, It was true in the most technical sense, but in his experience, if you disliked someone, there was usually a damn good reason why. Whatever that reason happened to be, it probably meant the person in question wasn't leadership material.

So, where did that leave him? One thing was clear: if Elias was working for Slade, he wasn't an obvious crony like Breslan. That would make this harder. "I want to ask you about one of your case files. Three years ago, you pursued a ship full of arms dealers out to the Fringe."

"What about it?"

"You were out of contact for three days." Long enough to

replace his symbiont with one of those twisted Nassai that Pennfield created. It was a noteworthy lapse. There were even notes in Elias's file. "That's a long time to go without checking in."

"The shuttle's comm-system was damaged in a firefight," Elias snapped. "I noted this in my mission report."

Jack narrowed his eyes as he studied the other man. "That doesn't make sense," he said, shaking his head. "Your multi-tool had a working comm-system. Your shuttle had a SlipGate. Why didn't you check in?"

The man's face went red, and he flinched like a dog who had been kicked. "I don't have to listen to this!" he growled, standing up. "If you're gonna come in here with these snide insinuations-"

"Answer the question."

Thon Elias leaned forward with his hands pressed to the table, glaring at Jack with nostrils flaring. "You want to make accusations?" he hissed. "You better show up with a whole lot more than a smile and scathing remarks."

He turned on his heel and walked out.

A groan escaped Jack as he leaned back in his chair with his arms folded and tried to plan his next move. "Wonderful," he said, eyebrows rising. "So, now you've gone and tipped your hand with nothing to show for it."

No sooner did he finish talking than the tiny woman with pink hair came striding into the conference room, marching past the table to stand at the window with her back turned. "Not bad," she said. "But not great."

Jack blinked a few times, then gave his head a shake. "And who might you be?" he asked, getting out of his chair. "No, wait, don't tell me. Larani sent you along to keep an eye on me."

She turned slowly, leaning against the glass.

The woman was actually quite fetching in that tight skirt and untucked blouse, but it was her smile that really got his attention. "How remarkably perceptive of you, Agent Hunter," she said. "But no, I'm not here to keep an eye on you."

She flowed around the end of the table with impeccable grace, then sat down on it with one leg crossed over the other. This close, he could sense that she had a symbiont. "Special Agent Cassiara Seyrus at your service," she went on. "You can call me Cassi."

"Well, if you're not here to keep an eye on me..."

She looked up at him, and he noticed that her eyes were a striking shade of purple, almost a perfect complement for her hair. "Haven't you figured it out yet?" she asked, arching a pink eyebrow. "I'm your new partner."

Jack scrunched up his face like a man forced to endure the stench of garbage, then tossed his head about. "Partner," he mumbled. "So...what? Larani just decided to assign another Keeper to this project."

"Partner," she said. "Get used to saying it."

"I've never even met you!"

Musical laughter was her first response, and then she threw her head back to direct a bright, vibrant smile at the ceiling. "Well, isn't this the perfect opportunity to do so? I'm even willing to help you hone your interview technique."

Jack fell back into his chair.

He shut his eyes, then pressed the heels of his hands to his forehead, fingers seizing clumps of his own hair. "Oh, this is gonna be fun," he whispered, turning away from her. "Did you, by chance, read my file?"

"You're Jack Hunter," she answered. "The first person from your world to receive a symbiont. I've read your personnel file, your mission reports, the piece on you in *Focus Magazine*. You might say I did my homework."

"There's a piece on me in *Focus Magazine*?"

"Is it really so surprising?" she shot back. "On your world,

Keepers are often the subject of headline news. Why should it be any different here?"

When he turned back to her, she was just sitting there, smiling at him in a way that was both reassuring and unnerving. "Now," she said. "Why don't we get an early dinner, and you can tell me about the next phase in your brilliant plan?"

A sleek robot of red plastic that glistened under the ceiling lights leaned over their table to fill Jack's cup with coffee. It stood up a moment later, fixed two glowing eyes on Jack and waited for a response.

Looking up to meet the thing's gaze, Jack smiled to show his approval. "Thank you very much," he said, nodding. "That'll be all for now."

The robot turned to go.

On the other side of the booth, Cassi sat with her hands folded in her lap, watching him with those gorgeous violet eyes. Damn it, but they were distracting. It didn't help that she was short and cute and just similar enough to Anna in appearance that his mind kept wandering throughout the conversation. "So, what brought you to Elias?" she asked with genuine curiosity in her voice.

Jack squeezed his eyes shut, then touched two fingers to his forehead. "The guy *did* work for Slade," he muttered. "And if you were listening, you know that he was strangely out of contact for several days a few years ago."

This place was probably about the closest thing that Leyria had to a 50's diner. The floor tiles were a black and white checkerboard pattern; the walls were a bright turquoise with bars of red neon lights, and the robots scuttling back and forth to keep an eye on the customers made him feel like he was in an episode of the Jetsons.

Speaking of customers, there were only two others besides Cassi and himself: an older man and his husband sharing a quiet meal a few tables down. Jack wasn't really all that worried about being overheard.

Cassi folded her arms and leaned forward so that he could only see a mop of hair. "That does look suspicious," she said, shaking her head. "But I think we both know that it's circumstantial."

"That's the thing about conspiracies."

She looked up at him.

Lifting his cup to his lips, Jack closed his eyes as he took a sip. It was good coffee, but Summer immediately felt a burst of anxiety. Nassai were very picky about what their hosts put in their bodies. "Everything is circumstantial," he said after a moment. "You've got hunches and hopes and not much else."

"So your next move?"

"Interview the next person on my list."

"And who might that be?"

He squinted as he studied her, chuckling under his breath. "Right now, it's you," he said, making no effort to hide his distrust. "So, why don't you tell me why Larani would assign me a partner without telling me?"

Her only response was a raised eyebrow, and when that failed to make him back down, she flinched and looked away. "Because she knows you're less than eager to interrogate your fellow Keepers," Cassi answered. "She wanted to see if you would do it without needling."

Typical.

Justice Keepers could shout day and night that they were the living embodiment of honesty itself, but they knew how to play the game with the best of them. Fortunately, he had learned from one very good teacher. *Thank you, Jena,* he whispered in the back of his mind. *You have no idea how much I wish you were here.*

"Now, I'm confused," Cassi said. "If you doubted my story, why not just call Larani and confirm it?"

Plunking his elbow down on the table, Jack leaned his cheek against the palm of his hand. "I like to see if I can catch someone in a lie," he said. "Maybe I was getting close to something, and you were planning to kill me."

"And if I had been?"

Tilting his head back, Jack blinked a few times. "You know, I'm really not sure," he admitted. "I figure the people out on the street would get one hell of a show. Two Keepers going at it."

She leaned in close with a smile that could melt butter. "If you and I were gonna go at it," she purred. "It wouldn't involve punches and kicks."

A year ago, a comment like that would have phased him, but thankfully, all those months dating Gabi had burned away any modesty he might have had left. "Tempting," Jack said softly. "I can't tell if the prospect of you going all Catherine Tramell halfway through makes it more or less appealing."

If she was confused by that little piece of Earth pop-culture, she gave no indication of it. "I tell you what," she said. "Why don't you call Larani, confirm everything I've told you, and help me plan our next step."

She practically crawled over the table to bring her lips to his ear. "After that," she whispered. "We can discuss the possibility of mixing business with pleasure."

Oh boy...I'm in trouble.

6

"I don't understand," Keli Armana said.

Tall, slim and gorgeous in a white dress with short sleeves, she sat in a simple gray chair with her legs crossed. Her dark face was as hard as granite, and she looked at Director Andalon as if she meant to stare through him. "You want to know if the man is lying; simply bring him to me, and I will tell you."

Jon Andalon stood before the window with his back turned, his knuckles whitening at those words. "It's not that simple," he grumbled. "We have rule of law here. You can't just go around reading people's minds."

For the fourteenth time that day, Melissa wondered why the telepath was allowed to be part of these meetings. Part of that resentment stemmed from the pain she had caused Raynar – those memories were a part of Melissa now – but when you got right down to it, she really didn't think that Keli was a good person.

The man in question was an efficiency manager named Miles Tarso; crime scene analysts had reported that it was his access code that allowed the arsonist to access the vertical farm.

Naturally, this made Tarso a prime suspect, but the man insisted over and over that he was innocent.

Of course, Keli wanted to read his mind.

"Why not take the opportunity?"

Jon stiffened but kept his back turned, his hands trembling as he tried to hold onto some scrap of patience. "Because there are rules, Keli," he snapped. "Rules that exist to protect a citizen's rights."

Keli slouched until her head hung upside-down over the back of her chair. "Rules," she said. "You Keepers and your obsession with protocol! Your choices are really quite simple, Jon; you can follow the rules, or you can win."

Clenching her teeth, Melissa turned her head to fix her gaze on the other woman. She narrowed her eyes. "You can't just go around reading people's minds," she growled. "They have a right to privacy."

Keli sat upright.

A cruel smile blossomed on her face. "And while you worry about that," she said, "your enemies will just do what needs to be done."

Ben stood in front of the wall across from her with his arms folded, frowning down at his own feet. " 'Doing what needs to be done' is just vague enough that you can use it to justify anything," he said. "Believe me, I know."

Thrusting her chin out, Keli squinted at him. "Yes, you do," she said, rising slowly from her chair. "Do you realize that, on my world, you would be celebrated as a hero for what you did?"

She was referring to Ben's decision to allow Fringe-World colonists to keep the weapons they had illegally acquired; that was public knowledge now. Though, Melissa was fairly certain that he didn't want to be reminded of it.

Ben went red, then shook his head in disgust. "I don't *want* to be celebrated," he said in a gruff voice. "What I did-"

"Was necessary."

"Enough!" Jon bellowed.

He spun around to stand in front of the window with his fists balled at his sides. "I don't like having to repeat myself," he went on. "We will *not* be employing your talents, Keli."

The telepath closed her eyes and sucked in a deep breath. "Then I have to wonder why I'm on this team," she said. "It's not as if you've made use of my abilities even once in the last three months."

By all means, Melissa thought, *leave at your earliest convenience.* She didn't say it, of course; it wasn't her place to say it. Working with Raynar had taught her the value of having a telepath in the mix, but there was one very important difference in this situation; she had *trusted* Raynar.

"Options?" Jon said.

"If we assume Tarso is telling the truth," Ben said, stepping forward, "then the next question becomes who hacked his access codes. That may be hard to answer."

Melissa strode toward the desk with her hands folded behind herself, keeping her head down. "I think we should continue looking at security camera footage," she offered. "If we can get a sense of who was in the area before the bomb went off..."

Jon looked up to study her with dark eyes, then nodded once to show his approval. "All right," he said. "If you believe that's wise, I'll assign a team."

"I'd like to work on this personally, Director Andalon."

"Your contributions have been noteworthy, Cadet Carlson," he replied. "But you've only just begun your training. This case is out of your depth."

"But-"

"Focus on your studies, Melissa," Jon cut in before she could voice her protest. "I will make sure that you get a chance to shadow the right people, but you are by no means ready to take the lead on this case."

"All right," she said. "If you think that's best."

Double doors in the shape of an arch – both made of polished mahogany – stood before her with light glinting off the brass door handle. The hallway outside the Hall of Council was lined with portraits on the white walls and lamps on golden stands that cast light down on the blue carpets.

Larani stood just outside the doors in a black skirt with a short-sleeved blouse and stockings, her black hair tied in a long ponytail. Sitting in on a session of Council always made her feel as if she ought to project a certain formality, even if there was no reason to expect she would be called upon to speak.

A hologram appeared before her: the image of a tall man in black pants and a white shirt under his maroon vest. "You may go in, Director Tal," it said before rippling away in a swirl of colour.

She pulled one door open.

On the other side, a set of steps formed an aisle between rows of blue cushioned seats that occupied the second level. She could already hear the raised voices of the speakers below radiating through this large room with its vaulted ceiling.

Larani closed her eyes, breathing deeply. *This is part of your job now,* she thought, taking that first step forward. *Sit through it, keep an eye on the political currents and use that information to your advantage.*

Larani had a talent for politics, though no love for it.

She chose a seat near the ledge that overlooked the first floor, sitting primly with her hands on her knees, hunched over to peer over the railing. If today's session followed the same pattern as the one she had attended last week...

Down below, 987 seats in a semi-circle along the opposite wall were occupied by councilors who represented various districts across Leyria, each one dressed in colours that showed party affiliation. That wasn't required, but it had become a tradition. The Reds were in the middle as the current dominant party with the Greens on their right and the Blues on their left.

One man in a blue coat with a high collar trimmed with silver was already on his feet and speaking in a clear, crisp voice. Jeral Dusep was of average height with bronze skin and black hair that he wore combed back. "The tide must be stemmed," he said. "At some point, we have to put a moratorium on this influx of immigrants."

Larani sat forward with her elbow upon her knee, covering her mouth with three fingers. *Well, this should be interesting,* she thought. *He's never been quite so...brazen about his views before now.*

On the red-carpeted floor at the base of the seats reserved for the councilors, a tall woman in a white coat stood with her back turned, a golden staff in the shape of a shepherd's crook in her hand. From this angle, Larani could only see the back of Sarona Vason's white-haired head, but she knew that the Prime Council had no patience for Dusep's open bigotry.

Sadly, there was little she could say; the Prime Council's job was not to argue but to mediate disputes among the councilors and to force a vote if necessary.

Dusep stood in the seventh row up, in the blue section, gesticulating wildly as he spoke. "They come to our world with backward ideas," he went on. "Violent and hateful ideologies! And worse yet, many of the Earthers that we take in as refugees are those who could not survive on their own world. Meaning it becomes our job to care for them."

Tapping her lips with one finger, Larani narrowed her eyes. *What are you playing at?* she wondered, sitting forward. *Your party isn't known for an anti-Earth stance; so, you can't think this will fire up the base.*

In fact, none of the parties were openly hostile to Earth. Few people saw the influx of immigrants – no more than a few thousand each year – as a threat or a problem. Was this simply Dusep's personal opinion?

"Now, look at the result," Dusep said. "Last night's attack on the vertical farm is a direct result of anti-Leyrian sentiment. They claim our society coddles its citizens."

A murmur rose up in response to that: most of it negative, but Larani was sure she heard the odd grumble of approval. Could the Sons of Savard be tapping into a sentiment that was taking root at the heart of Leyrian society?

"And so," Dusep shouted over the crowd. "They resort to violence to show us the error of our ways!"

On the floor, Sarona Vason turned and pointed the end of her staff at him. "There is no evidence to indicate that immigrants had anything to do with last night's attack." That was another facet of her job: fact-checking, holding councilors accountable for the things they said.

Larani didn't like where this was going.

"Is that a fact?" Dusep asked, stepping forward. "And this ideology of survival of the fittest that the Sons of Savard endorse? One of the guiding principles of Earth culture."

A woman on the other side of the room stood up, looking sharp in her dark-green dress with a V-shaped neckline. She was a blonde-haired beauty with a chin-length bob and a delicate nose. Gorgeous. It bothered Larani that her mind went to such places while she was trying to do her job, but there it was.

"Earth doesn't have a single defining culture," the woman said. "Their capacity for instantaneous planet-wide communication is less than one hundred years old. They have not had enough time to become homogeneous in the way other worlds have."

"Regardless," Dusep began.

Sarona Vason slammed the butt of her staff down on the floor, abruptly silencing him. "Regardless," she cut in before Dusep could begin protesting. "Instigating this kind of unfounded panic among our citizens will only make it harder for law enforcement to do their jobs. This line of discussion is over."

"But-"

The Prime Council pointed the end of her shepherd's crook at him, and Dusep shut his mouth so quickly that you might have thought Sarona Vason was a wizard on the verge of turning him into a toad.

Councilor Dusep sat down with a grunt, resting his hands on his knees and staring blankly into the distance. Something about his posture seemed to indicate that this line of discussion *wasn't* over, but he wouldn't press the point right now.

"We will resume our discussion on Bill 24C3," Sarona insisted.

Larani tuned the whole thing out; she wasn't the least bit interested in a bill about redefining the regulations governing medical bots. No, Dusep's latest ploy had her feeling very uneasy. After three years of running a Keeper team on Earth, she had seen just how destructive such divisive rhetoric could be.

The man was definitely up to something, and in taking on the role of Head of the Justice Keepers, she had made it her job to keep an eye on him. Worry gnawed away at her insides; she didn't like this.

She didn't like it one bit.

"So, explain the sitch to me again."

The auxiliary crime lab in the basement of the Denabrian Justice Keeper office was a cramped little room with no sources of natural light. Four spartan gray walls surrounded a control console in the shape of a horseshoe, and the entire place was just big enough to hold maybe a dozen people.

This room was used primarily for reviewing security camera footage; as such, none of the equipment that would fill other crime labs was present. The whole thing felt very much like a coffin to Melissa; she had never liked tight, enclosed spaces and sharing this one with her father and Anna was less than ideal.

Dressed in blue jeans and a plain, white t-shirt, Melissa leaned against the side of the console with her hands folded over her stomach, staring up at the ceiling. "Director Andalon says he doesn't want me getting near this case," she explained. "I'm supposed to focus on my studies."

Her father stood by the wall in an open-collared shirt and sport coat, heaving out a soft sigh. "Well put, Missy," he grumbled. "Way to make it sound like you're in the third act of a buddy cop picture."

Melissa grimaced, then touched a single finger to her forehead. "The point is that I can't access the train station's security camera footage," she said. "Cadets can't make use of this equipment without a supervising officer."

Anna stood behind the console with one fist on her hip, smiling down at herself. "You're nuts," she said, shaking her head. "Melissa, when I said I wanted to spend some time with you guys, this wasn't what I had in mind."

"But can you help?"

The other woman sucked on her bottom lip, nodding slowly as she thought it over. "I could," Anna said. "But you haven't given me much reason to think that I should."

"I want to be part of this."

"Why?"

Why? How did Melissa even *begin* to answer that question? Perhaps because she carried the symbiont of one of the best Keepers who had ever lived, perhaps because she was eager to prove herself. Maybe focusing on the job made it easier for both Melissa and her Nassai to deal with the sadness.

Closing her eyes, Melissa took a deep breath through her nose. "I just want to do something," she whispered in a soft rasp. "I was there when Jena fought that thing that Overseer made to defend the Nexus. I was helpless, and I hate that feeling."

With some reluctance, Melissa turned around to find the other woman watching her with those big blue eyes. Did her words make an impression? Her reasons did sound kind of hollow when she spoke them out loud, but...

Anna stepped up to the control console, her fingers dancing over its surface. "*You* are lucky that I'm a go with your heart kind of girl." There were a few soft beeps as she put in her passwords and brought up menus accessing the holographic imaging systems. "Besides, Jena was a force to be reckoned with because she relied on so many diverse perspectives, not just trained Keepers. Maybe that means a cadet has something to add."

White light streamed up from projectors on the wall across from Anna, forming a screen of light that was bright but not painful to look at. Colour seeped into the image bit by bit.

A long stretch of black pavement beneath an overhanging roof ran alongside a set of train tracks that stretched on for several dozen paces before entering a tunnel. By the warm light coming in from the west, it was clear that this footage was filmed at dusk.

No one was standing on the platform, not one soul. The place was so deserted that Melissa half expected to see a tumbleweed blow across the screen. It suddenly dawned on her that she had just asked permission to view hours upon hours of camera footage with no guarantee that she would see anything of significance.

A train emerged from the tunnel, hovering two feet above the mag-lev tracks as it settled to a stop next to the platform. Doors slid open, and then – twenty seconds later – they slid shut again. No one had disembarked.

Anna looked up at the screen with lips pursed, her brows

drawn together. “Hold on a sec,” she said, tapping at the console. “I'm going to run an algorithm that should speed up the process.”

The train zipped back into the tunnel at an accelerated rate, and the image darkened as the sun set. Lights in the overhanging roof came on, making it easy to see every square inch of the platform.

Another train emerged from the tunnel, settled to a stop for maybe half a second and then went back the way it had come. Once again, there was no one on the platform. And why would there be? The farms were automated; maintenance workers only came out this far once or twice a week.

She watched three more trains emerge from the tunnel without a single passenger getting off. Even with the film sped up, this was beyond frustrating. Her father was right; law enforcement was mostly a slow, tedious grind punctuated by brief moments of high intensity. But she was in it now.

Five minutes later, after what was probably the fourteenth or fifteenth train, Melissa perked up when the footage slowed down to normal speed.

A train on the platform had its doors open, light spilling out from within. Two people emerged, one after the other, and the image froze in place as orange rectangles surrounded each of them.

The camera zoomed in, and Melissa saw herself in profile. The figure behind her was obviously Aiden. “We were the first ones to arrive,” she whispered. “No one else came by train.”

Once again, the footage sped up only to slow down again less than five seconds later. Director Andalon stepped off the train, an orange box surrounding his body. He turned to face the camera with a stern expression and began tapping the screen of his multi-tool.

“What's he doing?” Melissa wondered aloud.

“Most likely, he's requisitioning the footage you're looking at," Anna explained. "Chances are he went through it himself and realized that the bomber didn't arrive by train. This was a duplication of effort, Melissa."

There was no venom in Anna's voice – in fact, her tone was incredibly gentle – but Melissa felt the sting of those words anyway. What was she doing, wasting everybody's time? She really should have left this to experienced Keepers. Stubborn resolve replaced self-pity mere seconds later.

Clasping her chin in one hand, Melissa shut her eyes. "No," she said, taking a few steps toward the hologram. "There's got to be something else we can try. Can you show me the farm's security cameras?"

Anna tapped in a few commands.

The hologram changed, turning white for a few seconds before it reformed into the image of a narrow road outside a gate. Once again, the sun was just a few minutes away from setting. She could see the train platform in the distance.

"Hang on," Anna said.

The footage sped up, though it was hard to notice with no obvious cues to mark the passing of time. The landscape darkened and then lights came on, shining down on the road. For the longest time, it seemed as if nothing was happening. Then her eye caught a glimpse of something. "Freeze it."

The image went still.

There on the road, roughly ten paces away from the gate, a smear of black and gray looked so very much like a fingerprint on the camera lens. There was no orange rectangle to identify this as a person; it was more like a camera distortion than anything else, but there was something odd about it.

"Resume playback," Melissa said. "Normal speed."

The smear of black and gray moved toward the gate.

"Reverse playback."

A few taps from Anna made the video play backward, the blur of colour moving away from the gate, back out to the road.

Something about it imitated human movements. "That's a person!" Melissa exclaimed.

Biting her lip, Anna looked down at the console, strands of blue hair framing her face. "I think you're right," she muttered. "A person using some type of jamming tech to prevent the camera from getting a clean image."

Harry stepped forward with his arms folded, shaking his head as he let out a deep breath. "That kind of tech exists?" he asked. "You can just disrupt a security camera with some kind of cloaking field?"

"It's basic holography," Anna said. "Spy movies on my world usually imagine a criminal using a complex hologram to make himself look like someone else, but that's unrealistic. Holograms are transparent. Even the best ones can't convincingly mimic a human face, but if you simply create a distortion field of refracted light around yourself, that'll do the trick."

"So we have no way to ID this man?"

"There has to be something!" Melissa protested. "Couldn't you at least estimate the height and build of the perpetrator from the size of the image?"

Anna was hunched over, tapping away at the control console with a sour expression on her face. "I could try," she mumbled. "But there's no reason the height of the hologram would have to correspond to the height of the subject. Our perp could be five feet tall and use a six-foot tall hologram. Also, how do you know it's a man?"

"Brilliant," Melissa grumbled.

She was out of options. Anxiety flared up when she contemplated the fact that she had no idea how to proceed from this point. Wasn't she supposed to know? *Of course not,* a small voice whispered. *You're a cadet.*

Harry shut his eyes and let out a sigh. "Okay," he said, coming up behind her. "If we can't ID the perp, we should look at the surrounding information. How did they get to the farm with a bomb in tow?"

Melissa stood with her arms hanging limp at her sides, her eyes fixed on the floor. "A car service," she whispered. "If he didn't take the train, maybe he hired a car to drop him off near the farm."

"We can check that," Anna said.

The hologram flickered out of existence to be replaced with a list of white text on a blue background. Addresses, Melissa realized. Some of them corresponded to Denabria's residential neighbourhoods, while others were in the downtown core. "Every destination requested by people using the central car service yesterday," Anna said.

She scrolled through them one by one until she found a drop-off point roughly half a kilometer away from the farm. "There!" she exclaimed. "Time stamp has the passenger arriving shortly after sunset."

"Who took the car?" Harry inquired.

"We don't know."

"There's no record?"

Anna squeezed her eyes shut, breathing in slowly. "Leyrian privacy laws are quite strict," she said. "The government can't just track your movements through the transit system. Usually, that's a good thing, but..."

"Can you tell where the car picked up this passenger?" Melissa asked.

A few taps of Anna's deft fingers brought up another list, side by side with the first. This one displayed pick-up addresses for every ride, cross-referenced by trip number. "I can indeed," Anna said. "The car picked up its passenger at 14 Elidrea Street and drove them to a spot near the farm."

"Elidrea Street," Harry mumbled.

"It's a residential neighbourhood."

"Well," Melissa said. "Looks like we have a place to begin."

7

It was hard to keep his mind off Anna.

He made a valiant effort – there was no denying that – but whenever he wasn't able to distract himself with work, thoughts of her crept into Jack's mind. Silencing them took a great deal of effort. Strangely, this wasn't the same as when he had broken up with Gabi just a few months ago.

Instead of feeling miserable all the time, he mostly just worried about Anna. And he missed her. Their long talks had become a fixed point in his life, a pillar that held up his world. Now, he was forbidden from speaking with her...Well, maybe not *forbidden* – she hadn't been *that* firm with him – but she did need her space.

That was one reason why he wasn't exactly thrilled about the prospect of having a partner that reminded him so much of Anna. Cassi was a fine Keeper, he was sure, but he knew that working with her was going to be difficult. Not because of anything the poor woman had done, but rather because Jack Hunter couldn't manage his feels. He wasn't planning to protest, but he did want to know the motive behind Larani's decision. Bright sunlight through the window of Larani's office left the desk and the woman herself as little more than silhouettes in the middle of a rectangle of light that stretched across the floor tiles. It was an unnerving sight, to say the least.

Jack walked through the door with his head down, heaving out a soft sigh as he approached his boss. "A partner?" he began. "Well, I certainly don't object, but I would have liked to have been told."

Craning her neck to study him, Larani blinked a few times. "You know, I thought you might," she said softly. "Which is why I decided to surprise you. I wanted to see how willing you are to follow my lead."

Jack crossed his arms with a grunt, backing away from the desk. "So, did I pass the test?" he asked with a shrug of his shoulders. "Are you ready to start trusting me? Or are you just gonna Walter Skinner me for the rest of my tenure as your attache?"

"Is that a director I don't know?"

"Never mind."

The warm smile that slowly spread on Larani's face was not the reaction he would have expected. "You've passed," she said. "This test, at least. I thought Cassiara might be agreeable to you. It seems you have a fondness for strong-willed women who speak their minds without hesitation."

Jack felt creases form on his brow. "Are you trying to find me a partner or a date to the ball at Netherfield Park?" he asked. "I'll tell you right now: I get plenty of action by standing awkwardly in the corner and casting disdainful glares at the dance floor."

His boss rose from her chair in one smooth motion, closing her eyes as she took a deep breath. "You and Agent Seyrus share something in common," she said. "A fervent hatred of Grecken Slade."

"Heh. I like her already."

"Before Slade revealed himself for the traitor that he was,

Cassiara made herself rather unpopular with a steady stream of criticisms of the man's policies."

Well...that made the prospect of working with her a little easier to swallow, but just the same, a part of him felt uneasy, and part of that uneasiness came from the fact that he was starting to accept the reality of Cassi as his new partner. It felt like he was betraying Anna, though he couldn't say how.

Was it because some of Larani's observations had sunk in? Somewhere in the back of his mind, Jack was beginning to wonder if maybe the woman he was meant to be with *wouldn't* just disappear on him for months. And thinking that – thinking that it might not be Anna – ripped him up inside.

God, he was so messed up!

To recap, he was uneasy about accepting a new work partner because he was afraid that getting to know Cassi would make him like Anna less. If anyone could over-think a situation, it was Jack bloody Hunter.

"Are you all right?" Larani asked.

Jack closed his eyes, touching two fingers to his forehead. "Yeah," he muttered in a breathy rasp. "I'm fine."

"Then perhaps you should speak to Agent Seyrus," Larani said. "I would imagine you have a lot of work to do."

Sunlight glinted off the windows on each floor of a long two-story building in the middle of a field of grass. To Jack, the Keeper office in Shilenar looked rather plain. Not a glittering tower or a masterpiece of architecture. Just a simple two-story rectangle about a hundred feet from the street.

He went inside and suffered through the rigmarole of submitting his badge to the holographic receptionist. A male hologram, this time, which was encouraging; Leyrians really didn't put much stock in antiquated gender roles. Once that was done, he made his way upstairs to meet the woman he would have to interrogate.

Reviewing her dossier on the screen of his multi-tool left him feeling more than a little apprehensive. Cara Sinthel had silver-blonde hair that she wore tied back, a sharp contrast to her tanned face with large dark eyes. Of course, she looked like a teenager, but her profile listed her age as thirty-two. Older than him by almost ten years; he was really going to have to project authority this time. No easy task for Jack Hunter.

The building was pretty much empty. He passed one or two people in the hallway that branched off from the lobby, but for the most part, every door he passed was shut, every office unoccupied. It was a civic holiday here in Kenthera Province, and most of the local Keepers had taken the day off. Why Cara Sinthel had suggested today of all days for their meeting was beyond him, but that already made him want to distrust her. Slade was exactly the kind of guy who would hate a holiday on principle, and he suspected the man's cronies would feel the same.

On the upper floor, white-walled corridors ran the length of the building with doors spaced at even intervals. Each office had a window that would allow any passersby to get a glimpse inside. Assuming the shades weren't drawn, of course.

Mostly, Jack saw only simple offices, about half the size of Larani's, with gray floor tiles and a desk in the middle. Rectangular windows on the back wall looked out upon the grassy field outside. The building was pretty much empty. It was a civic holiday here in Kentara Province.

He found the Keeper he was looking for.

Dressed in simple gray pants and a matching sweater, Cara Sinthel stood inside her office with arms folded, turned so that Jack saw her in profile. She seemed to be focused on some hologram on the wall.

He knocked on the glass door.

The woman stiffened, then shot a glance over her shoulder, squinting at him. "You can come in," she said, her voice muffled by the window. Pushing it open allowed him to detect the soft scent of lavender, but he saw no potted plants.

Jack shut his eyes, bowing his head to her. "Special Agent Sinthel," he said, taking a few cautious steps into the office. "My name is Jack Hunter; I work for Larani Tal. We were scheduled to have a little talk this morning."

Spinning on her heel, the woman strode toward him with arms folded, then craned her neck to stare up at him. "So, you're the one," she said. "The first Justice Keeper from your backward little world."

The heat in his face told him that his cheeks must have been a bright shade of red. Backward little world? "Yeah, that's me," Jack growled. "Now, if you don't mind toning down the nationalism, maybe we could have a chat."

"What do you want to talk about?"

"Grecken Slade."

Cara turned her back on him and marched over to the desk. "What about Slade?" she asked in a calm, controlled voice. "The man was a traitor, and I regret supporting his bid to become Chief Director."

Pressing his lips into a thin line, Jack narrowed his eyes. "I don't buy it," he said, shaking his head. "You were one of Slade's most dedicated supporters. You can't expect me to believe you did a complete one-eighty."

"A what?"

"Never mind."

The woman glanced over her shoulder, her face as smooth as silk. "Why is that so surprising?" she asked. "I agreed with Slade's policies, but not with his wanton acts of terrorism."

Jack crossed his arms with a sigh, approaching her with his head down. "Do you know anything about Grecken Slade's policies toward Earth?" he inquired. "Your people tried to manage us."

Cara turned around and sat on the edge of her desk, folding

her hands in her lap. "Well, perhaps that's because your people needed managing," she replied. "It's no secret that your world is a hotbed of bigotry and violence."

Red-faced and fuming, Jack squeezed his eyes shut. "Yeah, you *would* say that," he muttered, trembling on the spot. "Typical Leyrian arrogance! Just assume that you know what's best for everybody else in the galaxy!"

"And this is a crime to you?"

"I beg your pardon."

The woman looked up at him with lips pursed, her gray eyes like polished silver. "Why are we having this discussion, Agent Hunter?" she asked in clipped tones. "Surely, you don't plan to hold me accountable for a difference in political stance."

"We're having this discussion," he began, "because three years ago, you went to Petross Station on a mission assigned to you by Grecken Slade."

"What of it?"

"When you got back, your superiors noted a distinct change in your attitude. You were harder, quicker to advocate harsher sentences." That wasn't much to go on, but how exactly did you find a pattern that would indicate the presence of a corrupted symbiont? "You displayed an almost jingoistic Leyrian nationalism; on several occasions, you were written up for conduct unbecoming a Justice Keeper. The most recent of which – dated roughly two years ago – saw you reprimanded for openly declaring Antauran citizens to be sub-human scum in a public venue."

She was sweating, her face pinched into an uncomfortable expression. "So...Has Larani Tal's errand boy come to chastise me?" In the blink of an eye, she was on her feet and striding toward him, forcing him to back up. "Come to tell me that I'm no longer the model of an exemplary Keeper?"

"I want to know what caused that change in attitude."

"Perhaps I just started saying what I've always thought."

"No," Jack said. "That doesn't make sense. You see – in theory – if you were prone to such unapologetic prejudice, a Nassai would never have accepted you as its host in the first place. So...Care to answer my question?"

"There is no answer."

Jack turned away from her, clasping hands together behind himself as he walked to her office door. "You know, it's funny," he said, glancing back over his shoulder. "Calissa Narim had some interesting things to say about you."

It was a gamble; he hadn't been able to pull one useful tidbit of information out of Calissa, but he had to try something, and this lady was rubbing him the wrong way. If it paid off, he would have exposed one of Slade's minions; if not...Well, he'd end up tipping his hand for no good reason.

The tiny woman just stood there with stiff posture, her face twisted in disgust. "So, what did Agent Narim say?" she asked. "I suppose she offered you my name in exchange for some form of leniency after her debacle last year."

"Oh, she named you all right," Jack said, turning back to her. "Said it wouldn't be much of a betrayal since we were bound to find out anyway. She said that of all Slade's followers, you were the one who was least able to play the role of a good Justice Keeper. She was laughing at you, Cara."

The woman flinched.

Cautiously, he moved toward her, watchful for any sign that she might bolt like a cornered rabbit. "She was really quite thorough," Jack went on. "She said you got your new symbiont on Petross Station, but you weren't prepared for the sheer intensity of its emotions. She said you lacked discipline, and that's why you keep getting written up. A simple inability to control your-"

The woman jumped and kicked out.

Her foot slammed into Jack's face, filling his vision with

darkness, and applying a light Bending. He went flying backward, crashing through the window next to her office door. Glass shattered as he dropped to the floor in the hallway.

Jack curled his legs against his chest, flinging himself upright. His hands came up in a fighting stance. "All right," he said, shaking his head. "I suppose we could just go for the direct approach."

Cara stepped through the hole in the window.

She punched him in the face, blurring his vision once again, then spun for a back-hand strike. In a heartbeat, Jack reacted, turning his body and catching her arm in both hands. He forced her to double over.

Jack grabbed the back of her collar with one hand. Then he whirled around and sent her face-first through the window of the office across from hers. It was unoccupied, thankfully, but Cara was standing stunned in a pile of glass shards, facing a desk with picture frames on its surface.

Jack followed her in.

The woman faced him with an angry snarl, shallow cuts on her face leaking blood onto her creamy skin. "I'm gonna make you pay for that," she snarled, shaking her head. "Painfully."

She jumped and kicked out.

Jack brought one hand up to strike her foot, pushing it aside. The woman dropped to the floor right in front of him, dazed and off-balance.

He delivered an upper-cut to the stomach that lifted Cara off her feet, driving the air from her lungs. Then he brought his other fist down on the top of her head, knocking her senseless.

She fell and landed on her backside, staring up at him with tears glistening on her cheeks. Instinct took over, and he knew that he had to finish this before things got out of control. You did *not* give a Keeper a chance to get back up.

Jack tried to kick her face.

The woman's hands came up, grabbing his ankle,

preventing him from making contact. There was a twisting sensation that he recognized as Bent Gravity, and then he was thrown backward.

He went right through the shattered window, across the hallway and then through the window in Cara's office. The Bending fizzled out, dropping him onto his ass in the middle of the black-tiled floor.

Cara was on him in a second.

She leaped through the window like a cat pouncing on a mouse, landing on top of him and screaming. Her teeth were bared, and blood dripped from the cut on her cheek. "Slade was a great man."

Jack grabbed her shirt and applied a Bending of his own.

Cara was yanked upward until her back hit the ceiling, leaving a spider-web of thin cracks. A moment later, she fell, legs kicking wildly as she tried to recover her wits.

Jack rolled aside.

His opponent landed on all fours in the middle of the office, shaking her head to clear away the fog. "I can see why Slade found you such a nuisance," she said, struggling to get to her feet.

As he stood up and rounded on her, Jack pressed a hand to his chest and gasped for breath. "Well, tormenting him was so much fun," he said. "Hey, did Greck ever tell you about the time I said he looked like he'd just come from-"

Cara ran at him.

Stepping aside at the last second, Jack let her slip past him. He kicked out behind himself, striking the back of her leg. That sent her sprawling head-first into the dark gray wall with a *thunk.*

He whirled around.

Cara was already facing him.

The woman jumped and kicked high, striking his chin with the toe of her shoe. His vision darkened for a moment. Being a

Keeper, he was able to rely on spatial awareness to keep track of his opponent. She stepped forward, throwing a punch.

Jack turned his body so that his shoulder was toward her, catching her fist as it flew past. “You could at least...” He let go and spun around to face her, delivering a hard jab to the nose. “Let me finish my wisecrack!”

Cara went stumbling backward, blood leaking from her nostrils, spilling over her lips. She hit the wall and let out a grunt.

He charged at her, then jumped and turned his body for a flying side kick. The tiny woman ducked out of his path. His foot hit the wall instead, chipping the duroplastic, and then he landed.

Two hands seized the back of his shirt, whirling him around to face the window. Bent Gravity did the rest.

Jack went flying across the office with arms flailing, crashing through the window behind the desk. Glass rained down all around him as he dropped two stories toward the grass below. *This is gonna suck.*

He landed on his knees with enough force to crack a normal man's bones, his head spinning as a wave of dizziness washed over him. “Oh, god...” Jack pressed a palm to his forehead. “Why can't they ever go quietly?”

He looked up to see Cara leap through the shattered window, thrusting her hand into the air to reveal shards of broken glass that glittered in the sunlight. She flung them down at Jack with a touch of Bent gravity.

He rolled away.

Thin slivers of glass hit the ground where he had been like arrows loosed from a trained archer's bow, each one burying itself nearly to the tip. Had he remained there, they would have carved up his insides.

Cara landed in the grass maybe twenty feet away, crouched down and gasping for breath. Slowly, she got to her feet. “I'll give you this much credit," she said, whirling around to face him. "You provided a challenge."

Jack got up.

"You're not so bad yourself," he said, striding toward her. "So how 'bout it? You ready to finish this?"

Cara spun and back-kicked.

Doubling over, Jack caught the woman's ankle before her shoe made contact with his stomach. He gave a twist and flipped her around, throwing her flat on her back in the middle of the grass. Cara didn't stay down.

Curling her legs against her chest, she sprang off the ground and landed before him with her fists raised.

Jack punched her in the nose with a nauseating *crunch.* Seizing a fistful of the woman's hair, he forced her down and brought his knee up to strike her face. That left her dazed and disoriented.

Jack flung her sideways.

Cara went stumbling like a drunkard thrown out of a bar, her shoulder slamming into the building's front wall. A groan escaped her as she fell to her knees and pawed at the wall for balance.

She collapsed onto her stomach a moment later, lying stretched out in the grass. If you didn't know better, you might have thought she was taking a nap. "Well," Jack said. "I'm pleased to say you gave me a challenge too..."

He tapped quickly at the screen of his multi-tool, placing a call to the local PD. "This is Special Agent Jack Hunter at the Shilenar Keeper office," he rasped. "Requesting backup. Full tactical gear...We're bringing in a rogue Keeper."

"I cannot believe you went without me!"

Cassiara stood with her back turned, fists on her hips as she stared over the balcony railing at the city. The young woman wore dark green pants and a white tank top that left her shoulders bare. "Did it occur to you that we could have taken her together?"

In blue jeans and an unzipped sweater over his gray t-shirt, Jack leaned against the wall with a hand pressed to his stomach, his eyes downcast as he let out a sigh. "Did you ever *read* my personnel file?" he shot back. "Specifically, the part that says, 'does not play well with others?"

Cassi whirled around.

She stood before the railing with fists clenched at her sides, her gaze fixed on the floor. "You don't want to work with me?" she muttered. "Fine. Far be it for me to make a fuss if the great Jack Hunter has preferences."

Chewing on his lower lip, Jack shut his eyes. He was suddenly aware of sweat on his brow. "That's not what I meant," he rasped. "After Breslan, it's...hard for me to trust someone I don't know."

His new partner looked up at him with those gorgeous purple eyes, and for a brief moment, he felt like a ninth-grader at his first dance. "I thought we were getting to know one another," she said. "Was I wrong?"

Jack went red, then shook his head like a dog trying to get rain out of his fur. "We *are* getting to know one another." This next bit was going to hurt, but let it never be said that he wasn't willing to own his screw-ups. "And I shouldn't have just confronted Cara without telling you."

"Thank you."

"So..."

She just stood there with her hands in her back pockets, smiling down at herself. "You're something else, Jack Hunter," she said, stepping closer. "I've met a lot of Justice Keepers, but none quite like you."

And just like that, he was so very much aware of how close she was, close enough for him to feel the heat of her body despite the warm afternoon. God help him, he wanted to kiss her so badly. Anna's face flashed in his mind.

Clamping a hand over his mouth, Jack shut his eyes and coughed. “Yeah,” he said, backing away from her. “I get that a lot, actually. Everyone's always telling me that I'm one of a kind.”

Cassi was smiling, shaking her head with wry amusement. “Well, they are right about that,” she said softly. “But, just in case I haven't been clear, I happen to think that's a good thing.”

“Actually, you have been clear,” Jack said. “Refreshingly clear.” Maybe it was just him, but there was something so *hot* about a person who could just say what they wanted without reservation. He supposed it was because he had grown up on Earth where people got tongue-tied every time the subject of sex came up. Then again, from what he'd seen, that was equally true of Leyrians.

Dear god, he wanted to kiss her. Somewhere in the back of his mind, some muted voice was screaming that he loved Anna, but it was hard to focus on that right now. Oh, he would have no trouble putting Anna first if she, you know, actually *chose* him. But it was pretty damn difficult to be loyal to someone who gave absolutely no indication that she would be loyal to you. The last time they had spoken, Anna had told him they would see what happened when she was done getting over Bradley. That wasn't really a promise, and she had been incommunicado for nearly four months.

8

The sun was shining bright in the blue sky, silver rays falling upon small dome-like houses on either side of the street. Each one was surrounded by dense foliage, beautiful gardens and trees.

About a block away, an apartment building shaped like an hourglass stood tall with trees on its rooftop. Melissa still marveled at the beauty of Leyrian architecture. Months of living on this world had not changed that. In the end, she was glad that she had come here. Earth was a great big bundle of crazy compared to most Leyrian colonies – and she had worried that moving to a more peaceful planet would hinder her training – but it was worth it if only for the experience of actually being here.

She turned back to the man she had been interviewing.

An older fellow in gray pants and a simple blue t-shirt, he stood upon the sidewalk with sunglasses on his face, his white hair a total mess. “A Justice Keeper, huh?” he said. “Well, that's wonderful! You know I wanted to be one when I was young.”

Grinning ferociously, Melissa bowed her head to him. She had left her hair loose today, and she could feel the wind teasing it. "Thank you, sir," she began. "But as I said, I'm only a cadet."

"But you have the Nassai."

Melissa stood before him with her arms crossed, blushing as she smiled down at herself. "Yes," she said, nodding to him. "For almost four months now. I'm still learning how to work with it."

The old man smiled and chuckled. "Well, that's the biggest part," he said. "If the symbiont picked you, ma'am, it means you're worthy."

Ma'am.

It felt strange to be called that by someone so much older than her; she'd expected the man to call her "my dear" or something along those lines, but after many long years of struggle, Leyrians had overcome such sexist behaviours. Justice Keepers deserved to be respected regardless of age.

The man fidgeted, drawing her out of her reverie. "You said that you wanted to ask me a few questions, ma'am?"

"Yes, I'm sorry!" Musing on Leyrian history while the man patiently waited for her to get to the point! "Do you spend a lot of time outside, Mr..."

"Voren," he offered. "I sure do."

She looked to her left where a narrow cobblestone walkway led up to a house that looked like one large dome with two smaller ones pasted to either side, each with a roof that soaked up the sunlight. "That's your home?"

The man stood before her with his hands in his pockets, smiling down at his own feet. For some reason, he was blushing. "It is," he said. "A bit larger than necessary after my kids moved out, but my husband and I had so many memories."

Meaning this house was right across the street from the spot where a car would have picked up the bomber two nights ago. "You wouldn't have happened to have been outside two days ago, just a little before sunset?" Melissa inquired.

"I was, yes."

She had to suppress her elation. Maintaining *some* standard of professionalism was an important part of the job. Still, it was hard not to feel excited when things were finally starting to come together. "Did you happen to see a man getting picked up by a car?"

Mr. Voren frowned, turning his head to stare down at the ground next to him. "It's hard to recall," he mumbled. "I think a car might have passed by, but I don't remember seeing anyone get into it."

Melissa closed her eyes, breathing deeply. "Think back for a moment," she said. "Did you happen to notice the colour of the car? The model? Anything that might help identify the passenger?"

The man's face crumpled into a tense expression, and he shook his head. "No. I'm sorry, but no." He took a step back, letting out a deep breath. "I wasn't really paying that much attention. Cars come by sometimes."

"Could it have been your neighbour across the street?"

"Arrela?" the man scoffed. "Highly unlikely. She doesn't go out very much in the evenings, and when she does, she usually takes the train."

Most people did, so far as Melissa understood matters. Leyrian cities were designed to make public transit as accessible as possible. Major thoroughfares had no more than a few dozen cars on them at any given moment, and residential streets saw only one or two each day. "Nothing then?"

The man shook his head. "I'm sorry," he said. "If I remember anything, I'll be sure to call you."

"Thank you."

It was hard not to sound crestfallen. Professionalism was a must, but it was *so* hard to keep the disappointment out of her voice. For a moment there, she had really believed that she was making progress. "Thank you," Melissa said again. "We appreciate any help you can give us."

The sidewalk of Elidrea street was lined with small homes on one side, each with a gorgeous front yard. Some had flowerbeds and others tall trees that were already showing thick green leaves. It was a lovely neighbourhood.

Harry walked up the street in beige pants and a white shirt with the top two buttons left undone, his eyes downcast as he pondered his next move. *Canvassing the area like it's my first day with a shield on my belt,* he thought. *Some things never change.*

None of the homes had driveways, which made sense when you considered the fact that very few Leyrians actually owned a car. Possibly none at all. He wasn't entirely clear on that point.

Instead, each house had a pathway that cut through a lush green lawn on its way to the front door. To say the homes were dome-like was a bit of an oversimplification. They weren't all perfectly round. Some even had what he could only assume were the Leyrian equivalent of wings: smaller domes attached to the main building. In fact, no two houses were exactly the same.

He suddenly felt a little silly. When he had applied for a house in Denabria, he had simply accepted the standard model without any alterations. Still, it was a nice home.

At the edge of one yard, a woman in a blue dress was crouched over a flowerbed, pouring water on the plants. "Excuse me," Harry said as he approached. She stiffened, startled by his voice. "Can I talk to you for a moment?"

The woman stood up with a grunt. She was lovely: tall and slim with Asian features and black hair that she wore tied back in a long ponytail. "How can I help you, sir?"

Harry closed his eyes, breathing deeply. "I'm a liaison to the Justice Keepers," he said, stepping closer. "We have reason to believe that the person who bombed Vertical Farm 17 passed through this neighbourhood a few days ago."

The woman went pale and then lowered her eyes to stare down at the sidewalk. "I see," she mumbled. "And you want to ask me a few questions."

Crossing his arms with a grunt, Harry felt his mouth tighten. He nodded to her. "I do." It came out as a simple, matter-of-fact statement. "Specifically about whether you noticed anyone strange in the neighbourhood two nights ago around sunset."

"Two nights ago?"

"Yes, ma'am?"

The woman scrunched up her face, tossing her head about with such fury you might have expected her to get vertigo. "I was downtown two nights ago," she said. "I wouldn't have seen anything, but there was..."

"Yes?"

"It's probably nothing."

Chuckling softly, Harry bowed his head to the woman. "Ma'am," he began in the smoothest voice he could manage. "Anything you tell us could be an essential piece of information. Please don't hold back."

"Well, I've been on sabbatical from the university," she explained. "So, I've been home most days, working on my next book. And I've noticed a man who seemed to be wandering aimlessly through the neighbourhood."

"What do you mean?"

"Well, he wasn't..." The woman trailed off for a moment, a thoughtful expression on her face. "I mean to say I didn't recognize him. I know most of my neighbours, and I haven't seen this man before last week.

"At first I would have thought nothing of it – maybe he was visiting someone in the area – but I saw him several times over the course of one week, and he never seemed to have a specific destination in mind."

Harry's detective instincts kicked in. A young officer might look at something like that and think "But what about due process? You can't assume anything based on such circumstantial evidence," but after a few years, you began to develop a sense for these things. People, for the most part, were creatures of habit. They noticed when there was a change in their routine, and usually, such changes indicated something important.

"Could he have been out for a walk?" Harry asked. "Perhaps he was visiting one of your neighbours, and he wanted some fresh air."

"Well, that's what I thought," the woman said. "But it was weird. Once I started to notice him, I began to pay attention. He would stop at random points and...Well, there's just no good way to say this..."

"Go on."

"He'd *inspect* the area," the woman blurted out. "He'd pause on the sidewalk, take stock of how many trees were in the nearest front yard. Things like that. I almost thought he wanted to apply for a house here."

Rubbing his chin with the back of his hand, Harry squinted at the woman. "That *is* interesting," he muttered. "Think carefully. How many times did you see this man doing something like that?"

A touch of crimson painted the woman's cheeks, and she looked away to avoid eye-contact. "Twice, maybe three times," she said. "He would do it in the daytime, when most people are out of the house."

"Thank you. This might be useful."

Suddenly, the woman perked up, her eyes widening as if she had just seen a ghost. "I just remembered something!" she all but shouted. Taking control of herself, she let out a deep breath. "One time, he was near my house when he stopped and started looking at the homes across the street. I noticed a Talis Ring on his third finger."

"I'm sorry; what's that?"

The woman gave him one of those looks you'd expect to see from a mother whose child just asked why it was necessary to say please and thank you. "It's a symbol of the Holy Companion," she said. "Only members of the clergy wear them."

Harry squeezed his eyes shut, anxiety clawing at his insides. "Thank you," he said with a curt nod. "We'll be in touch if we need anything else."

A member of the clergy. Suddenly, the bombing had religious overtones. He would have to familiarize himself with the Layati doctrine, but he wasn't at all surprised. Most monotheistic religions had a certain paternalism that would fit nicely with the mandate of the Sons of Savard. He made his way back to Melissa. Maybe she had learned something they could use.

The office they had given her was a small, gray-walled room with a floor-to-ceiling window that looked out on a balcony. On the other side of the street, sunlight glinted off the windows of a cylindrical building with a field of green grass and trees on its rooftop.

Anna stood before her desk with her arms folded, frowning down at the report that scrolled across its surface. "The Sons of Savard," she said, eyebrows rising. "Fitting. You leave to Earth to get away from this toxic bullshit, and it follows you."

White text scrolled across the desk's surface, relaying the details of the bombing two nights ago. The Sons of Savard... She had been in her mother's living room when the news report came in. So far, she had never heard of a group like this. It galled her to think that the very things she had come to despise about Earth culture were now taking root on her own planet. She wanted to punch something.

A pang of grief hit her, and she had to force it down before she got trapped in the sadness. Thinking of Earth reminded her of Bradley. Why was it that her rational mind could be so convinced that she had made the right decision while her heart felt as if she had ripped out a piece of herself.

Closing her eyes, Anna tried to steady her emotions. "You don't have time for this," she said. "If you're gonna be any help to anyone, you can't afford to let yourself collapse into a pile of mush."

A knock on the glass door that looked into the hallway startled her. Nassai couldn't see through solid objects, even when they were transparent.

She spun around, expecting to see Larani Tal outside her door, and instead found the one person she really didn't want to talk to. Jack stood in the hallway in jeans and a gray t-shirt under a blue sweater he left unzipped. He was as handsome as ever with that unkempt hair and a mischievous glint in his eye.

Anna smiled, bowing her head to him. "You can come in," she said, striding toward the door. "I thought you might stop by."

He pushed the door open and stepped into her office, pausing for a moment to take in the total lack of décor. "Hmm," Jack said, deep creases forming in his brow. "I guess you really *haven't* had a chance to settle in."

"I'm only here for one day."

"I see," he mumbled. "Blue hair?"

Covering a grin with the tips of her fingers, Anna shut her eyes. "Yeah," she said, nodding once. "Just a whim I had about a month ago. After restricting myself to blonde and red-head so your people would take me seriously, I wanted to cut loose."

Jack turned on his heel, facing the wall to her left with his fists on his hips. "Well, maybe you should cut loose in here," he teased. "I mean, if this place gets any wilder, we might see accountants using blue ink instead of black."

Ordinarily, that would make her laugh. Well...Maybe not. Distracted as she was, she could still tell that Jack wasn't at the top of his game when it came to making quips. Maybe he was feeling the awkwardness as much as she was. "Did you need something?"

He rounded on her with his arms crossed, concern evident in his expression. "So, is everything okay?" he asked, raising one eyebrow. "I don't mean to pry, but you seem kind of tense."

"Now really isn't a good time," Anna said. "I have a lot on the go."

"I thought you were on leave."

"And that means I can't have a lot on the go?" she snapped. Bleakness take her, she did not need the awkwardness of this conversation on top of everything else that she was feeling. "I'm busy, Jack."

He blew out a deep breath, striding deeper into her office with his arms swinging. "Yeah, I can tell," he said, moving past her. "Four months go by without so much as a peep from you. You must be busy."

She whirled around to find him standing there with his back turned, staring out the window at the buildings across the way. The petulance in his tone made her want to give him a piece of her mind. Before she could stop herself, the words started spilling out.

"I told you that I need space," she said coldly. "What part of 'space' involves knocking on my door and demanding to have a conversation with me?"

Jack stumbled around to face her with his hands up defensively, his mouth hanging open. "I'm your best friend!" he sputtered. "It's been *four* months! Frankly, if our roles were reversed, I'd be offended that you *hadn't* checked in."

"I don't need you to check in."

"No, apparently not."

He marched past her to the door, pausing there for a

moment. “If that's the way you feel,” he began, “then believe me, I won't reach out again.”

And then he was gone.

Anna blew out a deep breath, trying to calm her nerves. The anger faded within moments, and she became aware of another voice in the back of her mind, a voice that cautioned her to hold back her harsh words.

Jack didn't deserve her anger...

Except, in a way, he did.

Gah! It was all so unbearably complicated. She could see that Jack had nothing but the best intentions, and there was really no way he could have known her state of mind, but at the same time, she was a grown woman. She didn't need him to check in on her. When she was ready to resume their friendship, she'd let him know.

Sadly, that might not be an option now.

The standard refrain about checking her impulsiveness rose to the forefront of her mind, but she silenced it. It wasn't her job to mute her feelings for someone else even if they were inconvenient.

Anna sat down on the gray-tiled floor, drawing her legs up against her chest. She pressed the heels of her hands to her eye-sockets. “I hate my life,” she muttered. “I really fucking hate my life.”

Pushing open a set of double doors that led to a large room in the church basement, Brinton strode through. There were boxes stacked against the cream-coloured walls, each containing copies of *The Light and the Way,* the holy book that detailed the covenant between Layat and the Holy Companion.

People stood in a circle in the middle of the room, their conversation coming to an abrupt halt when they saw him enter. Not a good sign, but he had larger concerns in his mind, at the moment. He took stock of the others.

Kaylia Sandez was a tall woman in a black skirt with white flowers and a blouse that revealed a hint of cleavage. Her long, black hair was left loose to frame a gorgeous face with olive skin and dark eyes that seemed to pull you in.

Across from her, Tran Sovala looked out of place in gray pants and a matching t-shirt. A short man with fair skin and tilted eyes, he wore his black hair up in a forest of tiny spikes.

And then there was Jarl.

Tall and imposing in a high-collared black coat that dropped almost to his knees, Jarl stood across from Brinton with a stony expression on his dark face. His eyes were narrowed in thought. "You're late."

With his mouth agape, Brinton looked up at the ceiling and blinked. "That's what you have to say?" he blurted. "A comment on my punctuality? We agreed that the Sons of Savard would not reveal themselves until we were ready!"

Jarl crossed his arms, frowning as he looked down at himself. He shook his head with a soft sigh. "We are ready, Brinton," he said. "Your assignment at the vertical farm was a complete success."

Brinton felt sweat on his forehead but resisted the urge to wipe it away. "I'm not sure," he muttered. "The event is getting all kinds of media attention; the Keepers are involved."

"We anticipated such eventualities."

"If they find me..."

Jarl reached out to clap a hand onto Brinton's shoulder, a lazy smile blooming on his face. "Then you will face that like a man," he said. "You cannot advocate the values of strength and independence and then become a coward when things get difficult."

"He was always a coward."

That came from Kaylia.

She stood there, yawning and covering her gaping mouth with three fingers. "Let's be honest with ourselves," she began.

"Brinton hasn't ever been fond of making the hard decisions. Of *course,* he would want to back down."

"I'm the one who planted the damn bomb!"

"And a very good job you did of it too."

Cutting them off with a soft sigh, Jarl turned his back on Brinton. He marched away from the group with his hands moving in emphatic gestures. "We have taken an enormous step forward," he said. "And we don't have the luxury of waiting for 'the right time' anymore."

He turned partway so that Brinton saw him in profile, then looked over his shoulder to fix smoldering eyes on the lot of them. "The Ragnosians could be crossing over to our side of the galaxy at this very moment."

"I'm aware of that!" Brinton shouted.

"We need to prepare our people," Jarl went on as if he hadn't even spoken. "We need to cut away the dead weight of those who cannot fend for themselves. A return to traditional values in preparation for the war that we know will follow. That is why we must begin the next phase of our plan."

"Next phase?"

"I've been in contact with other cells around the planet. They're coming here. In three days' time, we're going to destroy five more farms and two of the city's geothermal plants. That should create a little chaos, and chaos has a way of exposing the truth about human nature."

Brinton felt the blood drain out of his face, his eyes slowly widening as he studied the other man. "You're insane," he whispered. "We don't have the resources to pull off something like that."

"Ah, but you do!"

Brinton jumped at the sound of a voice that didn't belong to anyone in his group. It seemed to come from somewhere in the back of the room, near the boxes that were piled up along the wall.

The air seemed to ripple, forming the shape of what seemed to be a woman striding toward them, but it was just a silhouette. He could see right through her. It seemed as if he were looking at some ghostly apparition.

The illusion vanished moments later, the woman growing less and less transparent until she stood before them in a black dress and a cloak of all things. The hood was up, making it impossible to see her face.

Brinton found himself backing away from the newcomer with his hands raised up to shield himself. “Who are y-you?” he stammered. “What...Where did you come from? How did you do that?”

The shrouded woman offered only the tiniest shrug of her shoulders. “Ragnosian cloaking technology,” she answered. “It does very little to conceal you if you move too quickly, but it's quite useful if you want to watch someone without being seen. Life is a lot more interesting now that we can travel across the galaxy.”

“Who is this woman?” Brinton demanded.

Jarl stood in the corner with his arms crossed, smiling down at himself. “She's our benefactor, my friend,” he said. “The bomb you used to destroy the vertical farm? Where do you think it came from?”

Brinton didn't have an answer to that question. He had just assumed that Jarl had gotten his hands on explosives somehow. Acquiring the bomb wasn't his job, and he did *not* want to know too many details.

The woman came forward, inclining her head to meet his eyes, and he stared into the hood. A lovely face stared back at him, bathed in shadow, but he almost thought he had seen her before. “You wish to make your people strong again,” she said. “Hesitation is weakness.”

Brinton stiffened, trembling at the scorn in her tone. “You're talking about a large-scale assault on the city's infrastructure!”

he protested. "We are *not* trained soldiers. The Keepers will bring us down in seconds."

The woman flowed past him, tapping the side of her hip with gloved fingers. "You underestimate yourselves." She looked Brinton up and down. "Resources can be provided that will nullify many of the Keepers' advantages."

"Like what?"

"The cloaking technology for one. And this."

She reached beneath her cloak to retrieve something from a hidden pocket. A vial of small blue pills. How would pharmaceuticals help them fend off Justice Keepers? "Do any of you know what these are?" the woman asked.

Four heads shook.

"With these," she explained, "you will be able to mimic the strength, stamina and agility of a Justice Keeper. Did you think we would leave you without aid?" She tossed the vial to Brinton, and he caught it by instinct.

"But why?" he stammered.

The woman planted her fists on her hips and stood before him like a disapproving mother. "You say you want a return to the days when people had to fend for themselves," she intoned. "We agree with these goals."

"And who are you?"

The hooded woman strode forward as if she meant to mow him down, one hand lashing out to seize his chin with gloved fingers. She squeezed hard enough to bring pain, and Brinton grunted. "We are your benefactors," she said. "That is all you need to know for now. Do you have any further questions, Brinton?"

"No..."

"Good...Then in three days' time, you'll make a statement history will never forget."

9

The small outdoor patio was bathed in the light of early evening, a warm, golden glow that fell upon square tables with colourful tablecloths. A human-shaped robot came walking through on metal legs, carrying a tray of drinks and setting them down in front of three women who sat laughing and talking.

Across the street, a building that looked like a cone with the top sawed off stood proudly with a garden on its roof. The windows that encircled each of its seven floors looked in on apartments, though some had the shades drawn.

Ben knew when Jack called him up in the middle of the day that something wasn't quite right. It wasn't that his buddy didn't like to socialize in the daytime, but lately, Jack had buried himself in his work. Probably out of some sad attempt to take his mind off his complicated situation with Anna.

What little he understood of that tangled web said that his two friends had finally admitted their feelings for one another, but then Anna wanted to take some time to get over her relationship with that Earth guy. What's his name? Not that he didn't understand. Ben was still getting over the sting of losing Darrel.

There was nothing quite like hearing the person who had professed their undying love just a few months ago tell you that they never wanted to see you again to break your heart into a million pieces. So, he listened to Jack's story. With any luck, that would take his mind off his own problems. And he procured for them the one thing that would be a balm on any relationship troubles.

Alcohol.

Closing his eyes, Ben lifted a shot of whiskey to his lips and downed it. “Oh, that's rough,” he whispered, tossing his head from side to side. “So, she just booted you out of her office. Not even an 'I'm sorry?' ”

Jack sat across from him with his shoulders slumped, frowning into his own lap. “That's pretty much it,” he said with a shrug. “Just 'I told you not to talk to me; so why are you talking to me?' ”

Ben scrunched up his face, shaking with frustration. “Someone needs to have a talk with that woman,” he growled, sliding his chair closer to the table. “She was completely out of line.”

“She *did* ask me to stay away from her.”

Leaning back in his chair with arms folded, Ben shook his head. “And that meant you were never supposed to speak to her again?” he snapped. “Because if I were in your place, I'd want to know where I stand.”

Jack set his elbows on the table, lacing fingers over the top of his head. The man let out a soft groan. “Well, now I know,” he rasped. “Which should make it that much easier to put the whole thing behind me.”

“No, you *don't* know.”

“Dude, she said she doesn't want to talk to me.”

Ben slapped a hand over his face, grunting his frustration.

"You can be so dense at times," he muttered into his own palm. "Yeah, you should stay away from her while she sorts her shit out, but trust me, this isn't the end of the story."

Bleakness take him, if there was a way for Jack to find fault with himself, the man would find it and then shine a spotlight on it for all to see. It was mildly irritating as Ben had his own troubles to deal with.

Everywhere he went, he felt as though people's eyes were on him. The fallen LIS agent, the man exposed for smuggling weapons. Of course, that was absolutely ludicrous. The number of people who would know him on sight was so small that his chances of running into one of them at random were next to nothing.

But being a spy taught you to be paranoid.

"She's made her decision," Jack muttered.

Ben crossed his arms, hunching over in his seat and shaking his head. "Indeed she has," he said softly. "And you should respect that decision. But there's no reason to think that the woman who was your best friend for years will never talk to you again."

"If you say so-"

"I do."

He stood up, instinctively dusting himself off, and turned his head to stare off at the street. So little traffic. He had grown used to the constant bustle of Earth cities. "Look, I have a few things I need to take care of," he said. "But why don't I call you tomorrow and we can actually do something fun?"

"Sure," Jack mumbled.

Ben left his friend to work things out on his own; that was really the only thing you could do when someone was suffering from heartache; he knew that perfectly well. Pain still flared up in his chest every time he thought of Darrel.

As he made his way up the sidewalk, along a curving city street with tall apartment buildings on each sidewalk, he pulled up a document he'd been writing on his multi-tool. Black text scrolled across a white background.

Ben reviewed the words.

It was a letter of apology, an explanation for why he had done the things that he had done. Why he had given weapons to the colonists, why he had pleaded guilty, why he had been unable to return to Darrel despite his promise to do so. He had considered sending it to his ex-boyfriend many times. Every time his finger hovered over the button that would deliver this message to Darrel's inbox, he found himself unable to go through with it.

This time, his finger hovered over the button that would permanently delete this pointless message. He couldn't go through with that either. Ben growled like a hungry dog. Life was never simple. He put his ex out of his head for the moment.

There were more pressing concerns.

His fist pounded on the white front door of an apartment, and he took an instinctive step backward. This corridor was nicely decorated with paintings hung up on the pristine white walls and the odd potted plant near the bank of elevators.

Ben stood in the corridor with his arms folded, looking down at himself. "Don't tell me you're not home," he mumbled with a touch of venom in his voice. "Because we both know you never go anywhere."

The door swung inward to reveal a tall, dark-skinned woman in black pants and a blue tank-top. "Tanaben," Keli Armana said. "I could feel you coming for the last fifteen minutes. I considered opening the door before you knocked."

"Why didn't you?"

"It's my sad attempt to assimilate."

She stepped aside to allow him into her apartment, and he took a deep breath before venturing through the door. A telepath of average strength could cause him trouble with very little effort, and he had no doubt that Keli could kill with a thought. In fact, he had seen her do just that.

Hardwood floors stretched across a living room where a window along the back wall allowed golden sunlight to illuminate a white couch. A vase full of red roses was positioned in the centre of a glass coffee table. Simple décor, but Ben liked it. Though he *was* surprised to find the place so sparsely decorated.

Antaurans usually preferred to use furniture as a symbol of social status. The more elaborate the setting, the better. Sometimes people with a very low station tried to make themselves look more important by acquiring the best of everything. He wondered if Keli was the sort of woman to do that.

"I spent most of my life in a prison cell," she said, answering his unasked question. "I care nothing for social status."

Ben winced, touching two fingers to his forehead. "I keep forgetting that you can do that," he said, spinning around to face her. "I really wish you would resist the urge to poke around in my head."

Keli leaned against the wall next to the front door, her pretty face twisted in a scowl that revealed her contempt. "You normals," she muttered. "Verbal communication is slow and imprecise, but you still insist on it."

"It's how we function."

"Why are you here, Tanaben?"

Clenching his teeth, Ben gave his head a shake. "Blunt and to the point," he said, striding forward. "I guess that's how it works when every single thought in your head is laid bare for all the world to see."

"My question?"

He stopped a few feet away from her, slipping his hands into his back pockets and bowing his head to her. "I want your help," he said simply. "The other day, you suggested using your abilities to determine if a suspect was lying."

Pressing her lips into a thin line, Keli shut her eyes. She took a deep breath, then let it out slowly. "And you have decided to follow that suggestion," she said. "It's about time one of you displayed some sense."

"This isn't about Melissa's investigation."

"Then what-"

She squinted at him as if she were trying to read fine print at the bottom of a page, and suddenly, Ben felt pressure on his mind. Pressure that vanished before he could truly get a sense of it, but he knew she had read his thoughts.

"You want me to help you find rogue Justice Keepers," Keli said. "And you think my abilities can help you subdue the ones we do find."

Red-faced and fuming, Ben let out a feral growl. "I told you not to poke around in my head!" he shouted. "You can't just do that whenever you lose patience with this slow, imprecise form of communication."

"And yet you would have me violate the minds of Justice Keepers that you suspect of having betrayed their oaths." Embarrassment overwhelmed the anger he was feeling. He was hoping she wouldn't notice that contradiction. "A tidy little arrangement, isn't it? My abilities are abhorrent until the moment you need them."

"Keepers are different."

"How?"

Ben turned his back on her, throwing his hands up. "Because they're powerful!" he growled, marching over to the window. Outside, he saw a gorgeous park full of blooming maple trees across the street. Children were playing there, chasing each other in a game of hide and seek.

He loved his world, loved its people and all that they had accomplished. But Leyria owed much of what it had to the Justice Keepers, and if the Justice Keepers had turned against them...It wasn't something he wanted to think about.

"Does Larani Tal know about this?" Keli asked. Before he could answer, she took the words out of his mouth. "No, she doesn't, does she?"

He was about to chastise her for reading his thoughts.

The woman just leaned against the white wall with her arms folded, smiling down at herself. "I didn't *have* to read your mind, Tanaben," she mocked. "I am well aware of the Leyrian tendency to fall back on sanctimonious platitudes about rights. Larani would never sanction something like this."

She moved forward at a slow, even pace, shaking her head with a soft sigh. "Which means you're breaking the law again," she went on. "Haven't you endured more than your fair share of punishment already?"

"Larani wants us to stop the rogue Keepers."

"But not to violate their rights?" It was a question that hung in the air for a few moments until Keli decided that it had been answered without either of them speaking a word. "Leyrians... Always hesitating to do what's necessary."

"If that were the case," Ben countered. "Would I be here?"

"How do you plan to do it?"

Ben stood there with fists balled at his sides, hissing and shaking his head. "Larani gave me access to the prisoners we brought in," he began. "Calissa Narin and presumably the one Jack arrested yesterday."

He looked up to fix a steely gaze upon her, then stiffened as a shiver ran down his spine. "I'm going to interrogate Calissa again," he said simply. "And you're going to be there with me."

Musical laughter was Keli's response as she threw her head back. "Don't you think the guards might have something to say about that?" she asked. "You showing up with a strange woman they don't know."

"I can fabricate you an ID," Ben said. "And credentials to go along with it. You'll be a therapist."

"You really *are* eager to break the law."

"I am eager to protect my world," he said, marching forward. "If there are traitors hiding among the Keepers, I want them exposed."

Her eyes tried to draw him in, each burning with the heat of a thousand suns as she held his gaze without flinching. Finally, she nodded. "All right," she said. "I'd be lying if I said I wasn't itching for a chance to use my abilities. I'll do it."

"Thank you."

"Oh, don't thank me; I have a feeling we're both going to regret this."

Clack, clack, clack!

"Again!"

The field behind the Denabrian Keeper office was fenced in on all sides and dotted with a few elm trees with leaves that fluttered in the afternoon breeze. The air was warm and sweet, filled with the promise of an approaching summer.

Not far away, the cylindrical skyscraper loomed over them with windows on each of its fifteen stories, windows that reflected the bright blue sky. When she looked up, she saw a shuttle – a sleek little craft with curving wings – rise up from the rooftop and speed off toward the ocean.

Melissa stood in the grass in a pair of white shorts and a black tank-top, the wooden practice sword held horizontally over her head. "You're too fast!" she panted. "I just can't keep up."

Jack wore a simple pair of gray track pants and a matching tank-top, his blade held in a ready stance with the tip pointed at her. His face was glistening, his damp hair matted to his forehead. "You can," he replied. "Your Nassai will reinforce everything you learn until it becomes second nature. Trust your instincts!"

Melissa swung at his stomach.

In response, Jack hopped back and the tip of her blade

passed within inches of his shirt. Using her momentum, she spun and back-kicked to prevent him from moving in for the kill. Her foot hit nothing.

He had backed away.

Melissa charged at him, lifting her blade over her head and swinging it down in a sharp vertical slash.

Jack turned his shoulder toward her, raising the blade horizontally to intercept hers with a *clack.* "Good!" he shouted. "Press the attack. Keep me on the defensive."

Melissa lunged at him, trying to spear him through the stomach with her sword. His only response was a quick downward slash that ripped the weapon from her grip and left it lying in the grass.

Then his blade was touching the side of her neck.

Closing her eyes, Melissa shuddered as she tried to regain her composure. "It's no good," she said, shaking her head. "I'll never be as good as Jena was. Sometimes, I don't know why the symbiont picked me."

Jack's face was flushed, his expression stern. Fat droplets of sweat rolled over his forehead. "Melissa, you've made enormous progress," he said. "And may I point out that baseless self-loathing is *my* thing?"

She giggled.

"Come on," he said. "Again."

Melissa bent over and picked up the sword, doing her best to ignore her growing sense of inadequacy. Sure, Jack had told her over and over that he had needed practice too when he first started, but she had a hard time imagining him struggling this much. A part of her wanted to slip off to the sidelines and let the important people have the spotlight, but Keepers weren't afforded that luxury.

It didn't help that her father was standing in the shade of an elm tree with his arms folded, watching the whole thing with one of those unreadable expressions he'd learned after so many years on the force. The last thing she wanted was to screw up in front of him. But she could already hear her dad insisting that the only way to do that would be to give up.

She lifted the blade up in front of her nose, squinting at him. “All right,” she said, nodding once. “Let's do it.”

Jack didn't rush at her like some angry street tough. No, he just advanced with all the inevitability of an approaching tidal wave. His sword came at her in a sweeping cut aimed at her neck.

Melissa ducked, allowing the blade to pass over her head. She thrust her own sword forward, trying to skewer Jack through his mid-section.

At the last second, he moved aside and turned so that she saw him in profile. Then he brought his sword down on hers, tearing the weapon from her hands. It landed in the grass once again. *Not this time!*

Melissa dove, somersaulting across the ground beneath a cut that would have sliced through her chest if she had remained still. She came up on one knee, and she didn't even bother to reach for her sword.

Instead, she Bent gravity.

Her body was propelled upward, and then she tucked her knees into her chest to back-flip over Jack's head. Moments later, she dropped to the ground, raising both fists up in a fighting stance.

Jack rounded on her.

Melissa kicked him in the stomach, forcing him to double over and back off. That gave her the few seconds she needed to recover her weapon. Sliding one foot under the sword's blade, she kicked it up and caught the hilt.

Jack was already coming at her, spinning like a whirlwind with a blade that lashed out in a blurring horizontal arc.

Melissa turned her blade over her shoulder, parrying the cut before he could make contact. Wood met wood with an earsplitting *crack* that resonated through the yard, and she was forced to stumble sideways.

Her opponent faced her with a great big smile on his face, his blue eyes sparkling in the sunlight. "Not bad, kid," he panted. "You know how to improvise, but I still have you on the defensive."

Darting in on nimble feet, Melissa performed a quick cut that would leave a nasty gash in his upper arm if it made contact. Jack practically bent over backward, her blade passing over his chest.

With a casual flick of his wrist, he brought his own sword up to intercept hers and tear the weapon from her hand again. "Damn it!" Melissa shrieked as she backed away from him. "How do you keep doing that?"

"We're not finished yet," Jack said.

He was flowing toward her with that predator's grace, lifting his blade up vertically in front of his face. "Keep your head in the game, kid." He drew back his sword and tried to stab Melissa right through the chest.

Melissa dropped to her knees before him, reaching up to catch his blade between clapped palms. She gave a tug and pulled the weapon from his grip, tossing it aside. "See how *you* like it!"

Jack spun for a hook-kick, one foot whirling around...and stopping just before his heel made contact with her chin.

Melissa squeezed her eyes shut, a single tear rolling over her cheek. "I screwed up again, didn't I?" It came out as a squeak. "God damn it! No matter what I do, you always find a way to beat me!"

Jack stood over her with fists on his hips, shaking his head slowly. "It was a clever trick," he said, "pulling the sword out of my hand the way you did. But in falling to your knees, you sacrificed mobility."

Rubbing her mouth with the back of her hand, Melissa

winced. "Yeah...I can see that now," she muttered. "I won't make that mistake again."

"No, you misunderstand," Jack clarified. "Giving up your mobility doesn't make what you did the wrong move. But you have to be ready to counter whatever I throw at you next. If you had leaned back and caught my ankle, for instance, you could have held me pinned or thrown me to the ground."

He extended a hand to her.

Melissa took it and allowed him to pull her to her feet. Standing up with a grunt, she gave her head a shake. "But how..." It took a moment to gather her thoughts. "When I first started training, I often hesitated, trying to decide what to do. Now, I've learned how to react on instinct, but I seem to make the wrong choices."

"Practice," Jack said.

"That's it?"

His face was glistening as he hunched over and scraped a knuckle across his brow. "Learning to think outside the box takes time," Jack explained. "For instance, when you back-flipped over me and kicked me in the stomach."

"Yeah?"

"By doing something unexpected, you gave yourself an opening. You should have pressed your attack. Instead, you went for the sword. You were so focused on regaining the sword – on recovering what I'd taken away from you – that you missed opportunities to win. I was off balance. You could have followed it up with a kick to my face or a quick palm-strike. But all you could think about was the sword.

"A weapon is just a tool, Melissa; it's the Keeper's *mind* that makes the difference between victory and defeat. If I take one tool away from you, use others. Don't rely on a plan; adapt to each situation as it presents itself."

"I don't know how to do that."

"Yes, you do," Jack said. "You did it several times today."

He turned away from her, marching to the edge of their little practice area where his gym bag was sitting in the grass. Dropping to one knee, he retrieved a towel and cleaned the sweat off his face. "You did good, kid."

Melissa didn't feel very good about herself – it felt as if she had just played a game of Chess in which her opponent had been one step ahead of her with every move – but as the adrenaline rush faded, she noticed something. The symbiont within her. It wanted her attention, and it wanted it badly.

Her Nassai was like a third-grader with his arm in the air, begging for the teacher to call on him next. What could possibly be so urgent?

She had learned to commune with the symbiont after a few weeks of carrying it. At first, it had been difficult to focus – especially after the pain of losing Jena – but now, she could put her mind into a relaxed state at almost any time.

Melissa closed her eyes and let her cares drift away, focusing on the emotions that came from her Nassai. The world seemed to drift away, and she was floating. Floating in an endless expanse of nothing until her mind gave it form.

Ground sprang up before her: a gently sloping hill of lush green grass that curved around a river where waters babbled. Instead of filling in the sky with a standard blue, she left it dark but added millions of tiny stars. Not content with that, she added a bright pink nebula near the western horizon and a band of light across the sky that would be the nearest spiral arm of the galaxy.

Green grass as bright as if the noonday sun shone overhead under a starry night sky. She enjoyed the contradiction.

Melissa gave herself form, rippling into existence in a pair of black slacks and a matching blouse with short sleeves, her hair tied back in a bun. "You need to talk?" she asked, spinning around.

Further up the hillside, a woman in a white dress stood over her, and Melissa nearly jumped back in surprise. This was no ordinary woman. The newcomer had a pretty face of pale skin, short auburn hair that she wore parted in the middle and fierce brown eyes. The eyes of a leopard on the hunt.

It was Jena.

"That's not a form you should imitate," Melissa said. "Some people would be offended."

The Nassai frowned and bowed her head. "I'm sorry," she said, striding forward. "I did not mean to offend – I grieve for Jena as well – but I thought this might help me make my point."

"And what point is that?"

The other woman looked up at her with eyes as hard as cement. "I know everything that Jena knew," she explained. "All of her experiences remain with me. I know what she would have done in response to each of Jack's maneuvers, and I can share that knowledge with you. It will take time to build the necessary neural pathways, but I *can* do it."

"So I'd fight like Jena?"

"Yes."

Melissa closed her eyes, a single tear rolling over her cheek. "No," she whispered, shaking her head. "I appreciate the offer – I really do – but I want to succeed on my own terms, and it's hard enough to let Jena go without feeling like part of her personality has been grafted onto my own."

"I understand," the Nassai said.

She turned to go, marching up the hillside, then froze in place after a moment. "One last thing," she said. "You wanted to give me a name."

"I did."

The other woman turned around and stood with her hands clasped before herself, her head bowed respectfully. "Ilia," she suggested. "It was Jena's mother's name. I think she would like that."

"Ilia," Melissa said, testing the name. "Thank you."

Watching his daughter practice against Jack left Harry feeling a swell of pride that was almost enough to make him start crying. Almost. He had felt pride in his girls many times – when Melissa took first prize in her seventh-grade science fair, when he sat in the audience of Claire's first dance recital – but this was stronger somehow.

It was like watching his daughter learn to walk all over again. She had been reborn in that cavern beneath the moon's surface, and now she was learning all over again what her body could do.

He had resisted the urge to clap.

Standing in the shade of an elm tree with his hands shoved into the pockets of his beige pants, Harry frowned down at his shoes. "She wouldn't like that much," he said, taking a few steps forward.

For some strange reason, Melissa just stood there with the practice sword in one hand, staring blankly into the distance. She seemed to be in a daze. Jack's words hadn't been *that* hard on her.

The boy – Harry still thought of Jack as the nephew he'd never had – was crouched in front of his gym bag with his back turned, muttering to himself. Maybe now would be a good time to give Melissa his congratulations.

He made his way over to her.

At the sound of his footsteps, Melissa squeezed her eyes shut and shook her head as if to clear the haze out of her mind. "Hey, Dad," she said. "Don't take this the wrong way, but it's hard to practice when I know you're watching."

"Yeah, well," he mumbled. "That doesn't change the fact that you were amazing. You've really learned to adapt."

"No, I haven't."

"Stop being so hard on yourself."

That came from Jack, who was striding toward them with a

heavy sigh. "Even with Summer accelerating the rate at which I learned, I was still flailing about in my first fight with Pennfield."

Harry paused for a moment to consider that; he hadn't been there that night when Aamani had led Jack, Anna and a team of her best people to infiltrate Wesley Pennfield's skyscraper. He hadn't been forced to watch as the battle drones gunned down hardened CSIS operatives with casual disregard. There was a time when he would have considered himself lucky to have been spared such horrors, but after the skirmishes in New York, he could easily imagine the carnage.

He always pictured Jack fighting off Pennfield in some epic duel like the ones you saw in movies, a contest where both fighters were evenly matched, but if Jack had been scrambling to keep up...

"You're gonna do fine, kid," Jack said. Something in the kid's voice...There was sadness there. Which almost certainly meant it had something to do with Anna.

Harry let out a breath, shoulders slumping, then reached up to clam a hand onto the back of his neck. "Listen, Jack," he said. "We haven't seen you in a while. Why don't you stop by for dinner later?"

"Yeah," Jack said. "That'd be nice."

10

The blue-walled office they had given him was decorated with posters that Jack had put up on his second day here. One depicted Luke Skywalker holding his signature green lightsaber, and next to him was Rey with her staff.

On the opposite wall, a perfect recreation of *Amazing Fantasy 15* was hung next to a poster of Buffy Summers with her stake drawn. And there were pop vinyls on the desk: Spider-Man, Ms. Marvel, Vin from Brandon Sanderson's amazing Mistborn books. Anna was right; decorating his office *did* make it feel more like home.

Strange that he had never taken her advice until *after* they had stopped talking. It had been one of those things that he had always intended to get around to and somehow never found the time to do. Maybe following her suggestions was some sad attempt to hold onto her. Either way, he wasn't going to stop. He would follow every one. Because she made his life better...even after she was gone.

Jack lounged in a chair with his feet propped up on the desk, a tablet held in front of his face. "So, you interrogated

Cara," he began. "Were you able to get anything useful out of her."

Twenty feet away, Cassiara stood with her arms folded, turned so that he saw her in profile. She seemed to be fascinated by the posters. "Nothing much," she murmured. "No names or leads we could use to find other rogue Keepers."

Jack shut his eyes tight, trembling as he sucked in a deep breath. "Well, it's a start," he said. "I'm not surprised they've got her playing Jar Jar to Slade's Palpatine; she broke easily under pressure."

"You realize I don't get any of these references, right?"

"I know."

He stood up with a grunt, smoothing wrinkles from his shirt with one hand. Then he walked around the desk. "I guess it's just my way of holding on to some piece of my home," he said. "If I'm right, then Cara was never told the names of Slade's other agents. Possibly because that's their general policy, or possibly because they just can't trust her with the information. Look how easily I played her."

Well...It wasn't exactly *easy*. Cara Sinthel was no fool; as a young Keeper, she had displayed a knack for tracking down terrorist cells, which was no small feat. But a talent for exposing secrets wasn't exactly the same as a talent for keeping them.

As near as Jack could tell, Cara had lost faith in the Keepers as an institution when she joined up with Slade, and while some people might be able to smile the right smile, speak the right words and act as if everything was normal, Cara Sinthel just wasn't one of them. She spoke her mind.

It wasn't so surprising, really. Nassai valued honesty and a disinclination toward duplicity in their hosts. If a Keeper betrayed their oath because they truly *believed* that what Slade was doing was right, then it stood to reason that *some* of them would have a hard time hiding that belief. "She's like me," Jack went on. "She wears her heart on her sleeve...It's just her heart is in the wrong place."

Cassi turned to face him with her hands folded behind herself, bowing her head to him. "I think you're too quick to take her at face value," she said. "It's possible that Cara is just very good at *convincing* you that she knows nothing."

Biting his lip, Jack squinted at her. "It's possible," he said, nodding. "But I'm really not buying that theory."

He slipped his hands into his back pockets and moved past her, making his way to the office door. "If Cara is so good at playing us," he began, "Why'd she fall for my sad attempt at psyching her out?"

He spun around.

Cassi was hunched over, reaching up to thread fingers through her short pink hair. "I don't know," she answered. "Maybe she's feeling vulnerable now that Slade is dead."

"Could be?"

"But you don't believe it?"

Jack felt his mouth twist in distaste. "Not for a second," he growled, his voice full of contempt. "Slade may have been the leader, but he had lieutenants, people who would make sure that the grand plan kept unfolding on schedule."

"So..."

Leaning against the wall with his arms folded, Jack frowned down at himself. "So," he said with a shrug. "For now, we carry on with what we would have done if we'd never had this conversation. Tomorrow, you and I will interrogate Cara together."

When he looked up, Cassi was smiling at him, her violet eyes practically sparkling in the harsh light. "Well, at least we'll be doing *something* together," she said. "Don't look now, but this partnership might be working."

"Once again, I'm sorry for the lone-wolf routine."

"It's all right."

Jack stepped forward with his head down, clearing his throat roughly. "Look, if we *are* going to be partners," he managed, "then maybe we should get to know one another. I already have dinner plans, but I'll be meeting my friend Ben for a drink later. Care to join us?"

"Yes," she said. "Yes, I would like that."

"What did you say this thing was called?"

In her mind's eye, Melissa saw her father as a figure of swirling mist who stood in their living room with his arms folded. "A Talis Ring," he answered. "It's a symbol of the Covenant of Layat."

As a devout Catholic, it fascinated her to find so many similarities between Leyrian religions and those of her own world. The Church of the Holy Companion was founded over seven hundred years ago by a woman named Layat who was said to have performed miracles and taught the virtues of pacifism, charity and forgiveness.

It was a monotheistic faith with a loving god who granted salvation to anyone who tried to overcome their sins. Though an interesting quirk was the Companion himself...or *themself*. According to official texts, the Companion was neither male nor female, though adherents of the faith were allowed to picture their god in any way that pleased them.

Some people would say that such similarities were simply a quirk of the human condition – somewhere in the human brain was a collection of neurons that provided the impulse toward religion – but Melissa saw a cosmic order. A purpose to things. The individual trappings of a religion weren't important. It was the message at the core that really mattered. Perhaps Jesus and Layat were, in fact, the same person. Why shouldn't the Messiah visit all the worlds where God's children prospered?

Melissa sat at the desk in the corner with her hands on the keyboard, a rectangular sheet of SmartGlass on a metal stand acting as the screen. "I'm looking it up now," she said. "What's the Leyrian Wikipedia?"

Her father grunted.

"There," she said. "A Talis Ring."

Harry came closer, resting one hand on the back of her chair and leaning over her shoulder to study the image. "Interesting," he said. "The woman I spoke to said she saw a man with that ring wandering about the neighbourhood where our suspect got into the car that would take him to the farm."

Touching her thumb and her forefinger to the screen, Melissa spread them apart to enlarge the image. The ring was just a simple band of iron with the insignia of the Layati inscribed on it.

Tapping her lips with one finger, Melissa shut her eyes. "Hold on a moment," she said, sliding her chair closer to the desk. "It says here that not all denominations of the faith wear this ring. It shows up mostly in the Rokath and Lekanthi sects."

"Yes?"

Melissa swiveled in her chair, craning her neck to stare up at her father. "Don't you remember?" she asked, her eyebrows climbing up her forehead. "Miles Tarso – the man whose access codes were used to subvert the farm's security systems – is a church-going man. I looked up his profile the other day."

Swiping her finger across the screen, she flung the picture of the Talis Ring aside and brought up the desktop. A few quick taps at the icons displayed allowed her to access this computer's version of a web-browser...Link-browser. Whatever! She could get used to the new nomenclature later.

She Googled...er, um...*searched* for Miles Tarso's social media profile and found a plethora of pictures of him at church picnics, at parties and dinners with other members of the congregation. And of course, there were plenty of pictures of Tarso with his family, and some of him working with other technicians on the vertical farm systems.

Beneath a well-shot profile picture where Mr. Tarso stood in front of a tree with a great big smile on his face, his biographical information listed him as a member of the First Church of the Holy Companion, which preached the Covenant of Layat in the Lekanthi tradition.

"You see where I'm going with this, Dad," Melissa asked. "A suspicious man with a Talis Ring is snooping around the same neighbourhood where our bomber got into a car that would take him to the vertical farm. The bomber used Miles Tarso's security codes to bypass the farm's system, and Tarso just happens to attend a church where the clergy all wear Talis Rings."

Her father wore a great big grin as he stood before her with his head bowed. "I'd say you just made a significant connection," he replied. "So, Detective, what would your next move be?"

"Simple," Melissa said. "We interview people at that church."

"You're getting the hang of this."

At that moment, Claire came running into the living room from the front hallway, slamming into Harry so she could throw her arms around him. "Oh my god, Dad!" she squealed. "School today was *so* fun! We got to make holograms!"

Harry smiled down at his youngest daughter, chuckling softly. "Holograms?" he said, patting Claire's back. "How do you make those."

Stepping out of his embrace, Claire looked up at him with those huge dark eyes of hers. "There's this program on the computer," she began. "And it lets you...What are you guys working on?"

"Your sister is learning to be a Justice Keeper."

"Lame!"

Normally, that would have irked Melissa, but her spirits were so high just now, she couldn't help but laugh at it. Claire could give anyone a hard time, but nothing could spoil her good mood.

"Go get cleaned up," Harry said. "Jack's coming for dinner."

"He's lame too!"

Tossing her head back, Melissa rolled her eyes. "Ladies and gentlemen, I give you my sister." She let out a soft sigh of frustration. "The most aggravating person on not one, but *two* planets."

Claire stuck her tongue out.

Before Melissa could say one word, the girl turned and ran to the foot of the stairs where she proceeded to stomp her way up to the second level. Claire was ten years old now; at some point, this "I make it a point to annoy everyone in my life" phase of hers had to end, right? Right?

When the doorbell rang, Harry made his way over to the front hallway and let Jack in. Melissa caught the soft murmur of two voices talking, but she couldn't make out what they were saying, and that irritated her even more than Claire's practiced petulance. He was probably just saying his hellos, but she hated not knowing.

A moment later, Jack stepped into the living room with a great big grin on his face. "Hey, kid," he said, nodding to her. "Your father tells me you made a huge breakthrough on the case."

Blushing hard, Melissa squeezed her eyes shut. "He's exaggerating," she muttered, getting out of the chair. "I just noticed a pattern in several pieces of evidence we gathered and put together a plausible narrative."

"Melissa," Jack said.

"Yeah?"

"That's called 'detective work.' "

Her father was leaning against the staircase railing with his arms crossed, smiling down at himself. "It's no use, Jack," he said. "She's as bad as you are when it comes to not taking a compliment."

"Well, then I'm suing," Jack said. "Because I've patented that."

If she had been blushing hard before, her face was on fire now. Damn it, why couldn't she just say "Thank you" like a normal human being. Oh well. At least she *was* making progress in one aspect of her professional life, anyway. Jeez, things had become so very complicated in the last few months. Here she was, just seventeen years old, and she was already using phrases like "professional life."

"Thanks, you guys," Melissa said. "Come on. I bet Michael has dinner ready."

"I hate that robot," Harry muttered.

A large arch-shaped window with metal grating over its pane looked out on a patio where lanterns hanging from poles cast soft yellow light on round tables with umbrellas to shelter customers from the elements. People sat out there now, laughing, talking, lifting drinks in a toast.

Inside, the bar was hopping with a few dozen twenty-somethings shuffling about on the dance floor. Just the way Ben liked it. He was the kind of guy who liked to cut loose when it was time to relax, which was why – in a moment of unparalleled genius – he had come here with a man who wanted to mope.

Ben leaned over the table with his arms folded, smiling and shaking his head. "So, you're just going to sit there," he asked. "You do understand that the purpose of going out was to take your mind *off* your troubles."

Jack sat across from him in that light brown coat of his, frowning as he stared dead ahead at nothing in particular. "I'm sorry," he mumbled. "I guess I'm really not feeling the party spirit tonight."

No kidding.

By this point, Ben knew his friend well enough to know that Jack would be making some stupid wisecrack if he felt anything like his normal self. How exactly did you help a man get over the loss of his best friend? Especially when said best friend was also the woman he loved.

"They have a games table," Ben suggested.

If Jack heard him, the man gave no sign of it. Instead, he just stared blankly into the distance as if he had been hypnotized. Not good. Ben still had moments when he felt like his chest would cave in from the pain of losing Darrel; he really wasn't in a place to help anyone else through this.

Jack scowled, giving his head a shake, coming back to reality. "Sorry," he muttered. "I was thinking about ways we could put pressure on Cara to name a few more of Slade's operatives if she knows them."

"Really? That's what you were thinking about?"

"Well, it's-"

Closing his eyes, Ben buried his nose in the palm of his hand. "Listen to me, Jack," he said. "Tonight is supposed to be about having *fun*."

When he looked up, Jack seemed crestfallen. The man refused to make eye contact and just sat there with his shoulders slumped. "I'm not in the mood for fun. I just want to keep myself busy."

Ben stood up.

Slapping his hand down on the table, he turned away from the other man and put some distance between them. "Well, then *get* in the mood for fun!" His voice sounded a lot harsher than he would have intended.

Ben spun around to face his friend with his mouth agape. "Maybe you just want to sit here and mope," he went on. "But did it occur to you that you're not the only one who's in pain, and that I put aside my own-"

He cut off when he noticed someone behind Jack – a

woman in a pink, strapless dress to match her pink hair. She was quite short, only slightly taller than Anna, but she walked through the place as if she were a giant. *Well, hello there...*The stare she directed at Jack...Ben felt a moment of excitement when he contemplated the possibility that his friend might get laid tonight.

Jack seemed to notice her too because he twisted around in his chair to look over his shoulder. "You made it!" he exclaimed. "I'm glad! For a little while there, I thought I was going to have to attend Ben's lecture on what a boring person I am. And he's quite the stickler; he'd make me take notes."

The woman smiled and looked down at her feet. "Somehow, I'm having a hard time thinking of you as boring." She set her purse down on the table. "So, are you planning to introduce me?"

"Tanaben Loranai," Jack said. "Cassiara Seyrus."

Ben felt his cheeks burning, and it seemed as if his head had become too heavy to maintain eye contact. Companion have mercy, had he really just been lecturing his friend about being lousy company when Jack was clearly in pain. "You're Jack's new partner," he managed with just enough volume to be heard over the music. It wasn't too loud in this place. "Nice to meet you."

"Likewise."

"Jack didn't tell me you were coming."

Tilting her head to one side, the woman smiled at him. The kind of fetching smile that would set his blood on fire if he were straight. "Jack has a bad habit of not informing people of what he's planning."

"He's never been a planner, no."

Jack tossed his head back, rolling his eyes. "Yeah, that's exactly what I need," he teased. "A full accounting of all my faults! That'll make me feel better in no time!"

Rather than coming up with a zinger to win that little

verbal fencing match – Ben could if he put his mind to it; he really could – he decided to fetch some drinks and give the two of them a chance to talk.

Tension drained right out of him when he considered the possibility that maybe, just maybe, he wouldn't be solely responsible for keeping up his friend's spirits. If this Cassi liked Jack half as much as she seemed to...

He ordered three drinks from the dispenser along the back wall: a glass of whiskey for himself – he was growing quite fond of that – a Tropical Breeze for Jack and another for Cassi. Those were mostly fruit juice with just a little bit of alcohol. It felt a little silly to be ordering drinks that were intended for teenagers, but Keepers were forced to limit their alcohol consumption. That was one reason why he had never wanted to join their ranks. The idea of sharing his body with another life-form was...less than appealing.

When he came back to the table, however, Jack and Cassi were sitting side by side with their heads together, smiling and talking quietly. It made him want to melt into a great big puddle of feels.

Bleakness take him! That was one of Darrel's expressions. Ben *really* needed to get his ex-boyfriend out of his head. There was no fixing that relationship, and that was the end of it! If Jack was happy, then Ben would go and find some fun of his own.

He delivered Jack and Cassi's drinks to them, receiving a cheerful thank you from both Keepers, and then made his way over to the bar. A young man in a gray shirt with a high collar stood there, looking at Ben.

This guy had a handsome face of olive skin, short hair that he kept neatly trimmed and an infectious smile. *Well,* Ben thought. *Maybe I'll have some fun tonight after all.*

Jack found himself completely distracted by the gorgeous

young woman who sat next to him, close enough that her shoulder would brush his if she moved in the wrong way. Damn it, he knew – from various sitcoms – that sleeping with your coworker was almost always a bad idea, but it was hard to take his mind off Cassi. She looked amazing in that little pink dress, but that was only half of it.

The woman exuded confidence from every pore, and you only had to spend a total of five minutes with her to know she didn't take crap from anyone for any reason. That, more than anything else, let her get under his skin in ways that few other people had.

Cassi sat with one leg crossed over the other, a glass of fruit juice mixed with rum in one hand. "So..." She took a sip. "Ben said that you weren't feeling well. Anything you need to tell me?"

"Don't listen to Ben," Jack cautioned. "I'm just feeling a little..."

A glance over his shoulder revealed Cassi sitting there with her elbow on the table, her cheek pressed into the palm of her hand. Those purple eyes were full of curiosity. "A little what?" she inquired.

"It's Anna."

"Who?"

"Special Agent Lenai."

Crossing her arms over her chest, Cassi leaned over the table with a sigh. "Ah...You mean the Keeper you befriended four years ago," she said. "The one who helped you free your symbiont from Wesley Pennfield."

Pressing his lips together, Jack felt his eyes widen. "You're awfully well informed," he said. "But yes...The same Anna Lenai."

Of all the reactions he would have expected, soft laughter wasn't one of them. "It isn't hard to be well informed, my dear,"

Cassi said. "Just about everyone on this planet knows your story. I take it you were in love with Agent Lenai?"

To buy himself a moment to think, Jack took a sip of his drink. It was good: fruity, but not too sweet and something – probably lemon juice – gave it a nice sour twist. How to answer that question?

It wasn't so much that he minded Cassi knowing about his personal life – he wasn't the sort of man who felt the need to hoard his secrets like a miser – but he felt as though Cassi had him at a disadvantage. She had come into his life with all this knowledge about who he was; he knew next to nothing about her. Just how much did he want to tell this woman? Was any of this her business? Before he could even formulate a response, Cassi tapped her glass with one finger and said, "Ah..."

Jack felt his face heat up, then pressed a hand to his forehead. He scrubbed fingers through his thick, dark hair. "It's not what you think," he assured her. "We were friends for years before anything happened between us."

A small smile blossomed on Cassi's face, and she stared into her glass as though she could see the future in it. "Aren't those the best kind of love affairs?" she murmured. "The kind where everything is on the line."

"Not when you lose everything."

"Who says you've lost everything?"

Jack squinted into the distance. "Oh, I don't know," he said, shaking his head. "I suppose that would be Anna. Earlier this week, she told me that she pretty much wanted me to stay away from her."

"Did you two have a fight?"

Lifting his glass to his lips, Jack shut his eyes tight and downed half the beverage. "Nope," he said, slamming it back down on the table. "I just checked in on her after three months of silence, and she gave me the old heave-ho."

"I'm sorry to hear that." There was a surprising amount of sympathy in Cassiara's voice. "But Anna's loss is my gain."

"Is it, now?"

"Well, just in case you haven't noticed," Cassi teased, "I'm out with a hot guy for an evening that could be considered somewhat date-like."

"But Ben..."

Cassi gestured with her drink toward the bar where Ben stood chatting up another young man. It seemed to Jack that they were both enjoying themselves. "He's been over there for the last ten minutes," Cassi said. "Probably because he's smart enough to leave his friend alone with the adorable pink-haired pixie."

There was something so very Anna-like about this woman it left him feeling more than a little off-balance. She knew how to get his attention – there was no denying that – but a part of him felt weird. He had been starting to think of Anna as his soulmate, but could that be true if he was so easily attracted to someone else? It was all very confusing, and he just wanted to forget about it for a night.

"So," Cassi said. "How should we spend our evening?"

11

The small church on Lintal Street looked somewhat out of place when compared to everything else in this city; it was a small building with a stone facade and a gabled roof that rose to a peak a mere twenty feet above the sidewalk. Two arch-shaped windows on either side of the large wooden doors looked in on a room that might have fit nicely with just about every Catholic church Melissa had ever been to.

Dressed in black pants and a short-sleeved red blouse, Melissa stood on the front step with her arms folded. Working up the nerve to go inside took some effort. "You can do this," she told herself. "Stop dawdling."

In her mind's eye, Harry was just a short ways off behind her, standing on the path that cut through the church's front yard with his back to the road. "Are you sure you don't want me to come in with you?"

Melissa winced, shuddering as she sucked in a deep breath. "No," she answered truthfully. "But if I'm ever going to be successful at this, I'm going to have to learn to do it myself."

Harry shoved his hands into his pants' pockets and stood there with his head down. "Yeah, but you're still a rookie," he reminded her. As if she needed someone to point that out. "Back home, we wouldn't let a cop speak to a potential suspect on his first day unless his supervisor was present. Besides, I might notice something you don't."

"All right," she relented. "I guess you can come."

Pushing the door open revealed a large room with wooden pews at an oblique angle and stained-glass windows along each sidewall. Wooden beams along the vaulted ceiling were polished to a shine.

At the far end of the room, the altar stood solitary, unoccupied. It looked so very similar to the churches she had been to and yet different as well. The depictions in the windows weren't of saints but rather of scenes that Melissa didn't recognize. No doubt, they were important moments detailed in the Covenant of Layat.

Melissa started down the aisle between the pews with her hands folded in front of herself, her head bowed respectfully. It was a habit from years of taking Communion, and she broke it as soon as she realized what she was doing. A demure posture would not do much to convince anyone to respect her authority.

At the altar, she found a copy of the Covenant open to a page in one of the middle chapters. Melissa could read Leyrian now, but some of these expressions were from an older dialect of the language that-

"Can I help you?"

She nearly jumped.

To her right, a small door that led into what must have been the Reverend's Office was open, and a tall man with copper skin stood there in simple black clothing. "The next service will be three days from now."

Gathering her courage, Melissa turned to the man and began tapping the screen of her multi-tool. A hologram appeared before her, displaying her Justice Keeper ID. "My name is Melissa Carlson; I was hoping I could ask you some questions."

The man clasped his chin in one hand, frowning down at the floor. "Another Justice Keeper," he said, stepping out of the office. "And a cadet, no less. I thought I answered all the relevant questions the other day."

Melissa felt her eyebrows try to climb into her hair. "*Another* Justice Keeper?" she asked, approaching the man. "Someone else spoke to you?"

The reverend grunted, shaking his head. "I think his name was Director Andalon," he said. "And I will tell you the same thing that I told him; the person who stole Miles Tarso's access codes is not a member of my flock."

"How can you be sure?"

That put a touch of scarlet in the man's cheeks, and his lips peeled back into a sneer that betrayed his contempt. "Because none of my parishioners would ever consider doing something so sinful."

Crossing her arms with a heavy sigh, Melissa stepped forward with her head down. "I wouldn't be so sure of that," she said softly. "We have reason to believe that the person who planted the bomb wears a Talis Ring."

"Impossible!"

"We were-"

"Who's your supervising officer?" the man barked, and she was suddenly struck by a wave of panic so powerful she had to resist the urge to squeak. What would happen if he found out that she was here against Director Andalon's orders? "The arrogance! You would accuse a servant of the Companion of such things?"

Melissa closed her eyes, taking a deep breath to calm herself. "I wasn't accusing anyone," she said in an even tone. "I came here for information, and I was hoping you would be willing to share."

It took a moment for the reverend to calm down, but when he did, the anger visibly drained out of him. He slumped like a puppet with its strings cut. “What do you want to know, Ms...”

“Carlson,” Melissa said. “Let's start with your name.”

“Reverend Haran Vanorel.”

“And is it just you working here?”

The man clasped hands together behind his back and stood up straight as if he were about to give a lecture. “No,” he said in a crisp voice. “I have two acolytes – Sarellia and Brinton – who aid me in my duties.”

Sarellia and Brinton...

They were looking for a man; so that meant Sarellia was out of the picture for the time being. Which turned her attention to this Brinton. Unless Vanorel himself was the culprit; the man *was* strangely cagey about answering questions. “Would I be able to talk to your acolytes?”

“Brinton is tending the garden in the back.” The man suddenly looked up at her with eyes that were narrowed to slits. “You think he did it, don't you?”

“Right now, I don't have any firm opinions,” she lied. Ilia didn't care for that – the Nassai were sticklers for honesty – but telling the man that, in her mind, it was narrowed down to Brinton or himself wouldn't get her very far.

In her mind's eye, she spotted her father near the front entrance, leaning against the wall with a hand over his stomach. So far, Harry had been content to remain silent. Had he noticed something she could use? God have mercy on her; this was much harder than she would have imagined.

“I'd like to talk to Brinton,” she said.

“Through there,” the reverend muttered, gesturing to a door in the back wall. With a sigh, she turned away from Vanorel, and she was about to walk through that door when his voice stopped her in her tracks. “Carlson,” he said. “That sounds like an Earth name.”

Melissa rounded on the man, drawing herself up to full height and lifting her chin to stare down her nose at him. "It is," she said. "I'm surprised you noticed."

Vanorel's face twisted, and he shook his head with a growl that could have come from a rabid dog. "If you ask me," the man began, "your people should never have been allowed to join the Justice Keepers."

"What a saintly demeanour you have, Reverend."

She went through the door without giving the man a chance to respond – May the Lord Jesus Christ have mercy; she had believed that Leyrians had outgrown that kind of bigotry – and found herself in a garden where a cobblestone path slithered its way around flowerbeds where yellow tulips and white daffodils stretched for the clear blue sky.

A man in black was down on one knee in front of her, turned so that she saw his profile. He was using a watering pail to sprinkle a light drizzle on a group of tulips. The church could have requisitioned maintenance bots to do that, but from what she had read, plants held a sacred place in the Layati religion.

"Brinton?" Melissa called out.

He glanced over his shoulder, blinking at her. "Yeah, that's me," he said, setting the watering pail down and standing slowly as if his legs were aching. "Is there something I can do for you?"

Cocking her head to one side, Melissa squinted as she studied him. "Yes, there is," she said, taking a few steps forward. "If it's not too much trouble, I'd like you to tell me where you were four nights ago."

Colour drained out of the man's face. "The night of the bombing," he said. "I'm sorry. Who are you?"

She displayed her badge again.

Dusting his hands nervously, Brinton stepped forward and let out a huff of air. "A Justice Keeper," he said. "Well...four nights ago, I was visiting a friend, a member of our congregation who needed some counseling."

"And who might this friend be?

"Am I under suspicion?"

Through spatial awareness, she sensed her father coming through the door behind her and pausing there, watching as she conducted her questioning. Once again, he said nothing; he just waited. Time to prove herself worthy of his trust.

"What if I told you," Melissa began, "that we found the car that dropped the bomber off at the vertical farm and tracked it back to an address on Elidrea Street? What's more, an eyewitness claims that she saw a man with a Talis Ring get into that car." That last part was a lie, but she wanted to gauge his reaction, and he didn't disappoint.

With a squeak, Brinton ran for the back fence as fast as he could. Her first instinct was to chase after him, but...she was here without authorization. If she tackled him to the ground, would that be a crime?

"Melissa," Harry said.

Brinton had reached the chain-link fence, and he leaped to grab the metal bar at the top. Pulling himself up with a grunt, he awkwardly tumbled over into the field behind the church. Curse her hesitation.

Melissa charged after him.

Her multi-tool beeped with an incoming call.

Brinton was on the other side of the fence, scrambling through the grassy field like a madman, nearly tripping several times. He didn't even stop to look back.

With a touch of Bent Gravity, Melissa leaped and tucked her legs in toward her chest. She sailed over the fence with her arms spread wide.

Dropping to the ground a moment later, she was on her feet and chasing after him, the tall grass rustling as she ran. Her perp was only ten paces ahead of her. With Keeper strength, she'd overtake him in no time.

Her multi-tool kept ringing.

And then it started buzzing.

Maybe this was a bad idea, but curiosity and concern got the better of her. Melissa stopped to run her finger along the screen and check the text message that she had just received... from Jon Andalon.

Cadet Carlson, please explain why you have continued to pursue an investigation into the bombing of the vertical farm against my orders.

Answering the call filled the screen with an image of Director Andalon's face. And he was not happy. "Cadet," he said in a deep voice. "Would you care to tell me precisely what you think you're doing-"

"I'm..."

She looked up to see Brinton rush over a hilltop and vanish down the other side. If he made it to those trees in the distance...

"I was..." she stammered. "We found the man who planted the bomb."

"Who's we?"

Her mouth was moving, but she couldn't form words, and she was suddenly aware of sweat on her brow. How had the man figured out what she was doing? It was hard to concentrate with a voice screaming in her head that this was what happened when you broke the rules.

"Cadet," Director Andalon said. "I think you had better come to my office for a talk."

Melissa's stomach was doing flip-flops.

Outside, she was calm and collected, standing tall and proud before Jon Andalon's desk like a soldier ready to receive orders. Inside, however, she was a mess. A part of her wanted to squeak out an apology and slip away, but she knew better than to give in to that inclination. Besides, Director Andalon probably wouldn't be satisfied with an apology.

The man sat in his chair with his elbows on the armrests, his fingers steepled as he looked her up and down. "So," he began. "Despite my ordering you to keep away from this case, you've decided to get involved. And as for the rest of you..."

Melissa grunted.

The only consolation she had was the knowledge that she wasn't alone in this; the two people who had come here with her were in just as much danger of bearing the brunt of the good director's wrath. Not that she wanted her friends and family to get themselves into trouble, but these things were usually easier to deal with when you weren't the only one being chastised.

On her left, Anna stood with arms folded, frowning down at the floor. "If anyone deserves the blame here, it's me." She took one proud step forward. "I'm a fully-trained officer; Melissa's just a cadet."

Jon swiveled in his chair, his face twisting into the kind of expression you might find on a man who did not enjoy his very expensive meal. "You are correct there, Agent Lenai," he said. "Which makes me question your judgment."

"Sir, I-"

"And you, Mr. Carlson!" Jon Andalon snapped. "Do you have anything to say?"

Harry stood on her right with hands clasped before himself, his head bowed almost reverently. "Melissa wanted to learn about detective work," he explained. "I thought there were some things I could show her."

Leaning back in his chair with his hands folded over his chest, Director Andalon scowled up at the ceiling. "I'm sure there are," he said. "But none of that changes the fact that I gave her specific orders to stay away from this case."

Squeezing her eyes shut, Melissa ignored the heat in her face. "Leave them out of this," she said, approaching the desk. "I'm the one who coaxed them into helping me. I'm the one who disobeyed you."

Of all things, the director grinned at her as if he were surprised by her reaction. "A girl who's willing to fall on her sword to protect her friends." It galled her to be called a girl – and Melissa had to admit that part of that frustration stemmed from the fact that she *was* a girl and not yet a woman – but now was not the time to stand on indignation. She was on thin ice already.

"If I may ask, sir," Melissa began. "How did you find out?"

"When I learned that Miles Tarso's access codes were used to override the farm's security systems, the first thing I did was investigate his social contacts. This brought me into contact with the rather objectionable Reverend Vanorel, and I don't mind telling you that I wanted to hit a punching bag for half an hour after just five minutes in that man's presence.

"So, you can imagine how I might feel when the reverend called me earlier this afternoon to inquire about a cadet who had come down to his church to make all sorts of wild accusations."

Admitting this next part wasn't going to be easy, but she had to tell the truth if she wanted her new supervising officer to trust her. "We think we found the man who planted the bomb, sir."

The man looked up at her with hard, dark eyes. "Do you now?" he asked, arching an eyebrow. "Tell me, Cadet Carlson, how exactly did you put together the pieces of this rather ugly puzzle?"

She told the whole story: tracking the car back to Elidrea Street, getting witness statements from the people there, the man with the Talis Ring, her trip to the church and Brinton's sudden flight when she asked the wrong question. All the while, Jon Andalon just sat there with an unreadable expression. When it was over, he said, "So, why isn't this man in a holding cell?"

Melissa went red, then turned her head so that she wouldn't have to look at him. "I stopped to answer your call," she murmured. "And by the time it was over, Brinton was gone. We lost him."

She half expected a tirade and perhaps a warning that there would be a reprimand on her record, but the only response Director Andalon gave was a few tense moments where he tapped one finger on the surface of his desk. Finally, he let out a sigh and said, "This is why cadets don't take point on an investigation. You're not ready for this yet, Melissa. It takes years to develop the necessary experience."

"I'm getting that..."

Out of the corner of her eye, she saw Anna turn her head and direct a small smile her way. The other woman had been young and inexperienced when she chased a criminal all the way to Earth.

Jon Andalon stood up, running his gaze over the three of them. "I'm usually not in the habit of rewarding disobedience," he cautioned. "But I must admit that I'm impressed by your tenacity and by your ability to find the culprit."

Melissa felt a swell of pride.

Leaning forward with his hands braced on the desk, Jon nodded to each of them in turn. "Agent Lenai," he said. "Perhaps it's time you returned to active duty. We could use your expertise on this case."

"Happy to help," Anna replied.

"Very well," Jon said. "Melissa, if you're willing to follow my lead, I'm willing to let you be a part of this investigation."

It was hard not to jump for joy, but she contented herself with a warm smile and a curt nod. "Thank you, sir," she said. "I won't let you down."

"So, I'm confused," Anna said.

Sunlight came in through Harry's kitchen window, falling on a collection of dishes in a sink full of soapy water. He dunked a plate in the suds and began to scrub it with a sponge. Of course, the dishwasher could have done this – and when he had decided to forego that option, that blasted robot had come along offering to assist him – but he wanted to do it himself.

Wincing hard, Harry rubbed his forehead with the back of his hand. "What are you confused about?" he grumbled. "It seems to me Director Andalon was pretty clear about what he expects."

He looked over his shoulder.

Anna sat on his kitchen table with one leg crossed over the other, her hands folded primly on her knee. That blue hair of hers still looked out of place to him, but once again, he chose not to say anything. "Something doesn't add up," she said. "Why would Harry Carlson – the biggest stickler for the rules that I've ever met – decide to help his daughter disobey orders from her supervisor?"

Blushing hard, Harry closed his eyes and took a deep breath. "She needs to learn," he answered, scrubbing a plate well past the point where it was spotless. "And I needed to *do* something."

"See that's just it!"

Anna hopped off the table and shuffled over to stand beside him, bracing her hands on the counter. "Where did this obsession with being useful come from?" she asked. "For as long as I've known you, you've been the kind of man who wants to contribute, but now you're demeaning simple household appliances."

"I don't know...I guess I just feel out of place here."

"Come on, Harry."

The growing tightness in his chest made him want to shrink away from her. Harry really didn't want to have this conversation. "Can't we just have a nice dinner, Anna?" he implored her. "You're reading too much into this."

When he looked over his shoulder, Anna was squinting at him. He'd seen that look of suspicion on her a thousand times now. "Harry," she said. "Something's bothering you, and I think you should let it out."

"There's nothing for me to do here."

"There's *plenty* for you to do here."

God have mercy! What was Anna looking for? Back home, he'd had his job and his house and a thousand other little things to take care of. Not to mention keeping his girls out of trouble. But here...Claire loved her school; Melissa was doing well in her studies. The house maintained *itself,* for the most part, and he had no bills to pay. So, what was his purpose? He had to have a purpose, a reason for being, a reason that would make up for...

"It's nothing," he insisted.

"I don't believe you."

The tension in his chest was hard to ignore. "I just want to help," he whispered. "Why is it so unreasonable that I would go out of my way to help my daughters?"

He turned to find her facing him with her arms folded, staring up at him with those big blue eyes. "Because you're a by-the-book cop, Harry," she said softly. "Under normal circumstances, you'd tell Melissa to follow her supervisor's orders and stay away from the case. So, I repeat..."

"I *have* to do something!"

"Why?"

Gritting his teeth, Harry felt hot tears on his cheeks. "Because it was my fault!" he shouted. "Because I'm the reason it happened! All of it! I was there, in the Nexus...with Slade. I could have stood my ground."

He pressed hands to his eye sockets as sobs ripped through him. "But he threatened Melissa." The words came out as a squeak. "Slade...He said he would kill me on the spot, and then he'd go after Melissa.

"The N'Jal couldn't help me; he had EMP rounds. I couldn't shoot him. Slade would just deflect the bullets with one of those Bendings you Keepers are always throwing up. I had no options! So, I fled."

Anna stepped forward, slipping her arms around him, hugging him tight. This girl, nearly twenty years his junior, suddenly felt very much like the big sister he'd never had. "It wasn't your fault," she whispered. "You did the right thing."

"Don't you see?" Harry growled. "Jena is dead because of *me!* If I had found a way to stop Slade, she wouldn't have...She wouldn't have gone in there..."

"Or maybe Slade would have killed you too."

Anna stepped back, and when she looked up at him, her expression was stern. "You said it yourself, Harry," she went on. "You had no other options. It's time to stop blaming yourself for something you couldn't control."

"But Jena..."

"Might have died anyway!" Anna snapped. "Along with the rest of us, including your daughter. Think, Harry, if you hadn't come out to warn her, Jena would have kept fighting that Overseer creature until Slade turned the whole facility against us again. We all would have died on that moon, and nothing would be different."

Harry fell to his knees, doubling over and covering his face with both of his hands. "I know," he whimpered. "Believe me, I know that. But I keep thinking that there must have been *something* I could have done."

Anna knelt before him with her hands on her thighs, frowning into her own lap. "We always think that," she said. "Whenever things go wrong, we tell ourselves that if we had just done things a little differently..."

"But it's a lie," he whispered.

"It's *always* a lie."

Harry looked up, blinking tears away, and tried to regain his composure. "When did you grow up on me, Lenai?" he muttered. "What happened to the irritating, idealistic girl who threw her opinions around so casually."

"She's right here," Anna replied. "Casually throwing her opinions at you."

12

"One more time, Cara," Jack said.

The cell they'd given the woman was very much like many of the others Jack had seen: a bed in the corner, a nightstand, a table and some chairs. Large windows of bullet-proof glass looked out on a field. She could punch herself silly against that, and it would not even make a crack, but at least she had sunlight.

Cara Sinthel sat in a wooden chair with her hands upon her knees, a slaver's collar around her neck. And she glared daggers at him. Unlike Calissa, she didn't bother making taunts or insinuations; she just sat quiet and implacable like a glacier.

"I want names," Jack said. "You must have encountered other Keepers who have been working for Slade. Who are they?"

"You're not gonna get an answer."

That came from Cassi, who sat backwards in a wooden chair of her own, watching Cara the way a kid with a magnifying glass watches an ant. "She doesn't know anything, Jack; we're wasting our time here."

Cara said nothing.

Jack shut his eyes tight, sucking in a slow breath. "Perhaps," he said. "But I don't think Slade would go to all the trouble to recruit a Keeper unless he thought that Keeper was valuable to his cause."

Cara turned her head to fix gray eyes upon him, but she said nothing. You might have thought the woman was mute. Hell, she had responded to pretty much every single question with nothing but silence, and it wasn't as if they could do much to break down her resistance.

Offering leniency in exchange for her compatriots had produced nothing but a snort of derision; apparently, she wasn't frightened by the prospect of living out the rest of her days in a cell. Which meant she was either very stupid or she was expecting some kind of rescue. The latter was highly unlikely – no one had come for Calissa in the seven months since Ben had brought her in – but you didn't get to be one of Slade's people unless you were more than a little gullible. "Look around you, Cara," he said. "Nobody's coming to save you. Why protect people who sold you out?"

The woman said nothing.

Biting his lip, Jack pinched the bridge of his nose with his thumb and forefinger. He let out a groan of frustration. "All right, this is getting us nowhere," he barked. "What do you say we let her stew and see what Calissa has to offer?"

"If Calissa were going to tell you anything," Cara began, "she would have done it already. Nice try."

With his mouth open, Jack tossed his head back and rolled his eyes. "Lady, I don't get you," he said, striding toward her. "If it isn't entirely obvious by now, Slade's people think you're expendable. What do you get out of this?"

Cara looked up at him with rage in her eyes, and for a moment, he was tempted to step back. "Oh, I don't know," she murmured. "The favour of a god. The salvation of my immortal soul."

"Slade's not a god."

"Not him, you fool. Slade is just the emissary."

Wheezing with laughter, Jack let his head hang. He rubbed his brow with the back of his fist. "So, you're one of those idiots who worships the Overseers," he said. "Yeah. I heard all about that."

"Then you should know what happens to heretics."

He was about to reply with a witty retort when he noticed Cassi watching him with a worried expression. Maybe this was a bad line of questioning – or maybe she was upset that he hadn't told her about the Overseer religion – but he could deal with that later. For the moment, he had to know what made Cara Sinthel tick.

"You believe the Overseers are gods," Cassi said before he could think up his next response. "Why is that?"

Cara rose from her chair in one smooth motion, smiling down at herself. She shook her head with a soft sigh. "Because they are," she answered. "I've seen what they can do. Slade showed me the proof."

"What proof is that?"

"Give it time," Cara said. "You'll see."

The first rule of interrogation was to never lose the subject's respect. Your prisoner must always believe that you have complete control of the situation. If anything they say rattles you, you *must* hide. Jack knew this, but that didn't stop him from exchanging tense glances with Cassi.

Cara threw back her head and laughed.

Ten minutes later, Cassi was sitting on Jack's desk with her hands folded over her stomach, frowning into her own lap. "The Overseers are gods," she muttered. "What could possibly convince a grown adult to believe such a thing?"

Scratching his chin with three fingers, Jack squinted as he stared out the window. "You're right; it doesn't make sense," he mumbled. “But if you meet enough of Slade's followers, you'll realize they all believe it.”

“So, they're all insane.”

Jack wrinkled his nose and shook his head. “If only it were that simple,” he said, approaching the desk. “Generally speaking, crazy people don't make the best operatives, and yet Slade's people have proven effective time and again.”

Cassi looked up at him with purple eyes as hard as gemstones, and he could see the tension in her face. “You can't think there's any merit to this!” she growled. “Don't tell me you're starting to *believe* them!”

Crossing his arms with a sigh, Jack let his head drop. “Do I believe the Overseers are gods?” he asked with a shrug. “No, I wouldn't go that far. But Slade must have shown them *something* to convince them.”

“Like that?”

If only he knew.

The pieces fit, however; Leo had insisted over and over again that he was a servant of the one true god; Pennfield thought that he had been elevated above mere mortals like Jack. Then there was Slade's bizarre rant when he fought Anna behind that motel a few months back.

Jack had caught the tail-end of it, and Anna had filled in the rest while they waited in the ER. After looking into her eyes, Slade had gone nuts, shouting “How many times must I kill you?” The man was off his rocker, and yet he *believed* everything he said.

Jack turned his back on Cassi, slipping hands into his pants' pockets. He marched across the office. “I suspect it's something the Overseers do,” he went on. “Possibly some way they modify the human brain.”

Cassi was hunched over with her elbow on her thigh, her chin resting in the palm of her hand. “You mean they can turn a good Keeper into a traitor?" she exclaimed. "There's a terrifying thought."

"It's just a theory."

"A scary one."

"The point is that if we can determine what made these people follow Slade in the first place, we may be able to figure out how to make them change their minds. You won't get much out of a religious fanatic, but convince them zealotry won't earn them a place in heaven, and maybe they'll listen."

"No easy task."

"No," Jack said. "It isn't."

When he turned back to her, she was hugging herself and rubbing her upper arms, shivering as if a cold wind had blown through the otherwise comfortably warm office. "I think we both need a break."

"You took the words out of my mouth."

"Dinner?"

He was about to accept when something made him pause. It dawned on him that he was becoming more and more comfortable with the growing familiarity between himself and Cassi, and he wasn't sure what to make of that. Was this how life worked. When the person you loved went away, did you just start loving someone else? Even if you didn't really want that? He was happy to have Cassi as a friend, but...his heart still belonged to Anna. Didn't it?

Of course, it wasn't as if he had much choice in the matter. Anna had decided to push him away for reasons he didn't fully understand, and there wasn't much he could do about that. Life had to go on, one way or another.

"Yeah," Jack said. "Yeah, that would be nice."

Through his bedroom window, Harry watched his backyard under the deep blue sky of fading twilight. It was hard to make out the flowerbeds with only the soft light of two lanterns hanging from hook-shaped metal poles, but the image was pleasant nonetheless. His daughter had company tonight.

In light of that fact, he had suggested that Claire sleep over with her friend Ralita; his youngest was at a point where she tried to torment her older sister whenever possible, and he knew Melissa would want some privacy. Thankfully, the Savalis were more than happy to host their daughter's new friend from Earth.

Harry would have never imagined that he would be completely unconcerned about the prospect of his daughter dating, but after everything else they had been through? And besides, she was a grown woman, or close enough anyway. He had come to realize that he didn't want to be the overprotective father. Not anymore. Now, if only he could retain this level of inner peace when Claire eventually reached the age where she started seeing boys...or maybe other girls.

Harry stood with his hands on the windowsill, breathing slowly as he tried to ignore the guilt that he felt. His chat with Anna had been helpful, but there was still a small part of him that blamed himself. For all the good it did.

He turned and went to the dresser.

Pulling open the top drawer, he moved a few rolled up pairs of socks aside to reveal something nestled in the corner. A sphere of rolled up flesh about the size of a tennis ball. For almost four months, he had left the N'Jal hidden in this drawer without ever looking at it. Why would he want to be reminded of the day Jena died?

And he had done plenty of good as just plain old Harry Carlson. Maybe it was best to just leave the thing in there forever. Throwing it away wasn't an option when it twisted the mind of pretty much anyone who found it. He was still a little anxious about the fact that he seemed to be immune.

What had the Overseers done to him?

It didn't matter; he was still Harry Carlson. Shoving the

drawer closed, he went downstairs to say his hellos.

The last traces of daylight were fading from the sky as Melissa looked out over the backyard. Her eyes had never been very good at seeing in low light, but she could sense everything around her. Every flowerbed, every fence post. By this point, she had grown so used to being able to intuitively *feel* the world around her that she couldn't imagine going back to the way things were. She was intimately aware of everything in her world, including the young man at her side.

Aiden sat in a wooden deck chair with a glass of sparkling apple cider in hand, a distant look on his face as he watched the night sky. "So, he just brought you onto the case?" he asked. "Just like that?"

Melissa felt her lips curl, a touch of warmth in her cheeks. Closing her eyes, she nodded once. "It wasn't quite *that* simple," she said. "I think Director Andalon was quite annoyed with me, but...I guess we made progress."

Aiden was smiling into his lap, shaking his head. "You really are something else," he murmured. "You know, you might not be aware of this, but people tell stories about you and your friends."

"My friends?"

"Agent Lenai," he said. "Agent Hunter, that LIS operative who went rogue only to become a hero in the Battle of Queens – I forget his name – Even your father. You guys are the stuff of legends."

Now, she was *really* blushing.

Covering her face with both hands, Melissa trembled as she laughed. "I think you might be exaggerating," she said. "We're just a bunch of people who try our best to make the world a better place."

She turned to find him looking over his shoulder, watching her with dark eyes that were full of awe. Soft light from the lanterns cast shadows over his face. "You really *do* think that, don't you?"

"Of course! What else would I think?"

"Melissa, do you know how rare it is for a Keeper to Bond their Nassai outside of the official Bonding ceremony? Mine is scheduled for nine months from now, and that is only a formality to see if a Nassai will accept me.

"Your team has *three* Justice Keepers who received their symbionts under unusual circumstances, two of whom are now prominent figures in the history books. And if that wasn't enough, your friend from LIS is a convicted criminal. You work with a telepath – I'm not supposed to know that, but people talk – and you were in some way involved in the events that opened the class-2 SlipGates and allowed rapid transit across the galaxy. I'm still not entirely sure how that played out."

"Believe me, you don't want to." Didn't Aiden realize that it wasn't appropriate for him to ask? "It's a day I'd rather forget."

"Sorry," he muttered.

"It's okay."

The back door swung open, and Harry stepped out onto the patio, planting fists on his hips and staring off into the distance. "So, what do you say, Melissa?" he asked. "Did I do a good job with this place."

"A very good job, Dad."

He strode across the patio, extending his hand to Aiden. "Harry Carlson," he said. "Pleased to meet you."

Aiden smiled up at her father. "Likewise, sir," he said, taking Harry's hand and giving it a good squeeze. "I was just telling your daughter about how you and your team have become legendary."

Harry's brow furrowed, and he took one cautious step backward. "Legendary," he said in a gruff voice. "I don't know about that; we just did what needed to be done when it needed doing."

"With respect, sir," Aiden countered, "I'd imagine that's true of most legends."

"I like this kid, Melissa."

Leaning back in her chair with her arms folded, Melissa smiled down at herself. She shook her head slowly. "Well, as long as *you* like him, Dad; we all know that that's what really matters."

"Damn right."

Suppressing her irritation took some effort. She knew her father was only joking, but they'd had so many fights about Harry wanting to direct the course of her life in the last few months that she couldn't really find the humour in it. Especially when he made the joke right in front of the guy she liked.

Well...Sort of liked. She hadn't really spent that much time thinking about it, but they did have good chemistry, and he *was* very cute. Maybe inviting Aiden over hadn't been a good idea. With the way her luck was going, Claire would come stomping out the back door any moment now and start in with her usual antics.

When she looked up, she saw that her father had his eyes shut as he let out a long, slow breath. Maybe he'd noticed his faux-pas?

"So," Harry said. "When did you realize you want to be a Keeper, Aiden?"

"About five years."

Please, just go, Melissa thought at her father. Harry was just trying to be polite – she knew that – but there was really nothing worse than having one of your parents along for a non-date with the guy you may or may not have a small crush on.

"Five years," Harry said. "What made you-"

He was cut off by the sound of Melissa's multi-tool beeping like crazy. The thing was making so much noise and vibrating so hard that she half thought it would pop right off her wrist. Checking the screen revealed the source of the trouble.

The security systems at several vertical farms, two power plants and half a dozen food distribution centres had reported a breach. Keepers and local law enforcement were mobilizing. The situation was so dire that the automated systems had alerted anyone with a symbiont, even cadets. It must be that because Aiden's multi-tool was silent.

Melissa looked up at her father with eyes so wide it felt like they might fall out. "I think I have to go."

Her father's mouth twitched, and he gave his head a shake as if trying to get rid of an unpleasant thought. "You haven't exactly finished your training," he said. "And there are plenty of experienced Keepers-"

"Dad."

"-will be able to-"

"Dad!"

Harry stiffened.

Melissa stood up, putting herself face to face with her father, and did her very best to keep her voice even. It was a miracle she wasn't shaking. "This is an all-out attack on the city's infrastructure," she said. "I *have* to go."

In less than a second, Aiden was out of his chair and standing beside her. "Maybe I should..." The words died in his mouth, and he looked away, shame painting his face red. "There's not much I can do to help, is there?"

"No," Melissa said gently. "There isn't."

"No, son; you can't help her," Harry said. "But I can."

13

"You can't come with me!" Melissa shouted.

Harry winced, shaking his head. "You're a half-trained cadet!" he growled, racing up the stairs like some kid half his age. "I'm not going to let you face God only knows what on your own!"

He turned.

His eldest daughter stood at the foot of the stairs with the hem of her shirt clenched in her fists. "What about Claire?" she snapped. "What happens if you get hurt."

"Claire is sleeping over with her friend Ralita."

"Dad, that's not the point!"

He ignored her as he ran up the last few steps and pushed open his bedroom door. The room was dark, but lights came on as soon as he stepped inside, revealing a window on the back wall and a wooden dresser across from the foot of the bed.

Yanking open the top drawer – he practically threw the whole thing to the floor – he flung socks aside and uncovered the N'Jal. The Overseer device was still warm and when he picked it up and held it in front of his face.

The N'Jal uncurled, bonding with the palm of his hand,

microscopic fibers digging into his nervous system and flooding his brain with a new sense of awareness. He could feel the air pressure, the humidity, and a dozen other little things his mind didn't bother to identify. It drove away his sense of helplessness.

No one else was going to die because Harry Carlson had shied away from a fight. Least of all his daughter. Quickly, he pulled open the bottom drawer and retrieved the pistol Jena had assigned him when he joined her team. Technically, he was still a member of that team; so, no one had demanded that he return it.

With a grunt, he ran out the door and back down the stairs. Melissa was no longer waiting in the foyer. Damn that girl! She had no business rushing off to fight terrorists on her own!

He pulled the front door open.

A narrow stone pathway cut through his front lawn to a sidewalk at the edge of his property, and he could just make out lights in the windows of the house across the street. It wasn't hard to track Melissa.

Thrusting a hand out in front of himself, Harry let the N'Jal sense her pheromones. As expected, she was running for the nearest train station. And she had worked up quite a sweat along the way.

Harry chased after her.

He found her on the sidewalk maybe four houses away, jogging toward the subway terminal at the end of the block. The instant Harry got within a line of sight, she froze and spun around. "You're gonna follow me no matter what I do!"

Closing his eyes, Harry wiped sweat off his forehead with the back of his hand. "I am *not* letting you go alone," he panted. "You want to run? Go for it! There's no way that I can keep up with you!"

He started up the sidewalk at a fast jog, his shirt clinging to his back. Surprisingly, his daughter just waited there with her head thrown back, rolling her eyes. "But," Harry insisted. "I *will* follow you. So we're better off going together."

She seemed to accept that – grudgingly – and fell in beside him as they ran for the closest major thoroughfare to pass through their neighbourhood.

No one else was going to die because of him!

What will you do if these guys also have EMP rounds? some part of him wondered. He ignored it. Claire was safe, and that took away any hesitation he might have had about accompanying his eldest on this fool's venture. If anything happened to him, the Leyrians would contact Della, and while he cringed at the thought of the tirade she would kick up if he got himself killed...he'd be dead! He wouldn't have to listen to it. Claire was going to be all right whether he went or not. But Melissa...He was *not* going to let her face the danger on her own.

They ran for the subway entrance.

The instant Helina's nano-blade cut into the mesh of the chain-link fence, alarms started blaring, filling the night with noise. This much racket would put the whole damn neighbourhood on alert, but Aldin was prepared.

The food processing plant was a simple, box-like building with no real artistry to its design: a simple building that stood three-stories tall beneath a dark sky. Automated skids were carrying crates of processed food – cereals, canned vegetables, ready-made meals – down a wide road to the building next door where they would be sorted into grocery deliveries. Well, not after tonight.

He surveyed his little group.

Five people had come with him on this mission: three other men and two women, all dressed in dark colours. They shuffled about nervously, exchanging furtive glances and letting out the odd shuddering breath.

Helina was down on one knee on the sidewalk, carving a

hole in the fence with a blade that extended from her multi-tool. From this angle, Aldin could only see the back of her head, but he heard her panting.

A tall man in black pants and a matching jacket, Aldin wore his brown hair parted in the middle and pulled back from a pale face with a strong jawline. "Hurry up!" he said, stepping forward. "When we practiced this, it only took you fifteen seconds."

Glancing over her shoulder, Helina hissed like a cat. "You're not helping." She rose slowly, dragging her blade upward to complete the hole in the fence.

"I want to get inside before the security drones-"

Right on cue, several gray, egg-shaped robots rose from the roof of the building and began floating toward them. Each one had a cylindrical aperture on its front side – a gun that could pivot on a ball-joint – and a horizontal slit that glowed with blue light. Almost like a visor. "Please stand down," they ordered in a soft, soothing voice.

Aldin's group of half a dozen people backed up onto the sidewalk.

"Do it!" he shouted. "Now!"

His companions threw open their jackets, drawing pistols from concealed holsters. That action alone was enough to provoke a response. The drones reoriented themselves, pointing weapons at Aldin and his people. Stun-rounds erupted from those cylindrical nozzles.

One hit him right in the chest, but the electric current diffused into the protective vest he was wearing. That strange hooded woman had kept her end of the bargain. This was the worst he could expect; drones that used lethal ammunition had been outlawed when they proved to be a little *too* good at killing. Yet another sign that his culture had become weak and decadent.

The centre drone floated upward, trying to get a shot at his head.

Aldin threw himself down onto his belly, lifting his pistol in both hands, selecting EMP rounds. He fired and watched white tracers converge on the drone, striking it just below the glowing horizontal slit.

The drone fell.

"Hail our people!" Aldin shouted. "Hail victory!"

As she raced up the steps that led from the subway station to the street, Melissa felt her heart pounding. She stopped, halfway to the top, and looked back over her shoulder. "Are you okay, Dad?"

Her father was coming up behind her, gasping and shaking his head. "Hey, I might be middle-aged," he muttered, "but I'm still in pretty good shape. I used to run the track every day, remember?"

"I remember."

She ran for the top of the steps and found herself at the corner of an intersection where one of the streets that extended from the downtown core like spokes on a wheel intersected with one of the curving local roads. There were buildings on every corner, an arts centre that stood three stories high with a pyramid-shaped skylight on its roof, a tool library where residents of his neighbourhood could borrow household tools.

The food production centre was just a little ways up the road; of all the places to be hit, this one was closest to her house, only two subway stops away. "Come on," she said to her father. "I don't know if any other Keepers have responded to-"

She cut off when an explosion lit up the night sky.

Not the food processing centre – it was far too distant for that – but one of the many vertical farms along the city's perimeter. They had lost another one. "We have to move!" she told her father.

They turned down the curving street and ran hard. Only a block and a half from the intersection. To his credit, her father managed to keep up the whole time, though she was running at a slightly reduced speed.

When they reached the food processing plant, Melissa found a hole in the chain-link fence that bordered the property. Half a dozen people had slipped through and were now spread out in the grass between the fence and the building's front wall, firing on security drones that tried to hold them off.

"Hey!" Melissa shouted.

Two men at the back whirled around to face her, one slightly closer than the other. For a brief moment, they just stared, unsure of what to make of her. Then the nearest one lifted his pistol and tried to take aim.

Melissa ran for him.

She leaped, tucked her knees into her chest, and somersaulted through the air. At the apex of her jump, she threw up a Time Bubble – well, more of a tube than a bubble – and for an instant, she could see that it had saved her life.

The blurry images of both men had arms extended, pointing guns at her. Glowing white bullets hung frozen in mid-air, converging on a spot that she would pass through in her descent.

She fell through the tube, landing within a few feet of the nearest man. When she let the bubble vanish, bullets passed over her.

The man in front of her gave a start.

Melissa kicked high, striking the pistol and ripping it out of his hand. She brought her leg down, then spun and back-kicked. A quick hit to the chest made the man stumble and drove the air from his lungs.

Melissa rounded on him.

She lunged at him, seizing the man's vest with both hands and then quickly twirling him around so that he was between her and the other shooter. It was a well-timed move. Seconds later, the man's body spasmed as bullets hit the back of his vest. The current was absorbed into the material.

Melissa slammed her open palm into the man's chest and drove him backward with a surge of Bent Gravity. He flew toward his companion with arms flailing. The other man tried to get out of the way, but he wasn't fast enough.

They hit hard, like two cars colliding on the freeway, and dropped to the ground in a heap. "Justice Keeper!" one called out. "She's a Justice Keeper!"

If only...

The other four turned on her.

Harry charged through the hole in the fence to find his eldest daughter kicking the crap out of one of the terrorists. She grabbed him by the vest and spun him around to use him as a human shield.

He ignored that and focused on the three people – two men and one woman – who had their backs turned as they fired up at floating egg-shaped drones that bobbed and weaved to avoid their aim. White tracers flew into the night sky, but the drone managed to avoid them, swooping off to the side

Harry drew his pistol, setting it for stun-rounds.

Taking aim with the gun in both hands, he pointed the muzzle at the back of one man's neck and fired. A charged bullet hit that guy just below his hairline, and then he fell to the ground as the current knocked him out.

The other man and the woman whirled around to face him. In mere fractions of a second, they were raising their own weapons to take aim.

Harry was faster.

Thrusting his left hand out, he summoned a force-field with the N'Jal and watched as the air in front of him rippled. He loosed the force-field, angling it downward so that it sank into the ground and churned up a spray of dirt.

Both the man and the woman raised their hands up to shield themselves as chunks of soil pelted them. This gave him a moment to react.

Harry took aim with his pistol again, and he fired. One slug into the woman's chest; her vest absorbed the energy, but the impact staggered her. Another bullet hit her right in the forehead and bounced off, leaving nothing but a bruise. But the electric current that surged through her body knocked her out.

The man aimed.

Harry threw himself sideways, grunting when his shoulder hit the ground. White tracers sped over him, the air sizzling in their wake. He lifted his gun in both hands and fired several rounds.

The man stumbled as stun rounds hit his chest and fell uselessly to the ground. But it left him off balance.

Harry lined up the perfect shot.

Before he could squeeze the trigger, the other man stumbled as something hit him from behind. Flailing about like a drop of water on a hot skillet, the guy dropped to the ground, revealing the floating drone behind him.

That drone quickly reoriented itself to aim at Harry.

He raised a hand instinctively, the N'Jal erecting a force-field that intercepted stun-rounds before they hit him. This was why he would never trust robots! The drone didn't recognize him as a friend. Its software merely noted the presence of an unidentified man on its property, and so it responded accordingly. The worthless hunk of junk seemed to recognize Melissa as a Justice Keeper – it didn't bother targeting her – but it didn't know what to make of Harry and his force-fields.

Melissa ignored the man and woman who were currently fending off a spray of dirt that her father had unleashed. A grizzled old cop like Harry could handle himself. It was the other two – the ones nearest the building's front entrance – that concerned her. A man and a woman: they whirled around as soon as someone shouted. "Justice Keeper!"

Melissa turned and dove for the pistol that she had kicked out of the first guy's grip. Slamming her hands down in the moist grass, she grabbed the gun and then somersaulted across the field.

She came up on one knee.

Thrusting her hand out to the side – using her eyes wasn't necessary when she had spatial awareness – she fired blindly and mapped the path of each bullet with her mind.

White tracers sped across the field, struck the woman's vest and threw her to the ground with the force of their impact. The man didn't bother returning fire; he just fell to his knees.

Melissa could have put a bullet through his skull, but she wasn't a killer. She was a Justice Keeper, through and through.

The man pulled off his backpack, unzipped it and retrieved something from inside. "Back off!" he shouted. "Order the drone to stand down, Justice Keeper!"

He stood up and smiled at her with a small, rectangular device cradled in both hands. It was clear that this guy was the leader; tall and slim, he had an arrogant face and brown hair that he wore parted in the middle. "Tell the drone to stand down," he said again. "Or I will reduce this building to a crater and kill us all in one spectacular fireball."

"That's the bomb," Melissa mumbled.

"How very observant of you."

Squeezing her eyes shut, Melissa drew in a breath. "Security systems!" she called out. "Recognize Cadet Melissa Carlson, Justice Keeper serial number 5612578. I order you to stand down."

The drone stopped firing at her father, who was taking

refuge behind a force-field. It floated upward and then retreated to the building's rooftop.

A nasty grin spread across the leader's face, and he nodded to her. "Very good," he said, taking a few steps forward. "Now, you and your friend are going to drop your guns, and you're going to let us walk away."

Anxiety chilled her blood until it felt as if she had ice in her veins. What should she do? It felt wrong, just letting them go, but it wasn't just her father's life on the line. Or her own for that matter. There was no telling how powerful that bomb was.

"All right," Melissa said. "Go. But first, you put down your weapons."

"You're not in a place to be dictating terms."

Melissa stood up and faced him, lifting the pistol in both hands and letting out a deep breath. "Try me," she said. "I Bonded a symbiont that cut my lifespan in half. It's safe to say I have a death wish."

The man frowned and turned his head, staring at something off to her left. "Fine," he said after a moment. "I'll even make a show of good faith. My people will put down their weapons first, and then you do the same, or I activate this bomb."

The pair of men that she had disarmed earlier were groaning as they sat. One of them shook his head to get his bearings. "I don't like this, Aldin," he said. "We give up our weapons, and she'll be on us in seconds."

"Shut up, Roja!"

That silenced the man.

Aldin stood in front of the building with the bomb cradled in his hands, a great big grin on his face. "Now," he said, nodding to his people. "We're all gonna do what the nice lady says. Put down your weapons."

The woman who was lying on the ground after taking several hits to the chest threw her gun aside, as did Roja, though he grumbled about it under his breath. The two people that her father had dispatched were still unconscious.

"Your turn," Aldin said.

Dropping to a crouch, Melissa set her gun down in the grass. She craned her neck to fix her gaze on Aldin. "Sufficient?" she asked, raising an eyebrow. "I'm not carrying anything else on me."

"Your friend?" Aldin said.

In response, Harry threw his gun away and sat up. A grimace twisted his features, and he shook his head. "Run if you need to," he said. "You'll have a dozen Keepers on you before you reach the nearest SlipGate."

"Let me worry about that," Aldin said.

He dropped to his knees, setting the bomb down on the paving stones in front of the building. "There we are," he murmured. "Now, young Justice Keeper, a lesson for you in trust: it's a weakness."

He tapped a few buttons on the bomb, and suddenly the LCD screen on its surface lit up. Had he just armed the thing? Had he just armed the god-damn bomb with all of them standing here?

Aldin looked up at her and trembled with laughter. "You can chase me if you want to," he said. "But you have only five minutes to save this food processing plant, And I do hope there are no civilians in the area."

He got up and ran for the hole in the fence.

As did his comrades.

Melissa snatched up the pistol she had dropped, lifting it in both hands to point it right at Aldin's chest. "High Impact!" she growled. "Stay right where you are. I swear to God, I'll pull this trigger."

He stopped in his tracks.

The others did likewise.

Colour drained out of Aldin's face as he stared at her with

his mouth hanging open. "You wouldn't," he whispered, shaking his head. "Keepers don't kill."

"If I'm going to die here tonight," Melissa said, "then you're going with me. So, I'm thinking you might want to tell me how to disarm that thing."

Standing in the grass with a hand pressed to his chest, Aldin threw his head back and laughed. "It *can't* be disarmed!" he shouted. "We wanted to make sure no one had any second thoughts."

Wincing hard, Melissa felt sweat prickling on her brow. "Brilliant," she growled, standing up. "Then I guess we're all going to die here, tonight. You so much as twitch in a way I don't like, and I will *end* you."

"You don't have."

She lowered her aim and fired.

A bullet grazed his leg, then dug itself into the ground behind him, leaving a crater the size of a bowling ball. Aldin yelped, crouching down to slap a hand over the spot where he had been stung. God bless spatial awareness. Precision shooting was that much easier when you had an intuitive sense of everything around you.

After that little display of her sincerity, the woman and the two men who were still standing all backed up with their hands raised. Quite satisfying. Now, if only she could find a way to enjoy her pride for more than the next three and a half minutes. "Tell me how to disarm the bomb," Melissa said coldly.

"You *can't*!"

"I don't accept that."

Aldin was hopping on one foot with one hand pressed to his thigh. His face was so red that it looked as if he had acquired a permanent sunburn. "Idiot girl!" he squealed. "What does it matter if you accept it? It won't change anything."

"He's not lying!" the woman panted. "The bomb has no

disarm code. If you start poking around with its circuitry, it *will* explode. We have to run now! Or we're all going to die here!"

Suddenly, Melissa was very much aware of the pounding of her own heart. Was she ready to die? At seventeen? This *was* the life she had chosen. "Well, then I guess we're all going to die here."

"You're insane!" one of the men shouted.

"No," Melissa said. "Insane people use bombs to make their point." Gripping the pistol tightly, she strode forward, and it pleased her to see the lot of them backing up. Except Aldin, of course; he just kept hopping. "Up against the wall."

The woman and her two male companions pressed their backs to the front wall of the food processing plant, each one raising their hands. "I don't understand," the woman said. "You could have run."

Melissa felt her face heat up, fury burning in her veins. Her lip twitched, and she had to struggle not to snarl. "Any poor bystander who happens to be passing through this neighbourhood wouldn't have the chance to run."

She crouched in front of the bomb and saw that the timer was steadily counting down the seconds. At this point, less than two and a half minutes remained. "Harry, get over here!" she called out. Under no circumstances was she willing to call him Dad in front of the terrorists. That would just kill her credibility.

Her father rushed over, dropping to a crouch next to her with his hands resting on his knees. "What is it?" he asked, glancing over his shoulder. "Do you know some way to disable it?"

Closing her eyes, Melissa took a deep breath. "I was planning to ask you that," she admitted. "What do you know about defusing bombs?"

"Next to nothing."

"Damn it."

She tentatively reached out to touch one of the buttons on the bomb's surface only to yank her hand back when the terrorist woman shouted "No!" Melissa looked up to see the other woman standing in front of the wall with a hand outstretched, sweat glistening on her face. "If you touch that, it will explode."

"Then what do I do?"

The woman shuddered and shook her head. "Nothing," she whimpered. "Anything you try will only set off the bomb."

One minute and twenty-five seconds.

There had to be *something* she could do! But what? Was it too late to run? Maybe they could find cover in the time remaining? No...That was impossible. She had chosen her course, and now she had to stick with it.

If disabling the bomb was impossible, could she move it? A brief image of herself carrying the bomb down the street only to have it explode in her hands flashed through Melissa's mind. What good would that do anyway? Best case scenario, it would destroy some other building, and there could be people in those buildings. Not likely at this hour, but it was possible. If only she could move the bomb upward, but that was impossi-

Of course!

The calculations played out in her head. Physics was never her thing – she much preferred history and literature – but you gained a sense of these things if you carried a Nassai long enough. If she applied a Bending roughly ten times as strong as the planet's gravitational pull – but directed upward instead of down – the bomb would travel about five kilometers in ten seconds.

Of course, that was assuming the ideal conditions of a vacuum. There was terminal velocity to consider, and she didn't know how to do that math. But she figured she would at least get a few kilometers out of the deal.

The final issue to consider was just how long she could

make the Bending last. In general, the stronger the Bending, the longer it lasted, but even the most powerful ones fizzled out after about ten seconds.

Meaning she would have to time it well.

If she applied the Bending too soon, Leyria's natural gravity would reassert itself. The bomb wouldn't start to fall right away – an object in motion remained in its current state of motion unless acted on by an outside force – but it would begin to slow down. Every inch of distance she could gain was vital.

Twenty-four seconds remaining. Twenty-three, twenty-two..."Harry," she said. "Cover me."

Nineteen, eighteen, seventeen, sixteen...

Melissa touched the bomb with her fingertips, calling on the power of her Nassai. Energy surged through her body as she applied a Bending ten times as powerful as the planet's natural pull, directing it toward the upper atmosphere.

The bomb shot upward like a bullet loosed from a gun.

In less than a second, it was so far away that she couldn't track it with her eyes. Now, there was nothing to do but wait. Exhaustion hit her like a transport truck with the pedal to the floor. Her muscles felt rubbery, and her head was full of fog.

Melissa fell forward, slapping her hands down in the grass to catch herself. Her head drooped as dizziness came over her.

With an extreme effort of will, she managed to look up in time to see a bright flash of fire in the night sky. Like a new star birthed in the heavens. She was barely aware of the soft popping sound that must have been the explosion. It had worked; she had saved them, but now she was on the verge of passing out.

Her skin was on fire. It was like a million bees had decided to sting her at the same time. God help her; she was in no shape to defend herself.

The three terrorists along the wall stepped forward.

Before they could make a move, Harry stood up and thrust

his hand toward them, proudly displaying the N'Jal. “Don't even think it,” he said. “I swear by all that's holy, I will flatten you if you try.”

In her mind's eye, Melissa saw Aldin standing behind her with his back turned, bent over and rubbing his leg. The man seemed to think this was his chance to run for it; so, he began hobbling his way to the hole in the fence.

Melissa tossed the gun to her father.

He caught it in his right hand, keeping his left pointed at the other three and putting up a force-field to show he meant business. With an almost casual motion, Harry turned and shouted, “Stun-rounds!”

He fired.

A charged bullet hit Aldin in the back of the neck, and the man spasmed as current surged through his body. He dropped to his knees mere seconds later, then fell flat on his face in the grass.

Letting his arm drop, the force-field vanishing the instant he did, Harry showed them a wolfish smile. “Now,” he said. “Who wants to come quietly down to the nearest police station?”

14

Larani watched people scurrying about the Prep Room like ants gathering crumbs for...whatever it was ants did with crumbs. Eat them, she supposed. She had never been all that interested in insects.

Large enough to host a banquet with windows along the back wall that looked out on a city under the night sky, the Prep Room was mostly empty floor space with several computer consoles forming a ring in the middle of the floor. Monitors on the three other walls displayed news updates and incoming reports from the teams she had dispatched to protect the city's infrastructure.

Her stomach was in knots, but she managed not to show it. A good Keeper knew when and how to keep tight control of their emotions.

Dressed in black slacks and a white, short-sleeved blouse, Larani stood with her back to the windows. Everyone seemed to be ignoring her, but appearances were often deceiving; in reality, they were hurrying to fetch information she had requested.

Craning her neck, Larani squinted at a holographic display.

"Show me that last bit again," she said in crisp, cool tones, Always maintain your composure. "The report about the raid on the power plant."

The hologram that hovered over the ring of consoles rippled out of existence, and when it reappeared, it displayed white text on a blue background. A team of four Keepers assisted twenty-five police officers in apprehending eight terrorists who had attacked the geothermal plant in the city's eastern quarter. Her people had managed to apprehend the perpetrators before they set off a bomb.

Larani closed her eyes, breathing out a sigh of relief. "All right," she said, nodding once. "What's the status of the food distribution systems? Are any processing plants still being threatened by these cowardly..."

She didn't want to finish that sentence.

Agent Robert Caldwell – one of several Keepers who had transferred from Earth this past year – looked up from his station with a curious expression. "Ma'am," he said. "We just received the strangest report."

"Define 'strange,' Agent Caldwell."

The man shut his eyes, sucking in a deep breath. "The message came from Cadet Carlson, ma'am," he explained. "It seems she and her father managed to save the food processing centre in the Vaundren Heights neighbourhood."

Turning his head so that he wouldn't have to look at her, he cleared his throat with some force. "Police arrived on scene to find Cadet Carlson and her father guarding three terrorists while three more were unconscious."

"It seems praise is in order," Larani mumbled.

A young woman with long brown hair that framed an angelic face looked up to fix her blue eyes on Larani. "We still have a situation at the water purification plant," she said. "We haven't got an exact count on the number of hostiles there. Police have identified at least six, but they're wearing masks and they seem to be holed up in one of the inspection centres."

"What's the situation at Farm 21?"

"Stabilized, ma'am."

Pressing her nose into the palm of one hand, Larani massaged her eyelids. "Have Soras, Calivan and Lenai reinforce our people at the water treatment plant."

At the sound of his dearest friend's name, Jack Hunter came out of his hiding place in the corner. The young man wore a tense expression, and it was clear he wanted to rush out the door so that he could fight at Anna's side. He said nothing, of course. Larani had already chastised him for his sulkiness in private. Jack didn't like being forced to handle the logistics; he wanted to be out there, on the front lines with his fellow Keepers.

Unfortunately, that wasn't his job.

Being the personal attache to the Head of the Justice Keepers came with certain responsibilities; she needed him at her side, or she soon would in any event. Coordinating their efforts was the easy part of her job.

The hard part would come soon enough.

It went on like that for another hour: people giving her reports, her responding by redirecting her officers to this crime-scene or that one. It felt very much like a war. And that was a problem because she had never fancied herself a general.

Finally, it was over.

They'd lost another vertical farm, and there was minor damage to a solar field on the outskirts of the city, but otherwise, Denabria had come through this unscathed. The residents of certain neighbourhoods were being warned not to drink their tap water until city engineers could determine what – if anything – had been done to the water treatment plant. Luckily, there were emergency protocols in place in the event that something like this happened. Other treatment plants were shipping large bottles of water to distribution centres in the affected neighbourhoods.

Now, the hard part would begin.

"Hunter," Larani said. "You're with me."

The young man fell in step beside her, frowning intently down at the floor. "If you don't mind my asking," he began cautiously. "Where are we going."

Larani walked with her head held high, her eyes focused dead ahead. "Many of our best agents will be crawling into their beds for some much-deserved rest," she said. "Our work, however, is just beginning."

Large double doors split apart to reveal a corridor with soft blue walls. They would have to make their way down to the garage; the Keepers kept a fleet of cars at the ready in case of an emergency.

Larani strode through the corridor at a brisk pace, closing her eyes as she tried to put the stress out of her mind. "Jena began teaching you about politics," she went on. "I intend to continue those lessons."

At her side, Jack blushed and turned his head to stare at the wall. "I think that Jena found me to be a terrible student," he muttered. "You may want someone else with you for...whatever it is you're planning."

"On the contrary," Larani countered. "She often spoke of your keen mind. You have an ability to read people, Jack, and a talent for spotting discrepancies between someone's words and their actions. That's why you're here instead of fighting alongside your fellow Justice Keepers."

As the car emerged from the parking garage, Jack was surprised to see a deep blue sky through the windshield. The nearby buildings stood like shadows against the dawn's early light. Had *that* much time passed? He'd been cooped up inside the Prep Room with next to nothing to do, forced to sit and listen to reports while other people put their lives on the line. It left him feeling antsy. And now the night was over. He could feel Summer's fatigue as well as his own.

Chewing on his lip, Jack looked down into his lap. "So," he began, deep creases forming in his brow. "Are you gonna tell me where we're going?"

Sitting on his left with her hands folded neatly in her lap, Larani stared through the windshield with a blank expression. "Have you followed any Leyrian news outlets?" she asked. "What do you know about Jeral Dusep?"

"Not much," Jack admitted. "The few things I've heard make him sound about as bad as Earth's most vocal right-wing extremists."

Larani hunched up her shoulders, a shiver passing through her. She sat back in her seat and let out a breath. "That would be an accurate statement," she muttered. "The man is fiercely nationalistic."

"I thought Leyrians were above such things."

A quick glance over his shoulder revealed Larani staring at him with dark eyes that could drill holes through stone. "Society shapes us, yes," she said. "But even in the most miserable conditions, there will always be saints who share what meager possessions they have with others."

Her mouth twisted for a moment, and she shook her head with a sigh. "And even in a world that some would call paradise," she went on. "There will always be people who enjoy trampling on those less fortunate than themselves."

They were driving down a nearly empty road with dark skyscrapers on either side. Several blocks away, there was another car coming toward them, but other than that, he saw no one. The sky was growing brighter.

Leaning back in his seat with hands folded behind his head, Jack stared off into the distance. "So, we're going to meet this

Dusep?" he said. "I take it we should expect one of his standard speeches? Immigrants-bad, Leyria for Leyrians?"

"Something like that."

It left him feeling anxious.

As an immigrant to this world, he could very easily find himself the target of any hate Dusep stirred up. The law said that he had become a Leyrian citizen the instant he became a Justice Keeper – it was a reward for his service and dedication – but he didn't trust laws. Laws could be rewritten on a whim. Laws were nothing but ink on paper and had little to no effect on what people actually did.

Jack shut his eyes, heaving out a rasping breath. "So, what's your play?" he asked. "You want me to read this guy and tell you if he's lying? Because I might be a star in the interrogation room, but I've never analyzed a politician."

"I want you to tell me anything you find pertinent," Larani said. "Maybe some of it will be useful, maybe not."

It was a quick drive to the Hall of Council, an older building with two wings, both three stories high. The dome-shaped roof in the centre had a balcony that overlooked the front entrance. Jack half expected to see a flag rippling in the crisp morning wind, but of course, Leyrians didn't use flags.

In fact, he remembered Anna having some trouble trying to wrap her head around the concept. A piece of coloured cloth to designate one's nationality. What purpose could that serve? Jack had asked her what Leyrians did to differentiate different factions on a battlefield – and he had braced himself for some sanctimonious answer about Leyrians not participating in war – but Anna told him that soldiers had always known who to kill by their uniforms.

It turned out that Council was already in an emergency session when he and Larani stepped through the door. A holographic usher appeared to direct them to the third floor where they could observe the deliberations. This was a closed session, but Keepers had a right to sit in on all Council Meetings.

The upper floor gave them a good view of the councilors arguing down below. Less than half had made it this meeting – most weren't even in the city – and there were many empty seats in the semicircular rows along the far wall.

The Prime Council stood with her back to Jack and Larani, golden staff in hand as she tried to restore some semblance of order to a meeting that had gotten out of hand. At least five people in the Green Party were shouting at the Blues.

Sarona Vason banged her staff down on the floor tiles.

That silenced everyone.

"Order!" the Prime Council said, pointing her staff toward several Greens who had risen from their seats, "We *will* have order in this session. Councilor Dusep, please finish your arguments."

That was when Jack noticed a man in a blue coat standing on the other side of the room. Short – at least by Jack's standards – and slim, this guy had a handsome face of bronze skin and black hair that he wore slicked back. "Thank you, Prime Council," he said. "I maintain that any motion to upgrade the automated security systems at key points of city infrastructure *must* include lethal force as an option."

"Your thoughts?" Larani whispered.

Jack was sitting with his arms crossed, frowning into his lap. "Typical strong-man behaviour," he answered. "Demand harsh measures, and never mind whether your 'tough on crime' stance does anything to make people safer."

One of the Reds stood up: a woman in black pants and a crimson jacket who threw a harsh glare in Dusep's direction. With curly gray hair and a few wrinkles on her face, she reminded Jack of his grandmother. "Drones that use lethal force have proven to be a liability in the past."

Dusep twisted his face into an expression that made Jack

think he was about to vomit. "Oh yes," he said. "I've heard these arguments before, and the fact remains that the current security systems were obviously not a deterrent."

A man in red leaped to his feet, this one tall and broad-shouldered with dark skin and a gray beard. "The threat of force as a deterrent is rarely an effective policy," he said. "It's been researched quite thoroughly in papers by-"

"Hundred-year-old sociology experiments do not concern me," Dusep shot back. "Academics can make whatever claims they like, but simple common sense will tell you that the kind of people who would try to poison a city's water supply will only respond to one thing.

"Consider your hypothesis, Councilor," the man went on. "There is no poverty to be alleviated; these Sons of Savard are not destroying critical pieces of city infrastructure as an act of rebellion against an oppressive economic order. In fact, they wish to *create* the very conditions that many soft-minded politicians credit as being the root cause of crime. It should be obvious to you that a firm hand is needed."

Hard as it was to admit, Jack found himself agreeing with part of that. Not the plan to employ drones that use lethal force – that was ludicrous – but the man *did* have a point about poverty not being the root of this. So, why destroy the infrastructure that ensured everyone had access to basic living essentials?

Well, the answer was simple.

It was typical Social Darwinism and nothing more. To hear Anna speak about her world, you might have thought that Leyrians had shed such idiotic ideas like a layer of dead skin. But as Larani said, there would always be some folks who wanted others to have less. Not even so that they could have more but just because they *liked* the idea of there being an underclass.

Jack sat forward with his elbow on his knee, resting his chin on the knuckles of his fist. "It's funny," he said, eyebrows rising. "Normally a guy like Dusep would be telling anyone who'd listen about how much he loves the Sons of Savard."

Puckering her lips, Larani blew out a breath. "The man loves power more than anything else," she whispered. "And these terrorists are giving him the perfect excuse to accumulate it and then use it like a club."

"How does a guy like that become a councilor?"

"Power draws a certain type of individual," Larani murmured. "People like Dusep know how to say the right things and make the right gestures until they're comfortable. And when they do let their true colours show, most people think they couldn't possibly mean what they're saying."

"So, how come you weren't fooled?"

Glancing over her shoulder, Larani scowled at him. A heavy sigh exploded from her lungs. "Because I read a lot of history, Agent Hunter," she replied. "And I recognize these patterns when I see them."

Covering his mouth with two fingers, Jack shut his eyes. "Does Dusep know?" he muttered. "That you suspect his motivations for joining the Council aren't as pure as they should be, I mean."

"He knows I'm no ally."

Down below, the deliberations were coming to an end as Dusep took his seat again and someone from the Red Party began reviewing the morning's proceedings. Resource allocation algorithms had come up with half a dozen heavy-duty fabrication units along with a generous supply of copper, gold and dura-plastic to upgrade the security systems at power plants and food distribution centres. Council approved those measures.

The plan as laid out by the Prime Council's Planetary Security Team specified new biometric sensors on all systems and an increase in the number of security drones at each location.

The engineers who worked on those systems would be trained in new InfoSec protocols. Hopefully, that would make a difference.

"Come," Larani said.

"Where are we going?"

"To do the one thing that anyone in a leadership position dreads," she answered. "We're going to take the blame."

The double doors to Sarona Vason's office were shut, giving Larani a chance to study the polished wooden finish and the ornate, gold door-handles. This building had been rebuilt several times, but architects endeavoured to preserve as much of the original design as possible. It was one of the few remaining vestiges from that period of Leyrian history.

She waited patiently in a hallway with an arch-shaped vaulted ceiling and paintings on its cream-coloured walls. Really, it didn't bother her. She was tired and aching for just a few hours of sleep, but she was in no hurry to listen to a sternly-worded lecture about how her Keepers should have prevented this catastrophe.

Jack was at her side with his arms folded, his face as red as the setting sun. "You didn't tell me that I'd be meeting the Prime Council," he whispered. "God help me, I feel so under dressed."

Clamping a hand over her mouth, Larani shut her eyes and trembled as she laughed. "Relax," she told him. "You have an excuse for being somewhat unpresentable in light of the fact that you spent an entire night coordinating the defense of this city."

"Well...That's good then."

Larani clasped her hands together behind her back, smiling down at herself. "But it pleases me to see that you've begun to notice such things," she said. "Perhaps we'll make a model Keeper out of you yet."

"Heh," Jack grunted. "Don't count on it."

The door swung inward to reveal Sarona Vason standing there in white robes that went all the way down to her black boots. A tall woman with a leathery face of dark skin and silver hair that she wore up in a ponytail, she took one look at them and then jerked her head toward her desk. "Come on in then."

The woman turned gracefully, turning her back on both of them and striding across her office. "I'd imagine we have a lot to talk about," she went on. "It's not every day that someone threatens the Capitol itself."

The office was a simple room with blue carpets and white walls with bookshelves along them. A wooden desk – oriented to face the wall on her left – was littered with at least six Smart-Glass tablets. It seemed Sarona had been monitoring the situation.

The Prime Council stood in the daylight that came in through a narrow, rectangular window, gazing out at the courtyard. Unfortunately, she wasn't the only one present.

Councilor Derok, a tall man in a maroon jacket who wore his silver beard trimmed nice and neat, sat in a chair in front of the desk. He was the man who had tried to oppose Dusep's insistence that lethal force was the only thing that would deter a terrorist.

That wasn't what bothered her.

Councilor Dusep himself stood in front of the other window, stroking his chin as if lost in thought. "Director Tal," he said before anyone else could speak. "I imagine you'd like to explain yourself."

Larani squeezed her eyes shut, breathing deeply through her nose. "I was unaware that anything I've done requires explanation." She strode deeper into the office. "Perhaps you'd like to make a specific complaint."

Dusep turned to face her with one hand over his stomach, his face a mask of stone. "Very well then," he said in crisp, cool tones. "Would you care to explain how this lapse in our security happened?"

"No one is here to place blame."

That came from Voran Derok. Larani saw him in her mind's eye as a misty shadow rising slowly from his chair to stand behind her. "The purpose of this meeting is to assess our options going forward."

"I believe the plan put forward in today's emergency session covers that," Larani said. "In fact, I was one of the authors of that plan. So, you already know my position." Being the Head of the Justice Keepers guaranteed you a spot on the Planetary Security Team of pretty much any administration, though she often found that other members of that team treated her suggestions with suspicion. Was that because many of those people had worked with Slade when he filled that role?

The plan that Council approved this morning may have seemed rushed, but in truth, the PST had been working on it ever since the first attack on Vertical Farm 17. It should have gone through several more committee meetings before it was approved, but after last night's fiasco, Council was desperate to do *something*.

Spinning on his heel to face them, Dusep marched across the room as if he meant to mow her down. "I am uninterested in-" The man paused in mid-step, noticing Jack for the first time. "Who is this?"

Larani opened her mouth to answer.

Jack stepped forward with his hands in his pockets, smiling down at himself. "No one important," he said with a shrug. "Just a guy who thinks nationalism is an old song for small men with a lot of anger and no good ideas."

Sarona Vason laughed.

Dusep's mouth tightened, and his face went crimson, but he nodded and continued with his diatribe. "A situation like this should never have been allowed to happen in the first place," he rasped. "It shows how utterly unprepared we were for-"

"Yet another round of assigning blame will get us nowhere, Jeral." Sarona Vason had her hands on the windowsill as she spoke, and she kept her back turned as if this conversation were of no interest to her. "The plan has been approved."

"For the moment, but I intend-"

"Enough."

When the Prime Council rounded on them with her arms folded, her face as dark as a looming thundercloud, everyone else stepped back. "We've been over this more times than I can count," she snapped. "Make whatever motions you feel are appropriate, Jeral; I wish to speak with Larani."

The councilor strode past Larani on his way to the door. "Mark my words, Sarona," he said. "Sooner or later, someone will do something far worse than blowing up a few automated distribution centres. And on that day, you'll wish you had taken my advice."

He left without another word.

Grinning down at the floor, Jack rubbed his forehead with the back of his hand. "Guy's doing it all wrong," he muttered. "That kind of speech works better if you shake your fist and shout 'You'll rue the day you ever-' "

"Jack..." Larani hissed.

The young man really did need to do away with his habit of making jokes at the worst possible time. Jena may have put up with that nonsense; Larani would not. Not in front of the Prime Council, anyway. "You wanted to speak with me, ma'am," she said.

Instead of answering, Sarona Vason directed a motherly smile toward Jack. Some people found his impishness charming. "The man is a bit of a pompous windbag, isn't he?" she said softly. "Is it much the same on your world, Agent Hunter?"

"You know who I am?"

The Prime Council let out a peal of rich, satisfied laughter. "I wouldn't be much of a head of state if I didn't, now would I?" She sat down on the edge of her desk with hands folded in her lap, a position that looked oddly casual in light of the formal robes she was wearing. "I've read a bit of your history."

Closing his eyes, Jack nodded to the woman. "I figured you might have," he said, stepping forward. "That being the case, you know how dangerous a man like that can be if he gains momentum."

"All too well." Sarona let out a deep breath. "Which is why it is imperative that we restore order as quickly as possible. Voran, would you excuse us please?"

"Very well," he said. "Good luck."

When he was gone, Sarona hopped off the desk and flowed across the room to a small wooden table near a bookshelf. She poured herself a cup of tea from a pot that she found there. "Now then," she said after a moment. "I want an honest answer. How likely is it that Slade's people are behind these attacks?"

The woman spun around, and it was clear by the intensity of her stare that she was in no mood for sugar coating. Were Slade's people somehow involved with the Sons of Savard? The question made Larani somewhat uneasy.

It wasn't that she had never considered that possibility – after the last year, she had begun to see Slade lurking in every shadow – but she couldn't see anything that Slade's underlings might gain from this. Which, of course, meant that it was all too likely that they *were* involved in some way.

"Honestly," Larani said, "I'm not sure. I've considered interrogating the Keepers who joined Slade's cause, but if they do know something – and it's a big if – they likely wouldn't tell us."

"Slade did love a good terror campaign," Jack said. "But if his people were behind this, why use a bunch of untrained malcontents to do their dirty work? With all the other resources at their disposal, it doesn't add up. Where are the *ziarogati*, the battle drones?"

It was clear that Sarona wasn't convinced.

The Prime Council stood in front of a bookshelf with a teacup in hand, her eyes downcast. "If I recall your reports," she said. "Slade relied quite heavily on an untrained militia when he terrorized New York."

Jack squinted at the woman. "That's true," he said with a curt nod. "But Slade didn't rely on them exclusively. If Slade's people wanted to attack our infrastructure, they would have methods for dealing with Justice Keepers."

Stroking her jawline with the tips of her fingers, Larani shut her eyes and took a deep breath. "It *is* a possibility worth considering," she admitted. "I will have my agents look into it, but for now, I think that we should operate under the assumption that we're dealing with homegrown terrorism."

"Why would Leyrian citizens do this?" Sarona whispered.

In response to that, Jack stepped forward and stood before the Prime Council with his hands clasped behind his back. "With respect, ma'am," he began. "I would consider that to be Leyrian arrogance."

Sarona Vason lifted her chin to stare at him with dark eyes that seemed aflame with barely contained anger. "Is that so, Agent Hunter?" she asked, raising one gray eyebrow. "Do enlighten me."

Should Larani put a stop to this?

No. This wasn't one of Jack's ill-timed quips. She had brought him on as her attache because she wanted someone who would challenge authority. If Jack was going to do that effectively, she would have to let him off his leash.

"Don't get me wrong," he said. "I am *thrilled* to have the opportunity to live here. For someone who grew up on Earth, the prospect of a world without poverty is nothing short of miraculous, but I *have* noticed, in my many interactions with your people, that Leyrians seem to think they have created the perfect society. You're so pleased with it, you can't imagine why anyone would want to leave it."

"We're hardly keeping anyone here against their will, Agent Hunter."

"Aren't you?" he responded. "The Antaurans began raiding your outer colonies, and what was your response? You told the people living there to come home."

Sarona lifted her cup to her lips and took a long, slow sip, no doubt giving herself a moment to think. "You make it sound so one-sided," she said. "You *do* realize that taking aggressive action against the Antaurans could have started a war."

"I'm aware of that, ma'am. But I-"

"Jack," Larani cut in. "Enough."

She stepped up beside her subordinate, heaving out a soft sigh. "At the moment, we have no reason to suspect Slade's faction," she said. "What evidence we do have suggests a local terrorist cell."

"Then I suggest you find them quickly, Director Tal," Sarona replied. "Before the situation escalates."

A metal grating on a slanted glass roof filtered purple moonlight that fell upon a walkway lined with potted trees. On his right, the sidewall of the Music Therapy Centre was lined with arch-shaped windows with their own white grating. To his left, there was nothing but green grass that stretched on to a line of fir trees.

Brinton was curled up on a wooden bench with his cheek pressed to his forearm, trying to get some sleep. Trying and failing. Aside from the odd camping trip, he'd never had the misfortune of having to go without a bed. But he couldn't return to the church or to his own house; the authorities were looking for him.

Luckily, they would never think to look here. He had not set foot in this building in over ten years, not since his mother's failed attempt to turn him into a violinist during his teenage years. He had played for patients suffering from depression. Not with anything that could be called proficiency, mind you, but he *had* played.

The weather was warm enough to let him sleep outside, and the chances of anyone searching for him here were small. The Music Therapy Centre had no security bots and no cameras. Why would they? Theft was practically unheard of in a society where people could fabricate almost any material good at no cost.

"You look tired."

Brinton sat up.

The strange hooded woman who had given them weapons seemed to melt out of the shadows further up the walkway. Silhouetted by purple light, she wore a sleek black dress with thin straps, and her cloak hung limp behind her.

Squeezing his eyes shut, Brinton pressed fists to his eyelids and massaged them with his knuckles. "The explosions last night didn't exactly make it easy to rest," he said. "I take it the attack went well."

"You were absent."

He stood up with a grunt, hunching over and slapping a palm against his forehead. He raked fingers through his hair. "I've done my part," Brinton said. "I blew up the first one, remember?"

When he found the courage to look at her, the woman just stood there with her arms folded, her face hidden in the shadows of that hood. "Commitment to righteousness must be absolute," she said. "You of all people know that."

"I'm not putting myself in further danger!"

She flowed toward him in heeled boots that clicked as they struck the tiles of the walkway. "I thought you were a man of God." When she looked up into his eyes, Brinton could just make out the outline of her nose. “Is your faith so easily shaken?”

“I follow the Covenant of Layat! Brinton spat. “If you knew the first thing about that, you'd know the Companion is *not* a god.”

It was the living embodiment of the life force of the universe, the source of all light and warmth, but he supposed that for people who did not study theology, the distinction was somewhat irrelevant.

She reached up to touch his cheek with bare fingers, her caress leaving a tingle in his skin. “Yes,” she murmured. “You worship an abstract concept masquerading as a god. Would you like to see the real thing?”

“The real...”

Hair stood on the back of his neck.

When he turned, there was...something...in the walkway, a ripple in the light that he couldn't quite trace with his eye. But he could hear a faint scuttling as it came closer. And then there was pressure, pressure on his mind.

Brinton fell to his knees, touching fingertips to his temples. He felt hot tears leaking from his eyes. “What are you,” he whispered. “What are you?”

He barely noticed as the woman slipped up behind him, barely felt it when a knife slid into his throat. There was a brief ripping sensation, and then his blood was spattering against the gray tiles of the walkway.

He saw it on his hands, blood staining his fingers, dripping from them. It was hard to think, hard to focus. Dimly, he was aware that his body was heaving. He would have been coughing if he had been able.

May the light of the Companion guide you home, he thought, reaching for the words he had been taught from childhood. If he spoke the words – he couldn't speak the words – but if he focused on them the Companion...the Companion.

There was no Companion.

The darkness swallowed him up, and he found nothing there to welcome him. No loving presence, no guiding light. There was no Companion.

And his life was over.

Brinton woke to find himself curled up naked on a floor that felt soft and slimy to the touch. The room he was in...Was it actually a room? It looked more like a cavern, but the walls glowed with a soft blue light.

He sat up, gasping.

Closing his eyes, Brinton started pawing at his face with his hands. It certainly felt like the face he had always known. "Where am I?" he called out, surprised by the sound of his own voice. "Where..."

He scrambled backward across the squishy floor, panting and wheezing until his back hit the cavern wall. "Where am I?" Now he was screaming, his voice hoarse. Was this the afterlife then? It wasn't supposed to be a physical place. Everything he had been taught suggested that dwelling in the Light of the Companion was a state of mind. But there was no Companion...

As he gathered his wits, he noticed a strange pool just a few feet to his left, a pool filled with a viscous green sludge that seemed to drink in the light from the walls. It was a bad idea – he knew that – but he couldn't resist.

Brinton dipped his hand into the liquid, and when he pulled it out again, trails of slimy green goop dripped from each finger. "Companion have mercy," he whispered. He knew the afterlife legends of many primitive cultures, and some spoke of horrors beyond a man's wildest imaginings. "Can anyone hear me?"

"Calm yourself, Brinton."

A glance to his right revealed the strange hooded woman

coming through a hole in the cavern wall. She moved with ease as she stepped over a corpse that had been casually discarded near the doorway. "You're alive," she informed him. "By the grace and wisdom of the Inzari, you have been given another chance at life."

"How..."

The woman froze in her tracks, planting fists on her hips and staring down at him from the depths of that hood. "Did I not tell you that you would meet a god?" she asked. "Of all your fellow conspirators, I thought *you* would be able to listen."

Brinton shut his eyes, a ragged breath exploding from him. "I died," he whispered. "How did they...I mean this shouldn't be possible."

"They're gods, Brinton."

Tears streamed over his cheeks, and he shook his head, trying to get his bearings. "This isn't possible," he sobbed. "What are you going to do to me?"

"Nothing."

"But...Why did you kill me?"

She dropped to one knee before him and leaned in close enough for him to see that she was smiling. "As proof, my boy," she said. "False gods demand blind faith. True gods offer proof."

He winced so hard it made his temples throb. "It's a trick." Dropping to all fours, he crawled away from her as fast as he could. "You stitched me up, and you gave me a blood transfusion. I never actually died."

The woman said nothing in response.

She just rose gracefully and gestured toward the body that had been left to rot by the door. Deep down, Brinton knew that he didn't want to look; after all the horrors he'd endured, the last thing he wanted was to see a dead man's face. But some part of him had to know. Some part of him couldn't resist.

He crawled over to the body.

As he drew near, he saw that the corpse was wearing the familiar black clothing of an acolyte of the church. The dead man was sprawled out on his side, turned away from Brinton. *It can't be...It can't be...*

Gently, Brinton took the other man by the shoulder and rolled him onto his back.

His own dead face stared back at him, glassy eyes fixed upon the ceiling. The skin was a sickly shade of gray, and there was a deep gash across the throat. The man's shirt was stained with blood.

"Impossible," Brinton whispered. "If that's..."

The hooded woman approached him from behind and then bent over to offer him a pocket mirror. He took it and found the same face he had always known reflected in the silvered glass. He was Brinton...but so was the dead man lying next to him.

Craning his neck to stare up at the woman, Brinton squinted. "I was in there," he said, tapping the corpse. "And now I'm in here?"

She threw her head back and laughed. "An oversimplification." Her cloak flapped as she paced a circle around the corpse. "I lack the time to give you a proper understanding of metaphysics, but yes...For all intents and purposes, you have been given a new body, one in the peak of health."

"Am I clone?" It was hard to form words. Too many thoughts tried to force their way out of his mouth at once. "I remember dying. I remember the knife. I remember my training as an acolyte, my first crush..."

"You are Brinton," the woman said as if that settled it.

"What are you going to do with me?"

"Nothing."

She stopped in front of the hole in the wall and looked over her shoulder. Peering into that hood made him shiver. "We will not coerce your obedience, Brinton," she said. "You have been given proof of divinity; it is up to you to decide what you want to do with that knowledge."

"I...I want to serve."

"Good."

The woman strode forward, flipping her cloak back over her shoulder to reveal her gorgeous black dress. In the palm of her hand, she carried something, the disk of a multi-tool. "Then I will tell you how to begin."

She tapped one button on the disk, causing a hologram to appear over her upturned palm. The transparent image of a leggy young woman with smooth, mocha skin and long, black hair rotated slowly. Brinton recognized her instantly.

The Justice Keeper cadet who had exposed him.

"Your task is simple," the hooded woman said. "I want you to kill her."

15

Stirring a bowl of oatmeal for Claire, Harry threw in a few berries – his youngest always wanted fruit in her cereal – and then set it down on the kitchen counter. The damn robot was right next to him, watching him like some poor diva who had just been forced to let her understudy take centre stage.

"Michael" had long metal arms with hands of duroplastic and long metal legs that ended in plodding feet. Its all too human face was frozen in a blank expression, and that just made the damn thing even creepier.

Harry squeezed his eyes shut, grunting his disapproval. "Do you have to stand right *there?*" he asked, glancing over his shoulder. "Aren't you things programmed with *some* level of tact?"

Michael took a step back.

Its head came up, and the glowing eyes seemed to brighten. "This unit was trying to be of assistance," it said in pleasant tones. "Apologies, Mr. Carlson. This unit will remain at a more comfortable distance in the future."

"Looks like you made a friend, Dad."

He turned to find Claire sitting at the kitchen table with a big grin on her face, her hair done up in twin braids. The glass of orange juice he had given her was now only half full.

Harry grimaced, rubbing his forehead with the back of his fist. "I just find the damn thing creepy," he said, marching over to the table. "I've never needed a robot to make my girls' breakfast before."

He set the bowl down in front of Claire.

She looked up at him with those big brown eyes and blinked a few times. "So, are you gonna tell me about your adventure the other night?" she asked. "I tried to get details out of Melissa, but-"

"Your sister needs rest."

Plunking both elbows down on the table, Claire set her chin on her fists. "But you went and fought those terrorist guys," she said. "I want to hear about it. How did you beat them? Did you use that thing?"

What was going on here?

In the last few years, he had been in more than his fair share of scrapes, and Claire had always reacted with mild disinterest whenever he tried to share those stories. In truth, he always felt like some old grandpa trying to talk about how much better things were in his day while his grandkids played on cell phones.

Was it because they had moved to Leyria? Keepers were a bigger deal here, and Claire had always been the sort of girl to pick up on all the latest trends. Unlike Melissa, who enjoyed getting new clothes but was content to wait until she had earned enough to buy them herself, Claire had to have the latest fad *now*.

"It was pretty dangerous," Harry said.

"Did you almost die?"

He looked up to fix his gaze on his daughter, then narrowed his eyes to slits. "Why would you say something like that?" he asked, shaking his head. "Claire, I will *always* be here to take care of you."

The girl rolled her eyes and looked away, breathing out a soft sigh. "Whatever you say, Dad," she muttered. "I wasn't worried about you dying! But none of my other friends have Keepers in their families."

Harry sat down across from her with arms folded, his mouth twisting at the thought of his own mortality. "So, that's what this is about, huh?" he said. "I am not going to die, Claire. So, put that out of your head. Maybe you should focus more on school."

"It's hobby week."

"Hobby week."

Lifting a spoonful of oatmeal to her lips, Claire shut her eyes as she swallowed it. "School is different here," she said. "We're supposed to apply the things we've learned to our own projects this week."

"And that's a problem for you?"

He understood when his daughter gave him that glare that every kid unleashed at least once in their lifetime – the one that said: "my parents are so damn out of touch its embarrassing." Claire didn't have many hobbies.

Throughout her high school years, Melissa had shown an interest in baseball, in clothing design, in piano, but Claire had always been the kind of girl who just wanted to spend time with her friends; it didn't really matter what they were doing.

"Tell you what," Harry said. "I'll help you."

At that moment, Melissa came into the kitchen in black pants and a red t-shirt with a square neck. Her long hair was done up in a bun. You would never have suspected that she had pushed her symbiont to its limit just thirty-six hours earlier. "Morning, Dad," she said. "Just a bowl of cereal this morning, Michael."

"Certainly, Melissa."

The robot sprang into action, joints whirring as he marched over to the pantry and took out something that looked so very much like a large plastic container marked with a sticker that read "bran flakes." Leyrians believed in reusing packaging if possible. When that container was empty, it would be retrieved by the delivery bots and taken back to a food processing plant to be sterilized and refilled, and possibly delivered to someone else. Harry had never tracked individual packages.

Michael took the cereal over to the counter where he retrieved a bowl and promptly filled it. Damn it! Now, Harry was thinking of the robot as *he*. It wasn't alive, god damn it! Could he convince the department of housing to take the thing back? Melissa wouldn't like that, but they did *not* need a robot.

When his eldest sat down at the table, she took out her lipstick and began applying it with a pocket mirror. "So," Harry said after a moment. "You're going to class today? I thought they gave you a few days to recover."

His daughter glanced in his direction and arched a thin black eyebrow. "A few days that I don't really need," she said. "It doesn't take *that* long to recover from overworking your symbiont."

"If you say so."

"Tell me about fighting the terrorists!" Claire said with a big, bright grin. Her eyes were glued to Melissa. "Were you scared?"

Michael came over to set a bowl of cereal down in front of Melissa with something that looked like a bow, and then it straightened and backed away to stand in the corner. The girls barely noticed.

"Of course, it was scary," Melissa answered. "Who wouldn't be scared?"

"Did you use your powers?"

"That's enough for now," Harry cut in.

Two sets of eyes fell upon him, and it was clear that both of his girls were feeling no small amount of exasperation, but he remained adamant. "Your sister is tired, and she doesn't need the stress of reliving the event," he told Claire. "You just finish your oatmeal and get to school. I'll help you with your project later."

Claire sighed. "Fine."

When she walked into the classroom to find desks in a semicircle – all bathed in the light that came in through the windows – she wasn't expecting every head to turn. How did celebrities learn to put up with this kind of attention? She felt like she was giving a speech in her underwear.

Wil Asten spun to face her with a lazy grin on his face. "Cadet. Carlson," he said, taking a few steps toward her. "We were wondering if you were going to come in today. Your exploits have been on everyone's mind."

Melissa stood in the doorway with both hands gripping the hem of her shirt, unable to look up and accept the praise. "Thank you," she mumbled halfheartedly. "But it's really not a big deal."

"On the contrary," Wil said. "Few cadets have done what you did."

Blushing hard, Melissa closed her eyes and took a deep breath. "Thank you, sir," she said with a nod. "But if it's all the same to you, I'd rather just focus on today's lesson. I'm sorry if I'm late."

Chuckling softly, Wil bowed his head to her. "You're not late, Cadet," he said. "It turns out that when one of your students goes and makes herself into a hero, everybody else shows up early to catch a glimpse of her."

Making her way to her desk was incredibly difficult. People were tactful enough to not stare, but she still felt as if every eye was focused on her. Melissa had never been the sort of person who wanted to be the centre of attention; that was her sister. Strange that it had never occurred to her when she was putting her life on the line that doing so would thrust her into the spotlight.

Aiden flashed his winning smile as he leaned in close to whisper, “You were great! All the Keepers are talking about it.”

“Really?”

“Wil showed us the security camera footage yesterday. Where in Bleakness did you learn to *move* like that?”

Well then...Maybe all this extra attention wasn't *that* bad. She remembered meeting Anna for the first time and being blown away by what her friend could do. For years after that, every time she had a crush on some guy, she would fantasize about saving him from bullies with Keeper powers of her own.

Of course, that wasn't what had made her want to join the Keepers – Ilia would not have chosen her if fame was the only thing on her mind – but she had to admit that seeing Aiden smile at her was pretty awesome.

Today's lesson was about the ethics of government authority – specifically, what the limits of a government's power ought to be – but Melissa was having a hard time paying attention. Her mind kept drifting back to the other night. She'd spent most of yesterday sleeping and recovering her strength; she hadn't really taken the time to reflect on it.

Her life had almost ended two nights ago. If she hadn't been clever enough to come up with a plan to get rid of the bomb, she would be a pile of ash right now, and so would her father for that matter. She really shouldn't have let her father come along.

“What do you think, Ms. Carlson?”

Melissa froze.

Wil was standing at the front of the room with his hands folded over his stomach, poised like a statue next to a hologram. The transparent image of a country floated beside him. Melissa wasn't exactly well versed in Leyrian geography, but she was fairly certain that was Adune. It looked kind of but not quite like an upside-down version of Brazil.

Shutting her eyes tight, Melissa touched two fingers to her forehead. "I'm sorry, but could you repeat the question?" Damn it! She was blushing again. "I'm a little distracted this morning."

Wil smiled, shaking his head. "I'll forgive you," he said, stepping forward. "This *one* time. The question was about Adune's legalization of digital surveillance measures in the early 440s, something that became a problem in 462, when the Adunian parliament used those same measures to justify leaking private information collected from a gay and lesbian dating site, effectively outing thousands of their own citizens."

A young woman with blonde hair that fell to the small of her back rose from her chair and faced their teacher with a stern expression. "I don't understand," she said. "So what if people find out you're gay?"

Melissa understood.

The privilege of growing up on a world that had overcome homophobia could blind you to the severity of such bigotry, but she recalled a time, when she was very young, when the question of whether to tell your parents you were gay was a big deal.

"The government needs to have some degree of power," Melissa said, answering Wil's question, "but if surveillance becomes normalized, it becomes incredibly hard to make the government give up that power."

"Exactly."

Wil turned on his heel and paced a line to the window with his hands in his pockets. "In the wake of the recent attacks, some of you have questioned why we don't use more invasive forms of surveillance. Why don't we identify everyone who hails an automated cab and track their trips, for instance."

Melissa stood up, though it made her nervous to be the

centre of attention again. She really couldn't figure out why; it wasn't like her words would be more audible than they would have been if she remained seated. "Because that kind of data in the hands of law enforcement can be used to cyber-stalk individual citizens," she said. "Perhaps one day, a man with authoritarian inclinations becomes the Prime Council, and now he has a tool that he can use to determine if his detractors have been meeting each other."

"*Precisely,* Cadet Carlson."

Wil looked over his shoulder to study his students. "The benefit of any potential security measure," he began, "*must* be measured against the potential harm if that measure is misused."

The clock chimed.

"And that's it for today," Wil said. "Read chapters twenty-three through twenty-five for next week's lecture, and we'll see you soon."

After a brief lunch at the Student Centre – her courses were held on the campus of the University of Denabria – Melissa was ready to meet up with Jon Andalon. No doubt he would have spent the last two days putting together leads on these Sons of Savard, and he would want all the help he could get.

Double doors slid apart, allowing her to see a field of concrete where benches were positioned between tall, black lampposts. Beyond that, green grass stretched on to the Computer Sciences Lab, a square building with a cylindrical facade and windows lining all five stories.

She stepped out into the open.

Melissa closed her eyes, a cool breeze caressing her face. *If only every day could be this beautiful,* she thought, tilting her head back to feel the sun on her skin. *But I suppose you need winter to appreciate spring.*

"There's the girl of the hour."

Melissa turned.

To her delight, Jack was leaning against the brick wall of the Student Centre in gray pants and a black t-shirt. His eyes were hidden behind the dark lenses of sunglasses, and his hair was in its usual messy state.

Grinning sheepishly, Melissa bowed her head to him. "Good to see you too," she said, approaching him. "Don't tell me you came by just to tell me how good a job I did. Because I don't think I could handle it."

Jack took hold of the frame of his sunglasses and pulled them down to expose his bright blue eyes. "Perish the thought," he said. "Back in my day, we didn't slack off. No poorly armed terrorists for us; it was all Battle Drones and Death Spheres."

"I'm pretty sure Anna took out the Battle Drones."

"Quiet, you whippersnapper."

Melissa slammed into him, squeezing him tight, and when Jack patted her on the back, she couldn't help but laugh. "So, why did you come all the way down here?" she asked, stepping out of his embrace.

He tossed his head back to stare up at the sky, sunlight glinting off of those dark lenses. "Oh, no reason..." he mumbled. "It might have had something to do with wanting to say that was a very brave thing you did."

"I was just doing my job."

"It was more than that."

Melissa crossed her arms and shifted her weight from one foot to the other, refusing to look up at him. "It's no different than what you did," she said. "If I keep getting praise, I think I'm going to explode."

"There you go, stealing my bit again."

"Well, I-"

A shriek from some nearby girl cut her off, and she focused

on the awareness that came from her symbiont. The misty silhouettes of about a dozen students were backing away toward the lampposts at the edge of the grass.

"The roof," she whispered.

Jack whirled around to stand beside her, and together they backed up until they were a good distance from the building. That was when she noticed it – a figure in black standing on the rooftop.

The woman wore simple black pants and a matching t-shirt under a dark cloak that billowed in the wind. Her hood was pulled up to hide her face, but if she was walking around in *that*, she would draw attention. She must have come here in civilian clothing and then put on the cloak for effect.

"Two meddlers," the woman purred. "Excellent."

Craning his neck with a growl, Jack stared up at her. "And the lady who took last place in a ringwraith cosplay," he said, his eyebrows rising. "What is it with you villains and tacky bullshit?"

"Have you learned nothing about the power of theatricality?" the hooded woman mocked. "You of all people should know better, Jack Hunter."

Isara, Melissa realized. *This is the woman that Anna fought in Tennessee.*

Quick as a striking snake, Isara drew a pistol from the holster on her belt and thrust her arm out to point it at one of the students behind Melissa. There was a soft *buzz* as she fired, and then bullets ripped through a young man's chest with a spray of blood. Seconds later, he dropped to the ground. The other kids started running, turning their backs and sprinting through the grass.

Melissa reacted without thinking.

She ran for the Student Centre and then called upon Ilia's power. "No, wait!" Jack called out, but she wasn't listening. With a single thought, she Bent gravity and propelled herself upward like an arrow loosed from a bow.

Melissa crested the edge of the rooftop and then landed, raising fists into a fighting stance. "Do you wanna kill helpless kids?" she asked, striding forward. "Or do you want to fight someone who can-"

Isara struck in mere fractions of a second.

A pale hand lashed out to seize Melissa's jaw, fingertips digging into her cheek. For a moment, she could see into that dark hood, and she thought she might have recognized the other woman's face. But it was all over before she could think.

"Not interested," Isara spat.

Melissa was yanked backward as if someone had thrown a lasso around her waist and tied the other end to a galloping horse. She went over the edge of the roof and then dropped to the ground, landing hard on her ass with a jolt that sent shock waves of pain up her spine.

Isara stood on the ledge with one fist on her hip, the other pointing the gun down at the rooftop. "I prefer prey who can give me a challenge," she said. "Which means I shall have to settle for young Jack, there."

Jack rushed over to Melissa, crouching down beside her. He looked up at the other woman. "You want a challenge? I'm always available," he said. "But you should know I was trained by the best."

Isara chuckled.

She turned on her heel, pacing along the edge of the rooftop, her cloak flapping against the backs of her legs. "The irony is delicious!" she exclaimed. "But don't worry about your little friend there."

Isara looked over her shoulder, and malice seemed to radiate from inside that hood. "I have a trainee of my own!" she said. "And your little cadet should provide just enough of a challenge to keep his skills sharp."

Right on cue, a man in black came around the corner. This one was tall and slender with fair skin and short blonde hair. Melissa recognized him instantly. He was the acolyte who had stolen Miles Tarso's access codes.

Brinton.

Melissa sat up.

"Not sure if you realize this," she called out to the other woman. "But even a half-trained Keeper is more than a match for some guy who probably never fought a day in his life."

Brinton's lips pulled back into an ugly smile, and he chuckled softly. "The things you don't know..." He reached into his pants' pocket and pulled out a small bottle of blue pills. "I think I might surprise you."

Tilting his head back to stare up at the roof, Jack narrowed his eyes. "Amps?" he shouted. "You gave him Amps?"

"I thought it might be fun," Isara said.

She leaped and somersaulted through the air, uncurling to drop gracefully to the ground. She landed like Bat-Man with the cloak fanning out behind her. "Come on, Jack. Why don't we talk like adults while the children play."

Isara whirled around, pointing her gun at the door to the Student Centre. There was a soft *beep* from her pistol, and Melissa noticed the LEDs on its barrel turn red. She fired.

A high-impact round struck the door and ripped the whole thing right off its track, panes of frosted plastic falling to the tiled floor inside. Now, Melissa could see the many paintings lining the brick wall opposite the door.

Without another word, Isara ran inside, her cloak streaming out behind her.

Gritting his teeth, Jack shut his eyes tight. "Stay here," he ordered, getting to his feet. He broke into a sprint, chasing after the hooded woman, leaving her alone with the drugged-up psychopath.

Brinton flashed a toothy grin.

The man wore a pair of daggers on his belt, *shin-ral* knives unless she missed her guess. The blades were shaped like crescent moons with a handle connecting each tip so that he could punch with them like brass knuckles.

Curling her legs against her chest, Melissa sprang off the ground.

She landed upright with a grunt, assuming a defensive posture and backing away from the building. The sweat on her brow was hard to ignore. "We really don't have to do this, you know?"

Brinton smiled down at himself as he closed the distance between them. "When a god commands, you don't refuse." He retrieved both knives from his belt, gripping them until his knuckles whitened.

"The Overseers aren't gods."

"You can say that all you want," Brinton hissed. "But I've seen the truth with my own eyes."

Melissa wrinkled her nose, then gave her head a shake. "What did they do to you up there?" she asked, backing up until her body almost hit a lamppost. "A few days ago, you were dedicated to the Companion."

Brinton was deathly pale as he held her gaze, sweat glistening on his brow. "They showed me the truth," he whispered. "One day, you will see it true. I just pray you accept the Inzari before it's too late."

"I'll stick with Jesus, thanks."

"Isara will show you."

Closing her eyes, Melissa drew in a deep breath. "This is getting us nowhere," she said, shaking her head. "If you really want to solve this with violence, then let's just get it over with."

She charged at him.

The man slashed at her belly.

Melissa hopped back, the crescent-shaped blade passing within inches of her shirt. Brinton stepped forward and punched with the other fist. A gleaming, razor-sharp blade came at her face.

Melissa bent over backward, one hand coming up to strike the man's wrist and knock it aside. She snapped herself upright and delivered a fierce punch to the nose that made Brinton stumble backward. Trails of blood ran over his face.

She kicked him in the stomach.

Driven backward by the force of it, Brinton doubled over and let out a wheeze. A snarl twisted his features, and then he ran at her.

The man jumped, flying past her on the left, kicking out behind himself to strike her shoulder. It made her double over as a wave of pain went through her body. Melissa whirled around to find him standing over her.

Brinton raised the knives and slashed downward.

Bending her knees, Melissa reached up to seize both of his wrists, holding his arms extended. She brought one knee up to strike the man's chest, driving the wind out of his lungs. A second knee to the stomach forced him off her.

Brinton went stumbling backward until his ass hit the lamppost, hunching over on contact. "I don't want to kill you," he pleaded in a breathy rasp. "But you are not giving me much choice."

"Funny, I was going to say the same."

He spun in a blur, one arm lashing out to fling the crescent-shaped blade at her. It flew at deadly speed right for Melissa's throat.

Melissa leaned back, one hand reaching up to snatch the knife handle. "Okay," she said, standing up straight. "Well isn't this a fun new development? Teenager with a deadly weapon. Surely your god won't let you lose!"

Brinton rushed her, then leaped and raised his gleaming blade into the air. He tried to bring it down in a fierce, vertical cut. Instinct kicked in, and Melissa raised her own knife to intercept. Steel met steel, and Brinton landed before her.

He slashed at her face.

Melissa ducked, allowing the blade to pass over her head. She slashed at his belly, drawing blood, and then slipped past him on the right. She flung her arm out to the side to dig the tip of her blade into his back.

Brinton squeaked, stumbling away from her.

She spun on him.

Wiping her mouth with the back of her hand, Melissa turned her head and spit on the ground. "I've had months of training," she said. "You popped a few pills this morning, and you think that makes you powerful."

The man was doubled over with a hand pressed to his bleeding belly, wheezing as tears streamed over his face. "They saved me once," he whispered. "Even if you kill me, they will save me again."

"I'm not going to kill you," Melissa barked, striding forward. "But those god-damn pills might do the job."

He looked up at her, his face flushed, blood dripping from one nostril. "What are you talking about?" he whispered. "The drugs make me stronger."

Melissa tossed the knife away.

She crossed her arms and stood over him with a tight frown on her face. "You have no idea what they gave you," she mumbled. "Amps will make you stronger right up until the moment you stop taking it."

Melissa shut her eyes, knuckling her forehead. "No one told you that, did they?" If she ever got the chance, she would pummel Isara. "The people you work for don't have your best interests at heart."

Brinton dropped to his knees, hunched over and groaning. "It's too late," he rasped. "There's no turning back once the Inzari have you."

Melissa crouched down in front of him. "It's *not* too late," she assured him. "Come with me, and I can get you medical treatment. It's not too late to-"

His hand lashed out, and she had only an instant to react.

Melissa leaned back, but his crescent-shaped blade sliced into the skin just above her eyebrow, leaving a fiery gash on her forehead. With a grunt, she fell backward and tried to scramble away.

Brinton lunged at her like a feral animal, landing on top of her and seizing her neck with both hands. His face contorted with rage. "You don't believe me now," he said. "But you will. When they restore you, you will believe."

He began to squeeze the life out of her.

As he leaped over the broken door panes and landed inside the Student Centre, Jack stretched out with his senses, allowing Summer's awareness to fill his mind. Nobody was shooting at him; that was a plus.

This part of the Centre was essentially a wide corridor with a wall of yellow bricks on one side and windows that looked out on the quad on the other. Half a dozen college kids were making their way toward him, but they all jumped out of the way when they saw a wraith-like figure in black barreling down on them.

Isara ran as if her life depended on it, her cloak flapping against the backs of her legs. She was making her way toward the cafeteria at the end of this corridor. Who knew how many potential hostages she would find there?

Jack felt his face twist, then shook his head with a growl. "No, you don't!" he spat, chasing after her. "No, slipping away this time! I've got a nice, comfy detention cell set aside just for you!"

Without looking, Isara flung her arm out behind herself and pointed the gun at him.

There was no one behind him.

A thought was all it took to throw up a Time Bubble, power surging through Jack's body as he warped the very fabric of reality. Through its spherical surface, he saw Isara as a blurry, black image, the gun pointed at him.

A single bullet erupted from the barrel.

Jack took one step to the left.

He let the Bubble drop and leaped, hugging his knees as he somersaulted through the air. In an instant, he was uncurling to land just behind her.

Isara whirled around, swinging her arm to point the gun at him.

Crouching down, Jack brought his hand up to knock her arm away. He tried to jab with the other hand.

Isara's free hand came up to snatch his wrist before he could make contact. And then she was striking him across the face with the barrel of her gun. His vision darkened for half a second.

Isara's foot found a home in his stomach, forcing Jack to double over and wheeze. *No, no, don't let her!* She was trying to aim with the pistol again, trying to line up a clean shot to the head.

Dropping to his knees, Jack reached up to grab her wrist with both hands. He gave a twist, and the gun fell to the floor, landing beside him. The woman squeaked from the pain of having her wrist at an odd angle.

Jack slammed an open palm into her chest.

Bent Gravity hurled Isara backward like a piece of trash caught in a gale. She flew through the corridor with legs kicking, then jerked to a halt and hovered in midair for a moment. Her own Bent Gravity field.

The hooded woman dropped to the floor to land in a crouch, then stood up straight and laughed at him. "Did anyone ever tell you that you're remarkably irritating, Hunter?"

She started up the corridor toward him, and Jack felt very much like Frodo watching the approach of a Nazgul.

He picked up the gun.

Standing up, Jack lifted the pistol in both hands and snarled as he took aim. He set the gun for stun rounds. The LEDS on the barrel turned blue.

He fired.

A tiny slug sped toward Isara – moving slow enough for him to track it with the naked eye – but she raised a hand to shield herself. The air in front of her rippled, and his slug was caught in a Bending.

It curved to Jack's left, looped around and then sped off toward one of the students who was cowering by the wall. A red-headed man in a white t-shirt barely even noticed as a bullet hit his chest and jolted him with a surge of electricity.

Isara turned and ran, rounding the corner into the cafeteria.

"Wonderful," he said, running after her. "Just herd the crazy woman into the room full of helpless kids. You're doing *so* well today!"

When he reached the end of the corridor, he found himself in a large room where tables were spaced out on the gray floor tiles and banners hung from the incredibly high ceiling. And there were people. Maybe three dozen people.

The wall across from him was lined with windows that looked out on a path that cut through the green grass, and there were food stations along the other three walls. A salad bar, a pizza parlour, some other Leyrian delicacy.

As soon as he stepped into the open, he noticed movement on his left.

He turned in time to see Isara kick him right in the face. His head rang like a bell, and then Jack went tumbling back, landing hard on the tiled floor. The jolt knocked the pistol from his hand.

Tucking his knees into his chest, Jack somersaulted backwards. He came up on one knee, then rose in one fluid motion. "Okay," he said. "That sucked."

Isara came at him.

The woman threw a mean right-hook.

Jack leaned back, her fist swinging through the air in front of his face. He snapped himself upright in time to grab her arm with both hands before she could retract it. Then he whirled her around to face the brick wall.

Isara jumped, pulling free of his grip. She kicked out and struck the wall with one foot, then pushed off and flew backwards. Her other foot went into Jack's chest, and he was forced to stumble away.

Isara turned around to face him.

She spun for a hook-kick, her foot whirling around in a wide arc. Jack ducked and felt a leather boot passing right over his head.

He popped up in time to watch Isara come out of her spin. His fist went into the hood, striking her face with a sickening *crunch*. The woman stumbled backward, raising hands up to shield herself. "Not bad, boy!"

Jack ran in to finish this.

Falling over sideways, Isara caught herself by slamming one hand down upon the floor tiles. Her foot came up to hit Jack right between the eyes, and then his vision was blurry for a moment.

The fuzzy image of Isara stooped low to retrieve the pistol he had dropped, then stood up to point the muzzle at him. A slight beep from the weapon told him that she had set it for lethal ammunition.

Jack reacted by instinct.

His hands came up, warping space-time into a Bending mere fractions of a second before bullets appeared before him. They curved upward and sped up to strike the ceiling with deadly force. His skin was burning, a sign that Summer was nearing her limit.

Chunks of duroplastic rained down on him.

Jack redirected the incoming fire so that it would hit the ceiling above Isara's head, and then the debris was raining down on her. The woman screeched, crossing forearms in front of her face. Which meant she wasn't shooting at him for a moment.

Jack let his Bending drop.

He jumped and kicked out, the tip of his shoe landing in the soft flesh of Isara's stomach. The woman was thrown backward, propelled by Keeper strength. She grunted on impact with the wall.

Baring his teeth with a vicious growl, Jack felt his face redden. "Who the hell are you?" he asked, striding forward. "No more games, lady! I want to know who the bloody hell you really are!"

Isara leaped.

She flipped through the air, passing right over Jack's head. A moment later, she was straightening to land behind him. Rage flared within him, set his blood on fire and made him react without thinking.

Jack spun around.

When the woman turned to face him, he moved like a striking snake. His hand flew into the hood with enough speed to make Isara grunt when he seized her jaw. The shock was so great she actually dropped her gun. He clutched the top of her hood and yanked it back, exposing her face.

And his blood froze.

Gaping at her, Jack felt his eyes pop out. "No," he whispered, shaking his head. "No, it's not possible!"

It was a face that he had seen countless times: a pretty face with a pointed chin and deep brown eyes that were a perfect compliment to her boyishly short auburn hair. If she had decided to attack him right then and there, he would have been unable to react. Not when she was wearing *that* face.

Jena's face.

"What's the matter, Jack?" she asked. "Aren't you happy to see me?"

The End of Part 1.

INTERLUDE

Jon was exhausted.

As he strode through the front door of his apartment, he let his arms hang limp and kept his eyes focused on the ground. "Bleakness take me," he muttered, shutting the door behind himself. "Why did I let Jena talk me into this?"

A large rectangular window along the back wall of his living room looked out on a balcony and allowed sunlight to spill in on the hardwood floor and the blue couch to his left. To his right, white cupboards at hip and shoulder height surrounded an island in the middle of his kitchen.

The serving bot was there, waiting patiently with hands clasped in front of itself. Its blue eyes lit up when he entered. "Hello, Jon," it said. "You're home earlier than I would have expected. Would you like me to prepare some lunch?"

Jon shut his eyes, sucking in a deep breath. "No, thank you," he said, shaking his head. "Just a cup of mint tea if possible."

"Certainly."

The robot went to work.

Clasping his hands together behind his back, Jon paced across the living room to stand in the light that came in through the window. By the Companion's good name, he *was* tired! Two nights ago, the Sons of Savard had attacked Denabria's infrastructure, and it seemed as though every hour that followed had been filled with a hundred things that demanded his attention.

Already, he had Lenai working her way through a list of over two dozen terrorists they had managed to capture that night, interrogating each one. So far, she had not found much useful information, but it had been less than forty-eight hours, and if the Sons were as organized as they seemed, the men and women they used as cannon fodder wouldn't be told very much about their larger plans.

He sensed the robot approaching on his right, moving across the room on legs that made soft whirring noises and carrying a cup of tea in its right hand. "Thank you," Jon said, accepting the cup when it was offered.

Beyond the edge of his balcony, two tall buildings stood on the other side of the street, each with sunlight glinting off its windows and lush trees rising from its rooftop. It was a strange quirk, he knew, but whenever he applied for a new apartment, he went out of his way to select one on the top floor of a tall building. He liked a view.

Such accommodations weren't always available; sometimes he had to settle for a place on the sixth or seventh floor, but most cities had more homes than people to live in them and had to rely on robots to maintain the upkeep. Sometimes vacant houses were actually *deconstructed* so that the city wouldn't have to expend so much energy looking after them. It really made no difference. New houses could be constructed in a matter of days if they were needed.

This way of life was built upon the abundance that the Leyrian people had created for themselves. Why would anyone want to destroy that?

He lifted the cup to his lips and slurped as he took a sip.

"Fools," he said, spinning on his heel and turning his back on the window. "No matter how enlightened we become, there will always be those who believe that suffering is the only way to become strong."

He set his cup down on the coffee table and went to his bedroom.

It was a simple room with white walls where sunlight through a large window fell on a bed where the blue blankets were pulled right up to the pillows. He retrieved his tablet from the dresser and powered it on to begin reviewing his notes. So far, no one had been able to locate the young man who planted the first bomb at Vertical Farm 17.

Jon really should have forced himself to eat something; he wasn't hungry, but he would have to meet with his staff in two hours, and he suspected that coming up against more dead ends would be stressful, to say the least. Incorporating Melissa Carlson into this investigation would be easy – trained Keepers often allowed cadets to shadow them – but what should he do about the girl's father? Or that disgraced LIS agent that Larani had foisted on him? How Jena had managed such a hodge-podge team was simply beyond him.

Jon stepped into the living room again and froze.

The front door was open just a crack.

Touching his chin with three fingers, Jon squinted. "Service robot active," he called out, striding across the room. "Did I leave the front door open?"

When the robot didn't respond, he felt a chill and looked up to find it slumped over in front of the kitchen sink, its eyes dark. Someone had deactivated it, and it wasn't Jon. He wasn't alone in this apartment.

He turned to face the couch on the wall opposite the kitchen and found that the door to his bathroom was somehow moving of its own accord. There was nothing but darkness in the other room, but *something* was moving in there.

His eyes saw nothing but a faint ripple in the air, like waves of heat rising up from black pavement, but his *mind* sensed something through contact with his symbiont. The silhouette of a tall man in a loose-fitting jacket was coming toward him with a stun-baton in one hand.

The man swung for Jon's temple.

Jon ducked, allowing the invisible weapon to pass over his head. He threw a punch into the phantom's stomach, then rose to back-hand his opponent across the face. A loud *crunch* told him that his enemy was solid enough.

Jon leaped, somersaulting through the air.

In an instant, he was landing behind the other man, spinning around to grab the guy by his invisible collar. His mind sensed another intruder coming in through the open front door, and this one was also invisible. If you looked right at him, you would see nothing but a shimmer in the air, and only if he moved too quickly.

Jon whirled around, shoving one invisible man toward the other. The first guy went stumbling across the hardwood floor and collided with his companion. Perhaps the fact that neither one had tried to step aside meant they couldn't see each other.

Baring his teeth in a snarl, Jon winced and rubbed his forehead with the back of his hand. "Neat trick," he said. "I've never seen a functioning tactical cloak, but it's useless against a Justice Keeper."

Both men were lying on the floor, but the first one had rolled off the second, and now they were stretched out on their backs, staring up at the ceiling. The one on the left was still clutching his stun-baton, and he got up to charge at Jon, swinging like a maniac with a club.

Jon leaned back, the crackling tip of an invisible baton passing within inches of his nose. He snap-kicked and drove his foot into an invisible stomach. The silhouette went stumbling backward, bumping into its companion.

This second man came forward with a pistol in his hand, a pistol that he lifted for a shot at point-blank range.

Falling over backwards, Jon caught himself by slapping both hands down on the floor and brought one foot up to strike the underside of an invisible wrist. The gun went tumbling from the man's hand, rippling back into visibility before it hit the wall and fell to the floor.

Jon snapped himself upright.

A ghostly figure stood before him, staring into its own empty hand before it looked up to fix an eyeless gaze upon him. The man drew a small knife from a holster on his belt and ran forward with a growl.

Jon sidestepped.

He let the spectre run past on his left, then flung his elbow into the invisible man's back. This sent the guy stumbling into the kitchen where he crashed into the island and wheezed on impact.

The first man had recovered and now stood hunched over with his stun-baton in hand. He raised the weapon above his head and suddenly charged forward as if he meant to bludgeon Jon to death.

Jon jumped.

He turned belly-up in mid-air, kicking out to slam both feet into an invisible face. This knocked the man to the floor and caused him to lose his grip on the baton. It became visible as it tumbled end over end toward the ceiling.

Back-flipping through the air, Jon landed on the floor and reached up with one hand to catch the baton's grip as it fell. He spun and flung the weapon point-first at the man in the kitchen.

The tip of the baton hit the invisible man as he turned around, and sparks flashed over his body. He seemed to flicker, appearing and disappearing so quickly it was almost disorienting, and then his cloaking device shorted out, revealing a tall man with fair skin and a blonde goatee who dropped to the floor and passed out.

"Now," Jon said to the other one. "What to do with you."

Life aboard a starship was cramped.

Her office was just one example. Though it was large enough to hold a horseshoe-shaped desk between its four gray walls, the room had no windows. It felt very much like being trapped inside a coffin, and she wanted to look out at the stars. Of course, that had a lot to do with ship's design. You didn't put key areas near the hull where a stray particle beam might expose them to vacuum.

Telixa sat with booted feet propped up on the desk, a tablet held up in front of her face. "More hand-wringing," she muttered, reading through the latest deliberations of the Parliament. "You've had all the information for months now. Either use it or admit your own ineptitude."

She tossed the tablet onto the desk.

Reclining in her chair with hands folded behind her head, Telixa frowned as she stared up at the ceiling. "Idiots, the lot of them," she added. "Trust a politician to put off making a decision as long as possible."

The president was pushing for an immediate reconnaissance mission through the SuperGate to properly assess what the Leyrians were planning. There was really no way to know short of sending a ship through and seeing for themselves. Probes were only so useful, in the end; there wasn't much a probe could do if a hostile ship tried to destroy it. But Parliament was, as usual, determined to hem and haw until the Leyrians showed up on their doorstep with bombs armed.

The door chime rang.

"Enter!"

Her door slid open to reveal Lieutenant Janis looking prim and proper in his fine gray uniform. The young man wore a grim expression as he offered a curt nod. "We've just received orders from Fleet Admiral Loth."

Closing her eyes, Telixa tilted her head back. "Let me guess," she said, spinning in her chair and rising quickly. "Parliament has denied the president war powers and the fleet is to maintain a watch on the Class-2 Gates indefinitely."

The young man bowed his head and cleared his throat as if trying to hold down the urge to cough. "Just the opposite, ma'am," he said. "We've been authorized to send three ships through the Gate on a scouting mission."

"Will wonders never cease."

Telixa strode around the desk and stood before her subordinate, and despite the fact that the top of her head was barely in line with his chest, Janis still took a step backward. A sign that her reputation was still well known among the crew, and a very good thing in her estimation. When you were short, you had to learn to act tall. "Let's go," she said. "I believe we have work to do."

Outside her office, a white-walled corridor encircled the bridge with cleaning bots polishing the floor. It was a little too bright for her taste – she had sensitive eyes – but the lights on the ship were designed to simulate real sunlight, and it was just past noon.

The Bridge doors opened, allowing her to see men and women at the stations and the Captain's Chair – her chair – sitting empty. There were soft beeps and clicks from the various computer consoles.

At the front of the room, the large screen displayed an enormous diamond-shaped SlipGate silhouetted against the backdrop of a blue star. It hung there, beckoning her to come through.

Clasping hands together behind her back, Telixa turned on her heel and approached the screen with her head down.

"Status report," she ordered. "Has there been any activity from the Gate?"

"No, Ma'am."

Telixa squeezed her eyes shut, sucking in a deep breath. "Have the Alethi and the Elendel form up on our flank," she said. "Interface with the Gate's systems and prepare for transit. We're going through."

"Yes, Admiral."

It took about five minutes for the other ships to get into position and for her people to program the Gate accordingly. Telixa couldn't help but note a small pang of anxiety in her stomach. True, they'd sent probes through this thing, but she didn't trust alien tech one bit. It wouldn't surprise her if her atoms were scattered across a thousand solar systems.

Telixa sat in her chair, fingers gripping the armrests, and leaned forward to stare at the screen. "Activate the Gate," she ordered. "Let's see what life is like on the other side of the galaxy."

On the screen, she watched as a bubble surrounded her ship and the other two as well, a bubble large enough to encompass an entire city. It made her shiver just to think about it. The sheer power these Overseers displayed.

They were pulled forward, through a dark tunnel where stars seemed to wheel by on either side, above and below. Hundreds of little flecks of light. Should she have felt something? For all her body could tell, the ship might have been stationary.

Suddenly, they jerked to a halt.

The bubble surrounding all three ships vanished, allowing her to see yet another diamond-shaped SuperGate floating in front of a distant white star, "Status report!" she growled. "Where are we?"

"We can confirm a successful journey," Lieutenant Janis said.

The image on the screen changed, displaying a map of the galaxy with a red line drawn from their point of origin in the upper right all the way across the Galactic Core to a system on the lower left.

"Ladies and gentlemen," Telixa said. "I welcome you to Leyrian space."

PART II

16

A hush fell over the Student Centre cafeteria as college kids who had taken refuge under tables poked their heads out to see what made the shooting stop. In that moment of calm, a young man's quiet sobbing echoed through the room.

Jack backed away until his body hit the brick wall, then hunched over with a hand pressed to his chest. "It's a trick," he whispered, shaking his head. "Whoever you are, you're not Jena."

Spreading her arms wide, Jena bowed to him like an actor on a stage. "A genuinely magnificent performance, wouldn't you agree?" Her words were delivered in that strange accent, but it *was* Jena's voice. How had he missed it?

Jack stared at her with an open mouth, blinking slowly. He shook his head. "I don't believe it," he said. "The Jena I knew would never hurt her friends like this. Who are you really?"

She drew herself up to stand before him with one hand on her hip, then threw her head back and laughed. "I tried to teach you how to play the game, Jack," she said. "Did it never occur to you that you were learning from a master?"

He lunged at her.

Jena leaped, turning belly-up in midair and bringing one foot up to hit the underside of his chin. Pain nearly drowned out all awareness, but he saw her backflip and drop to the ground before him.

Jena tried to kick his stomach.

Jack brought both hands down to strike her foot and push it away before she made contact. That threw her off balance, but she recovered quickly. She charged at him, drew back her arm and punched.

Jack ducked, allowing her fist to pass right over him and hit the wall with enough force to crack the bricks. He slipped past her on the left and then flung his elbow into the soft spot between her shoulder-blades.

That sent her face-first into the wall.

Whirling around to face her, Jack raised his fists into a boxer's stance and backed away. "You died in that Overseer base," he growled. "Our science teams investigated the wreckage. We *found* your remains!"

She turned slowly, looking over her shoulder with a predatory smile. "Did I not tell you that the Inzari are gods?" she snapped. "Did you think I was making it up? Clinging to the false hope offered by so many of your false religions?"

Rage tightened his chest until it felt like he couldn't breathe. He had trusted Jena, listened to her, and all the while, this woman – this *monster* – had been playing him! He should have seen it; Jack Hunter didn't trust anyone. Why would he let his guard down simply because someone came along with just the right anti-establishment buzzwords to win his confidence?

He thought of Anna, of Harry, of Melissa. Of all the people Jena had screwed over in her manipulations! Damn it! Slade had figured out the locations of the first and third ciphers; was Jena the one who betrayed them? Had she led them all into a meat grinder back in New York?

Was Raynar dead because of her?

The fury bubbled up, and Jack charged at her again.

Two hands squeezing her throat.

The only thing that Melissa saw was Brinton's sweaty face contorting against the backdrop of a clear blue sky. And her vision was starting to fuzz anyway. She had to get him off her! Now!

Grabbing each of his wrists with her hands, she tried to pull free of his grip, but the man was insanely strong. He just kept pushing. She couldn't breathe! God help her, there had to be something she could...

She slapped her open palm against his forehead.

Power surged through her body as she twisted gravity around him, and just like that, Brinton was yanked upward as if caught by some invisible fishhook. He flailed about as Bent Gravity propelled him above the rooftops of all the nearby buildings, and then the Bending she had crafted fizzled out, and he began to fall.

He screamed, legs kicking, hands grasping for something – anything – to hold onto, as he plummeted a good hundred feet back to the concrete. When he hit, he actually bounced and then flopped over on his side. The man was still alive. She could tell because he was still wheezing.

Melissa sat up.

Wincing as tears ran over her cheeks, she touched her fingers to her forehead. "For fuck's sake!" she spat, ignoring her usual dislike of profanity. "I was trying to help you! What is *wrong* with you?"

When she pulled her hand away, there was blood on one of her fingers. The gash on her forehead...Now, she would have to check in at a medical centre.

She stood up.

Brinton was stretched out on his side, sobbing and clutching a leg that was almost certainly broken. The man just shook and spasmed as breath exploded from him. What did these Overseers do to people to make them so insane?

The doors to the Student Centre slid apart and four college-aged kids came running out, two of whom were sobbing as hard as Brinton. Isara...If she started letting loose with that pistol before Jack could contain her...

Melissa had work to do.

Brinton wasn't going anywhere, which meant she had to focus on the greater threat. Hopefully, there wasn't too much internal bleeding – she didn't want him to bleed to death before she had a chance to question him – but right now, protecting these kids was her first priority.

She ran into the Student Centre and found the wide hallway just inside the doors completely empty. There was silence from the cafeteria at the end of that hallway. Not a good sign.

She ran.

When she burst through the doors to the cafeteria, she slid to a stop, and her blood turned to ice. To her left, in the narrow space between the brick wall and the first set of tables, a woman in black stood with her back turned and her head exposed. But Melissa recognized that haircut.

Further away, Jack stood with his fists up, his face as red as a ripe tomato. "Kid!" he growled. "Get the hell out of here!"

"No," Isara said. "She wants to stay."

The woman turned smoothly, and Melissa's heart sank when her fears were confirmed. Jena Morane wore a cruel smile as she chuckled softly. At the sight of her former host's face, Ilia became frantic. The Nassai's emotions were so strong that they almost overpowered Melissa. "Hello, dear," Jena said. "It's been a while. How's my little friend been treating you? Well, I hope."

Melissa immediately assumed a fighting stance of her own, backing away from the other woman. "Two against one!" she called out to Jack. "Even Jena would have a hard time against both of us!"

"You'd like to think that, wouldn't you?" Jena purred.

With two hands, Jena undid the clasp that held her cloak in place and shrugged out of it one shoulder at a time. The garment fell to the floor behind her. Before Melissa could so much as blink, she was moving forward, closing the distance in seconds.

The woman kicked high.

Melissa ducked and felt a boot pass over her head. She popped up in time to see a fist clip her cheek in a back-hand strike. Everything went fuzzy for half a moment. Half a moment too long.

A foot landed in Melissa's stomach.

She stumbled backward, doubling over and clutching her belly with both hands So much pain! This wasn't like fighting Brinton. As her vision cleared, she saw Jena running toward her.

Melissa jumped, back-flipping through the air, allowing the other woman to run past underneath. She turned upright and landed on the hard floor tiles, trying desperately to catch her breath.

Jena came up behind her.

An arm slipped around Melissa's throat, forearm applying pressure to her trachea. "Pitiful. It seems my all my lessons were wasted on you." Jena whispered in her ear. And then the woman gave a shove that sent Melissa stumbling toward Jack.

He moved past her.

As he closed in for the kill, Jack found his former boss standing there with her fists up, an arrogant smile on her face. Beating up a half-trained cadet? That was low even for one of Slade's lackeys.

Jack didn't hesitate.

He threw a punch, but Jena leaned back, one hand coming up to deflect the blow with casual disregard. Her other fist came at him.

Jack's left hand shot up, clamping onto her wrist before her knuckles could touch his nose. He used his right to deliver an uppercut to the stomach that made Jena wheeze as the air fled her lungs.

The woman pulled free of his grip.

She spun for a hook-kick one foot wheeling around in a tight horizontal circle. By instinct alone, Jack leaned back in time to watch a black leather boot pass within inches of his nose.

Jena came out of her spin, facing him.

She leaped and flew right over his head, kicking the back of his skull as she passed. Dizziness washed over him like a wave as he went sprawling face-first toward the brick wall, and he barely caught himself in time. *Melissa...*

Melissa recovered in time to watch Jena jump over Jack's head and kick him. The other woman landed on the floor tiles as Jack went stumbling toward the wall. *So much for two against one...*Terror filled her mind as she watched the woman she had grown to love move toward her on nimble feet and close the distance within seconds.

Jena spun and back-kicked.

Melissa hunched over, catching the woman's ankle in both hands before she made contact. The woman jumped, turning her body like a corkscrew, her other foot coming up to strike the side of Melissa's head.

Vertigo! Terrible vertigo!

Melissa stumbled backward.

As her vision cleared, she saw Jena striding toward her with a murderous grin on her face. *How could you do this?* she wondered as her opponent drew near. *We trusted you! We believed in you!*

A pair of jabs to the chest drove the air from Melissa's lungs, and then five fingers were seizing a handful of her hair, yanking her head down. Jena's knee came up to hit her face, and everything went dark.

She landed on all fours, groaning as she struggled to clear her head. Jesus Christ, the woman could hit hard! Through contact with Ilia, Melissa was able to sense the other woman walking away.

She seemed to be heading toward a door in the back of the room, one that led out to the field behind the Student Centre. Melissa didn't know what to make of the fact that her former mentor hadn't bothered to finish her off. Was there some spec of mercy left in the other woman? Or was it that Melissa was too unimportant to bother with? An obstacle to be removed and then promptly forgotten.

Jack ran to her side.

He dropped to his knees in front of her, gently cupping her chin in both hands, and then his face filled her vision. He seemed to be staring into her eyes. "Are you all right?" he asked. "How many fingers am I holding up?"

"Two," Melissa groaned. "We have to go after her."

"You're not going anywhere." He stood up with a sigh. "Except to a med-centre! You're in no condition to fight that woman."

"But..."

"No buts," Jack insisted. "I'll handle her. By this point, campus security will have been alerted, and we have cops on the way."

Revealing herself had not been part of the plan. The Inzari had been quite specific in their instructions; she was to stir up chaos and add to the climate of distrust they were fostering on this planet, but her identity was to remain a secret. Leave it to Jack Hunter to throw a well-crafted plan right out the window.

Still, Isara couldn't say she was unhappy with the result. Now that she was finally free of the lie that was Jena Morane, she would no longer be consigned to those dreadful hoods and masks. For over a hundred years, her face had brought fear to those who saw it and to become the symbol that these idiots rallied around was simply galling.

She stepped through a door and found herself on a concrete path that ran through a field to the nearby arts building, but that wasn't what got her attention. Three egg-shaped drones floated in front of her, each one with a nozzle on its front side and a horizontal slit that glowed with blue light.

Beneath them were three officers in the black pants and white shirts of the campus security squad. Two men – one dark, the other pale – and a woman with red hair that she wore in a long braid. It was pathetic, really. These people weren't even allowed to carry firearms. What could they do against her?

"Stay where you are," the woman said.

Isara smiled, bowing her head to them. "Or what?" she asked in a voice as smooth as the finest silk. "I just threw around two Justice Keepers like a pair of rag dolls. Do you really think your *toys* frighten me?"

The drones floated higher, pointing their weapons at her.

At the last second, Isara raised a hand to shield herself and created a Bending that refracted the light until it seemed as though she wasn't staring at three people but rather at a swirling whirlpool of black and white and green and blue.

Stun-rounds hit the patch of warped space-time, curved away from her and flew off to hit the two men. She let the Bending drop to find them collapsing to the ground while the woman backed away.

The drones floated further upward and split apart so that one was on her left, one was on her right and the third was dead ahead. From multiple angles, they pointed their weapons at her.

Isara ran forward.

Without even thinking, she erected a Time Bubble in the shape of a long tube that ran along the pathway. Just ten feet long – not even half the distance between her and the frightened redhead – but it was enough to let her evade incoming fire. When she reached the end of the tube, she let it vanish.

Charged bullets hit the ground behind her.

Isara leaped, using a surge of Bent Gravity to propel herself forward. Her skin was burning from the strain she had put on her symbiont, but a warrior learned to ignore pain. She flew right over the uniformed woman's head.

Isara landed behind her.

She whirled around to find the redhead backing up toward her. Isara grabbed the woman's shirt with one hand and clamped the other onto the woman's throat. "No sudden movements, dear," she cautioned. "We wouldn't want to make a mess."

The three egg-shaped drones had turned around to point their weapons at her, but none fired. Their software was sophisticated; they wouldn't fire when there was a good chance of hitting someone in a friendly uniform.

"We're just gonna move nice and slowly to the subway terminal," Isara said. "No need to make a fuss"

The security officer squirmed in her grip.

Gritting her teeth with a hiss, Isara brought her lips to the other woman's ear. "I said there was no need to make a fuss," she growled. "Good children obey their elders. Nasty children, however..."

She squeezed the girl's throat.

The drones moved a few inches closer, but they didn't fire. They just floated above the path and waited for their opportunity. Not that she had any intention of providing one. This was getting tiresome.

Tilting her head back, Isara narrowed her eyes. "Multi-tool active!" she called out in a gruff voice. "Execute Program 3."

The Student Centre was a box-like, yellow-bricked building with windows on the first floor that looked into the cafeteria. She had watched Melissa for half an hour before choosing this place as the venue for her attack.

A Death Sphere that she had left on the rooftop suddenly floated over the edge and reoriented itself to point its lens at the three floating drones. Recognizing the new threat, those egg-shaped robots turned around to face her sphere.

They fired stun-rounds, but the Death Sphere didn't even bother to move. Bullets hit the sphere's surface at too low a velocity to do any real damage, and the charge they carried was too weak.

The sphere's lens began to glow with orange light, and then it spat a bright orange particle beam that it swept through the air in a horizontal arc. The beam cut through the security drones one by one, leaving chunks of metal that fell to the ground.

"Follow," Isara ordered.

Her multi-tool chirped its confirmation.

She dragged the redheaded security guard up the path while the Death Sphere floated just a few paces behind them. Not far ahead, the path forked with one branch running straight toward the arts building and another heading off to her right, toward the edge of the campus.

It wasn't very long before she found herself on a gently-sloping hillside, and at the bottom, a narrow street that bordered the university was packed with black police cars, each with flashing yellow lights.

Officers in gray uniforms were taking refuge on the other side of the line of cars, over two dozen people, all pointing guns at her. There were drones as well. Six of them floating above the cars. "Director Morane," said a man with dark hair. "You're ordered to stand down."

The name sickened her.

Isara shut her eyes, trying to calm herself. "Really now, Sargent?" she said, pulling the frightened security officer hard against her own body. "Do you expect me to believe that you're going to fire when I have this lovely young lady with me?"

Gripping the girl's chin in one hand, Isara squeezed until she heard the sweet *snap* of breaking bones. The redhead whimpered, and tears streamed over her face. "Now step aside," Isara ordered. "Or she dies."

At that moment, she sensed movement behind her. The silhouette of Jack Hunter came up the path, stopping a few feet away and lifting the pistol she had discarded in his hands. "Jena..." he called out. "Stand down."

"We have you surrounded," the lead cop said. "Be reasonable, Director Morane. You're not walking out of this-"

"Let me pass!" Isara screamed. "Or I kill the girl."

Scrunching up his face with a groan, the cop shook his head. "I don't think so," he replied. "The girl is your only bargaining chip, and you know it. You're not going to kill her just to prove a-"

Clamping one hand onto the girl's chin and the other onto the side of her head, Isara gave a quick twist and snapped the young woman's neck. The body slumped against her, and she let it fall to the ground.

The lead cop gasped. "Take her!"

"Program 3!" Isara bellowed.

The Death Sphere floated off to her left, pointing its lens at the cop cars. Before it could fire, EMP rounds from Jack's gun struck its body in a flash of sparks. The sphere fell to the ground, landing in the soft grass and exploded.

Isara barely noticed.

Fifteen police officers began firing stun-rounds at her. Thrusting her hand out, she crafted a Bending that stretched the image of those cars into a streak of black that seemed to curve around her. Her Bending was in the shape of a dome, causing incoming bullets to flow around her on either side and hopefully cause Jack some trouble. Her skin was on fire, but she tried to hold on.

A moment later, the Bending vanished. She was still concentrating on maintaining it, but her symbiont was too exhausted to continue...And so was she. Isara dropped to her knees, panting from the exertion.

One stun-round hit her and then another, sending jolts of current through her. As consciousness fled, her last thought was a silent prayer that no other slugs hit her. Too many in quick succession could kill, and if she died *here,* the Inzari would be unable to restore her.

She passed out right there on the path.

17

Jena was alive.

That was the gist of a report that had shown up in Anna's inbox just over half an hour ago. Oh, there were some details about an attack on the university, and about the police bringing her in along with a suspect in the vertical farm bombing. But you could hardly expect Anna to focus on those details in light of the fact that Jena was alive. Alive and evil, it would seem.

Anna strode through a corridor with her arms swinging wildly, shaking her head with a growl. "Just what I need," she muttered. "One more way for this world to kick me in the gut."

The silhouette of Ben came jogging up behind her, huffing and puffing with every breath. In seconds, the man was falling in beside her. "Is it true?" he asked. "Is she really still alive?"

"It's true."

Ben stared into the distance with his mouth agape, sweat glistening on his brow. "But we found her remains," he mumbled in disbelief. "The science teams confirmed it! How can she be alive?"

Glancing over her shoulder, Anna squinted at him. "What makes you think I have the answer to that question?" she snapped. Bleakness take her, the rage was like a fire in her chest. "I just found out myself!"

She squeezed her eyes shut, then gave her head a shake. "I'm sorry! I'm sorry!" It was hard to keep her tone civil. "I'm already feeling a little overwhelmed, and this on top of everything else..."

Of all things, Ben hugged her.

Anna slipped her arms around him and buried her nose in the side of his neck. "Oh, thank you," she whispered. "I really am sorry."

"Don't worry about it."

At the end of the hallway, double doors split apart to reveal a room with black floor tiles and blue walls. Hospital beds were positioned at even intervals, each one with three or four screens that could monitor a patient's vital signs.

Only one of those beds was occupied.

Larani stood just inside the door with hands shoved into the pockets of her black pants, her hair pulled back in a dark bun. "Agent Lenai," she said with a curt nod. "I'm glad you came so quickly."

Dressed in gray pants and a blue t-shirt with a white collar, Jack stood over one bed with his arms folded, his short brown hair in a state of disarray. Anna's first instinct was to say something comforting, but...Given the situation between them, maybe that wasn't such a good idea.

Her eyes fell on the bed.

A woman in black pants and a sleeveless t-shirt was stretched out there: a woman with boyishly-short pixie hair. Her eyes were closed, her face serene. Jena. It was really Jena. Until now, some part of her had been holding out hope...

Covering his mouth with one hand, Ben shut his eyes. "Sweet Mercy," he rasped, letting his arm drop as he stepped forward. "How did she survive...Does that mean Slade is alive too?"

Jack looked over his shoulder with blue eyes that seemed to blaze. "Yeah, I've been wondering the same thing," he muttered. "No one really saw what happened in that room. For all we know, they left some organic material behind, set off a bomb and then took off together."

It was a fair question. At the moment of Jena's death, Anna had been recovering her strength with Ben, in a room littered with the bodies of soldiers who had rallied to Slade's call. All of them had suffocated when the Overseer sucked the air out of a narrow tunnel that connected the chamber she and Ben had taken refuge in with the main corridor.

Anna crossed her arms with a sigh, shaking her head. "Melissa might know," she said, stepping forward. "She Bonded Jena's symbiont. If the Nassai knew anything about what Jena was planning..."

"Where is Melissa?" Ben inquired.

Fists clenched at her sides, Larani turned her head to stare at the wall. "The girl was beat up pretty bad," she murmured. "We've got her recovering in Med-Lab 2. I don't want her here if that...*woman* wakes up."

Dr. Sarela came around the corner. A short woman with olive skin and dark brown hair that she wore in a braided ponytail, she took a moment to survey each of them and then let out a sigh. "Director Morane's vitals are stable," she said. "A few stun-rounds are nothing to laugh at, but her symbiont seems to be healing the damage. I think it would be prudent to subdue her."

Jack nodded.

He lifted a thin metal band from the table next to Jena's bed and snapped it around her neck with a *click.* A slaver's collar? Anna felt her stomach turn at the sight of such a thing, but then there really wasn't much else you could do to keep a Justice Keeper under control. At least this way, Jena wouldn't be able to go on another killing spree.

Anna felt her knees weaken at the thought, and somewhere in the back of her mind, Seth groaned in sadness. This was the woman who had advised her, who had guided her. Anna knew it was only practical advice, but she couldn't help but relive some of those old arguments where Jena had insisted that she learn to make "the hard choices."

And then her confrontation with Slade on Station One...

The man had stood there in front of the SlipGate with a mocking grin, insisting that she lacked the stomach to do what was necessary. At the time, his words seemed to be a twisted echo of Jena's advice, but now...Was it possible? Had Jena been grooming her to take her place as one of Slade's agents?

Hugging herself and rubbing her upper arms, Anna stiffened as a chill went through her. "I'm with Larani," she said, though she didn't really believe it. "Whoever this woman is, she is *not* Jena."

"You'd like to think that."

Jena's eyes fluttered open, and she tossed her head from side to side. "Really, Anna, I thought you of all people would know I can survive anything."

"You'd never work for Slade."

Jena laughed.

It was cruel laughter, vicious laughter, the kind you would expect from a bully who had cornered you on the playground. Had she ever heard Jena laugh like that? Something about this woman was different. There was no humour, none of Jena's acerbic wit. It was all rage and hate.

No, Anna had never heard Jena laugh like that. But then if everything that she knew about Jena was a lie...

Jack flinched, turning his face away from the woman he had once called a friend. "Well, since you're feeling better," he began, "I'm sure you'll be quite comfortable inside a holding cell."

Jena stretched out on the mattress, arching her back and

then smacking her lips a few times. "Well, then perhaps we should be on our way," she said. "This bed has wheels, doesn't it? Start pushing."

"This isn't a hotel."

"You're right, boy; it isn't," Jena mocked. "But I have no intention of walking."

Boy, Anna noted. *Jena used to call him "kid."* She filed that little tidbit away in the back of her mind and took some small comfort in the possibility that maybe this woman wasn't the person she had come to think of as a friend.

"How long have you worked for Slade?" Larani asked.

Instead of answering, Jena smiled up at the ceiling and batted her eyes. "You know, I think I'd like some french toast," she said. "All that time on Earth has given me a taste for their food. Fetch some for me."

"How *long*?" Larani growled.

"With blueberry syrup, please," Jena went on. "I've come to prefer it."

Larani grunted, turning her back on the other woman. She marched to the door and stood there with trembling hands. "Throw her in a holding cell!" she barked. "Leave her there until morning; she can eat then."

Laughing hysterically as she sat up, Jena pressed a hand to her forehead. "So, I'm going to be sent to bed without supper?" The sheer pleasure in her voice sent a chill down Anna's spine. "Honestly, you Keepers have such brutal interrogation techniques, I'm sure I'll be revealing all my secrets in no time!"

The woman curled her legs against her chest and hugged them, burying her smiling face between her knees. "Come on then, Jack!" she teased. "You'd better start pushing me down there. I have no intention of walking."

She suddenly looked up at him with a cold expression. "You could use the collar, I suppose," Jena said, arching one eyebrow.

"Force me to obey. Tell me, Jack, do you have the stomach for it? Are you willing to torture another human being?"

Jack didn't answer.

He just started wheeling the bed toward the door, and everyone who had come to this impromptu meeting jumped out of the way. Jena cackled with giddy delight. "Oh, I love it!" she exclaimed. "Give me three days, and I'll be running this place!"

Jack looked like he was ready to spit bullets, but in that moment, Anna was proud of him. Prouder than she would like to admit. A Justice Keeper would resort to violence in defense of their own life or the life of another, but never as catharsis for the indignities they were sometimes forced to endure. Jena could taunt all she wanted, but Jack wouldn't let her bait him... and Anna loved him for it.

It can't be Jena, she told herself yet again. Jena was focused, methodical. Not cold by any stretch of the imagination, but she had a way of zeroing in on a goal like a laser. What little Anna knew of "Isara" suggested a similar tenacity, but this woman was almost manic in her demeanour. She took a kind of sick pleasure in causing pain.

They're more alike than you'd care to admit, Anna thought. *It took Isara less than ten seconds to establish herself as the dominant personality in this room. Just like Jena would have.*

She felt sick inside.

Melissa floated in an endless expanse of stars, a white dress with a frayed hemline falling almost to her bare feet and billowing in the non-existent wind. She moved her arms as if swimming, though there was no water. No air either. This was a place of the mind. A place where she could get answers.

Closing her eyes, Melissa focused her thoughts. "Ilia!" she called out, diving like a fish through the endless void. "I need to talk to you!"

Ground rose up to meet her, lush and green and dotted with trees. She noticed a river carving its way through the landscape and flocks of birds moving past underneath her. Boy, her mind could conjure some amazing imagery.

Melissa landed on bare feet at the top of a grassy hill, lifting her hands up in front of her face to study her fingers. It felt strange to be so *solid* in what was essentially a very vivid dream.

Another woman materialized before her, dressed identically in a white dress that left her shoulders bare. This lady was tall and slim with a pretty face and short hair that she wore parted in the middle.

Jena.

Melissa let her head hang, then rubbed her eyes with the back of one hand."That might not be the best form to choose," she said. "Right now, everything is very confus-"

"It isn't Jena."

"I'm sorry?"

"The woman that you encountered at the university!" Ilia said. "The one who names herself Isara! She is *not* my former host!"

"Can you be sure?"

Ilia strode through the grass in a way that reminded Melissa of the moments right before her father launched into one of his most scathing lectures. In the blink of an eye, she was towering over Melissa. "I remember *everything* that Jena experienced!" Ilia said. "She never fought Anna in Tennessee. She despised Grecken Slade with every particle of her being! Under no circumstances would she ally herself with that...traitor!"

Hearing those words was such a relief; Melissa felt every muscle in her body relax. She was about to thank the Nassai for setting her mind at ease, but Ilia was still fuming. "Jena believed in the ideals of the Justice Keepers!" she insisted. "And she would *never* kill indiscriminately the way this Isara does. More to the point, I would not have allowed it! This woman may look like Jena – she may *sound* like Jena – but she is *not* Jena!"

Melissa crossed her arms, frowning down at herself. "Well, all right then," she said, nodding slowly. "At least that much is settled. So, all this time, Jena had an evil twin. Or maybe...a *clone*!"

"A clone?"

"Think about it!" Melissa exclaimed. "You're Grecken Slade, and this one annoying Justice Keeper has been a thorn in your side for years. So, how do you deal with it? You make a copy of her, your very own Jena."

Ilia didn't look convinced.

The Nassai stood before her with a hand pressed to her middle, a tight frown on her face as she stared down at the ground. "Jena was a formidable enemy because of *who* she was. You can't clone life experience."

"No, but...Maybe that wasn't the point." A thought occurred to her, accompanied by a feeling that reminded her of the times when she couldn't wait for the teacher to call on her because she just knew she had the right answer. "Maybe the point was to destabilize us, make us doubt one another."

"Then why would Isara hide her face?"

Melissa turned her back on the other woman, trudging up the hillside and stopping there with her hands clasped in front of herself. "I don't know," she said with a shrug. "It could be that she was trying to get information, use Jena's access codes."

Ilia leaped off the ground like a ballet dancer and floated up the hill, passing right over Melissa's head. She landed in the grass, then promptly turned around. "You should know it doesn't work that way," she said. "Having Jena's face doesn't give you her access codes. You can't clone a fingerprint."

Tossing her head back, Melissa shut her eyes so tight it made her tremble. "Then I don't know!" she snapped. "But I'd better go tell Larani what you just told me. And one more thing."

"Yes?"

"You offered to help me learn how to fight like Jena," Melissa said. "I accept."

It was hard to keep the tears off her face.

Larani was the sort of person who prided herself on a certain amount of emotional control, but discovering that Jena was not only alive but also one of Slade's most trusted lieutenants was like a kick to the stomach. Her insides felt as if someone had tied them in knots. It was a shock to realize that she cared this much.

Well...No, not really.

Months ago, she had smothered her feelings the instant she first recognized them for what they were. Jena had been unavailable at the time, with Melissa's father, no less. Not that Larani had time for such indulgences. It was a source of irritation for her to feel like she had been reduced to a babbling school girl. Romance was for the young; she was in her mid-forties, which was old for a Justice Keeper.

Her office was lit only by a single lamp on her desk. How long had she been sitting here anyway? Several hours? She remembered making her way down to the cafeteria and forcing herself to eat a bowl of soup, but for the last few hours, she had just been lost in her own thoughts.

Larani felt tears on her cheeks, then buried her nose in the palm of her hand. She massaged her tired eyes. "You have work to do," she reminded herself. "You don't have time to sit here and mope about-"

The door chime cut her off.

"Come in."

When the double doors slid open, Melissa stood in the blue-walled corridor with her head down. "I'm sorry to bother you, ma'am," she began. "But there's something you should know."

"What is it?"

The girl took a hesitant step forward, and the door slid shut behind her. She forced out a deep breath. "She's not Jena," Melissa said. "The woman we've got locked up in a holding cell? She's not Jena."

Larani stood.

She leaned over the desk, pressing her palms to its surface, and shook her head. "I don't mean to be harsh, Melissa," she said. "But we took a sample of that woman's DNA. It's identical to Jena's."

Melissa jumped and clapped her hands so hard it sounded like someone had set off a firecracker. "Then I was *right*!" she exclaimed, striding toward the desk. "Ma'am, Isara is a clone!"

Lifting her chin to study the young woman, Larani narrowed her eyes. "A clone," she said softly. "I wish that were true, Melissa, but she also has Jena's fingerprints. You can't clone a fingerprint."

"Okay, so she has Jena's fingerprints," Melissa said. "And Jena's DNA as well. But she *doesn't* have Jena's memories, I can guarantee it. My symbiont remembers Jena's life backward and forward, and Jena never did any of the things Isara did."

Clamping a hand over her mouth, Larani shut her eyes. A mystery. Normally, she liked mysteries. "I don't know," she muttered. "We know Slade's people have the ability to swap out a true Nassai for one of those corrupted symbionts."

"What's your point?"

"Perhaps Jena...exchanged the symbiont you carry for one that would let her attack Anna without consequences."

"Ilia would remember that."

Crossing her arms, Larani hung her head. A heavy sigh escaped her despite her best efforts to suppress it. "I see you've also named your Nassai," she grumbled. "A practice I would rather discourage."

The girl held her gaze with dark eyes that – just for a moment – seemed to belong to a woman twice her age. "Ilia is a person," she said firmly. "Why shouldn't she have a name of her own?"

So much was changing.

Larani had never considered herself a traditionalist – in fact, she prided herself on being able to adapt to new situations – but the Justice Keepers had certainly morphed into something very different from what they had been twenty years ago, when she was just a raw cadet. She supposed that was a good thing, but it did take some getting used to. Over four hundred years of humans Bonding with Nassai, and it took some cheeky kid from a backward world in the middle of Dead Space to come up with the idea of naming them.

Melissa looked flustered; it was clear the girl was adamant about proving that this Isara was not the Jena Morane she had come to love. So, why was Larani so dead set on believing the worst?

Turning her back on the girl, Larani went to the large window behind her desk and braced her forearm on the pane. "It's possible, Melissa," she admitted. "But the truth is we don't know what to make of Isara."

"Quiz her," Melissa suggested.

"Hmm?"

"Ask her things only Jena would know."

Well...That really should have been the first arrow in her quiver. Why was she so willing to believe that Jena had betrayed them? Was it because hate was easier to handle than... whatever else she might have felt? "That's a good idea, Melissa," Larani said softly. "I'll have someone look into-"

The door slid apart again, and this time, there was no chime to announce the new visitor. Instead, Jon Andalon came striding through as if this were his office. "We have a new problem," he said. "A big one."

Larani spun around.

The man stood on the other side of her desk, breathing slowly. "I was attacked in my apartment today," he went on. "By two men who used a kind of cloaking technology I've never seen before."

Larani felt her jaw drop, then shook her head to clear her mind. "We've never been able to make a working cloaking device," she replied. "And to the best of my knowledge, neither have the Antaurans."

Jon crossed his arms and grunted his displeasure, approaching her desk with his head down. "That may be so," he said. "But clearly someone has. I've got the two men who did it in lock-up."

"A cloaking device..." Melissa whispered.

At times, the girl was so quiet, it was easy to forget her presence. She seemed to be putting the pieces together in her head. "And Director Andalon was attacked on the same day that Isara hit the university. It can't be a coincidence."

"Who?" Jon snapped.

"A woman who's given us some trouble in the past," Melissa answered. "We just found out she's a clone of Jena."

"I beg your pardon, Cadet."

Larani raised a hand to forestall any further argument. She needed time to think, to analyze the factors. Every instinct she had told her that Melissa was right; there was just no way these two incidents were unrelated. But if Isara had been the one to provide the cloaking devices to the men who attacked Jon... "I take it you recovered the devices they were using?" she inquired.

"Yes."

"Then let's go have a look."

The Science Lab was a large room on the sixth floor with windows that looked out on a skyline that was lighting up as evening set in. A series of consoles arranged to form a circle took up much of the floor-space.

Dr. Maz Atero was in an uproar.

A short man in a white lab coat, he paced a line across the room with his hands in the air. His round face of smooth, dark skin was handsome enough, Melissa supposed, but the mop of brown hair gave him a boyish look. "I don't believe it!" he shouted. "An actual working cloaking device."

As usual, Melissa waited in the corner with her hands clasped before herself, her head bowed respectfully. Do a lot of listening and a little talking; that was advice she had once heard her father offer to a young cop on his way to his first meeting. She had taken those words to heart.

Larani was hunched over with a palm pressed to her forehead, and it looked as if she might collapse from fatigue. "So you can confirm it?" she mumbled. "This isn't just some complex holography?"

"I did say as much, didn't I?"

That came from Director Andalon, who sat on the windowsill with his hands on his knees. He shook his head slowly in exasperation. "Two men attacked me this afternoon, and they were invisible."

"I just want to be sure," Larani muttered.

Dr. Atero lifted something that looked like a loose-fitting smock and pulled it over his body. His head popped through the neck hole, and he blinked several times. "See for yourself," he said.

The man touched a button on the garment, and just like that, he seemed to ripple out of existence, leaving only a slight shimmer in the air that you might have missed if you weren't paying attention. To Melissa's eyes, he was gone, but Ilia could still sense him. It was somewhat disorienting.

That shimmer in the air moved as Atero made his way around the ring of consoles. "The device creates a field that refracts light around the body," he said. "It would make incredible camouflage if not for the fact that it runs out of power in about ten minutes."

"Still," Larani said. "It's an advantage."

It was hard to resist the urge to begin dry-washing her hands, but Melissa was able to maintain her composure. Anxiety was like a lump in her stomach. Enemies that could make themselves invisible? True, she could sense them, but the Sons of Savard could do all sorts of damage with that technology.

Jon was on his feet in an instant, pacing across the room with an expression that made it look as if he had just bitten into a lemon. "Could this be used on starships," he asked, "Or other military tech?"

"No, it wouldn't work."

"But a ship can generate enormous amounts of power."

The shimmer moved away from Jon, and when Melissa focused on the awareness that came from her symbiont, she could see that Atero was fiddling with his multi-tool. "The device bends light around my body," he said. "But that only prevents EM waves from reflecting off of me. If I happen to be the *source* of those waves..."

Suddenly, there was light shining in the middle of the room. Light so bright it made Melissa shield her eyes. The flashlight on Atero's multi-tool. It was somewhat distorted by the cloaking field – almost if someone had held up a prism that broke the white light into a rainbow of colours – but still clearly visible.

A moment later, Atero reappeared, and the rainbow of light reformed into a single white beam from his multi-tool. He turned it off with a few taps. "Ships emit all sorts of energy: thermal emissions, radar pings. You name it."

He sat down in the chair in front of one console, muttering to himself as he tried to pull the smock off. "Bleakness," he said at last. "A simple pair of infrared goggles would render this device useless."

"Well, there's that much," Larani said. "Keep studying the tech. I want a full report on my desk as soon as possible."

"Yes, ma'am."

She just prayed the Sons of Savard didn't have any other nasty surprises in store for her people.

18

Melissa felt her mouth stretch into a great big yawn and then covered it with one hand, groaning as she fought through her fatigue. She was tired. "Goodness," she muttered into her own palm. "You'd think Keepers would have more stamina."

A ceiling of gray clouds threatened to spit rain down on Riado Street, but somehow, they never made good on it. Buildings on either side of the street stood five or six stories high, and trees along the curb sighed in the wind. The architecture was a little different here on Leyria. There were still highrises, but many buildings were shorter, and some were designed with odd geometry in mind.

Sliding her hands into her back pockets, Melissa closed her eyes tried not to yawn. "That's what I get for only sleeping four hours," she mumbled. "And after getting my ass kicked to boot."

On the nearby street corner, she spotted Aiden standing in shorts and a light green t-shirt. He was staring off into the distance, unaware of her presence. Melissa had briefly considered canceling their lunch date, but she needed to unwind.

When Aiden noticed her, he perked up and started up the

sidewalk with a big smile on his face. "Hey!" he shouted. "I was worried you weren't gonna make it. I heard about what happened yesterday."

Melissa smiled down at herself, then shook her head slowly. "Well, you can take it as a complement," she replied. "I don't know...I'm still reeling from the fact that there's a murderous religious zealot who wears the face of someone I grew to love and respect."

Aiden crossed his arms as he stood before her, bowing his head as if he couldn't bring himself to make eye contact. "Yeah," he said. "Have you thought about speaking to a counselor?"

"Oh, believe me, I have."

And she wasn't particularly enthused about the prospect of having to go through *that* again. She had only just been cleared to end her therapy sessions with the counselors who had treated her after she bonded Jena's symbiont. If being a Justice Keeper meant a constant strain on her mental health...

Well, actually, that was exactly what it meant. She had signed up for a life of near constant danger and political intrigue. She couldn't exactly act surprised when that took a toll on her emotions.

Aiden jerked his head toward the cafe on the street corner. "Shall we..."

"Yes."

Inside, the place was quaint with silly paintings that reminded her of Picasso's work hung up on the pastel-green walls. A counter with a display case that showed off cakes and other delicious goodies was operated by a woman who...

A woman. A *human* woman.

This lady was short with olive skin and dark hair with a streak of teal through it. She smiled when she saw them, gesturing to one of the many empty tables that sat in the light of a store-front window. "Please, come in! Sit wherever you like!"

"You're a person!"

The woman's face took on an expression that you might expect to see on someone who had just picked up a whiff of garbage. "Thank you?"

Melissa felt her cheeks burn, then turned her head to stare at the wall. She cleared her throat. "I'm sorry," she mumbled. "It's just...I grew up on Earth, and most restaurants I've seen since moving here have been automated."

A bright beautiful smile replaced the woman's scowl. "Oh!" she exclaimed. "I see. No, this place is mine. The name's Tesia."

"And you run this place?"

"Yes, I've known I wanted to be a pastry chef since I was about eight years old. We do have robot waiters for the busy hours, but they're all on standby for the moment."

Aiden seemed a tad chagrined by her touristy behaviour, but what could she say? She was still new here. They chose a small table by the window, but with an overcast sky, there wasn't much light to be had.

The menu came in the form of a hologram that floated above the table, and Melissa selected something that was kind of like a fajita. Grilled chicken, green and red peppers and shredded cheese in some kind of tortilla shell.

Tesia approached their table mere moments later, standing with her hands behind her back as she smiled down at them. "I should tell you that we're out of chicken for the next little while," she explained. "Ever since those idiots hit one of the cloning facilities the other night, deliveries have been behind schedule."

"Oh that's all right," Melissa said.

Aiden leaned back with his arms folded, grinning up at their server. "You should thank this one for the fact that you still have bread and pie crusts," he said. "She saved a food processing plant."

Tesia blinked.

A moment later, she pulled up a chair as if she had been invited to join them and sat with her elbows on the table. "You're too young to be a cop," she said, studying Melissa. "But you might be a Keeper."

"Yes," Melissa answered. "But it's really not a big deal."

"On the contrary," Tesia insisted. "It's a *huge* deal" It was hard not to feel just a tad uncomfortable after that. All Melissa wanted was a quiet lunch. She wasn't looking for a generous helping of praise along with her food. "And you're from Earth? How long have you carried a symbiont?"

"Just a few months."

Tesia flinched as if someone had splashed cold water over her face. "Only a few months...Cadets don't usually go on...Are you Melissa Carlson?"

Squeezing her eyes shut, Melissa pressed the heels of her hands to her forehead. "How do you know that?" she whimpered. "I've turned down every reporter who asked me for an interview."

And there had been plenty of those. In the few days since the attack on the city's infrastructure, she had received at least half a dozen calls and almost as many e-mails from journalists who wanted to hear from the city's youngest hero.

Tesia sat with her hands folded over her stomach, a great big grin on her face. "You can turn them down," she said. "But it doesn't prevent them from doing their jobs. When a cadet saves a major piece of the city's infrastructure, that's news."

"Oy..."

Hunching over the table with his arms crossed, Aiden shook his head. "Well, I say you should enjoy it," he said. "Come on, Melissa! You put your life on the line! At least enjoy the rewards a little!"

"You could let me serve you dessert," Tesia suggested. "We have the most delicious key lime pie in the city. My own recipe."

"Okay, okay," Melissa relented. "I'll try the pie."

"Good." Tesia stood up and nodded curtly as if the matter were settled. "And one small piece of advice? You may want to agree to at least one of those interviews. People need to know that someone is protecting them."

A shivering Brinton sat with his elbows on the surface of a metal table, his fingers laced over the top of his head. The young man looked wan and pale, his brow glistening with sweat. Amps withdrawal was a terrible thing to witness. From what Anna had been told, the doctors were trying to wean him off the drug.

Another man sat on Brinton's right.

This one was tall and lean in a gray jacket and high-collared white shirt. His thin face of chocolate-brown skin was marked by high cheekbones, and he had shaved off his hair. "Agent Lenai," he said. "Clearly my client is in no condition to answer questions. I submit that anything he tells you in this condition is inadmissible."

In gray pants and a black blouse with the collar open, Anna sat with her hands on the armrests of her chair, staring into her lap. Lawyers. Sure, it was their job to protect a suspect's rights, but she had no intention of maneuvering Brinton into saying something that would incriminate himself; they had all the evidence that they needed to convict him several times over. All she wanted was to know *why*.

Biting her lip, Anna shut her eyes and nodded. "You make a good point, Mr. Pellan," she said. "But I just want to clarify a few things. Brinton, I understand that you're in pain, but if you cooperate, it will go a long way toward helping your case."

"I will cooperate."

Rax Pellan was not satisfied; the man shot a glance toward his client and frowned as if someone had dropped rotting garbage on the table. "You're sure?" he said. "Brinton, you can't be forced to answer questions if you can barely think."

"I want to answer."

Closing her eyes, Anna breathed slowly to steady herself. "All right," she said. "I want to know why you attacked the university, and what made you ally yourself with the Sons of Savard."

Brinton looked up at her with bloodshot eyes, and he blinked as if trying to moisten them. "I attacked the university because Isara told me to," he answered. "She said it was the will of the gods."

"More religious nonsense," Ben muttered.

Anna could perceive him with spatial awareness. The man was leaning against the wall behind her with hands in his pockets and shaking his head in disgust. "You've gotta love the human condition; we can go to the stars, but we're still taken in by superstitious nonsense."

Restraining herself from snapping at Ben required a little effort. Only a little. She lacked Jack's flair for putting a suspect on the defensive, but there were other ways to get information. Belittling people wasn't one of them.

Anna felt her lips curl, then bowed her head to the young man. "Isara told you that it was the will of the gods," she said. "Brinton, you're an acolyte of the Holy Companion. You don't believe in gods."

Brinton slouched in his chair, his head lolling to the side as if he couldn't find the energy to stay awake. "I was an acolyte of the Holy Companion," he murmured. "Then Isara showed me the truth."

"What did she show you?"

"That the Overseers are gods."

Everyone was silent for a moment, and Anna found herself exchanging looks with Mr. Pellan. It was clear that the lawyer was growing uncomfortable with this particular line of questioning. "How did she show you that, Brinton?"

The young man wheezed with laughter, doubling over and

trembling with every breath. "She killed me," Brinton whispered. "She killed me, and then the Inzari brought me back to life."

Anna felt a lump of ice in her stomach. Was this man insane? A victim of some sort of brainwashing? Was that how the Overseers turned Keepers to their cause. She shivered at the thought that it might happen to her.

Ben was less than pleased with the answer. He was standing by the wall with his hand pressed to his stomach, growling as he stared down at the floor. Perhaps asking him to be part of this interrogation had been a bad idea.

Rax Pellan forced a smile and then shook his head slowly. "Agent Lenai, you must see that Brinton is suffering from delusions," he said. "I'm going to recommend that the court remand him to a rehabilitation facility where he can receive the-"

"I'm not delusional!"

When Brinton looked up, his face was red, and for a moment, it looked as though he might launch into a fit of rage. "I was there! On their ship!" he squealed. "I saw my own dead body lying on the floor."

Once again, the room fell silent. How exactly did you respond to something like that? Brinton certainly sounded delusional, but she couldn't really discount what he was saying simply because it seemed incredulous. The Overseers had re-engineered planets to make them suitable for human life. Who could say what they were capable of?

Tapping her lips with one finger, Anna shut her eyes tight. "That's very interesting, Brinton," she said gently. "Maybe it's time for a change of subject. What can you tell me about the Sons of Savard?"

"They want Leyria to embrace traditional values."

"What do you mean?"

The young man covered his face with both hands and groaned into his own palms. "It shouldn't be that hard to understand," he said. "We've eliminated poverty. There's no struggle to life anymore. This made us soft."

"So, you *want* people to starve in the streets?"

"I accept it as a necessary evil if we want a populace strong enough to deal with the threats represented by the Antaurans, the Ragnosians and anyone else who might want to encroach on our borders."

Restraining her hot temper required a miraculous effort of will. This was the kind of stupidity that only a privileged Leyrian could articulate with any degree of sincerity. Anna had been to Earth; she had seen the horrors of homelessness, deprivation. She had witnessed the deleterious effect poverty had on the human soul. Destroying their social infrastructure wouldn't produce a generation of hardy Leyrians willing to defend their home against any threats; it would produce a generation of people so desperate for any kind of relief that they would sell themselves into slavery.

"Is this what the Overseers want?" she asked.

Brinton winced, shaking his head so quickly he was likely to make himself dizzy. "No," he replied in a strained voice. "The Sons have nothing to do with the Inzari. Isara gave us weapons but..."

Anna sank into her chair with arms folded, frowning at the young man. "So, Isara gave you advanced weaponry?" she said. "Why?"

"I don't know."

"Everything Isara does is done with only one purpose," Anna said. "To further the ends of her so-called gods. Clearly, the Overseers see your group as a convenient tool."

Before she could say another word, Rax Pellan stood up with a hand over his chest. He looked to Anna and then to Brinton. "I think that, in the best interests of my client," he began, "it would be best to suspend these proceedings for now."

"He's willing to talk, Mr. Pellan."

"There's no point in hiding it," Brinton said. "You cannot deny the truth of divinity itself. Only a fool would try."

Anna stood up.

Heaving out a breath, she let her head sink and rubbed her brow with the back of one hand. "All right, that's enough for now," she muttered. "Come on, Brinton. Let's get you back to your cell."

Mr. Pellan stood with hands behind his back, nodding his approval. "It's clear to me that Brinton needs help," he said. "I'll draw up the paperwork to have him transferred to a psychiatric care facility."

Anna wasn't quite so convinced that these were mere delusions – she had seen the devotion that the Overseers inspired in their servants – but she wasn't willing to put up a fight about it. A therapist might do a better job of getting Brinton to confess whatever it was he knew about the Sons of Savard anyway.

"Ben," she said. "Contact Jack. Tell him what Brinton said. Let's see if he can get something out of Cara."

The screen of Jack's multi-tool was filled with the image of Ben grimacing as he relayed everything he had learned from Brinton. "Jon wants you to ask Cara about it," he said. "See if you can corroborate any of this."

Standing in the hallway outside Cara's cell, Jack heaved out a breath as he stared at the gauntlet on his forearm. "All right," he said with a nod. "Cassi's in with her now. We will see what we can dig up."

"Thanks, man."

"No problem."

The screen went dark.

Jack pressed his palm to the scanner beside the door, allowing the computer to read his biometrics. Then he typed in a security code and waited for the soft beep that told him he had been granted access.

When the door slid open, he saw Cassi in profile, seated on a stool just in front of Cara's bed. His partner wore a gray skirt and a sleeveless fuchsia blouse that was a near-perfect compliment to her short pink hair. And she seemed to be concentrating on something.

On the other side of the room, Cara Sinthel was dressed casually in track pants and a tank-top with spaghetti straps, her silver-blonde hair done up in a ponytail. "We've been over this, Cassiara."

"And you still haven't given an answer."

Leaning against the wall with a hand over her stomach, Cara tilted her head back and rolled her eyes. "I don't know anything about these Sons of Savard," she said. "Or the proliferation of Ragnosian weapons or the true identity of this Isara."

Jack strode into the room with his arms swinging, shaking his head as he let out a growl. "What about the Overseers?" he demanded. "You must know all the juicy gossip about them."

Cara watched him for a long moment, her gray eyes sizing him up. "You wouldn't be interested in anything I have to say about them," she muttered. "You've already made your opinions clear."

"Did they bring you back from the dead?"

The woman's mouth dropped open, and her skin visibly paled. "How do you know about..." She closed her eyes and gave her head a shake. "Impossible."

Jack crossed his arms with a chuckle, bowing his head to her. "Is that so?" he said, stepping forward. "You know, we've got a guy two cells over who insists that the 'Inzari' brought him back from the dead."

"Then perhaps you should believe him."

Cassi sat on her stool with such poise you might have thought it was a throne, and she watched the other woman the way a mother bear watches a hunter. "So, you're saying the Overseers can resurrect the dead."

"They did for me." Cara lifted a hand up in front of her face, studying her nails as if she had just applied a fresh coat of polish. "Slade stabbed me through the heart, and when I woke up, I was fine, but my symbiont was gone. It was disorienting, losing my sense of spatial awareness.

"They left me alone in a room that felt very much like a cavern with walls made of skin. Naked and terrified. I'd never been more afraid in my life. After what felt like hours, Slade showed up and offered me the chance to join him."

"And what did you say?"

Soft laughter was Cara's first response to that. "I was a good Justice Keeper," she said. "A bit out of step with my colleagues, sure, but I *believed* in what we stood for. You want to know my response? I spat in Slade's face."

"What changed?" Jack murmured.

"They took me to a room where my own corpse was stretched out on the floor, its skin glowing as the Nassai I carried grew more and more desperate for a living host. I reached out to Bond the symbiont again, but Slade stopped me. He told me that if I chose to serve the Inzari, they would give me a much more powerful symbiont, but if I refused, I would be killed and my soul would be thrown into a void of endless darkness, cut off from everything I'd ever loved for all eternity."

Cara slumped against the wall, sliding downward until her bottom hit the floor. Then she drew her legs up and hugged them. "Do you understand now?" she asked. "The Inzari did nothing to coerce my obedience; they simply provided the right incentive."

It was...fascinating.

Jack wasn't sure what to make of all this, but if Cara was telling the truth, it would confirm his suspicion that some part of the human consciousness continued to exist after death. He could already feel himself getting excited, and *that* was a bad thing. His mind could spin all sorts of hypotheses, but it was time to be a scientist, and a scientist would approach this whole situation with guarded skepticism.

Biting his lip, Jack closed his eyes and took a deep breath. "Okay," he said with a nod. "Let's start with the obvious question. What makes you so sure the Overseers could make good on their threat."

"Because they're gods."

"I highly doubt that."

With her mouth agape, Cara looked up to blink at the ceiling. "I stand before you as living proof!" she insisted. "The Inzari killed me and then restored me to life. What else could do that?"

Cassi sat forward with her hands on her knees, her face scrunched up in obvious disgust. "They didn't kill *you*," she said. "They killed the original Cara Sinthel, and you are just a clone."

"Oh, you're very wrong about that."

"Really? Prove it."

"I have Cara's memories."

Rising gracefully with a soft sigh, Cassi paced across the room in high heels that clicked on the floor tiles. "So, they scanned Cara's memory engrams and then duplicated them. It doesn't prove anything."

"*All* of her memories," Cara insisted. "Including the brief period where I was dead. I remember it quite well: the light and warmth, a feeling of absolute calm serenity. It was like nothing I'd ever experienced; I was connected to everything, and yet I was still Cara, still me. I remember feeling free. It was like I could see the universe in its entirety, know it completely from the moment of the Big Bang all the way through to its conclusion.

"And then suddenly, I was ripped away from all that, trapped in a cramped little space that I didn't recognize as my own body. When I finally got my bearings, I thought it was all a vivid dream or some drug-induced hallucination, but my Nassai was gone...and they showed me my other body with a knife through its chest."

"That doesn't prove anything," Cassi insisted. Jack couldn't blame her for feeling skeptical; even if Cara was telling the truth, there were a dozen possible explanations for what she had experienced. Still, it wouldn't be wise to jump to any conclusions.

Pressing his lips together, Jack closed his eyes. He let out a deep breath. "Cassi, I think we should consider the possibility that she might be telling the truth."

His partner whirled around to look him up and down with a glare that could peel strips off his skin. "You can't be serious!" she snapped. "Jack, they rebuilt Cara's brain! They could have implanted any memories they wanted!"

Backing away with his hands raised defensively, Jack stared at her with his mouth hanging open. "I'm just keeping an open mind," he said. "We don't know enough about how the human mind works or whether there is some part of it that survives after death."

"So what? We should start worshiping the Overseers?"

"I didn't say that!"

Cara threw her head back with a peal of soft laughter. "See how easily you turn on one another?" She grunted as she got to her feet, dusting off her track pants. "It goes well beyond proof of life and death, Jack Hunter."

The tiny, silver-haired woman strode toward him with an expression that sent chills down his spine. "I serve the Inzari because they are morally superior to us," she went on. "They bring unity instead of this divisiveness."

"What you call divisiveness, I call individuality."

Cara turned to face the window, unconsciously touching the collar that prevented her from using her powers. "Call it what you will," she said. "But unity is the reason why my side will prevail in the end."

It was time to end this interrogation; never let the subject see that you were rattled; that was one of the cardinal rules. More to the point, Jack suspected that he couldn't get anything more useful out of Cara anyway. She had left him with a lot to think on.

Could the Overseers really bring people back from the dead? It seemed impossible, but...No. Actually, it *didn't* seem impossible, and maybe that was the problem. Death was one of those things that people just didn't question. When you were gone, that was it. But Jack Hunter questioned everything.

He had no firm belief in any kind of afterlife – just a niggling feeling that there was more to existence than what he could perceive with his physical senses – but he wasn't so opposed to the idea that he was willing to dismiss it out of hand.

Maybe Cassi was right; maybe this Cara was just the clone of a woman who had lost her life years ago. A clone with brain patterns duplicated so precisely it reconstructed her entire personality. But maybe that wasn't the point. Maybe the totality of everything that was Cara included the woman in that cell and the woman who had died years ago and something else that connected both of them.

But he was sure of one thing.

The Overseers were *not* gods.

He had no solid argument to back up that position. Just a feeling. A feeling that said anything that claimed the mantle of godhood should be above the disgusting displays of violence he had seen from the Overseers. Besides, it wouldn't matter if they were. If the only way to get into Heaven was to violate his conscience, then Jack Hunter was going straight to Hell.

19

A long lunch in which she'd fielded questions from Tesia – you couldn't be blamed for thinking the woman wanted to be a reporter more than she wanted to be a baker – left Melissa feeling even more tired than she had been that morning. She was burned out, and that made the prospect of having yet another difficult conversation less than appealing to say the least. But she owed her friends this much.

Melissa was beginning to suspect that they might have pieced some of this together on their own. Director Andalon had been kind enough to e-mail her a summary of what they had learned from Brinton. A shiver went through her when she thought about it. Just two weeks ago, she would have insisted on being part of that interrogation, but after the incident at the university, she was more than happy to avoid Brinton whenever possible. Still...The Overseers could bring people back from the dead? And duplicate people? That would explain Isara.

When she pushed the front door open, she saw, on her right, the staircase that led up to the second floor. The hallway that ran alongside that staircase to the kitchen at the back of the house was being vacuumed by a small robot about the size of a footstool.

"Is everyone here?" Melissa called out.

"In the kitchen!" her father responded.

She shut the door with a deep breath and braced herself for a dozen questions that she probably couldn't answer. But her father more than anyone else needed to know what she knew. He had loved Jena.

"Sorry I'm late," Melissa said, stepping into the kitchen. "I got caught up with someone who...Does everyone on this planet idolize Keepers?"

"You don't want to meet the ones who don't," Anna said.

She sat on the kitchen table with her knees together, smiling into her own lap. "I'm sure you'll get used to it soon enough," she said. "So...Your dad said you had something to tell us?"

Jack slouched in a chair with his hands on his thighs, blinking as he stared up at the ceiling. "I think she just wanted to have a party," he teased. "Station Twelve crew unite! Can I get a what-what?"

Her father had his back turned as he stood over the counter, stirring a cup of coffee. "Very Nineties, Jack," he said. "Good to see you're still listening to your father's music."

"My father's music was Fallout Boy."

"Still, it's-"

Closing her eyes, Melissa took a deep breath and then stepped forward. "Isara isn't Jena," she interrupted. "They may look the same, but they are two different people. My Nassai doesn't remember doing any of the things Isara did."

"Well, at least there's that much," Anna said. "So, what does that mean in terms of our investigation?"

Jack exhaled slowly. "It means we have to consider an unappealing possibility." He slid his chair back over the floor tiles and stood up with a grunt. “Maybe The Overseers can create duplicates-”

“Are we sure the Overseers made her?” Anna asked. “Leyria has had cloning tech for over two centuries now.”

“True, but who else would-”

Melissa tuned them out, allowing them to discuss the matter among themselves. This wasn't an argument she wanted any part of; it didn't matter *where* Isara came from. What mattered was that someone had violated the form of a person she had come to love like a part of her own family.

Someone had taken the face of a woman she looked up to like a surrogate mother and made it into the face of an enemy. That was something she couldn't forgive. Melissa was a person of faith, but she had never been offended by religions other than her own. She had never been threatened by Allah or Vishnu or the Leyrian Companion. But for the Overseers to call themselves gods in light of all they had done? That *sickened* her.

She made her way to the living room, where the pastel-blue walls looked a bit off in the gray light of an overcast afternoon and the glass coffee table reflected a window that displayed a cloudy sky.

Melissa fell onto a comfy couch, setting her elbows on her thighs and covering her face with both hands. *Is this what it means to be an adult?* she wondered. *Feeling strung out all the time.*

“You're upset about Jena.”

She looked up to find her younger sister standing at the foot of the stairs in green jeans and a black t-shirt. Claire wore her dark hair up in a bun. Dear Lord, she was only ten and she was already starting to look like a teenager. She still had the body of a child, but there were little things.

“How do you know that?” Melissa asked.

Claire folded her arms and marched into the living room with her head down. “I'm not stupid, you know,” she began. “I hear you and Dad when you talk. There's someone who looks like Jena?"

Pressing the heel of one hand to her forehead, Melissa groaned. "Yeah," she said in a strained voice. "It's the same woman Anna fought a few months ago in Tennessee. She's very dangerous."

"How come they look the same?"

"I don't know."

Claire plunked herself down on the white carpet and stretched out her legs. The girl wore a lazy smile as she shook her head. "Do you ever think that maybe if you guys just leave these aliens alone, they'll leave you alone?"

Melissa sat back against the couch cushions, turning her face up to the ceiling. "All right, Claire," she said, rolling her eyes. "Think long and hard and then tell me why that's a bad idea."

"I don't know."

"Where are we?"

"Home?"

Melissa gestured to the window, where she could see the front lawn and the houses across the street under a thick blanket of clouds. Aside from the fact that the architecture was a little different, it might have been any neighbourhood on Earth. She still marveled at that. The similarities... "Be more specific," she said. "Where are we?"

The girl frowned as she looked down at herself, her brow furrowing. "Do you mean Leyria?" she asked. "The planet?"

"The planet," Melissa said. "Which the Overseers specifically terraformed to be a near-perfect copy of Earth. They moved our people across the galaxy and settled us on dozens of worlds. Do you really think they'll just leave us alone?"

"I didn't think of that," Claire said.

Melissa stood up, heaving out a deep breath, and carefully maneuvered around the coffee table. She made her way over to the window. "Well, it's my job to think about that stuff now," she said. "Like Jena did."

"Why would they copy Jena?"

Closing her eyes, Melissa let out a soft hiss. "I don't know," she answered. "They seem to be trying to mess with us. Maybe they think that we wouldn't be willing to fight someone who looks like one of our own."

With spatial awareness, she could perceive her sister sitting on the carpet behind the coffee table. Claire was tense. In fact, something in her posture reminded Melissa of the time her little sister had insisted on watching *The Lady in the Window* only to have some pretty terrible nightmares later.

"It's gonna be all right."

"I know," Claire said petulantly.

Bracing her hands on the windowsill, Melissa hunched over. She shook her head with a sigh. "You know, you could let me be a big sister just once," she said. "It wouldn't kill you."

To her surprise, Claire got up and came toward her. Melissa turned around just in time to let her slam into her with a fierce hug. "You *are* a big sister," Claire said. "You're the best big sister."

"Thank you."

Mere moments later, Jack came out of the kitchen and paced through the hallway between the living room and the staircase. "We'll go over it tomorrow," he said, glancing back over his shoulder.

Harry came out behind him with arms folded, frowning and shaking his head. "The pair of you are going to drive me nuts," he said. "You realize that we don't have time for whatever it is you're fighting about."

Jack said nothing.

He just went to the door, pulled it open with a violent twist of the knob and left. Melissa had a sinking feeling that she had missed something important. She absolutely hated it when her loved ones fought.

Harry turned around. “Well?”

Anna emerged from the kitchen with her head down, her cheeks flushed to a faint shade of pink. “Well what?” she snapped. “You can't force emotions to just line up the way you want them to, Harry.”

Her father had his back turned, but Melissa could easily imagine the glare that he directed at Anna. She had been on the receiving end of it a million times. “I'm aware of that,” Harry said. “But you two shift uncomfortably and barely acknowledge each other's presence. I made it a point to let you sort out your own drama, but we have much bigger problems, and I need you two to work together.”

Oh no...

This was one of Harry's cop speeches. Tuck in your shirt, and do your job. He was famous for giving them to officers of the Ottawa PD who failed to live up to his lofty expectations. They usually went hand in hand with one of his glares. Melissa could recall the many times she had received a lecture just like this one; they almost never produced the result Harry was looking for.

To her credit, Anna didn't snap or snarl. She just looked up at Harry with hard blue eyes, and somehow – despite the fact that she was barely five-foot-three – she seemed a giant. “I'll thank you to let me sort out my own personal life, Harry.”

It wasn't cold; it wasn't mean.

It was just a simple statement of fact.

Harry stepped aside.

As soon as he did, Anna rushed down the hallway to the door. She paused there for a moment, taking hold of the knob. “It'll be all right,” she said almost reluctantly. “Jack and I will sort it out...somehow.”

She left without another word.

Harry stood in the hallway with his shoulders slumped, closing his eyes as he let out a deep breath. "Kids," he muttered. "How did I end up with four of them?"

"What happened?" Melissa asked.

"Neither one has been very forthcoming with details," Harry replied. "What makes you think today would be any different? I know pretty much what you know. They were in love, one of them rejected the other..."

Melissa felt her mouth tighten as she looked down at the floor. "Yeah," she said, nodding. "But it's so obvious how they both feel! Someone needs to sit them down and make them sort this out."

Her father squeezed his eyes shut and grunted his agreement. "What do you think I was trying to do?" he exclaimed. "It was stupid of me to think I could change anything. They have to work this out on their own."

"Yeah..."

"So..." Harry said. "Wanna help me make dinner?"

"Sure."

As she walked into the Science Lab, Larani found Dr. Atero standing so that she saw him in profile, frowning at the screen on the wall that displayed schematics of the cloaking technology. With any luck, the man had called her down here because he had found something useful. A countermeasure or a way to duplicate the technology.

The work table along the sidewall was clear, which surprised her. She would have expected Atero to be tinkering with the cloaking devices, but he seemed to be focusing on their design specs instead. "I trust you have those things under lock and key," she said.

"Yes, ma'am."

Larani blew out a breath, then reached up to scrub fingers through her thick black hair. "All right. What do you know?"

she asked. "Do we have anything solid on where these damn things came from?"

Atero faced her, chewing gum quite thoroughly. His eyes were marked by dark circles, and his mop of brown hair looked even more unkempt than usual. Had the man been up all night? "I checked the cloaking device against schematics we received from the Ragnos Confederacy back when we were still exchanging information."

"And?"

"There's no doubt about it," he said. "This is Ragnosian tech."

Hearing that left her feeling tense. Ragnosian tech on this side of the galaxy? That meant *someone* had been using the Class-2 SlipGates. Council had ordered starships to keep a watch on every star system with a Gate in it, but their resources were finite. There were Gates in Dead Space that they couldn't monitor, for instance.

Larani approached the ring of consoles in the middle of the room.

Gripping the edges of one in both hands, she stood with her head hanging. "Do we have any indication of how the Sons of Savard got this technology?" she asked. "Is there any reason to think the Ragnosians are sponsoring them?"

"That's outside my purview."

"Yeah...I suppose it is," Larani muttered. "All right. Let's focus on what we can control. Do you have an effective countermeasure?"

Atero stood with his hands pressed to his sides, his eyes downcast. "Well, as I told you last night," he began. "The cloaking device does nothing to limit EM emissions from the subject it's cloaking. Simple infrared visors will work."

Larani rounded on him.

She narrowed her eyes as she stared him down. "Something doesn't add up here." This strange niggling feeling had been tormenting her ever since she saw the cloaking devices in action. “These cloaks...They're not very useful.”

“Well, it's a matter of perspective.”

Larani shut her eyes tight, then gave her head a shake. “No...” she said, stepping forward. “What would be the point in delivering this technology to Leyrian terrorists if it can be so easily countered?”

Spots of colour appeared on the good doctor's cheeks, and he kept his gaze fixed on the floor. He reached up to clamp a hand onto the back of his neck. “Well, I think maybe they weren't expecting the average person to have IR visors lying around.”

“And Keepers with spatial awareness?”

“Maybe the Ragnosians don't know the limits of Keepers power.”

Larani traced her fingers along the top of each console as she paced a slow circuit around the room. “It's possible,” she said. “But if you're looking for allies, giving them useless tech, won't help.”

“I don't follow-”

She whirled around to face the window and found herself staring at a beautiful city under a cloudy sky. There had been no further attacks on infrastructure since the incident last week; she was beginning to suspect that Sons of Savard had been crippled when her people brought in over two dozen of them.

So, why was Isara affiliated with them?

A clone of Jena...

It occurred to Larani that while they may have some extreme differences in terms of personality, in some ways, Jena and Isara were very much alike. Both natural fighters, both able to dominate a conversation through sheer force of personality. It brought up some uncomfortable questions in terms of the nature vs nurture debate. Jena and Isara shared many of the same skills but used them for different ends.

That being the case, perhaps the best way to determine Isara's motivations was to ask what Jena would have done in her place. It had taken Larani some time to warm up to a junior director with boyish hair and a tendency to throw the rule book out the window, but she had come to respect Jena. The woman could play politics with the best of them.

Larani often wished she could have been there on the day that Jena had stormed into a meeting between Slade's cronies and a dozen Canadian law-enforcement officials. She would have loved to have seen the looks on their faces when Jena defied protocol and simply revealed the existence of Amps.

The move made her look impulsive and reckless, but it had also thrown Slade off balance and ensured that Jena would be in charge of the investigation. Which was the whole point. Jena was the sort of woman who would aim every weapon in her arsenal at one target so that you wouldn't notice when she pointed one tiny pistol at another.

If aiding the Sons of Savard wasn't Isara's true purpose...

"What if the tech was an end unto itself?" Larani whispered.

"Ma'am?"

Larani's eyes flicked back and forth as she went over it in her mind. "What if there was no military objective?" she murmured. "What if getting Ragnosian tech onto Leyria was the goal? And making sure we found it..."

She spun around.

Dr. Atero jumped back in surprise and put a hand over his heart. His face contorted into an ugly snarl that he smothered half a second later. "Sorry," he muttered. "I still don't understand what you're getting at."

"Who else knows about this cloaking tech?"

"I...I haven't spoken to anyone else, but..."

"But what?"

The man's mouth worked silently for several seconds before he touched the tips of his fingers to his forehead. "The logs," he said. "I've been recording them, of course, and I've made them all publicly available in case any of our people encounter this tech in the field. It's standard procedure!"

As if on cue, Larani's multi-tool chirped with an alert. She had programmed it to e-mail her every time Councilor Dusep gave a speech or an interview. She wanted to keep tabs on what that man was up to.

Larani tapped at her multi-tool, opening the link to Dusep's livestream and sending the feed to the screen on the wall. Moments later, she was looking at a small crowd of reporters standing on the steps of the Hall of Council.

Dusep stood behind a podium with his hands gripping the lectern, and his face was grim. "Cloaking technology," he said. "*Ragnosian* cloaking technology used on our planet against our citizens. It's exactly what I've been warning about!"

Larani felt her lips peel away from clenched teeth. She shook her head with a feral growl. "How did he find out about that?" she snapped. "I want a list of everyone who has accessed those logs."

On the screen, Dusep assumed the role of the noble statesman, standing tall and proud with his head held high. "Since the day news broke about the Class-2 SlipGates, Leyrian citizens have been justifiably concerned about the threat posed by hostile powers from across the galaxy."

He ran his gaze over the assembled reporters and practically sneered. "It's no secret that the Ragnos Confederacy holds us in contempt," he went on. "Our many attempts to share information, to build diplomatic ties, were met with hostility. They've stonewalled us at every turn!"

Larani cursed.

As if he could sense her reaction, Dusep offered a small

smile. More likely, it was duping delight. Some people displayed such tells when they knew their manipulations were successful. "Now that it's possible for the Ragnosians to physically come here..."

He left that sentence unfinished, but the implication was enough to send murmurs through the crowd. "I share your concern!" Dusep went on, pouncing on the unrest at the first opportunity. "I have shared your concern from the very beginning! But Council has repeatedly opted to ignore the justifiable fears of their own constituents! And as a result, we have Ragnosian cloaking devices in our cities!"

Of course, he'd do this, Larani growled inside her own head. *When I find whoever told him about the cloaking devices...*

Gripping the sides of the lectern with both hands, Dusep leaned forward with a grin that belonged on a raptor. "It makes me question the leadership among the Keepers!" he thundered. "Yes! We place too much faith in them!"

People muttered angrily in response.

"I hear your frustration!" Dusep shouted. "But consider the simple facts! Grecken Slade, quite possibly the worst terrorist we've seen in four centuries, was able to infiltrate the highest echelons of the Justice Keeper hierarchy.

"It was a team of Justice Keepers who *allowed* Slade to activate the Class-2 Gates, thereby exposing us to the Ragnosian threat. And now...And now! Ragnosian cloaking devices have found their way into *our* capitol!

"This very morning, a conscientious young Justice Keeper informed me that two of these devices were being stored in the Denarian Keeper Office!"

By this point, Dusep's face was so flushed that you might have expected his skin to catch fire. "And if you want proof," he said. "Then I'm happy to offer it."

He drew aside his jacket to reveal one of the cloaking devices clipped to his belt. Then, with a few quick taps, he began to disappear, his body fading away until he was completely invisible.

Gasps filled the air.

Moments later, Dusep returned, his body rippling like water disturbed by a rock until he was solid again. "You see?" he exclaimed. "The Justice Keepers have known of this threat for some time, and did they report it to Council? No! They are untrustworthy!"'

"Kill newsfeed!" Larani barked.

As soon as she spoke, Atero jumped backward and raised a hand to his temple. His face was bone-white. "I...I...I..." The man gasped. "I don't know how he could have gotten his hands on that."

"Check the safe you used to store the two devices."

The man hopped, then quickly shuffled around and practically tripped over his feet as he made his way to the locked cupboard in the corner. He dropped to one knee in front of it and began typing in his code.

Moments later, the door snapped open with a *ca-thunk.* Atero knelt there with his back turned, slowly shaking his head. "Only one," he whispered. "They...they...they...Um. They took one of the devices and gave it to-"

"Yes, Doctor," Larani said. "That much is obvious."

"I...I...I didn't..."

"I know...If you'll excuse me, Doctor. I have matters to attend to."

Ten minutes after she left the Science Lab, the double doors to her office slid apart, and Cassiara Seyrus came striding through. The woman wore a skirt and dark pink blouse along with a pair of high heels, and she moved with a grace only a Keeper could manage. "You wanted to see me, ma'am?"

Sitting back in her chair, Larani closed her eyes and took a deep breath. "I did," she said. "I trust you've seen the latest press conference."

"I have."

Larani stood, smoothing her shirt with one hand, and stepped up to her desk with her head down. "Then you know that someone took one of the cloaking devices without authorization," she said. "I want to know who."

Cassiara stared vacantly into the distance for a moment, and then she nodded once in confirmation. "Yes, ma'am," she said, turning to go. "Jack and I will start looking into it immediately."

"Just you, Agent Seyrus."

Cassi froze in mid-step. "Ma'am?"

"Tell Hunter I want him to interrogate Isara," Larani replied. "I want to know everything that woman knows."

"Yes, ma'am."

When Cassi was gone, Larani dropped into her chair and tried her best to calm her frayed nerves. The pieces were there in her mind, but she didn't like the image they were forming when she put them together. Isara had gone out of her way to smuggle foreign weapons onto Leyrian soil. Now Dusep had them, and true to form, he was using them to stir up fear and controversy.

When they had first discovered the SuperGates, Anna had said that it was only a matter of time before Leyria and Ragnos found themselves in conflict. And who knew what the Antaurans would do with this third player on the map?

So, the Overseers had used Slade to open massive SlipGates that could transport starships across the galaxy, and now one of their agents was stirring up fear and mistrust between two of the galaxy's major powers. It didn't take a genius to see what the end goal was. She just prayed she could stop it before it was too late.

Isara relaxed as she stretched out on the soft bed in her cell. Comfortable sleeping arrangements were a luxury she sometimes had to do without. Serving the Inzari was not always a pleasant experience, but it was necessary. One did not deny a god. She smiled to herself as she considered how well her latest gambit was unfolding.

Everything was proceeding according to plan.

20

"I think you had better tell me everything, Larani."

Cradling a warm cup of tea in two hands, Larani felt steam waft up to wash over her face. She breathed deeply, inhaling the scent of mint. "For starters, Dusep was less than honest in his press conference."

With the onset of early evening, Sarona Vason's office was lit by small lamps on small tables in two corners. Lamps that cast warm golden light on the many bookshelves along the white walls. The furniture here was archaic – except for the desk, of course – but this office had existed for centuries, and the traditionalists worked to ensure that it remained in its current form.

The Prime Council sat patiently in a large blue chair, folding her hands in her lap and smiling as she waited for Larani to finish her thought. Seeing the woman in simple casual clothing always felt disorienting, but of course, Sarona would only wear her robes when Council was in session.

"We've known about the cloaking devices for less than twenty-four hours," Larani explained. "There was no conspiracy to keep them hidden from you."

With a grunt, Sarona stood up. Her face twisted in a wince. "Old bones," she said. "I believe that you had no intention to hide anything, but you can see how this looks."

Lifting the cup to her lips, Larani closed her eyes and slurped as she took a sip. "I suppose it would be too much to hope that people should care more about how things *are*," she said. "And less for how things look."

Sarona turned her back and shuffled over to the window, pausing there with her hands upon the windowsill. "That is exactly what I would expect to hear from a Keeper," she said. "You *must* know most people don't think in those terms."

Larani did know it; in fact, she knew it all too well. Most people were pretty decent on the inside, but they panicked easily. You had to be made of sterner stuff if you wanted to Bond a Nassai. "And if I told you that Dusep is almost certainly playing into Isara's hand?" she asked. "Tension between Leyria and Ragnos seems to be the point here."

"And how did you reach that conclusion?"

"Isara served Slade."

The Prime Council stiffened at that, but she kept her back turned and stared through the window pane. "Keepers and their games," she grumbled. "I begin to wonder if maybe Dusep has a point."

"Slade was never a Keeper."

"Can you be sure of that?" At last, Sarona turned around, and her face was haggard. "I've read your reports about corrupted symbionts and plots to serve the Overseers. How do you know the man wasn't just like the rest of you?"

Larani couldn't be sure, and that was a big part of what bothered her. There might have been a time when Grecken Slade was an ideal Keeper. When exactly did he fall? Did he start his career with good intentions, or was he corrupt to the bone from the very beginning? Not knowing bothered her.

Larani set her cup on a nearby table.

She stood up and paced across the room, reviewing everything she had learned. "The exact circumstances of Slade's betrayal are tangential," she said. "We know that Slade was responsible for opening the Class-2 SlipGates."

"Indeed."

"Slade made it possible for the Ragnos Confederacy to access our little corner of the galaxy," Larani went on. "And now, one of Slade's minions is taking actions that will almost certainly increase tensions between our two worlds. It's not hard to see what the end goal is."

Leaning against the windowsill with her arms crossed, Sarona frowned and shook her head. "Justice Keepers," she whispered. "The lot of you are so very good at spinning a yarn, you might have found prestigious careers in film-making."

"So, you *don't* believe Slade's people are trying to start a war?"

"That is *one* potential motivation for their actions," Sarona answered. "But it could just as easily be a case of Isara wanting to destabilize our economy and using the Sons of Savard to do it. Perhaps the cloaking devices were only a means to that end."

Larani snapped her mouth shut before she succumbed to the urge to say something entirely inappropriate. Spending so much time with young Hunter had earned her some bad habits, it seemed. The cloaking devices were next to useless against a Justice Keeper; Isara would know as much, and since people without a symbiont could overcome them with a simple pair of IR goggles, it wasn't likely that she would believe the devices could offer much of an edge to a rag-tag band of terrorists.

But they would stir up all kinds of controversy.

"I will make a public apology, of course," Larani said. "Maybe that will be enough to mitigate some of the damage Dusep has done."

"It's a start."

The last thing Jack wanted to do was spend an hour in an interrogation room with a woman who wore the face of someone he once loved. Someone he still loved. Even after learning that Isara was a doppelganger, he still couldn't help but see Jena each and every time he thought of her.

But Larani wanted to get to the heart of what this woman knew, and that meant he was stuck trying to ferret out the goods. One downside to developing a reputation for being able to smell a lie from half a mile away: you were the first person people went to when they wanted someone questioned.

Jack walked through the gray-walled hallway in black pants and his brown jacket, heaving out a deep breath. "Think of it as a challenge," he muttered to himself. "Besides, you need a new story to tell at next week's Masochists Anonymous."

As he neared the door to Isara's cell, he noticed Anna standing there with her back turned, rocking on the balls of her feet. His one-time best friend wore gray pants and a black blouse, and she kept her hair up in a ponytail. The sight of her made his heart skip a beat and left him feeling uneasy.

Running into her at Harry's place had already left him feeling more than a little off balance, and Harry's insistence that they "sort out their issues" didn't help matters. Jack was afraid that Anna would think he'd put Harry up to it. Well... maybe not. You only had to spend a few days with the grizzled old cop to know that he expected everyone to be on their best behaviour all the time.

Anna turned around.

Jack grinned, then shook his head. "Wasn't expecting to find you here," he said, stopping right in front of her. "Do you want first crack at her? Or should we try to do this together?"

Anna looked up at him, blinking slowly as if she had never seen him before. "Isara was involved with the Sons of Savard," she said. "Jon wants to know everything that she knows; so, here I am."

"Like old times then."

"Let's just get this done, okay?"

Biting his lower lip, Jack felt his face burn, but he nodded to her just the same. "All right," he said. "Should be all kinds of fun."

Inside the cell, they found Isara facing the door with arms folded, lost in the kind of intense focus you would expect from one of those British guards who weren't supposed to move or speak. Because, you know, she wasn't creepy enough already. Looking at her and seeing Jena's face...It didn't matter what Melissa said. It was still unnerving.

Jack stepped in first, clasping hands together behind his back and striding toward her with his head down. "Good to see you're settling in," he began. "Hope you like the place; you're gonna be seeing a lot more just like it."

Isara didn't react.

Pressing his lips into a thin frown, Jack studied her for a long moment. "So, that's the way you wanna play it, huh?" he asked. "You refuse to eat, you refuse to answer any questions."

"She refuses to eat?" Anna broke in.

His partner – for lack of a better term – stepped forward with her scowl that would shatter mirrors. "I suppose that solves one problem," Anna said. "I figure she'll last a few weeks, tops, and then we get our cell back."

I guess that makes me the good cop, Jack noted. His talent for snark urged him to make a joke about how much he liked it when Anna was the bad cop, but that would *not* go over well under the current circumstances. Damn it! The world was tilted off its axis when Anna wasn't in his life.

Isara said nothing.

Still as a statue, she watched the wall with such intensity

you might have thought someone had scrawled a best-seller on white duroplastic. What the hell was that woman thinking? She might not be Jena, but she had Jena's talent for controlling a room. Were they sisters? Summer was tense. "This isn't working," he said. "So how about-"

"When did you two turn against each other?"

"Excuse me?"

The victorious grin on Isara's face hit him like a knife to the gut. "Not so long ago, you two were professing your undying loyalty to each other," she said. "Now it's all icy stares and awkward silences. What happened?"

"That's not your business."

"Oh, if Slade could see this."

"Is Slade alive?"

Turning her back on both of them, Isara faced the wall. "Mmm...Wouldn't you like to know?" she mocked. "Come on, Jack; I trained you better than this. So, use that keen mind of yours and put the pieces together."

Jack strode toward her, shaking his head in disgust. "It's not gonna work," he said, stopping before he got within arm's reach. "I know that you're not Jena. Melissa carries Jena's symbiont."

Isara stiffened at that.

So, she didn't know. Which only served to confirm the fact that this woman as *not* the person who had mentored him over the past year. The relief he felt at that was beyond description. Now, they just had to figure out why someone else was walking around with Jena's face.

Anna stepped forward and looked the other woman up and down. "The question we should be asking is 'Who are you?' " she said. "More importantly, why would Slade need to clone Jena?"

Isara's cruel laughter was so sudden, so vicious, Jack nearly jumped backward in response. Jesus, he really *was* afraid of this woman. "Foolish children," Isara said. "You still haven't figured it out."

"Figured *what* out?"

When Isara turned and looked over her shoulder, her eyes cut like daggers. "Jena was the clone!" she spat. "One of my worst decisions. I never imagined that she would give me such trouble when I squeezed her through my loins."

"You're her mother?"

"Her biological mother."

Grabbing one of the plastic chairs, Isara turned it around and sat down backwards, hugging the thing as she spoke. "Slade was operating in Ragnosian Space back then," she said. "So, I came here.

"I was the only one of his lieutenants who could even come close to challenging him, but even I wasn't a match for his power. But what if there were two of me? Together, we could throw him down and take his place.

"I had a geneticist engineer a clone and impregnate me with the embryo. He offered to accelerate the clone's growth so that Jena would be an adult in a matter of months. But such accelerated growth rates tend to produce an unstable cellular structure. No, I wanted a daughter, and for a brief time, I had one.

"My intention was to raise her as my own, teach her everything I knew. I hid on the Fringe, on the colony worlds that had largely gone unnoticed by the major powers in this part of the galaxy. But Slade began to suspect, and when he learned of what I'd done, he ordered me to destroy the child."

Isara winced, tears streaming over her cheeks in glistening trails. God in Heaven, was she actually being sincere? "I arranged for Jena to find a home with two engineers who worked on orbital space stations," she whispered. "They never told her of her true parentage; she grew up thinking she was theirs."

Jack sat on the edge of the wooden table with his hands on his knees, smiling into his own lap. "Yeah, I get it," he said. "You and your ego decided that it was time to take your relationship to the next level; so, you brought home a little bundle of joy, and then you gave her up because...parenting fail!"

"Slade would have killed her."

"Well, you know what they say," Jack muttered. "All's fair in narcissism and war."

Next to him, Anna still had her arms crossed, and her gaze was locked on the other woman. "Here's what I don't understand," she said. "Why are you telling us all this? Why give us the answers?"

Good question.

It occurred to Jack that this could all be lies, but...Why? The most Isara could gain from this little performance was to keep them distracted for a day or two while they tried to find some record of Jena's adoption. Usually, when someone lied, they did for a reason. Isara seemed to just be sharing like this was some kind of therapy session.

All you needed was one glance at Isara to see that she was strung out. The woman was slumped over with her arms wrapped around the back of the chair, exhaustion plain on her face. "Because you took her from me," she said. "You made her small. You made her one of you."

"Jena saved lives."

"Meaningless lives."

Jack grimaced, touching two fingers to his forehead. "Don't you see what's going on here, An?" he asked. "She's about to launch into one of those patented 'I am evil, hear me roar,' speeches."

Anna moved forward until she was right in front of the

other woman. "Let's stick to the basics," she said. "I want to know how you mimicked Jena's biometric ID."

"They have the same DNA," Jack said.

His former best friend shot a glance in his direction, and the ferocity in Anna's stare made him flinch. "But not the same fingerprints," she snapped. "Those are shaped by life experiences, not DNA."

That was a good point. Sometimes Anna had a better head for the logistics of *how* something might work. How one might bypass a security system, for instance.

Isara lifted both hands, palms out, and wiggled her fingers playfully. "Actually, we *do* have the same fingerprints," she said. "Which shouldn't surprise you. The Inzari sculpt flesh to serve their will, remember?"

"So, they gave you Jena's fingerprints?"

"Oh, it went well beyond that," Isara replied with disdain in her voice. "When Jena was twenty-three, she lost a tooth in a fight with a particularly nasty arms dealer. She had it replaced shortly afterward."

Isara narrowed her eyes and shook her head slowly. "The Inzari pulled my tooth out and replaced it with one of your primitive synthetics." She stood up and spread her arms wide, bowing to them. "These clothes, this hair, the way I carry myself. They made me a perfect match for her in every way."

Jack shivered.

"Ironic, isn't it?" Isara went on. "I created a copy of myself, and as penance, they turned me into a copy of the copy. It was Slade's idea. He enjoyed the...symmetry."

"Okay, Izzy," Jack said. "That'll be enough for now."

He had already learned more than he would have liked to, and he could see that Anna was getting flustered as well. Better to end this now before they lost control of the situation. By the look on her face, he could see that Isara had guessed his intentions.

And that made him very uneasy.

Anna sat on Jack's desk with one leg crossed over the other, her hands folded on her knee. She looked down into her lap and tried to calm herself. "So, what do you think? Is there any chance she's telling the truth?"

Jack was leaning against the wall with his arms folded, smiling up at the ceiling. "Well, that's the thing about subjects like her," he muttered. "Nuggets of truth are buried under layer after layer of lies. Lady makes Elim Garak look honest."

"Who?"

"Deep Space Nine."

"Oh."

The reference brought up painful memories. Sitting on Jack's couch and watching *Star Trek* with a bowl of popcorn. Noticing the way he smiled at her when he thought she wasn't looking. They should have been happy memories, but grief had a way of twisting everything.

Setting her elbow on her knee, Anna rested her chin on the knuckles of her fist. "I was about to lose it in there," she mumbled. "I don't know what I would have said if you didn't pull me out when you did."

When she let her hand fall, Jack was still standing by the wall, but he was blushing and looking down at himself. "Don't be so hard on yourself," he said. "I lost it in there a few times as well."

Anna hopped off the desk, pressing a hand to her stomach, and grunted as she made her way to the door. "Well...I'm sure you can take it from here," she said. "I need to write out a report for Director Andalon."

"Wait."

She turned.

Jack came toward her slowly. "I could really use a fresh

perspective," he said. "Someone to bounce ideas off of, and you were always really good with that."

Anna shut her eyes tight, drawing in a deep breath. "I'm sure you'll be fine," she said, turning away from him. "You're the brainstorming king, Jack. I think you can figure out Isara's evil plan."

In her mind's eye, he was a silhouette that stared over his left shoulder at the wall. "Maybe that's true," he countered. "But you were the practical one, the one who could synthesize all those ideas into a cohesive picture. I *need* you, An."

"No, you don't."

"Yeah, I do!"

Anna crossed her arms with a heavy sigh, hunching up her shoulders in some lame attempt to make herself as small as possible. "I haven't been much use to anyone lately, Jack," she mumbled. "So wrapped up in myself."

"You're strong, you're capable," Jack said. "I wish I understood what it is that's got you so down, but whatever it is, I know you'll face it with your usual brand of courage and practical wisdom."

Tears welled up when she heard those words. It was *so* sweet...and it made her feel so very, very guilty inside. The emotion was there in an intense flash and smothered by anger before she could really analyze it. *Why* she felt so guilty was secondary. She could deal with that later.

Anna whirled around to face him.

"Will you stop it?" she shouted. "In case you haven't realized, Jack, I'm trying to make a polite exit here. I don't need you to put me back together or...find the words that will take all the pain away!"

He stared at her with a gaping mouth, then shook his head to clear his thoughts. "I didn't mean to..." The words came out so fast they were almost incoherent. "I know that you can sort out your own problems; that's what I was-"

"Then let me sort out my own problems!"

Jack raised both hands defensively and backed away from her as if he thought she might pounce and go for the throat. "Anna, I'm not trying to solve your problems," he said. "But I've always been there for you in the past, and it seemed like the right-"

"The *past*, Jack," she said. "Times change."

Why was she doing this? Bleakness take her, she was insulting someone who was just trying to love her and that... infuriated her. It was a rush of anger that came on before she could really analyze it. She had a glimpse of it, of a grounded logical explanation for her fury, but it vanished before she could put it into words.

Seth was panicking in the back of her mind. The Nassai clearly didn't want her to go down this path, but it was her life, damn it! Sure, okay, Jack was only trying to love her, but she didn't ask for his love. She didn't *want* him to love her.

Because she didn't deserve it.

After what she had done, the pain she had caused, the look in Bradley's eyes when she told him that she didn't love him. Her ex-boyfriend had known all along. He had seen what was going on between her and Jack. And she had let it continue!

She had carried on an emotional affair with her best friend for months without even realizing what she was doing, and now she was supposed to what...Jump into Jack's arms and let him kiss the pain away?

Maybe she deserved a little pain.

Any relationship she might have with Jack was going to be tainted by the memory of what she had done, and...No! If there was ever a time for the two of them, it certainly wasn't now.

First Harry pesters her to sort this shit out, and then Jack starts in with his "Help me solve this case" routine. She needed out.

"Leave me be," she said.

Before he could open his mouth, she was whirling around and walking out the door. Was her impulsiveness getting the better of her? Maybe. At some point, she would have to deal with the fallout from this argument. But right now…

Right now, she just needed out.

21

Sparring was *not* one of Melissa's favourite activities. Some Keepers developed a craving for the thrill of besting an opponent, but she was not one of them. However, even a Justice Keeper had to develop muscle memory, and this was really the only way to do that. The Nassai could help accelerate the process – and Ilia seemed to be doing just that – but they could not simply "beam" knowledge into your mind.

Most matches were tame compared to the pounding she had taken from Isara; you might endure the odd punch to the face, but nothing too serious. That didn't mean she was eager to participate.

The matches were held in the basement of the Justice Keeper HQ, in a large box-like gym with a ring in the middle and young people in sweat pants who milled about, waiting for their turn. She would be fighting people a little older than herself. Because she carried a symbiont, she was prohibited from fighting cadets who had not yet Bonded a Nassai.

That meant she was fighting young agents.

Jack might have been one of her opponents if not for the fact that his experiences had forced him to learn at an accelerated rate. She was nervous. And she desperately hoped that no one would notice.

It was your standard square-shaped arena with ropes along each side. Right now, Tavis Arveri was bouncing on the balls of his feet in the middle of the ring. Tall and fit, with skin as dark as her father's, the man was gorgeous.

Melissa wore gray sweat pants and a white tank-top as she stood in the corner with hands folded over her stomach. Her eyes were glued to the floor. *Please, don't call me,* she thought at the referee.

Operative Sarl Venson was leading this session. A tall and pale man with blonde hair that he wore in spikes, he paced a line in front of the ring. "First match," he shouted. "Akiri Tenabra and Tavis Arveri."

A young woman climbed into the ring with Tavis.

Melissa shut her eyes, breathing deeply, trying to remain calm. *It's just a sparring session,* she reminded. *Nothing to get upset about. You've been through like twenty of these by now.*

Of course, she had lost most of them.

Melissa had a bad habit of hesitating when it came time to throw a punch. Deep down, she wished she had natural instincts for this like Jack or Anna. She had become a Keeper to help people, but...

Ilia wanted her attention.

It was a strange feeling to be summoned by her symbiont, but the Nassai was quite content to let her live her life unless she had something important to share. *Here?* Melissa thought. *In front of everyone?*

The emotional pressure became more insistent; so she calmed herself and put her mind into a relaxed state. Luckily, she could manage this without very much effort. Some Keepers had trouble communing with their Nassai.

The world slipped away, and Melissa was floating in a void full of stars, descending slowly to a city street below. An Earth street at night; she recognized the architecture of the houses. In fact, she knew this street well.

It was the street she had grown up on.

Melissa landed on the front lawn of her father's old back-split house with its bright yellow porch light. It was a warm summer night, and she could feel the humidity, the warm air on her skin.

"Hey, kid."

Melissa turned around.

Jena was standing in the grass with hands shoved into the pockets of her blue jeans, looking very much like her old self in a black t-shirt with a bright yellow happy face on it. Her hair was cut short and parted in the middle. "Thought you could use a good talk. So, I tapped you on the shoulder."

"Ilia?"

"Not quite."

Crossing her arms, Melissa backed away from the other woman with her head down. "Jena?" she stammered. "Is it you?"

The other woman smiled, nodding to her. "Yeah," she said, stepping forward. "It's me...For all intents and purposes, anyway. Everything I was exists within Ilia, and now that knowledge is yours."

"You're...a simulation?"

Jena shrugged, then turned on her heel to pace a line in the grass. "That's one way to put it," she said, glancing over her shoulder. That hawk-like gaze...So familiar. Perfect in every detail. "A part of me will always live on inside Ilia. She knew every tiny corner of my mind."

"So, you're a very *accurate* simulation."

"That's a very human way of looking at it," Jena said. "From a Nassai perspective, Jena and Ilia are the same person. Everything that was Jena exists within Ilia, and so it's simply a matter of Ilia expressing herself as Jena would."

Closing her eyes, Melissa sucked in a deep breath and nodded. "I get it," she said. "So, what did you want to talk about?"

"You're nervous."

"Well...Yeah."

Jena's grin was infectious as she stared down at the grass. The woman reached up to press a hand to the top of her head. "Think about what I just told you, kid," she muttered. "Ilia knows everything I know...which means you know it too."

"But...Nassai can't just beam knowledge into your mind."

"No, they can't," Jena said. "But they can accelerate the rate at which your brain forms neural pathways, and Ilia has been structuring yours to match mine."

"What...What are you saying?"

Tilting her head to one side, Jena smiled like a mother who had just watched her little girl win a talent show. "Get ready to pull a Neo," she sad. "Because, sweetie...You know Kung Fu."

"Oh."

"Now, it's time to use it."

The dream world seemed to fuzz, colours and objects blurring together until they were gone, and Melissa felt herself being pulled back into the moment. The voices of the other Keepers chatting, the cheers as the match went on.

She opened her eyes.

A small crowd stood between her and the ring, but she was tall enough to see Akiri jump and perform a spin kick that took Tavis across the cheek. The man dropped to one knee, rubbing his smarting face.

Sarl Venson stood on the steps that led up to the ring with his arms spread wide. "It is over!" he shouted, nodding. "Both of you grab some water and recuperate. You're done for the day!"

People started clapping.

"Next match," Venson said, scanning the crowd for a victim.

"Reiko Corthali and Melissa Carlson."

Damn it.

Melissa hung her head, then wiped sweat off her brow with one hand. *You can do this*, she thought, making her way through the crowd. *Jena just told you that Ilia found a way to impart some of her knowledge.*

As she ascended the steps, Sarl Venson stepped aside and offered a wolfish grin. "Good luck," he said. "You're gonna need it."

Melissa climbed over the ropes with only a little awkwardness and moved into the middle of the ring like a prisoner on his way to an execution. People were chattering all around her; ignoring them was difficult.

On the opposite side of the ring, Reiko Corthali pulled himself over the ropes and landed nimbly on his feet. The man was tall and slim with Asian features and short hair that he wore in spikes. Melissa knew that "Asian" was the wrong word to use, but she was used to thinking in those terms.

Reiko clapped his hands and then moved into the middle of the ring, standing in front of her with his feet apart. "Don't worry," he said. "I'll go easy on you."

Melissa held his gaze for a moment, then squinted. "Don't hold my account," she said. "I'm not going to learn a damn thing if you don't push me to my limits."

"All right."

Melissa backed away from him, adopting the proper defensive stance. Her stomach was churning, her face drenched in sweat. And then suddenly...she was calm. Somehow, this didn't seem like such a big deal.

"Begin!" Venson shouted.

Reiko moved forward like a man dancing on a cloud, and despite herself, Melissa backed away. Something in the way he moved his feet felt significant. *He's going to lead with his right hand,* she noted, allowing him to close the distance.

Reiko threw a punch.

Melissa ducked, allowing his fist to pass right over her. She slipped past him and then counted. One breath...two breaths. She jumped and kicked out behind herself.

Reiko spun around just in time to take a sneaker to the face, a hit that landed with enough force to make his head jerk backward. The man stumbled away until his body hit the ropes at the side of the ring.

When Melissa landed, she turned to find him down on all fours, shaking his head to get his bearings. Reiko was on his feet again in a heartbeat, coming toward her with that look in his eyes, the one that said he wanted to prove a point.

Melissa backed away with her fists up in a guarded stance, sweat prickling on her face. The fear in her belly was too much to ignore. *Stop being so timid,* the quiet voice whispered. *You know what to do.*

Reiko closed in on her.

He threw another punch.

Melissa ducked, evading this blow as cleanly as she did the last one. She threw a pair of jabs into his belly, forcing him to back up, then rose to deliver a devastating right cross to the nose.

Reiko stumbled.

Melissa jumped and snap-kicked, sending her foot into the man's chest. The raw power of it sent her opponent stumbling backward again. Reiko hit the ropes and then fell face-down on the floor.

People cheered.

"This match is over!" Venson cried out.

As she stood in the middle of the ring with her arms hanging limp, Melissa frowned down at herself. The sweat on her brow tingled. "I'm sorry," she mumbled, though no one heard a word of it.

Venson was standing on the steps, facing the crowd and

gesturing for the next two combatants. "Rael Tarvo and Max Jefferson!" he called out. "You two are next, and I do not want to see a repeat of last week. Do I make-"

"Wait?"

That was Akiri's voice.

Melissa stepped forward, moving close enough to see the tiny woman shove her way through the crowd to stand on the bottom step. Akiri was at most five-foot-three, short and slim with pale skin and a bob of brown hair. "I want a crack at her," she said. "She's gotten pretty good."

Venson kept his back turned as he stood on the top step with arms crossed, shaking his head. "You've both already been in the ring," he said. "I'm not willing to put two of my pupils in the medical centre."

Planting fists on her hips, Akiri craned her neck to stare up at him. "Come on!" she pleaded. "I'm fine, and Melissa didn't take a single hit."

"Melissa?" Venson asked.

"I'd rather not."

"There's your answer."

Akiri wasn't satisfied, however. The woman leaped with a surge of Bent Gravity, tucking her knees into her chest and flipping through the air. She went over Melissa's head and landed in the middle of the ring.

Melissa spun to face her.

Akiri turned partway around, glancing over her shoulder with strands of brown hair falling over her face. "You're not scared, are you?" she asked, raising one eyebrow. "This is only a sparring match."

Crossing her arms, Melissa strode toward the other woman with her head down. "I don't want to fight you," she said. "I do this because it's necessary to hone my skills, but I don't *enjoy* fighting, even when it's practice."

Tilting her head back, Akiri blinked at her. "Well," she

began, "then why don't you 'hone your skills' against someone who will give you a challenge?"

"Fine."

Without warning, Melissa bent her knees and leaped. She somersaulted over the other woman's head, then dropped to the mat a few paces away. "You really want to do this? We'll do this."

She spun around.

Sarl Venson was standing on the top step with one hand clutching the top rope, shaking his head. "We're gonna have words about this, Akiri," he said. "But if you insist on going through with this, let's get it over with."

"Trust me," Akiri said as she moved forward to put herself within arm's reach of Melissa. "This will be over soon enough."

Akiri was much shorter than her, and she bounced from one foot to the other like a rabbit ready to flee from some hungry wolf. This woman was cagey; Melissa could tell. Something in the way she moved suggested speed and evasiveness.

"Begin!"

Akiri turned her body for a high roundhouse kick.

Melissa leaned back in time to see the sole of a training shoe pass right in front of her nose. The other woman brought her leg down and spun for a back-kick.

Melissa doubled over, slapping Akiri's ankle with both hands to deflect the blow. Thrown off balance, the other woman stumbled with her back turned and tried to regain her equilibrium. *Now!*

Melissa ran in, slipping one arm around Akiri's throat, holding her in a choke-hold. *Oh, no, no, no! That was a mistake!* Panic welled up inside her. *She's a Justice Keeper, remember? Different rules!*

Akiri jumped, throwing herself backward and taking Melissa with her. They both fell to the floor with Melissa's body hitting the mat first and providing a nice cushion for the other woman. The wind fled her lungs.

In an instant, Akiri rolled off her and started getting to her feet. *Have to move fast,* the voice whispered. Without thinking, Melissa rolled away from her opponent to put a little space between them.

She got to her feet with a grunt and raised her fists into the proper stance. The fear in her stomach was noticeably absent. Why was that?

Wiping her mouth with the back of one hand, Akiri winced and let out a groan. "All right," she said, striding forward. "I really wasn't expecting that. Have to give you some credit for surprising me."

Watch her feet, the voice warned. *Get ready, she's getting close.*

Akiri threw a quick right-hook.

Crouching down, Melissa reached up to clamp both hands onto the other woman's wrist. She gave a twist and forced Akiri to double over with her arm extended. *You know what to do.*

Then she rose, bracing one hand upon Akiri's shoulder while leaving the other on her wrist. In this position, it was easy to turn and send her opponent stumbling head-first toward the ropes at the edge of the ring.

Akiri staggered like a drunken sorority girl, barely able to slow herself before she hit the ropes and bounced off. The woman was dazed! Now was the perfect opportunity to move in and finish this fight.

Melissa spun on her.

She charged across the ring, then jumped and curled her legs as she flew gracefully through the air. *A swift kick to the face should do it,* she thought. *Just wait for her to turn around and then-*

Akiri blurred into a streak of colour, solidifying once again just a few feet to the left. Time bubbles! They ought to be illegal. Melissa landed with a loud *thump* and spun to face her opponent.

A fist hit her right between the eyes, blurring her vision for a moment. Another fist struck her chest with enough force to drive the wind from her lungs. She was backing off, trying to get her bearings. *Come on,* the voice whispered. *You know how to handle this! You've done it a million times.*

Akiri came at her.

Melissa jumped, turning belly-up in midair. Her feet came up to strike Akiri's chin, and then Melissa flipped upside-down, pressing her hands to the mat. She was upright again in an instant.

Melissa charged in.

She punched the other woman's chest with one fist, then followed that with a quick jab to the nose. Akiri stumbled, blood leaking from her nostrils. Time to end this.

Melissa spun and back-kicked, her foot slamming into Akiri's chest with strength only a Keeper could manage. The other woman was thrown backward, knocked onto her ass ten feet away.

Groaning, Akiri tried to sit up and then flopped back down onto her back. She just stretched out there, blinking tears out of her eyes. "Bleakness, Melissa," she said. "How did you learn to fight like that?"

Venson was on the far side of the ring with the top rope gripped in both hands, watching her with skepticism on his face. "Where indeed," he said. "You two are both done for the day; go get changed."

Melissa quickly made her way to the change room, hoping that no one wanted to talk about her unexpected victory. That look on Venson's face...Did he suspect that her Nassai was accelerating the rate at which she learned? That could be dangerous. There was a not entirely insignificant chance of brain damage. It didn't matter. This was her only option. Sooner or later, she was going to have to face Isara again.

And when that happened, she would be ready.

22

This gray-walled corridor in the detention centre went on for what seemed like forever with photographs on the walls depicting scenes of nature. This close to the Detention Centre, there were very few windows; so Ben figured that the designers tried to compensate for that by hanging pictures of waterfalls and gardens. Prisoners had windows, yes, but those were made of glass strong enough to stop bullets.

Ben walked along with his arms swinging, smiling in an attempt to look casual. "It can be done then?" he asked his companion. "You're sure?"

In a blue skirt and a turquoise t-shirt, Keli moved through the hallway with her hair done up in a bun. "I can handle it," she muttered in a voice so soft it was barely audible. "In case you've forgotten, I've overpowered Keepers before."

"Don't remind me," Ben said, shaking his head. "If you can manage it, try to be subtle. I'd prefer it if she didn't know you've read her mind."

"That will be difficult with a two-soul."

"I know."

"Just make sure you do your part."

Ben shoved his hands into the pouch of his sweater and hung his head as they made this final leg of the journey. "I know my part," he whispered. "Bleakness take it all, I am ready to betray my friends *again*."

The corridor ended in a set of metal doors that were gleaming under the fluorescent lights. A biometric scanner on the wall would be their first obstacle, but with any luck, he wouldn't have to hack that. Hopefully, he would convince one of the guards to simply *let* him in.

The weakest part of any security system was always the human factor. Computers would do as they were instructed without variation, and almost all of them had protocols that would make it impossible for external attacks to do very much damage. If you really wanted to fuck with a system, you had to con some poor dupe into opening the wrong file and letting a script run on his machine.

It was the same everywhere.

Exploit humans; with proper persuasion, you could talk them into doing just about anything. Ben touched the door chime just below the scanner. Moments later, a woman's voice came through the speaker. "Yes?"

Closing his eyes, Ben took a deep breath. "My name is Tanaben Loranai," he said. "I'm a consultant with the Director Andalon's team, and I've been ordered to interview one of the prisoners."

"Ordered by whom?"

"Larani Tal."

Moments later, the doors slid apart, and he was looking at a cramped room with a desk next to a door along the back wall. A blonde woman sat there, reading a report on her monitor. "Who are you again?" she asked.

"Tanaben Loranai."

"And Larani Tal sent you down here?"

Ben grinned, bowing his head to her. "Yeah, that's right," he said, approaching the desk. "She's had me interview Calissa Narin at least half a dozen times. She wants me to take a crack at the new prisoner."

When the blonde woman looked up, her green eyes were like lasers that threatened to scorch the flesh off his body. "The new prisoner," she said, arching an eyebrow. "You mean the one who looks like Director Morane."

"Yeah. Her."

The woman leaned back in her chair, folding arms over her chest and shaking her head in disbelief. "You expect me to believe that Larani Tal wants you to interrogate this prisoner," she said. "I didn't receive notification of your orders."

"Well, that's embarrassing," Ben replied. He rolled up his right sleeve and began tapping commands into his multi-tool. "I've got the orders right here; she must have just forgotten to CC you."

In truth, he had forged the e-mail, using several proxies to make it look like it had come from Larani's address. No easy task, that. Official Keeper communications used a verification code that the user never saw. It had taken him close to four months to figure out how that code system worked and to design an algorithm that would duplicate it. He had never used those tools until now.

Ben wasn't sure what it was that compelled him to find a way to break every system or circumvent every rule. He knew it would get him in trouble – Bleakness, it had already gotten him into trouble – but Isara was a gold-mine of information, one of Slade's most trusted lieutenants. She would have intimate knowledge of his plans.

Larani and the others would never do what was necessary to get at that knowledge, but if they wanted to ferret out the crooked Keepers who were still at large, they had to know what Isara knew.

"Everything seems to be in order," the blonde woman said.

Her eyes fell upon Keli, and her expression hardened. "Who's this?"

"An associate," Ben said. "She works for LIS."

His chest tightened when it seemed as though this lady might demand to see Keli's credentials. Keepers weren't entirely immune to telepathy, but as Keli had said earlier, influencing a two-soul without her knowing would be extremely difficult.

"Fine," the woman said. "Go on in."

The door behind her desk opened, leading to yet another gray-walled hallway with doors at even intervals along each wall. His heart was pounding. This was not going to be an easy session.

Isara's cell was the third door on the left. Ben paused for a moment to collect his thoughts before approaching. He hadn't been able to rig up some special workaround to bypass the biometric scanners, but hopefully, that wouldn't matter. Larani had given him access to the prisoners when he had interrogated Calissa, and with any luck, that access had not been revoked.

He pressed his palm to the scanner and let it take a reading. After that, he typed in his code. *Please, please work...* If it didn't, then he'd gone to a lot of trouble – including forging Larani's credentials – for nothing.

The doors slid apart.

The cell was dark with only moonlight coming in through the window. Ben was suddenly apprehensive about the prospect of being in a confined space with a person who could snap his neck within seconds. True, the collar prevented her from using any of her fancier powers, but she was still deadly.

"Lights!" he ordered.

The cell lit up, revealing a small table with chairs, a nightstand and a bed along the wall to his left. Isara was under the covers, clearly unhappy to have been disturbed from what looked like a peaceful slumber.

She sat up, clutching the sheets to her chest, her head hanging as she tried to wake up. The woman's shoulders were bare. Bleakness take her, was she naked under there? "I normally enjoy company," she said in a voice remarkably similar to Jena's. The only real difference was the accent. "But perhaps you could come back at a more civilized hour."

She looked up at him.

Ben stepped forward.

He pressed his lips into a thin line and held the woman's gaze without flinching. "I want to ask you some questions," he said, surprised by the firmness in his voice. "And I figure now is as good a time as any."

Isara's mouth stretched into a yawn, and she shook her head like a dog trying to get water out of its fur. "Oh, very well," she muttered under her breath. "I suppose I could do with a little more entertainment."

She got out of bed and let the covers fall off her body, padding across the room with no concern at all for her lack of clothing.

Ben looked at the wall.

It was a good wall, sturdy and well constructed. It wasn't as though he was bothered by the female form, but this woman was a near-perfect copy of Jena Morane. It felt like he was peeping on his friend and disrespecting her memory at the same time.

Of course, Isara noticed his embarrassment and froze in the act of putting on her pants. "Are we having difficulties, Tanaben?" she asked. "Maybe we should conduct the interview like this?"

Ben scrunched up his face and shook his head. "Just put your damn clothes on," he said, moving deeper into the room. "The sooner you answer my questions, the sooner you can go back to sleep."

Isara was doubled over in a pair of track pants, pulling a t-shirt over her body. Her head popped through the neck-hole, her short hair a mess. "Yes, I would prefer to remain undisturbed."

"Well, then-"

Glancing over her shoulder, Isara studied Keli for a long moment. "I see you plan to violate the privacy of my thoughts," she said. "You're welcome to try."

Bleakness take that woman! She knows!

Gliding forward with her arms swinging, Keli smiled down at herself. "So, you've heard of me," she said. "I guess I shouldn't be surprised that one of Slade's minions is so well informed, but how-"

"I slaughtered half that ship to free you," Isara said. "All so that you could make trouble for me. It's rare for something to upset one of the Inzari, but you've developed a talent for causing trouble. Watching you flee across that beach...quite satisfying."

"You!" Keli shouted.

"You know her?" Ben spluttered.

His companion stepped forward with her fists clenched, her teeth bared like some she-wolf who wanted to rip into the throat of an unsuspecting sheep. "Your doppelganger put me on that ship."

Isara covered her lips with three fingers, her eyes slowly widening. "And I freed you," she said. "Fitting, no?"

"We don't have time for this," Ben growled.

"No, indeed!" Isara exclaimed. "You're much too busy violating my rights. Well, let's be on with it then!"

Ben felt his face heat up, sweat beading on his forehead. "Bleakness take subtlety," he growled at Keli. "Do whatever you have to do. Rip through her defenses. Leave her a vegetable if you have to."

Tanaben gave his permission – and Keli had to admit that

she had no love for the woman who had gleefully watched while one of the Overseers tried to kill her – but she hesitated just the same. Oh, she was willing to do whatever was necessary to survive, but she took no joy in inflicting pain. The men in that base had made her do it to Raynar over and over. She had no love for the boy, but that didn't mean she wanted to harm him.

And now he's dead...

Isara just stood there with her back to the window, half-dressed and smiling like a teenage girl who had caught her best friend in the closet with a boy. "Well, Keli?" she mocked. "Will you take your revenge?"

Keli focused.

She had grown so used to blocking out her telepathic awareness; the new sensations were overwhelming at first. When she threw all of her strength against the other woman's defenses, the symbiont reacted.

It wasn't the focused, deliberate resistance that she had encountered when disabling that poor young Keeper on Station Twelve. A Nassai's mind was orderly, disciplined. This was pure rage, feral thrashing. The effect was the same however, she had to work to get through the cloud of fog that obscured Isara's thoughts.

Isara crossed her arms, smiling down at herself. She shook her head slowly. "Is that really the best you can do, Keli?" she said. "Perhaps Slade was wrong to feel intimidated by your abilities."

"Don't listen to her," Tanaben murmured.

Keli tuned him out; the man's encouragement was worse than useless, and she did not need the distraction. Every time she pressed her attack, the Nassai – or whatever it was – resisted with violent emotions that turned her stomach.

Keli pushed.

The symbiont resisted, but she was able to punch a hole in

the wall of fog, a crack through which light spilled forth. Memories flooded her mind before she could make any sense of them, and then the light was gone.

Keli fell hard on her ass, raising a hand to her temple instinctively. A groan that she couldn't hold back sounded strained even to her own ears. "She's strong...That symbiont she carries won't let me through."

To her surprise, Isara sank to her knees on the floor and reached out to grab Keli's face with both hands. The woman stared into her eyes as if she thought she might find gold within them. "If you want to know about me," Isara said. "All you have to do is ask. I'm an open book."

"Why did the Overseers clone Jena?" Tanaben demanded.

"Ask Hunter," Isara said. "I've already answered this."

"You will tell me-"

The cell door's opened, and Keli sensed a new presence in the room. A presence that she could identify without having to look. Larani Tal had come down here to see what they were up to.

And she wasn't happy.

"You know," Larani said, "when someone presents orders from me that look a little suspect, they usually call me to confirm."

Ben shivered.

"I think we should talk, Mr. Loranai."

23

"I wish I had an answer for you, Larani."

The head of the Justice Keepers stood behind the desk in her office, her face a thundercloud that threatened to spit lightning. It was all Ben could do not to groan. This was the woman who had given him a chance after he'd been convicted of a crime. And he had let her down.

Ben sat in a chair with his hands on his thighs, trying his best to collect himself. "I'm sorry," he mumbled. "But we *need* to know what Isara knows, and I don't see any way to get her to tell us willingly."

Backing away from the desk, Larani scowled and shook her head. "Isara may be a criminal, maybe even a monster," she said in a voice like ice. "But she's still human, and forcibly scanning a prisoner is a gross violation of their rights."

"Oh, come on, Larani!"

"You're on thin ice as it is, Mr. Lorenai."

Before he realized what he was doing, Ben stood up and leaned forward with his hands on the desk. He stared the woman down as best he could. "You can't be serious," he said. "That woman gave up her rights a long time ago."

He didn't want to say it, but Larani understood. The only way to deal with Isara – the only way to be sure – was a bullet to the head.

For a brief few seconds, there was silence while Larani stared blankly ahead with a face made out of granite. "Council may agree with you," she said. "They do not seem to care *what* I do with her, but I am still a Justice Keeper and bound by a code of ethics!"

"I can't believe I'm hearing this!"

Ben turned away from the desk, marching toward the door with his fists clenched. It was all he could do not to scream! Keepers and their codes of honour! Even Jena, the most reasonable of them, still got prickly on certain issues. It was why he'd never wanted a symbiont. Too much rigid thinking.

"What do you expect, Tanaben?"

He looked up to find Keli standing next to the door, yawning and then covering her mouth with one hand. "She's a two-soul," Keli went on. "If I thought Keepers were able to do what was necessary, I wouldn't have fled Station Twelve."

"Ah yes," Larani said. "Ms. Armana."

The head of the Keepers stepped out from behind her desk, sighing with frustration as she made her way across the room. "The x-factor in this equation," she said. "I would think you would understand by now that rules here are a little different from what you're accustomed to?"

"And what, pray tell, am I accustomed to?"

Ben could only see the back of Larani's head, but he knew that withering glare of hers all too well. It had been directed at him more than once. "Telepaths are afforded a great deal of latitude on Antaur," Larani said. "Isn't that so?"

"Maybe it is," Keli answered. "But I didn't spend most of my life on Antaur. The rules to which I am accustomed say that I will perform feats of telepathy when instructed to do so, or my captors will shock me again."

"You won't perform them at all here," Larani rasped. "Not without the expressed consent of anyone involved."

The smile on Keli's face was positively wolfish. She wasn't afraid, not even a little bit. "And how do you propose to enforce that particular restriction?" she asked. "Even if you monitored me, would your people even know if I misused my talent?"

"You certainly did so tonight."

Ben squeezed his eyes shut, a growl rumbling in his throat. "Enough!" he shouted, striding forward until he was right beside Larani. "This gets us nowhere. We still have to decide how to handle Isara."

At his side, Larani stood with her hands clasped behind her back, her head bowed as she fought off a grimace. "Jack has already gotten quite a bit of valuable intelligence from her," she said. "I have faith in my people."

Doubling over with arms crossed, Keli shook her head. "Of course you do!" she said through a fit of laughter. "Leyria's terrifying interrogation techniques. Why, if she doesn't talk, you might send her to bed without her supper."

"That's it. You're both dismissed."

Keli snorted as she turned quickly and made her way to the door with a spring in her step. "Mark my words, Larani," she said on her way out. "One day, these principles you cling to so rigidly are going to be the end of you."

Pressing the heel of his hand to his forehead, Ben sighed as he reluctantly followed the telepath. "I'm sorry," he said softly. "For what it's worth, Larani, I never wanted to let you down."

"Mr. Loranai."

He turned around.

Larani's brows were drawn together as she shook her head. "Your services are no longer needed," she said. "Your access codes have been disabled, and I must ask you to stay out of restricted zones of this building."

"I understand."

Once again, he'd broken the system and paid the price for it. He had come to like having Larani's respect; now, that was gone. This was his life, the life of a man who just couldn't do what was expected of him. Maybe Darrel had been right to end it.

Stirring her drink with a straw – it was a habit her mother had never been able to squelch – Anna watched the ice cubes swirl around in a mixture of vodka and orange juice. Not much vodka; Seth wouldn't appreciate it if she got drunk. She had never really been the sort of woman who regretted her inability to imbibe. The experience of sharing her life with a Nassai was more than worth it, and...Well, she kind of liked being a bad-ass.

But these last few months had seen more than a few nights where Anna had wished that she could drown her problems in alcohol. Jena was dead; her friendship with Jack was in ruins; she had broken not one but *two* men's hearts. And now, on top of everything else, Isara was perverting the memory of everything Jena stood for.

Shelves on the wall behind the bar counter were lit up to display liquor bottles, but the bottles were empty and just for show. This place was automated with drinks prepared out of sight.

All around her, she sensed people – some congregating at the small, square-shaped tables on this side of the room, others moving about on the dance floor. The music was fast and upbeat, and she might have considered joining those people if she didn't feel like pulling a pillow over her head and hiding from the world.

Anna bit her lip, strands of blue hair falling over her cheeks. She grimaced and shook her head. "You're the life of the party, Lenai," she muttered. "Keep this up, and a funeral might just break out in here."

The silhouette of a tall and well-muscled man came up behind her, pausing just a few feet away. By the way he was looking at her, she could tell that he was working up the nerve to say something. “So-”

Tilting her head back, Anna rolled her eyes. “Whatever it is you're about to say,” she began. “I'm not the one you want to try that line on.”

She swiveled around on the bar stool.

The man who stood before her was quite handsome, with dark skin and a jaw that could have been chiseled from granite. His short hair was trimmed close, and he looked gorgeous in a gray, high-collared shirt.

He lifted a glass of something that looked like whiskey to his lips, took a sip and then cleared his throat. “I see,” he replied. “Then I suppose the best thing I can do is just leave you be.”

“Sorry to disappoint you.”

“I'm not disappointed.”

Tilting her head back to stare at him, Anna felt her eyebrows climb slowly upward. “Oh no?” she asked. “That's a little rude, don't you think?”

“Disappointment implies that you failed to live up to my expectations,” the man explained. “I expected to learn that you were unhappy. I could tell that much from fifty paces away. I guess I'm just the sort of man who feels compelled to do something when he sees someone suffering.”

Without another word, he turned to go and lifted his glass to his lips. Maybe it was months on Earth that made her do it – fending off the constant unwanted advances of men who thought they could persuade her with a little more persistence – but she blurted out a response before she knew what she was saying. “That's it?”

Her would-be suitor stopped in his tracks, but he didn't

turn back to her. "You made it clear you aren't looking for company," he said. "I'm not inclined to push."

Once again, she was blushing, and this time, it felt like the sun had come out of the sky to take up residence on the tip of her nose. "I'm sorry," she said. "I'm just used to men who have trouble with the word no."

This time, he did turn around, and he stood there with his mouth open, blinking as if he'd never seen a woman before. "Where do you find these men?" he asked. "Don't the authorities do something if they harass you in that way?"

"It doesn't work that way on Earth."

"You're Terran?" he asked. "You sound like you're from Iyra Province."

The man had a good ear.

Anna stood up with a sigh, crossing her arms and frowning down at herself. "I grew up in Iyra Province," she explained. "But I spent a few months working on Earth, and the culture is very different there."

The man closed his eyes and took a deep breath. "Sounds like one very harrowing experience," he said, nodding to her. "I've read the odd news story about the differences between our culture and Earth's, but..."

"You have *no* idea."

"Well, I'd love to..." The man stiffened and then turned his face away from her. "Never mind. Have a nice evening."

Anna grinned, a touch of heat in her face. She rubbed her forehead with the back of her hand. "You can stay if you want," she said. "I'll tell you all about Earth and its insane politics."

"I'd like that."

"My name is Anna," she offered.

"Devin."

A little while later, she was sitting at one of the square tables with her elbows on its surface, her chin resting on the knuckles of both fists. “It gets worse,” she said, eyebrows rising. “*Then* they tell me my judgment is impaired by volatile female hormones because I don't want to shoot a kid while he's under the influence of Overseer technology.”

Devin lifted the glass to his lips, closed his eyes and drank the last of the whiskey in one big gulp. “You're kidding me,” he said after a moment. “And they were eager to kill this kid because-”

“Because he was black.”

“Like me?”

“What you need to understand,” she began, “is that things are very different on Earth. People like you are trying to end the oppression inflicted on them by people like me.”

“That's...absurd.”

It was, but Anna had come to realize that many people looked at Earth's particular forms of bigotry through a very Leyrian-centric lens. The concept of race didn't exist on her world in the same way it did on Earth, which wasn't to say that Leyrian history wasn't littered with its own forms of bigotry.

Many centuries ago, in the days of wooden sailing ships, the Entareli Empire had extended its reach to much of the known world. Citizens of the Empire were considered enlightened, wise, while outsiders were savages.

Though there was a great deal of variation in skin tone among the Empire's citizens, Entarel was a sub-tropical nation. Many of its citizens were superficially similar to Latinx people on Earth. The sad irony was that, six centuries ago, white people like Anna would have been called savages.

Devin leaned over the table with his arms crossed, shaking his head. “I was under the impression that Earthers had developed an understanding of genetics,” he said. “How can they be so stupid?”

Slouching in her chair with hands folded in her lap, Anna bit her lip as she stared at the ceiling. “Because there's nothing empirical about racism," she said. "It's a belief that exists for one purpose."

"And what purpose is that."

"People at the top of an unfair social hierarchy always need the appearance of a meritocracy to justify their position."

It got her thinking about her own people's history, the many stupid and downright *evil* justifications that Leyrians had used for bigotry throughout their checkered past. And now, they were doing it again, looking at Earthers as savages. Even she was guilty of it to some degree.

The very first generation of Justice Keepers had played a pivotal role in uniting humanity on her world. The Nassai would Bond anyone who would use their power for good, regardless of race or gender or sexual orientation. Any human being willing to use that power to save lives was accepted, and those who would use it selfishly were rejected. It was a very powerful statement, one that – among many other advancements – had helped usher in a new age of tolerance and acceptance.

So, what did it say that Nassai were perfectly willing to Bond people from Earth? She wished other people would consider that question.

Plunking his elbow down on the table, Devin leaned his cheek against the palm of his hand. He smiled at her. "Well, you must be happy to have come home after all that. I know I would be."

Anna shut her eyes, breathing deeply. "Yeah," she said, nodding to him. "But it also made me see failings in our society that I never realized were there. Issues that we would prefer to sweep under the rug."

"Like what?"

"Like this," she said. "Look at the way we talk about Earth. We weren't so different, once upon a time, but we shame them because it's an easy way to hide the shame we feel about our own past."

"I never thought of that."

Grinning as her cheeks grew warm with chagrin, Anna stared into her own lap. "I had to think about it every single day," she said. "Every time I got frustrated, every time I complained. Every time Earthers told me that Leyrians were arrogant."

Devin looked up at her, and his sly smile made her blush. "So," he said, raising one eyebrow. "Is it all right if I ask a personal question."

She chuckled. "Go ahead."

He stretched out in his chair, lacing fingers over the back of his head and directing that grin up at the ceiling. "It's been a long time since I've seen someone that unhappy," he said. "Who broke your heart?"

Anna wrinkled her nose and shook her head in disgust. "No one broke my heart," she answered. "Just the opposite, really; I broke a wonderful man's heart. Two wonderful men...Still want to get to know me?"

"Sounds like there's a story there."

Anna sank deeper into her chair, pressing the heels of her hands to her eye-sockets. "Oh, there's a story," she admitted. "But not one I want to revisit. The truth is I came here to forget it for a few hours."

Devin stood up with a grunt, nodding to her. "I get that," he said. "And it seems to me there's only one way to forget it."

"What's that?"

"Dance with me."

Covering a smile with the palm of one hand, Anna shut her eyes and trembled as she laughed. "Either you don't listen," she said. "Or you're braver than most people. I've left two broken hearts in my wake, remember?"

"I remember."

"Do you really want to be the third?"

His grin widened. "I think maybe it might be worth it," he answered. "Besides, I really don't think you'll have to worry about bruising my feelings."

"Oh no?"

"I'm not looking for anything serious."

"That's what everyone says," Anna countered. "Right before they fall madly in love and get hurt."

"Try me."

It was a tempting offer, she had to admit. A little intimacy without all the drama and pain? Who wouldn't be tempted by that?

But she wasn't in a place where she could give her heart to someone, and she was terrified of hurting someone else. Life was complicated and love even more so. What she needed right then was *simplicity.*

There were moments when you looked at someone, and you knew that you weren't going to spend your life with them. It was a gut reaction, not something you could easily put into words. An emotional certainty that every part of you believed without question.

Yes, there were definitely moments when you looked at someone, and you knew with perfect clarity that you were *not* going to spend your life with them. Whatever you felt for each other would be a brief flash of passion. Here and then gone. You knew this...

And you went through with it anyway.

"Okay," Anna said. "Let's dance."

The hallway outside Devin's apartment was dimly lit and just a little stuffy, but none of that mattered to Anna as he pushed her back against the door and kissed her lips. The man had a talent for this. Just the right amount of pressure.

Seizing his face in both hands, Anna returned the kiss,

gasping softly with every breath. "Nice neighbourhood," she murmured before his lips were on her again. "Have you lived here very long?"

He pulled back from her with eyes closed, sucking in a deep breath. "Only a few months," he said in a rasping voice. "I moved to the capitol for a job."

"And what would that be?"

Devin slammed his palm against the door scanner, allowing the biometrics to read his hand print. Then he synced his multi-tool to the building's computer systems, and the door was unlocked with *a click*.

Gently, he pushed her in.

Spatial awareness allowed her to perceive the entire apartment without having to look. The place was nice with an open living room where two couches were positioned on either side of a table that supported a vase of flowers. The kitchen was off to her left, but she barely even noticed it. Fridge, cupboards, a serving bot in standby mode. All of the usual amenities.

Devin shut the door behind himself, then strode toward her with a great big smile on his face. "I'm part of the Artist's Coalition," he said. "We're putting together a major show with a new statue as the centrepiece."

"Uh huh...And what's your preferred art form?"

His cheeks went red, and he shut his eyes tight, shaking his head as he closed the distance. "You're gonna laugh," he said shakily. "I'm a poet..."

Anna jumped, wrapping her legs around his waist. Her arms went around his neck, and then she was kissing him again. "Mama always told me to date a poet. She said no one could sweep you off your feet quite like a poet."

"Should I talk about your eyes?"

"Maybe later."

He carried her down a short hallway to a bedroom with wooden nightstands and lamps that lit up when they sensed motion. He threw Anna onto the mattress, and then he was kissing her again.

Her neck, her collarbone...

As she watched the early morning sunlight through Devin's bedroom window, Anna smoothed the wrinkles from her shirt and let out a soft sigh of contentment. Her one night stand was still sound asleep; she could see him in her mind's eye, clutching the blankets to his chest, breathing softly. This close, she could make out the features of his face.

Anna turned silently.

Bending over, she pressed her lips to his forehead, and then pulled back. "Thank you," she whispered. "You will never know how much last night meant to me."

The hastily crafted note she had typed out on her multi-tool and forwarded to the apartment's central computer would tell him much the same thing when he woke up. She had been granted a brief reprieve, a few hours of peace.

But now it was time to go back to being Anna Lenai.

24

As he walked into a kitchen filled with soft morning sunlight, Harry saw his eldest daughter sitting at the table with her elbow on its surface, massaging her eyelids with her fingertips. "Hey!" he said. "You look stressed."

"I'm fine."

Harry stood in the doorway with his hands shoved into the pockets of his robe. "I think you push yourself too hard," he said, moving into the kitchen. "It's not good to take on so much responsibility."

The automated coffee maker already had a pot brewing, and there were cups on the counter. Harry took one and filled it. He went to the fridge for some almond milk – sadly, he was still getting used to that; Leyrians cloned meat, but not cow's milk – and then he joined his daughter at the table.

Melissa sat across from him with her face buried in her hands. "It can't be helped," she murmured. "I have to push myself this hard if I want to get good enough in time for-"

Harry sat back with his arms folded, frowning at his daughter. "In time for what?" he asked, shaking his head. "In time to throw yourself at the next bad guy who wants to blow something up?"

"I-"

"Melissa," he cut in. "I support *what* you choose to do with your life, but not *how* you choose to do it. You're a cadet. It's time you accepted your limitations."

When his daughter looked up at him, her face was strained with dark circles visible under her eyes. "I understand how you feel, Dad," she said in a hoarse voice. "But I need you to trust that I know what I'm doing."

Licking his lips, Harry shut his eyes and took a deep breath. "If you insist," he said, nodding to her. "On this planet, you're past the age of majority, and I really can't tell you what to do anymore, but I will never stop worrying."

"That's why I love you."

He sipped his coffee and focused on one of his other worries. Isara, the woman who looked just like his dead girlfriend. Maybe it should have bothered him that a murderous demon of a woman was walking around with Jena's face, but really it didn't. Superficial appearance didn't matter. It was who you were inside that made the difference.

But the woman's existence raised several questions about Jena's past. Jack had sent him an update on what he and Anna had learned in their last session. Jena was a clone. Or so Isara claimed.

He had to know the truth.

Melissa was slumped in her chair, her eyes closed as she teetered on the edge of sleep. The poor girl really was pushing herself too hard.

Bringing the mug to his lips, Harry slurped as he took a sip. "I think maybe you should call in today," he said. "I think the hero who prevented a food processing plant from becoming a pile of rubble deserves a little rest."

"Maybe you're right," she murmured.

Harry watched as his daughter got out of her chair and shuffled out of the kitchen, tapping away at her multi-tool as she did. “Hello?” she said from the hallway. “Yeah...it's me, Director Andalon. I don't think I'll be able to make it...”

Harry sighed.

Now, what to do about his other problem.

Through his living room window, Jack saw the sun as a red ball sinking toward the western horizon, painting the sky in bands of orange and red and violet. There were more than a few buildings that rose up like shadows before him, but for the most part, his view was of Alari Park – a large patch of green with trees that were already showing leaves.

He stood by the window in jeans and a white tee under a black dress shirt that he left unbuttoned. It had been a long day, and Anna was on his mind. Somehow, he knew that she had moved on from him. It was something he felt in his gut. Probably just a case of paranoia, but you never know...

Tilting his head back, Jack squinted through the window pane. “What do you think, Summer?” he asked in a rough voice. “Am I just stressing about nothing? Or is it time to move on myself?”

His Nassai responded with grief.

Jack shut his eyes, breathing deeply. His head sank from the weight of his sadness. “Yeah,” he said, nodding. “That's what I thought you'd say.”

A knock at the door.

He took in the sight of his living room, hunting for any sign that it was as messy as he feared. A gray couch was positioned smack dab in the middle of the tiled floor, facing a rectangular sheet of SmartGlass on the wall to his left. A makeshift TV.

To his right, the kitchen with its stainless steel cupboards and a large refrigerator was home to a serving bot that stood in the corner. It was slumped over, in standby mode. He had tried to engage the thing in conversation several times, but despite his secret hopes that Leyrian machines might be sapient, this robot was nothing like Ven. Not a true AI by any measure.

Jack strode across the room with his head down, heaving out a breath. "Come in," he said, approaching the door. "It's open."

When the door swung inward, he found Cassi in the hallway, dressed in a pair of green skinny jeans and pink tank-top that displayed more than a little cleavage. Damn it! Why did she have to be so hot?

"Thought you could use some company," she said.

"Sure...What's up?"

Cassi stepped into the apartment with arms folded, smiling down at herself. "Well, you've been moping around the office for the last few days," she said with a shrug. "It's almost like you forgot all about the gorgeous woman who has told you several times now that she's into you."

"Yeah...I'm sorry about that. I've just had a lot on my mind for the last little while."

"She's not worth it."

"I'm sorry?"

Cassi looked up to stare at him, and those purple eyes were...bewitching. "The lady you're fretting about," she said, raising a thin eyebrow. "I suspect it's Lenai, but of course, I can't be sure."

"You think-"

"She's not worth it."

Clasping her hands together behind her back, Cassi paced through the living room like she owned the place. "Anybody worth crying over," she began, "wouldn't make you cry in the first place."

Jack turned slowly on the spot.

He stood by the door with his hands in his pockets, refusing to look up. "That's an interesting opinion," he said, nodding.

"Big with the oversimplification, but hey! Good on you for streamlining the grieving process."

To his surprise, Cassi didn't get mad; she just stood behind the couch with her arms folded, biting her lip as she looked him up and down. "A bit of advice," she said. "People will let you down every time."

"Gee, I feel *so* much better."

She moved toward him like a leopard, cocking her head to one side and flashing a smile that left butterflies in his stomach. "Which is why," she added, "you avail yourself of opportunities for happiness when they present themselves."

Chewing on his lower lip, Jack felt his eyes pop out. "Interesting," he said, stepping forward. "And I'm guessing that one of those opportunities might be presenting itself this very moment?"

Her finger touched his chest, trailing a line down the white fabric of his t-shirt. "A beautiful woman is standing in your living room," Cassi said. "And she is willing to do *anything* you want to do."

Oh boy...

"So, tell me, Jack: what do you want to do?"

Five minutes later, Jack was sitting on his couch, listening to a powerful orchestral score while the words "Star Wars" receded into the distance on the TV screen. Jack read the opening title crawl for his guest. It was the least you could do when you were trying to share one of Earth's cinematic masterpieces with someone who could speak English but not read it.

Cassi was curled up by the couch arm with a bowl of popcorn on her lap, smiling and shaking her head. "This is how your people imagined space travel?" she asked. "Big triangular ships with rayguns?"

Jack slouched with his arms spread over the back of the couch, chuckling softly. "I would like to see some of your planet's early cinema," he said. "I'm betting there's all sorts of silliness there."

"You're probably right."

The movie went on, and despite the original scoff, it was clear that Cassi was really enjoying herself. That opening sequence had her on the edge of her seat, and she actually gasped when Vader made his first appearance.

Somehow – and Jack was certain that he didn't remember doing it – the lights were dimmed and Cassi was sitting close enough that he could feel her body heat. It was quite distracting but in a pleasant way. "Hmm," she murmured. "So, this is how your people imagined serving bots?"

Grinning with a wheeze of laughter, Jack closed his eyes and shook his head. "No, it's not like that," he said, sinking deeper into the couch cushions. "C3PO and R2D2 are both genuine AI, fully sapient."

"They're people?"

"Indeed."

Cassi yawned and covered her open mouth with one hand. "And yet, the princess feels no compunctions about ordering them into the line of fire," she said. "And Luke's family treats them as property."

"The movie doesn't really delve into the rights of droids."

"Apparently not."

It was a minor complaint, however, and she very quickly lost herself in the story. Talk of serving bots gave Jack an idea, and he asked the one in the kitchen to bring them each a glass of sparkling water. With a "please" and "Thank you," of course. You could take the boy out of Canada, but you couldn't take Canada out of the boy.

Cassi gave him an odd stare when he made it a point to be polite to the robot; after all, it had no feelings, but it couldn't hurt! No one had planned on Ven becoming a fully autonomous AI. Granted, Ven had started off as a program designed to manage the entire planet's natural resource base – and this minor serving bot was nowhere near that level of sophistication – but it couldn't hurt!

Toward the end of the movie, Cassi perked up as the rebel fighters made their run on the Death Star. Jack was almost sad when it was over; he didn't want her to leave. He didn't want to go back to thinking about all the topics he had been avoiding.

Luckily, he didn't have to.

Cassi scooched closer, leaning her head against his chest and letting out a soft sigh of contentment. "I like you," she said. "In case that wasn't clear from the dozen times I've already said it."

"I like you too."

"Well then?"

He ventured a glance at her and found himself transfixed once again by her lovely violet eyes. Before he could react, Cassi touched his cheek with one hand and kissed his lips. God have mercy! He was returning the kiss.

"Wait..." Jack mumbled.

She straddled his hips and seized his face with both hands. "Stop over thinking it," she whispered between kisses. "For once in your life, just do what feels good."

An hour or so after that, Cassi was lying flat on her stomach on Jack's bed, her chin resting on folded arms. "That...was fantastic," she murmured. "You should consider doing this professionally."

Jack closed his eyes, breathing in as his head sank into the pillow. "Well," he said. "I always appreciate an evening that defies my expectations. You weren't so bad yourself, you know."

"Thank you."

Rolling onto his side, Jack dug his elbow into the mattress and leaned his cheek against his fist. "So," he began. "Where exactly does this leave us? Because I'm thinking beaucoup de awkward when Larani starts asking questions."

Cassi shut her eyes, then buried her nose in her arms. "Why do we have to tell her anything?" she replied, her voice muffled. "There's no rule that prohibits relationships between Keepers."

"Is that what we have?"

Cassi's head came up, and she blinked several times as she considered the question. "Is that what you want?" Of course, she wouldn't just give him a straight answer! People never gave you a straight answer.

He flopped onto his back with hands folded on his chest, chewing on his lip as he thought it over. "I don't know," he answered. "To be perfectly honest, I was planning on staying single for the next little while."

"She's not worth it."

Jack sat up, hunching over and pressing a hand to his forehead. He ran his fingers through his hair. "You know, I'd appreciate it if you stopped giving me input on that," he said. "I can figure out my own personal life."

Soft laughter was Cassi's response; not anger, not indignation. It left him feeling uneasy. Like she knew something he didn't, understood something he couldn't. What *was* he supposed to do now?

Deep down, he knew that he would never stop loving Anna. Not after everything they had shared. But if she didn't want him...

This was what he was supposed to do, wasn't it? Meet other women, date them, fall for them? Maybe if he grew to like one of them enough, he wouldn't be tempted to call his former best friend. He wouldn't feel the need to ask her if there was some way they could work this out. Anna had made her wishes clear; his job was to respect them. Would that be easier if he found someone else to love?

But did he love Cassi?

No...

Jack winced, shaking his head. "I'm sorry, Cassi," he said, sitting back against the headboard. "Maybe this was a bad idea; I don't want to lead you on or do anything that might hurt your-"

She crawled over him, gripping his shoulders with both hands and pushing him back against the headboard. Her lips found his before he could say one single word, and then all he could think about was how good it felt to have this goddess in his arms.

"Do I look like I'm hurt?" Cassi asked. She gently sank her teeth into the soft skin around his collarbone, nipping at him. "You worry too much, Jack Hunter."

"But-"

"Shut up, and enjoy yourself."

Metal doors slid apart to reveal a cramped room with a sleek, curved desk along the back wall. The man who sat behind that desk was short and slim with pale skin and black hair that he wore in spikes. "Mr. Carlson," he said without looking up. "What brings you by at this hour?"

Harry stood in the doorway with his shoulders slumped, his eyes downcast. "I want to speak to the prisoner," he said, stepping forward. "I have several questions that I need her to answer."

The young Keeper – Harry didn't know his name – sat back and smiled in the way a father might smile after listening to a lengthy argument about why his daughter just *had* to have the latest iPhone. "You realize that just a few nights ago, we had someone forge Larani's credentials to get in here."

Wetting his lips, Harry shut his eyes and tried to remain composed. "Look, I'm not going to commit fraud," he said. "But that prisoner has critical information that I'll need if I'm going to assist Director Andalon in tracking the Sons of Savard."

"That's still not very compelling."

Harry leaned against the door-frame with his arms folded, tilting his head back to blink at the ceiling. "Then what *would* be compelling?" he asked. "I realize that I'm not exactly on the payroll...or whatever you call it around here."

The other man was smiling into his lap, shaking his head slowly. "Mr. Carlson, you are listed as a consultant with Director Andalon's team," he said. "You have been granted access to many restricted areas of the building."

"But?"

The young man stood up and tugged on the hem of his shirt. His face hardened with stern resolve. "But Chief Director Tal has made it clear that no one is to see the prisoner without her direct authorization."

"What's your name, son?"

"Jensen Noralis, sir."

Harry closed his eyes, breathing deeply to work up the nerve for something that he really didn't want to do. He was a stickler; coaxing someone to break the regs was not in his genetic makeup, but he *needed* to know what Isara knew. Even Harry had his limits. Most cops would follow the rules to the letter – unless they were crooked, of course – but these Keepers were a little different.

Years of working with Jack and Anna had convinced him that they were guided by their emotions. In some ways, that made them more compassionate – more focused upon the spirit of the law – but it was also a weakness that he could exploit.

If he had to.

"Did you know Director Morane?" he asked.

"No," Jensen replied. "We never met."

"I knew her," Harry said, striding across the room. "She was my partner, and that woman in there has her face. I *need* to know the truth."

Harry stepped up to the desk with hands clasped behind himself. "I could be wrong," he went on. "But I was under the impression that you Keepers were the experts in finding an exception to every rule."

"What is it you think you can learn from Isara?"

Now to play his hand; he would have preferred to have avoided this necessity, but he needed a compelling reason.

Slipping a hand into his jacket pocket, Harry retrieved the N'Jal in its curled up ball form. He held it up in front of the other man. "Do you recognize this?" he asked. "Do you know what it is?"

Jensen shook his head.

"It's an Overseer device," Harry explained. "A powerful weapon, a scanning tool, and it probably has several other functions we haven't discovered." He wasn't going to mention his ability to reprogram a *ziarogat* on the fly. "Just about everybody who bonds with it becomes unstable, paranoid. But I can use it just fine. Isara tried to get her hands on this thing a few months back, which means she probably knows *why* I can use it just fine. So, I want answers."

All of that was true; Harry Carlson was no liar. In fact, he had brought the N'Jal specifically to ask what Isara knew about it. But that only scratched the surface of what he wanted to know.

The other man stared at him with an open mouth, then blinked and tossed his head about as if to clear away an unpleasant mental image. "Right," Jensen said. "That makes sense...I'll trust you, Mr. Carlson."

"Thank you."

"But please," Jensen implored him. "Don't do anything that might compromise her rights. We're in enough trouble as is."

"I won't."

The doors behind the desk slid open, and Harry stepped into a long hallway with cells in both of its gray walls. The third door on the left: that was where he was headed. His heart was pounding.

Closing his eyes, Harry sucked in a deep breath. "You can do this," he whispered, nodding to himself. "She's just a woman, no different from any other Keeper."

He placed the N'Jal against the palm of his left hand and felt the little ball uncurl, tiny fibers bonding with his skin. Using this thing always felt like a shot of adrenaline. His senses were sharper, his mind focused. He could *feel* things that were imperceptible to any other person.

If he concentrated hard enough, he would know – intuitively – the composition of the air in this hallway. He would be able to sense even trace amounts of other chemicals. It was exhilarating...and terrifying.

He went to Isara's cell.

After going through the necessary security checks – he had to remember to use the hand that didn't have the N'Jal attached to it – he watched the door slide open to reveal a cell where Isara sat in a simple wooden chair with her back turned. "Harry!" she said without looking. "It's so nice to see you again! It's been what? Six months?"

"Seven."

Isara stretched, fingers straining for the ceiling, and then she got out of her chair. "Far too long," she murmured. "To what do I owe the pleasure of your company."

She faced, and Harry felt the frigid sting of grief, like an icicle piercing his chest. Her face was a perfect match for Jena in every way, right down to the boyish hair that she wore parted in the middle. *Christ...I thought I could handle this.* Now was not a good time to lose his composure.

Thrusting his hand toward her – palm out – Harry gave her a moment to take stock of the N'Jal bonded to his skin. Then he marched forward while the door slid shut behind him. "You know what this is?"

Isara nodded.

"It's the one we found in Tennessee," he added. "Why did you want it so badly?"

A wry little smile appeared on Isara's face, and she shook her head. "I should think you would know that by now," she replied. "No doubt you used it to discern the location of the Key."

Isara slipped her hands into her back pockets and stood with her head held high. "I want to know when you bonded with it," she said. "It can't have been long ago, or you'd be a quivering ball of paranoia."

Harry squinted at the woman. "Well, it's funny you should ask," he said. "Turns out I can use this thing with no unfortunate side-effects. And I'm betting you know why."

Isara froze.

He'd caught her off guard. This exchange went to him, but Isara would come back with something devastating. Was it possible that she didn't know what the Overseers had done to him when he and Jack had found the first cipher?

Isara turned on her heel, pacing a line across the room with a smile on her face. "I see," she murmured. "What makes you think *I* know anything about your predicament? Better to ask the Inzari, yes?"

"I thought you had the inside track."

Isara stopped at the side of her bed, her chest swelling as she took in a deep breath. She let it out slowly. "I am just a servant," she said. "They tell me what they want me to know and nothing more."

Harry felt his face twist, then tossed his head about with a rough growl. "Not good enough!" he snapped. "You're one of their most trusted agents. You expect me to believe you don't know how their tech works?"

"What you believe is irrelevant."

"We'll see about that."

As he closed in on her, Isara turned on him with her arms folded, raising her chin. “Really?” she asked, arching one eyebrow. “What exactly do you expect to accomplish here, Harry?”

“I'm gonna get some answers.”

He strode forward.

Isara spun for a back-kick that would throw him across the room if it connected. By instinct alone, Harry reacted. His left hand came up, and the air before him rippled with a force-field.

Isara's foot touched the curtain of electrostatic energy, and she was flung to the floor. The woman landed with a grunt, shivering as she let out a ragged breath. “You've grown stronger, Harry.”

Harry let the force-field vanish.

Dropping to one knee beside her, he clamped his left hand onto the back of Isara's neck and felt the N'Jal's fibers dig into her skin. Instantly, he was aware of every last bit of Isara's nervous system, and he used that knowledge to his advantage. He flared pain receptors throughout her body.

Isara shrieked, arching her back and then flopping about like a fish that had been left on dry land. “You think that will contain me?” she bellowed. “I have known every torment the Inzari can visit upon-”

Harry intensified the pain.

Her screams were loud enough that they would have drawn attention if not for the fact that this cell's walls were soundproof. Not that the Justice Keepers were in the habit of torturing their prisoners – the idea would be abhorrent to them – but they didn't want prisoners talking to and possibly plotting with the person in the cell next door.

Isara kicked her feet and pounded her fists on the floor. Every time she tried to get up, Harry only intensified the pain. He wasn't likely to get her in this vulnerable position again, and she would kill him if he let her take control of the situation.

"Tell me everything you know about the Overseers!" Harry shouted. "No more secrets, no more manipulations, no more lies! WHAT ARE YOU HIDING?"

The door slid open.

When Harry looked up, he was expecting to have to explain himself to Larani Tal, but instead, Jensen Noralis stood in the hallway with his hand on a holstered pistol. "Let her go," he said, stepping into the cell.

"You don't understand."

Jensen drew his pistol and pointed it at Harry. The LEDs on the barrel were dark. No stun rounds; a shot from that gun would kill. "Let. Her. Go." the man insisted. "Get up and back away."

Harry did so.

Getting to his feet, he backed away from the man with his hands raised defensively. "Don't get close," he said, shaking his head. "She's dangerous."

Grinning as his face went red, Jensen shut his eyes and bowed his head. "I know," he said, moving deeper into the cell. "Are you all right, ma'am? I wouldn't have let him in here, but he claims to be able to use the device without side-effects. I thought you would want to examine him for yourself."

Isara pushed herself up on extended arms, and when she looked at Harry, her face was crimson and tear-stained. "That's quite all right, Jensen," she assured him. "You did well. I take it we're on schedule?"

"Yes, ma'am."

Isara stood up, wiping tears off her cheeks with two fingers. "Excellent," she said with a curt nod. "Now, if you please..."

"No!" Harry shouted. "You can't!"

The other man produced a key from his pants' pocket and slid it into the locking mechanism on Isara's collar. The collar popped open with a *click* and then dropped to the floor. Terror was like a fist squeezing Harry's heart.

Isara turned to the man who stood beside her, smiling the kind of smile a mother bestowed on her favourite son. "You have proved yourself." Abruptly, her attention was focused on Harry again. "Kill him, recover the device, and then join us at the SlipGate terminal."

When she stepped into the hallway, Isara found Cara Sinthel and Calissa Narim waiting for her. Both stood before her in rumpled track pants and sweaters, each with hair in a state of disarray.

"What now?" Calissa said.

Isara turned and started up the hallway, flanked by the other two women. "Well, there are several options," she said. "But right now...I'm thinking violence."

25

The cell wasn't that big; once, Harry would have thought that these Leyrian prisons that were basically like small hotel rooms would have been excessively lavish – criminals did *not* deserve furniture, books or tablets with interactive games – but now, he regretted those hasty sentiments.

It was a small, box-like room with a table on one side and a bed on the other, and he stood by the window along the back wall. The exit was blocked by a short and slender man whose pale skin was contrasted by his black hair.

A short and slender man who could rip him to pieces.

Closing his eyes, Harry took a deep breath. "You don't have to do this, Jensen," he said, stepping forward. "I don't know what they did to you, how Isara convinced you to join her misguided cause, but-"

Jensen pointed the gun at him.

Harry raised his left hand, a force-field rippling into existence, blurring the other man as if a curtain of falling water stood between them. Slugs hit the wall of shimmering energy, and Harry caught them each with his mind, holding them all in place instead of allowing them to fall to the floor.

He thrust his hand forward.

The force-field *flexed* and vanished, throwing half a dozen bullets back toward the man who had loosed them. Jensen became a streak of colour, resolidifying in the corner and lifting his weapon to point at Harry. "EMP!"

I'm a dead man.

Years of training kicked in, pushing that voice to the very back of Harry's mind. He threw himself down on the floor as the other man's gun beeped its confirmation, landing hard on his belly.

White tracers flew through the air, striking the wall.

Harry rolled onto his side, stretching his left hand toward the other man. A small force-field – no larger than a tennis ball – appeared in the palm of his hand. He loosed it with a thought.

A ball of rippling electrostatic energy sped across the room and hit Jensen's knee. The man let out a squeal as he fell forward, catching himself by bracing his hands on the floor. He was gasping. The shock of touching a force-field wasn't pleasant. Hopefully, it would give Harry a few moments.

Harry stood up.

He rushed across the room and then dropped to one knee in front of his opponent. Without even thinking, he slapped a palm against Jensen's forehead, and the N'Jal's fibers dug in. He activated Jensen's pain receptors.

The other man screamed, dropping to the floor and flailing about like a mugger hit by a taser. Crude but effective. Now to end this.

Harry scooped up the pistol that had fallen to the floor.

He stood up and pointed it at the other man. "Stun rounds." Of course, nothing happened. The gun was keyed to Jensen's voice print. It wouldn't do if an enemy could change your weapon's settings simply by shouting. Fortunately, Leyrian pistols could be activated manually.

Harry set the weapon for stun-rounds and fired.

A charged bullet hit the back of Jensen's neck and bounced off, causing the man to flail about almost as much as he had when Harry had tickled his pain receptors. When the spasms had subsided, the man was lying face-down on the floor.

Chuckling softly, Harry shut his eyes and rubbed his forehead with the back of one hand. "Justice Keepers," he said. "You're not so tough."

He ran out the door.

Skidding to a stop just outside the cell, he spun around and began tapping at the door controls. "Thank you, Jensen," he said. "You just happen to be in the best place you could possibly be right now."

The door slid shut.

The doors to the cell-block slid open, allowing Isara to step into the small reception area outside. The desk was unoccupied, of course, but she found a small pile of weapons on the floor. Pistols, ammo cartridges and even a shotgun. Jensen had done as he was ordered and readied supplies for them.

Isara squatted near the pile, smiling down at the weapons. "Well done, my boy," she said. "Quickly, arm yourselves."

Cara and Calissa both did as they were told, each woman snatching up pistols and sliding magazines into place. "What do we do now?" Cara asked. "It's only a matter of time before they realize we're gone."

"Both of you will take the south-east stairwell to the first floor and exit the building as quietly as possible," Isara said. "Keep your heads down until you reach the apartment complex on Third Street. Our contact is hosting us in Unit 108."

"And you?" Calissa asked.

Isara picked up the shotgun and laughed softly as she caressed the weapon. "I'm going to make some noise."

Harry stumbled through the door to the reception area with a hand pressed to his chest, gasping for breath. "You're getting too old for this, Carlson," he wheezed, shaking his head. "Way too old."

He looked around.

There were half a dozen ammo cartridges and a few pistols scattered on the floor. More than enough for one person. Which meant Jensen had let out someone else. He had to hand it to these evil Keepers; when they turned bad, they did it big.

"Think," Harry said. "You're only a few minutes behind them. They can't have gone very far."

But how to find them.

Now that he wasn't fighting for his life, his cop instincts kicked in and he recalled his training. Going after them alone would be stupid. He rolled up his sleeve and began tapping at the screen of his multi-tool. "Full security alert!" he said. "Prisoners escaped. Activate containment protocols."

Alarms started blaring. Having access to the building's restricted areas meant that he had many of the same computer privileges as any Justice Keeper. Including the ability to declare an emergency.

What to do next? He had to find Isara!

The answer was there in his mind in an instant. He lifted his left hand and allowed the N'Jal to scan the air. Trails of pheromones drifting through the room. They were still quite distinct, meaning the women who had created them had been here just a few short moments earlier.

He rushed through the door and found himself in a long gray-walled hallway with bright lights in the ceiling. Some had turned red to indicate a state of emergency. The trail of pheromones extended through this corridor to an intersection maybe fifty feet away. There it split in two. So, the women – somehow, he could tell they were all female – had split up, had they?

Harry ran through the corridor.

When he reached the intersection, he noticed three distinct trails, two heading into the corridor on his right, the other going left. It was likely that Isara was the one who had decided to go solo; it was what Jena would have done.

What to do...

He went after the other two, huffing and puffing as he ran like a mad-man. He was in pretty good shape for a middle-aged man, but it had been over a year since he had left the Ottawa PD. Not much opportunity to run when you were working as a diplomat.

This corridor was far shorter and ended in a hallway with windows along one wall. He ventured a glance around the corner.

A tiny blonde woman ran side by side with a taller raven-haired woman through a hallway where trails of smoke were curling at the ceiling. Unless he was mistaken, these two were Cara Sinthel and Calissa Narim.

As they approached a stairwell door at the end of the corridor, a force-field sprang to life in front of them, a wall of white electrostatic energy that cut off their escape. Cara pointed her gun at the ceiling.

She loosed a single white tracer that struck the force-field emitter and caused it to short out in a flash of sparks. EMP rounds. His own force-fields would be useless, and he wasn't wearing body armour.

Both women had their backs turned, but Keepers didn't need eyes to see you. Cara noticed him and then spun around to point her pistol in his direction.

Harry jumped back into the adjoining corridor just before a flurry of white tracers sped through the intersection. The cautious voice in the back of his mind whispered that going out there would be suicide. Justice Keepers could react several times faster than an ordinary human being, and his force-fields were useless.

He should just leave – his first responsibility was to his daughters – but memories of confronting Slade on the moon bubbled up. He would *not* be a coward again. Harry Carlson was not going to run every time he came up against a Keeper. Still, if his force-fields were useless...

Or were they?

Harry aimed around the corner, firing blindly with his pistol. Stun-rounds only, but they would knock out a Justice Keeper if any of them hit their target. With any luck, Cara and Calissa would react the way Keepers always do.

He stepped into the other corridor to find the two women standing side by side, each one a smear of colour as they used Bendings to redirect his bullets into the wall or the windows. They couldn't return fire so long as they were taking refuge behind warped space-time.

Harry raised his left hand, crafting a force-field as tall and as wide as the corridor itself, filling every inch of space from floor to ceiling. Then he sent it flying toward his opponents like a truck barreling down the highway.

Cara and Calissa tried to dodge, but there was nowhere to go.

The force-field hit them both and threw them backward with incredible momentum. Each woman was flung about like a rag-doll. Calissa even went shoulder first into the wall next to the stairwell door.

Cara landed on her side, grunting and wheezing as she tried to catch her breath. *Now,* Harry thought. *Take her down.*

He aimed for Cara and fired.

The tiny woman rolled aside just before his bullet hit the floor where she had been. In the blink of an eye, she was a streak of colour, a streak of colour that reformed into a woman who stood with her arm extended, the gun pointed at Harry's chest.

Harry wasn't sure what he did.

Something very much like a force-field rippled into existence and sped toward the woman in the instant before a single white tracer erupted from the barrel of her gun. The charged bullet passed through the curtain of rippling energy, and just like that, it wasn't charged anymore.

But it was still a bullet.

Still moving at incredible speed.

The slug pierced Harry's chest on the right side and ripped right through him. He was barely even aware of the sting. Then, for some reason, his legs gave out, and he was falling to his knees in the middle of the hallway.

He couldn't breathe. It was like someone had sucked the air away or filled one of his lungs with fluid...with blood. His own blood. He had been shot in the chest. That fact was only beginning to register with him.

Cara marched through the hallway with her arm extended, pointing the gun at his face. “Idiot!” she snapped. “Even with that toy, did you really think you could stand up to *both* of us?”

At only five-foot-three, she towered over him. Close enough that he could almost reach out and touch her. “I regret this,” she said. “I feel no animosity toward you, Harry Carlson, but you have chosen to oppose-”

It took some effort – a great deal of effort – but Harry managed to lift his left hand. And then he flung something at her.

A force-field the size of a tennis ball hit Cara right between the eyes and pushed her head back with enough force to snap her neck. Breaking a Justice Keeper's bones was no easy task – their bodies were incredibly durable – but he had managed it. With the side-effect of quite literally smashing her face in.

Harry would have vomited if not for the fact that he could barely even breathe.

The woman dropped to her knees and then toppled over, landing sprawled out on her side. Damn it! Nearly twenty years as a police officer, and he had never been forced to take a human life...Until now.

At the far end of the hallway, Calissa turned her back on him and kicked open the stairwell door. She was gone before Harry could even think to do anything to stop her. Apparently, the woman wasn't willing to risk her life attacking a man who would likely bleed to death anyway.

Bleed to death.

Oh, God help him, what had he been thinking.

Harry fell over sideways, groaning when he hit the floor. "Help...me..." he croaked out. "Help me..."

Anna was in a good mood.

Bleakness take her, she had been in a good mood all day. It was amazing what a night off from your worries could do to improve your disposition. Months of beating herself up for the way things had ended with Bradley...For one night, she'd been able to put all of that out of her head, and she was eternally grateful for it.

In beige pants and a navy-blue t-shirt, Anna stood inside an elevator as it descended to the first floor. She had been working late, catching up on reports that she had filed after interviewing several members of the Sons of Savard.

The elevator came to a halt.

Fluorescent bulbs in the ceiling went out to be replaced with the hellish red glow of emergency lighting. Why oh why did building designers think horror movie cliches were the best way to alert a passenger to a potential crisis. "Security alert," the computer said over the loudspeaker. "All elevators have been shut down."

Biting her lip, Anna looked up at the ceiling and blinked. "Recognize Special Agent Leana Lenai," she barked. "Authorization 2774-*Vaela-Trialasi.* What is the nature of this security alert?"

"Prisoners have escaped from detention cells."

Anna winced, trembling as she drew in a slow breath. "Of course they have," she muttered, stepping forward. "Reinstate this elevator and reset the destination for the third floor. Resume standard security protocols once I've exited."

She was descending again.

Moments later, the metal doors slid apart to reveal a gray hallway where red lights in the ceiling cast an angry glow upon the walls. Luckily, there were still enough white lights to allow her to see. Not that she needed it – spatial awareness was a blessing – but there were some things you could perceive with your eyes that remained undetectable to any Nassai. The ability to look through windows, for instance.

She stepped into the corridor and began making her way to the Detention Centre. There wasn't much else on the third floor. Her multi-tool identified her as a Keeper and prevented the computer from raising force-fields to block her path.

It was pure dumb luck that brought her around a corner to find Isara in the middle of the adjoining hallway. The other woman stood there in a pair of gray track pants and a tank-top, carrying a shotgun in both hands. Why? How? Who would let her out? *The very same people who let Pennfield out of his cell. There are moles among the Keepers.*

One look at the ceiling told her that most of the force-field generators in this hallway had been shorted out. Trails of smoke descended from several of them, and the stench of burnt circuitry was unmistakable. No doubt Isara had blasted them all to clear a path for herself.

A rictus smile was Isara's first response. "Well, well, well," she said with a nod. "I came to kill Larani, but you'll do."

Anna set her jaw, squinting at the woman as she strode forward. "Just a thought," she said. "If you're going for intimidation, you might not want to rely on the 'just spent a week on the couch, eating cheese puffs' look."

"I'm glad to see your wit is intact."

Anna strode through the hallway with her fists clenched, shaking her head as she made her way toward the other woman. "Your wits are about to be splattered all over the floor," she said. "Or the chunks of brain that are responsible for them, anyway."

"Why, Anna, you've grown violent."

"I learned from the best."

Isara hoisted up the shotgun in both hands, squinting as she took aim. "I think you might be forgetting something," she said. "I'm the one with the gun."

She charged the weapon.

Thrusting her hand out, Anna threw up a Bending without thinking, curving space-time to form a convex shield in front of herself. There was a soft buzzing sound, and then several dozen pellets were hanging in the air before her. They curved around her body on either side and sped off down the corridor.

Anna let the Bending drop and ran forward.

Isara charged the weapon again.

Turning her shoulder toward the other woman, Anna brought her fist up and crafted the same Bending. Once again, pellets hit the patch of curved space-time and then curved around her on either side. Isara was just a few feet away.

Anna let the Bending vanish.

She leaped and turned her body for a flying side kick that took her opponent in the chest, pinning the shotgun between them. The impact was enough to throw Isara to the floor, where she slid backwards across the tiles.

The woman lost her grip on the shotgun, and it slid to the side of the hallway and hit the wall. For a moment, Anna was tempted to grab the damn thing and use it on Isara, but while she was willing to take a life if it was necessary, she wouldn't ever be truly comfortable with lethal force. If you were at a point where taking a life was your only option, then you had already lost.

Placing her foot on top of the shotgun, Anna slid it backward across the floor tiles, a good twenty paces down the hallway, where it would not be in arm's reach. "Who needs accessories? This girl is hot enough without the accouterments."

Isara was lying flat on her back.

The woman curled her legs against her chest and then sprang off the floor, landing on her feet with fists raised and teeth bared. "Not bad, girl," she murmured. "Seven days of being cooped up must have left me a little off balance."

"Yeah...I'm sure that's it."

Tilting her head to one side, Isara flashed a smile that was almost flirtatious. "Shall we do it the old-fashioned way then?" she asked, stepping forward, closing the distance in one long stride. "I'd enjoy a good dance."

Isara threw a punch.

Anna ducked and felt a fist pass over her head. She stepped to the left, then popped up and delivered a mean right hook to the cheek. Isara stumbled, a bright red welt on her creamy skin.

Anna spun and back-kicked, driving her foot into the other woman's side, right into the rib-cage. The ferocious impact made Isara stumble backward and sideways until her shoulder hit the corridor wall.

She recovered quickly.

Isara leaped, doing the splits in mid-air as she sailed through the corridor. In her mind's eye, Anna saw a shadowy figure drop to the floor behind her and turn around to finish this altercation.

Anna spun to face her.

Bending her knees, she punched Isara's chest with one fist then the other, then rose to deliver an uppercut to the chin. The impact made her opponent's head jerk back.

Falling over backward, Isara caught herself by pressing two hands to the floor. She brought one leg up to hook her foot around the back of Anna's neck. Then she flung Anna sideways. Painfully.

Anna's shoulder hit the wall, her head rebounding off the duroplastic. Pain and dizziness made it hard to think, her vision blurring as she watched the other woman in pop up right in front of her.

Isara tried to back-hand.

Anna ducked, evading the blow but just barely. She slammed one fist into Isara's stomach, then pulled back her arm and drove that same fist into the other woman's nose. A sweet crunching sound was her reward.

Anna jumped and snap-kicked.

Her opponent leaned back, two hands coming up to seize Anna's ankle and fling it upward. The sudden reversal turned Anna upside-down. She slapped her hands down on the floor and flipped upright.

Isara moved in closer.

The woman kicked high, striking Anna's chin with the tip of her boot. Everything went fuzzy, which made it hard to react when she saw the woman's hazy image spin for a hook-kick.

The heel of a boot came round to clip Anna across the cheek, knocking her sideways, right into the wall. Disorientation set in, and before Anna even realized it, she was falling to her knees.

Her brain full of fog, Anna watched as her opponent turned and ran up the hallway. Isara threw her shoulder against a door that led to a stairwell, and then she was gone. It took a moment for Anna to let out the breath she had been holding. Isara hadn't even gone for the shotgun that was lying at the far end of the corridor.

Perhaps, she was more concerned with getting out.

Tapping at the screen of her multi-tool, Anna activated the building's PA system. "Third floor, east stairwell," Anna shouted. "She's here."

And then she chased after Isara.

26

When the fog receded from Harry's mind, he found himself in dreadful pain. It was like someone had dropped a pile of bricks on his chest, and now he could barely breathe. Trying to sort out the logistics of how he had ended up in this condition was beyond him at this point.

His vision slowly came into focus, a hazy smear of colours slowly resolving into a woman in black who stood over his bed with arms folded. Not his daughter. Larani Tal. Why was she here?

She wore an ugly scowl as she stared down at him, shaking her head in dismay. "I think we have a few things to talk about, Mr. Carlson," she said. "Like the specifics of your skirmish with Cara Sinthel."

Harry felt his face twist, tears leaking from the corners of his eyes. "I tried to stop them," he wheezed, surprised by the hoarseness of his voice. "She was...Someone had to do something. I had the N'Jal."

The N'Jal...

He felt a brief moment of panic at the thought that they might have taken it away from him, but the Overseer device was still firmly attached to his palm. Why hadn't they removed it? Taken it from him. No one really liked the fact that he had kept the thing, but they had tolerated it since he was the only one who could use it.

"And why were you in the cell?"

Grinding his teeth, Harry drew in a soft hissing breath. The pain was intense, and his anxiety seemed to make it worse. "Isara...I wanted to know about the N'Jal," he said. "And... About Jena."

Larani stood with her arms crossed, her eyes fixed upon the floor. "You loved her, didn't you?" The words were so soft he might have imagined them. "It rips you up to see a murderer with her face."

"I..."

Did he love Jena?

The question was oddly specific, specific enough to tickle his detective's instincts. Could it be...Was Larani...It was too hard to form a coherent thought, but somehow, he suspected there was something between Larani and Jena.

"It's not what you think," she said as if reading his thoughts. "Yes, Mr. Carlson, I did have feelings for her, but it was one-sided. She never knew."

"How?"

The tiny smile on Larani's face told him that he had just asked a stupid question. "You aren't the only one who spent twenty years in law-enforcement," she said. "After a while, we start to think alike."

"Why didn't you tell her?"

Laughing softly, Larani fell into the chair at the foot of his bed and doubled over. "I am not the sort of woman who breaks up relationships," she answered. "Jena was happy with you, and I had other concerns."

Harry could understand that; mere weeks after Jena had arrived on Earth, Larani had become acting Chief Director, and shortly after that – after Slade's betrayal had been confirmed – the promotion became permanent. A good manager just did not fraternize with their subordinates.

"You realize you've left me with a bit of a predicament," Larani said. "Just the other day, I revoked Mr. Loranai's clearance for doing exactly what you did."

"And what do you plan to do with me?"

"I don't know."

Placing a hand over his chest, Harry spasmed as he coughed. The pain that brought was enough to cloud his vision with tears. "I broke the rules," he whispered. "You should exercise your authority in whatever way you see fit."

Larani sat forward with elbows on her knees, her chin resting on laced fingers. "I am not so concerned with rules," she began. "I'm more concerned with doing things right. With rules that make sense."

She lifted her forearm and began tapping at her multi-tool, a look of concentration on her face. "It shouldn't surprise you to know that holding cells are monitored," she said. "The security cameras were running while you spoke with Isara."

A hologram appeared between them, displaying a wide-angle shot of Harry down on one knee with his hand on the back of Isara's neck. The woman was lying flat on her stomach and thrashing in pain.

"What do you make of this, Mr. Carlson?"

Harry winced.

"Well..."

He turned his head so that his cheek was pressed to the pillow and let out a grunt. "I have no excuse," he said. "It's exactly what it looks like. I was inflicting pain to make her tell me what she knew."

"Torture."

Harry would have preferred not to use that word, but there was no sense in dancing around the point. Torture was what it was. "Yes," he admitted. "Something that I would never condone for anyone-"

"Who didn't wear the face of your dead girlfriend," Larani said. "Or maybe it's the blood on Isara's hands that makes you feel justified in your actions."

Larani stood up and heaved out a breath. "Have you considered another possibility, Mr. Carlson?" she asked. "Has it occurred to you that perhaps you are not so immune to the N'Jal's influence."

"I don't know what you mean."

"I should think it would be obvious." She turned on her heel and began pacing a line at the foot of his bed. Something in her posture told Harry that she was really quite uneasy. "Does torture sound like something Harry Carlson would do? I've read your file, Mr. Carlson; I made it a point to familiarize myself with everyone on Jena's team."

He had to admit that it *didn't* sound like him. It was the sort of thing that he would never have imagined doing, not once. Not ever. And yet...The image of himself in that cell, tormenting Isara like a psychopathic twelve-year-old who had decided to rip a worm in half just to see what would happen was something that he couldn't get out of his head. "Why didn't you take it from me?" Harry asked. "The N'Jal."

"Surgically removing a N'Jal has been known to put a great deal of stress on the patient," Larani answered. "You were already choking on your own blood. You would have died if Operative Velarese hadn't found you and declared a medical emergency."

"My daughters?"

"Melissa has been notified that you're all right and that you're expected to make a full recovery." Larani turned to face him, her lips pressed together in a thin line. "You are very lucky, Mr. Carlson."

"What about Isara?"

"Gone," Larani said. "She leaped through a window on the second floor, and now she's somewhere out in the city."

Harry raised his left hand, and with a thought, he ordered the N'Jal to disengage. There was a slight tingling sensation as its fibers retracted, and then a thin sheet of flesh in the shape of a hand fell onto his chest.

It quickly rolled up into a little ball.

Closing his eyes, Harry breathed slowly. "Take it," he said in a hoarse voice. "You were right; that thing has been influencing my thoughts." He didn't feel as if his thoughts had been influenced in any way; in fact, he felt like himself. Good old Harry Carlson, the cop with the stick up his butt.

But if he was torturing people.

Are you sure that's not just a convenient excuse? he asked himself. *Blame the N'Jal for your own failings?*

It was a surprise to him when Larani didn't accept his offer. Granted, most people were unwilling to touch the N'Jal with bare skin – Kevin Harmon had made that mistake – but surely Larani would have left to fetch a HAZMAT team or something along those lines.

When he opened his eyes, the woman was still standing there, still frowning down at him. "I'm afraid it's not that simple, Mr. Carlson," she said. "I was there with you, on Earth's moon, if you recall. Your ability to interface with Overseer technology is the only reason we're still alive."

"I..." He coughed. "I remember."

"This is an advantage we cannot afford to lose. You walk a dangerous line, Mr. Carlson." She turned her back on him and made her way to the door that led out to the hallway, pausing there for a moment. "By rights, I should press charges for what you've done."

"Yes...You should."

"I won't because I'm fairly certain that even with the video evidence, a jury won't convict you. Isara has become somewhat infamous; news reports of the strange woman who shot up Denabrian University have stirred up quite a panic. I suspect that may have been the point. But have a care...Violate a prisoner's rights on my watch a second time, and I won't be nearly so lenient."

Harry breathed out a sigh.

When she stepped through the door to her father's room in the Medical Centre, Melissa found him lying on the bed with his eyes closed, breathing softly. Sound asleep so far as she could tell. She toyed with the idea of waking him but decided it would be better to let him get his rest. Her father, on the other hand, had other plans.

Harry placed a hand over his heart, turning his head so that she saw him in profile. "Hey, kiddo," he grunted in a strained voice. "Sorry I gave you such a scare.

Crossing her arms, Melissa frowned down at her father. "You're crazy," she said, shaking her head. "What in God's name would compel you to take on not one but *two* Keepers at the same time?"

"Hubris?"

Melissa chuckled.

Her father looked all right, though the doctors had told her that he would have to take it easy for a month. Thankfully, Leyrian medical tech was more advanced than what they had back home. Harry would make a full recovery.

"I wanted to know..." Harry said. "About Isara."

With her mouth open, Melissa looked up to blink at the ceiling. "So, you decided to bust into her cell and interrogate her?" she grumbled. "You realize this woman has been tortured, right? Standard cop techniques not gonna cut it."

Melissa sank into the chair across from the foot of the bed, setting her elbows on her knees and burying her face in her hands. "I'm not gonna get on your case about doing dangerous things – I'm hardly one to talk – but could you at least wait until Claire is just a *little* bit older before you get yourself killed?"

Her father smiled, wheezing and gasping as his body shook with laughter. "Come on," he said. "My job put me in dangerous positions before. You girls handled it just fine if I recall."

"We had Mom back then," she said. "And Grandpa, and Nan. Maybe you forgot, but Mom is five hundred lightyears away."

"Fair point."

Of course, Melissa's head would choose that moment to flare up with pain. Another reaction to Ilia accelerating the rate at which she learned. Those headaches were now less severe than they had been just a few days ago – she assumed that meant she was reaching a plateau in her training – but her luck would a flash of pain to remind her of her own dangerous choices just when she had lectured her father about doing the same thing. "Did you learn anything useful?"

Harry shook his head. "No," he said. "The woman has an iron will. It shouldn't surprise me, given..."

"Yeah."

Melissa stood up.

She made her way over to the bed, then bent over to press her lips to her father's forehead. "Get some rest," she said. "Claire is with the Savilis. I've got a few things that I need to do."

She turned to go.

It was time to put an end to this once and for all. From what she had heard, Isara had smashed and trashed her way out of this building, knocking down everyone in her way, including Anna. That was no small feat; Anna was one of the best.

The sad reality was that the only person who had any shot of putting Isara down was someone who thought like Isara.

Jena would have been able to do it, but fate was a cruel mistress. They didn't have Jena anymore.

But they did have the next best thing.

The orange ball hit the wall and then bounced off, flying back to Ben's outstretched hand. He closed his fingers around it. That was thirty-seven. At this rate, he was probably going to leave scratch marks on the wall. Not that it mattered all that much. Such things were easily fixed.

In black pants and a gray t-shirt, Ben sat on a stool in his living room with his head down. His dark hair was cut short and parted in the middle. "You should give it a try," he said, throwing the ball again. "It's fun."

Light through the large window that looked out on his front lawn illuminated the big easy chair and the glass coffee table. This place had finally begun to feel like home; six months ago, when he had first moved in after being released from police custody, he had thought that staying was out of the question.

But then all his friends moved to Leyria...

Keli was in the corner with her arms folded, her head turned to direct a frown out the window. "You're going to drive yourself mad," she muttered. "You're already driving *me* mad with that noise."

Ben squeezed his eyes shut, breathing through his nose. "It's not like there's much else to do," he muttered. "I made sure of that, now didn't I? Ruined any chance we had of being useful."

"Stop sulking; it's unbecoming."

"Yes, Mother."

The woman forced out a breath and strode across the room with her arms swinging, passing in front of the window. "You want to do something useful?" she asked. "Gather some of those wonderful tools I saw you use on Ganymede, find Isara and kill her. I'd be more than happy to help."

News of the woman's escape had come this morning

when a furious Jack had called to give him an update. Ben didn't know why his friend bothered; it wasn't as though there was any chance of regaining Larani's trust. It seemed that Jack was just the sort of person who wanted to believe that the people he cared about would overcome their differences.

Keli wasn't much help in that regard. In the days since his dismissal, Ben had spent most of his time with her, and the woman talked of little except how ill-prepared Leyrians were for the threats that lurked beyond the edges of known space. Truth be told, she was beginning to sound like one of the Sons of Savard.

"I heard that," Keli said. "If you believe I'm anything like those idiots who insist on dressing up and playing revolutionary, then you really don't know me."

Touching his fingertips to his forehead, Ben shut his eyes. "You're really something else," he muttered. "How many times have I asked you to stay out of my head? Must be at least fifty by now."

"I can hardly help it if you insist on broadcasting your thoughts."

He threw the ball again, watched as it bounced off the wall and then caught it on its return flight. Thirty-nine. Keli was antsy; he didn't have to be a telepath to see that much. When she wasn't talking about her disdain for the Justice Keeper – and Leyria in general – she was listing all the reasons why Isara had to die. "Why do you hate her so much?" he wondered aloud. If the woman was going to read his mind against his wishes, then he may as well voice his thoughts. "Didn't she save you from people who wanted to dump you back in another cell?"

Before he could throw the ball again, Keli positioned herself in front of him and stood with hands clasped behind herself, her head bowed. "Have you seen an Overseer?" she asked. "Have you come face to face with one of those monstrosities?"

"No," Ben said. "I mean...There was an Overseer in the Key when we tried to take control of it, but I didn't see-"

"I *have* seen them." The look on her face was frightening; her cheek twitched, and her forehead glistened with sweat. "More than once; believe me when I tell you that they desire our extermination, and Isara *serves* them."

"That doesn't make sense."

"I beg your pardon."

Ben wrinkled his nose, then shook his head vigorously. "If the Overseers wanted to destroy us," he began, "they could do so. Their technology is so far beyond ours we can't even comprehend it."

A knock at the door spared him from further elaboration. Now, who could that be? Jack came by once every few days, but always in the evenings, and it was only just past lunchtime. "Come in!"

He got off his stool and turned to find the door in his kitchen swinging slowly inward. His "front door" was actually built into the side of the house. A curious features, but he didn't really mind it. It struck him that only recently had he begun to evaluate the house's design. For the longest time, he hadn't planned on staying.

When the door was open, he found Melissa Carlson standing before him in a pair of gray jeans and a matching tank-top. The girl's face was flushed, and she seemed unable to take her eyes off the welcome mat. "Hi, Ben."

"Melissa."

"I hope I'm not disturbing you."

Clasping his hands together behind his back, Ben studied the girl with pursed lips. "Oh, not really," he said with a shrug. "I was just in the middle of putting a nice dent in my living room wall. Care to join me."

"Maybe later," Melissa said. "I need to talk about something."

All the while, Keli stood by the front window with her arms folded, watching the young woman like a hawk. "Hear her out, Tanaben," she said softly. "I suspect that she has something very interesting to tell you."

Melissa drew herself up to assume the posture of a confident Justice Keeper, lifting her chin to stare over his head at the living room wall. "Isara," she said. "You know that she got out last night."

"I'd heard."

"I want to go after her."

Covering his mouth with one hand, Ben shut his eyes and chuckled. "Okay, kid, I get that you're eager to prove yourself," he said. "But there's no way in the Companion's Grand Vision that you're up for that challenge."

Melissa strode forward at a brisk pace. "If we get close enough, I can bring her down," the girl said. "All we have to do is find her."

"She's being sincere," Keli murmured.

Melissa turned narrowed eyes upon the telepath, and for a moment, you might have thought the girl was a wolf who intended to pounce on some poor deer. "How would you know that?" she demanded. "I thought you couldn't read Keepers."

"Ordinarily, I can't," Keli answered. "Not without considerable effort, at least. But it seems your symbiont is willing to let me have a peek."

"Grand."

Throwing his hands up, Ben shook his head and let out a grunt. "Okay, so Melissa *thinks* she can take on Isara," he cut in. "But even if that were true, why would you think *we* could find her."

"You have a telepath," Melissa said.

Keli's throaty laughter shot down that idea. The telepath

was hunched over with a hand pressed to her stomach. "If I could find Isara on my own," she began, "the woman would be dead already."

"You sensed Anna when she was in orbit of Ganymede."

"Yes, but there were less than two hundred people on that base," Keli replied. "My talents are refined enough to pick out a new voice in that din. But Denabria is a city of two and a half million people. Imagine yourself in a crowded stadium where everyone is talking at once. You might be able to make out the words of the person next to you, but everything else is just a hum, a buzz."

"Even if we could find her," Ben added. "You're just a half-trained kid, and Isara has smacked around some of the best Keepers in the business with little difficulty. She's as good as Jena was, and I can't back you up."

Melissa blinked.

"I'm sorry; I thought you knew," Ben muttered. "They took away my weapons, Melissa. All of that illegal tech I spent years accumulating? It's gone."

He marched forward to stand in front of the young woman and looked up to gaze into her eyes. "I fought Isara on Palissa," he went on. "I had all my best gadgets with me then, and I *still* barely got out with my skin on."

"What about Vetrid Col's suit of armour?"

"What, you think they let me keep it in my bedroom closet?" Ben snapped. Really, it *was* a stupid question. "It's buried in some vault beneath the Keeper building, and my access codes aren't working right now."

Not that they would have granted him access to that particular vault anyway. Larani had been quite clear that letting him use that tech during the Battle of Queens was a one-time deal. "I'm licensed to carry a single pistol," Ben said. "And right now it's locked up in a cabinet upstairs. Not exactly the kind of high-powered ordinance you want to bring against a Keeper."

He really hoped the girl would let this drop. On top of everything else, he really didn't need a reputation for being the man who took a kid with him on a suicide mission. Granted, Melissa was above the age of majority, but only just.

"Fine," she said. "You're right; I'll go home."

"Melissa...Your father..."

She spun around, turning her back on him, and raised one hand to silence him. "It was a stupid idea," she said. "Experienced Keepers can handle Isara much better than I can. Let's leave them to it."

She slammed the door shut on her way out.

As she leaned against the side of the house with her arms folded, Melissa closed her eyes and tried to calm down. "So, what now?" she growled, hoping that her Nassai might have an answer. "If Keli can't find her, we've got *no* chance of-"

Melissa...

It wasn't a voice that intruded upon her thoughts so much as it was an idea forced into her mind. An urge to pay attention, the feeling of being summoned. Ilia quivered at the sudden emotional pressure.

Biting her lip, Melissa felt her eyes widen. "Keli?" she asked in a soft whisper. "Is that you?"

You want to find Isara?

Melissa stiffened, sweat prickling on her brow as she inhaled through her nose. "Of course I do," she answered. "But if you can't locate her, then I'm at a loss for what to do. It's a big city, and she might not even *be* here."

There might be a way.

"I'm listening."

Not here. Meet me at Letasarin Station in half an hour. We'll find Isara, and then we will end her together.

27

Letasarin Avenue was a street that curved slightly as it made a circuit around the downtown core, a street lined with glittering buildings that stood six or eight stories high and trees on each sidewalk. Tall maples and elm trees with bright green leaves drank in the light of a clear afternoon.

The air was warm with a sweetness in the breeze, and despite the fact that summer was just a few weeks away, the temperature was still quite comfortable. The juxtaposition was not lost on Keli; every time she imagined a setting in which she might take another human being's life, she always came up with a dark, musty warehouse or an empty space station. She never pictured the bedroom or a mansion or...wherever it was Isara had gone this afternoon.

Melissa Carlson was hugging herself and rubbing her arms as she came up the steps that led to the subway platform. Odd...The girl had seemed so intent on this less than an hour ago. Why would she be squeamish now?

Keli stood on the sidewalk in white shorts and matching tank-top with thin straps, her hair up in a bun. “You came,” she said with a nod. "Good. I believe I just might have a fix on our...friend."

Melissa's face crumpled, and she gave her head a shake. "I thought you said you couldn't track her," she muttered. "Something about too much noise to pick out any one individual voice."

Images floated around Melissa's body like steam rising from a pot of boiling water – the girl's thoughts made manifest to Keli's eyes – but they were nothing but wispy bits of fog. Unreadable. Melissa's Nassai was shielding her thoughts again. Keli disliked the creatures, but now was not the time to say as much.

Tilting her head back, Keli studied the girl with her lips pursed. She blinked a few times. "That was for Tanaben's benefit," she said. "It's true, I can't pick out an individual human in a city of two and a half million."

"But..."

"But there are far fewer Nassai."

Keli fell in beside Melissa, marching up the sidewalk with her head down, passing under the shade of a maple tree. "Only a few dozen of the creatures in this city," she said. "Most of them concentrated in Justice Keeper Headquarters."

A moment later, Melissa fell in step beside her, staring straight ahead with a blank expression. "You can find them?" the girl asked in a voice so soft no one who stood more than five feet away would hear.

"I can try."

The street was curving slightly to her right, lined on both sides with sidewalk cafes, fabrication centres and the odd church, public pool or apartment complex. They were in a residential neighbourhood near the downtown core.

Up ahead, a group of four young women in colourful dresses stood on the sidewalk, gossiping with one another. Images fluttered around their bodies only to disintegrate like smoke blown away by a strong wind. Most thoughts lasted only seconds, not nearly long enough for Keli to get much from them. Not unless she pushed.

Some were easy to make out, however. The lady in the middle kept picturing a man with stubble on his olive-skinned face and flecks of gray in his black hair. There was no need to guess at her desires. Keli couldn't understand why people were so eager to have sex with each other. The thought of anyone touching her in that way made her shiver.

"Do you have anything?" Melissa asked.

Closing her eyes, Keli turned her face up to the afternoon sun. The warmth on her skin was pleasant. "It's difficult to say," she whispered. "The mind of a Nassai is nothing like the mind of a human; there is a different flavour."

"How so?"

Keli grimaced, tossing her head about as she tried to forget her frustration. "It's not something I can describe in words," she said. "And I doubt your symbiont would wish me to show you."

"I see."

"These...corrupted symbionts were even more distinct." She felt their presence as a throbbing pressure against her mind, like waves crashing over her body, only they were waves of emotion. Somewhere to the south...It was hard to be specific; all those human minds tended to drown out awareness of everything else.

It wasn't very long before they were standing on the corner of Letasarin Avenue and Third Street. There were very few cars on the road – most people used public transit – but a few drifted through the intersection.

Melissa stepped up to the curb with fists on her hips, shaking her head slowly. "It still amazes me," she murmured as if speaking to herself. "No traffic lights."

"Traffic lights?"

The girl put herself in front of Keli with arms crossed, frowning down at herself. "Back home, we use coloured lights to direct traffic," she said. "Green means go through the intersection, red means stop."

Keli felt a smile blossom. "Such technology is obsolete in a world where the cars drive themselves," she said. "I should think it wouldn't be *that* strange to you."

She pointed up Third Street, in the direction that led away from the downtown core. There were more small buildings on this road and more trees with bright green leaves that had come into full bloom. "The corrupted Nassai are in that direction," she said. "And I'd suggest that we hurry. I'm feeling...tension."

Before they could activate the crosswalk, a blue car with tinted windows rolled up to the curb and came to a stop. Keli felt a rush of emotions – irritation with minute traces of concern – and she knew that they were caught.

The car's front door swung open, and Tanaben emerged, shaking his head as he let out a growl. "What in Bleakness do you two think you're doing?" he asked. "I thought we agreed that this was a foolish plan."

The car drove off once he shut the door.

Keli folded her arms with a sigh, lifting her chin to stare down her nose at him. "So, how did you find us?" she asked, raising an eyebrow. "I wasn't aware that you possessed the ability to track people, Tanaben."

"You think I haven't kept tabs on you?" He stepped forward to stand in front of her, and despite the fact that she was an inch taller, Keli still felt the force of his stare. "Every time we meet, I sprinkle your clothes with nanobots."

"Why?"

"Because you're unpredictable, that's why."

Melissa shoved herself between them, pushing the both of them apart, and directed a fiery glare at Ben. "Enough," she said. "If you don't want to help us, you don't have to, but we're doing this."

"And if I call your father?"

Melissa went beet-red, but to her credit, the girl composed herself quickly enough. The images that radiated from her body seemed to be just a little more solid. "If you want to disturb a wounded man's bed rest, be my guest," she said. "But Harry is in no position to stop me, and neither are you."

Ben stepped away from them, arms hanging limp at his sides. He let his head sink. and forced out a deep breath. "You're both insane, you know that?" he muttered. "You're gonna get me killed."

"You don't-"

He drew aside his light spring jacket to reveal a pistol holstered on his hip. "Good thing I brought this," he grumbled. "Were the two of you at least smart enough to bring weapons of your own."

Melissa opened the purse she carried, allowing them a glimpse of a pistol that was almost identical to Ben's in every way. "It's all I could get," she whispered. "Cadets are allowed access to weapons, but if I sign out half the armory, it will raise suspicion. I was thinking Keli could use it."

Keli had to admit that she liked that idea; she had no weapons of her own and no way to acquire them. Also, the thought of being the one who put a bullet through Isara's head had a certain appeal.

"Well, then let's go," Ben said. "Before I come to my senses and remember that this is suicide."

As the car pulled up to the curb, Isara ventured a glance out the window to her right. Her own face was reflected in the tinted glass – and it was *her* face, no matter what those idiots who had loved her daughter insisted – but beyond that, she saw a small park where a concrete path led to a round fountain that sprayed water into the air, a fountain that was surrounded by a ring of lampposts.

There were trees as well, tall ash trees with leaves that had blossomed bright and green. Children played in the grass near the fountain, kicking a ball while their parents watched and made small-talk.

In beige pants and a red tank-top, Isara sat with a briefcase in her lap, impatiently drumming her fingers on it. "It's time," she said, peering over her shoulder at the two who sat behind her.

Calissa Narim wore gray pants and a simple blue t-shirt, her long black hair a sharp contrast to a face of milky-white skin. Eyes like emeralds fixed themselves on Isara. "I'm ready," she said.

Next to her, Tarell Sakarai sat with his knees apart and his jacket open. A tall man with olive skin and brown hair that he wore combed back and gelled, her stared somberly into the distance. "For the glory of the Inzari."

Squeezing her eyes shut, Isara slapped one hand over her face. "Yes, Tarell," she muttered into her palm. "Your devotion is duly noted."

She opened the briefcase to reveal three pistols inside, each one powered down for the moment. It was the most that she could manage to bring without attracting too much attention. As it was, she had already received a few raised eyebrows. Briefcases were all but unheard of in a society that did not conduct correspondence by paper. But then most Leyrians were fools who had grown so used to their comfortable life-style that they couldn't fathom why someone would commit a violent crime.

"Take one," she said, offering the weapons to her companions.

When they did so, she claimed the last pistol for herself, shut the case and opened the door. The air was warm as she stepped out onto the sidewalk, the sun shining high in the sky. It was a beautiful afternoon in the Leyrian capitol.

Not the sort of place where you would expect a massacre.

Pressing her lips into a thin line, Isara turned her head to survey her surroundings. “Lovely,” she said, eyebrows rising. “Have you spoken with the others? Venez, Taliok? Do they have transportation ready?”

Without waiting for a reply, she put the briefcase down on the sidewalk – it was useless to her now – and started up the path toward the bubbling fountain. Once you were committed, there was no point in stalling.

Calissa fell in beside her, walking stiffly with her shoulders hunched up and her head down. “We're ready,” she whispered. “Venez has commandeered a shuttle, and he's waiting in orbit. He can be here in just under ten minutes.”

“No sooner?”

“If he comes in hot, it will trigger every sensor on the network, and they may shoot him down before he gets here.”

Closing her eyes, Isara let out a sigh. “Order him to begin his approach,” she said, nodding to the other woman. “We'll be finished in less than ten minutes.”

The other woman looked tense, but she did as she was ordered, tapping a button on her multi-tool that had been programmed to send a signal to Venez. Six months in a cell had rattled Calissa. The woman had become far too timid for Isara's liking. “If we time it appropriately, we should be able to avoid drawing too much attention until just before Venez arrives, and then we can-”

“Where's the fun in that?” Isara said.

She jumped, Bending gravity to propel herself upward. Tucking her legs into her chest, she somersaulted through the air and then landed gracefully on the small concrete circle that surrounded the fountain.

Tarell landed on her left and Calissa on her right, the three of them pausing for a moment to allow nearby spectators to get a good look at them. Parents and their small children stood in awe of the display. A heavyset man in shorts and a t-shirt stared at her with a gaping mouth; a tiny woman in a green sundress smiled and giggled. Some of the younger children squealed with delight.

One man on the other side of the fountain started clapping, and pretty soon they all were doing it, a round of applause that echoed through the whole park. Idiots! It did not even occur to them that they were staring death in the eye.

A great big smile stretched across Isara's face, and she ran her gaze over the crowd. "Yes...You people do love your Justice Keepers, don't you?" she shouted. "The stalwart defenders of the common good!"

Isara thrust her hand out, pointing her gun.

She fired.

The woman in the green sundress staggered as a bullet ripped through her chest, blood spraying into the air. She took a few shaky steps backward and then fell hard into the grass.

Isara adjusted her aim, pointing her weapon at the heavyset man who stood there like a cow that didn't realize it was about to enter the slaughterhouse. Bleakness take her, *everyone* in this park looked as if they were wondering if they had really just witnessed a Justice Keeper killing in cold blood.

Isara fired.

The man spasmed as a bullet pierced his chest, his arms flailing about before he fell to the ground. That was when the screaming started! People finally realized that this was *really* happening.

Everyone turned and ran from the fountain like a herd of buffalo in stampede, fathers scooping up young children and carrying them in their arms, teenagers shrieking as they scrambled through the field. Some took refuge behind trees.

A young woman in shorts and a halter top fell to one of

Calissa's bullets. A middle-aged man in a high-collared shirt fell flat on his face, a pool of blood spreading from his broken body.

Throwing her head back, her mouth a gaping hole, Isara roared with cruel laughter. “Do your worst, Larani!” she bellowed. “Send your little minions! But we both know that the only Keeper who could defeat me is dead!”

28

Finding Isara wasn't difficult when Melissa spotted the flood of people flowing out of a park on Third Street. Maybe two dozen of them in total, all in summer clothing, all bolting in different directions. Some ran into the road, and she cringed at the sight of that. Luckily, traffic was sparse. No one was hit.

Doubling over with her hands on her knees, Melissa shook her head. “Oh god,” she panted. “What has she done?”

Ben skidded to a stop on the sidewalk beside her. The man stared into the distance, his face so gray it looked as if he was about to throw up. “It's a slaughter,” he whispered. “She's going to kill them all.”

In her mind's eye, Keli was right behind them, a wispy silhouette who stood with fists clenched, shivering. No doubt the woman could feel what those people were feeling. All that fear. All that pain.

Melissa stood up straight. “No,” she whispered, striding forward. “No one else is going to die today. God puts you where you need to be, and he put us here!”

When she spun around, Ben and Keli were standing together on the sidewalk, both with nervous expressions, both watching her as if they weren't quite sure whether or not they wanted to believe her. People rushed past all around them; no one seemed to wonder why Melissa and her friends weren't fleeing for their lives.

She was keeping tabs on Isara as well; the woman and her goons were focused on victims on the other side of the park.

"We have the power to stop her," Melissa said.

Ben flinched as if someone had struck him, then shook his head slowly. "Maybe *you* do," he said, stepping forward. "But I remind you that any hope I had of besting a Keeper went away when they took my tech."

Keli was shivering, gripping the fabric of her shorts as she trembled. Her lips were twitching. "There are three of them," she said. "The other two have symbionts as well. I can handle one."

"I'll take Isara," Melissa said.

With his mouth hanging open, Ben tossed his head back and blinked at the clear, blue sky. "Is *anyone* gonna listen to me?" he moaned. "I *can't* take on a Justice Keeper. I don't have the tools!"

"You'll think of something," Melissa assured him. "Do everything you can; trust in God to make up the rest."

"Great advice for an atheist!" Ben protested.

Retrieving the gun from her purse, Melissa threw the weapon to Keli. The telepath caught it awkwardly, stumbling backward and nearly dropping the damn thing. Had Keli even handled a firearm before?

Melissa flung her purse to the ground – there was nothing in it that she would mind losing anyway – and then took off at a dead sprint through the grass. The park was a large field with trees that took up most of a city block between Third Street and Balin Avenue.

Four concrete pathways spread out from the fountain in each of the four cardinal directions, but no one was keeping to those. The last few stragglers ran through the grass or took refuge behind trees.

Isara was at the fountain with her back turned, as were her two minions. Had the woman noticed that someone was running *toward* her? It didn't matter. It was time to end this once and for all!

When Melissa took off through the field, Ben didn't even try to stop her. Charging headlong toward death itself was something that Keepers just did. Those Nassai messed with your brain; only an idiot would want one.

He rounded on Keli.

The woman jumped and then backed up on the sidewalk. Her face hardened after a moment. "Are you just going to stand there?" she demanded. "If we don't help, that girl's going to get herself killed."

Licking his lips, Ben looked down at himself. "We need to create a distraction," he said. "Can you do anything to those other two with Isara? Mess with their minds the way you did with the guards on Ganymede?"

"Their symbionts will make it difficult."

"Try," Ben said.

He detached the metal disk that contained his multi-tool's processing unit and then handed it to Keli. Of course, the woman was baffled, but he had no time to explain. "I'm gonna go right, you go left," he said. "Set this down in the grass. It doesn't matter where, but make sure it's out in the open."

"All right..."

"Let's go!"

He broke into a sprint, tracing the circumference of a circle around the open field, using the trees to make sure the enemy Keepers wouldn't notice him until he was ready for it. Not that it would do much good. *You're an idiot, Tanaben Loranai,* he told himself. *Always letting these insufferable do-gooders drag you into trouble.*

Melissa skidded to a stop some fifty feet away from the fountain. Close enough for Isara and her pair of jackals to notice. Keepers using their gifts to kill and wound instead of protecting the innocent! It sickened her. "Isara!" she growled.

The woman twisted around to face her and flinched as if she hadn't really taken note of Melissa's presence. A mocking grin spread on her face. "Well, well," she said. "It's the Carlson girl. I thought you had enough of a beat-down last time to put the idea of being a hero out of your mind."

"I lack Jack's talent for quips," Melissa said. "Let's just fight."

"Very well!"

Isara raised her weapon.

By instinct, Melissa jumped and curled up in a ball, back-flipping through the air. Bullets rushed past underneath her. She uncoiled and then fell to land poised in the lush green grass.

The other woman adjusted her aim.

Crouching down, Melissa felt another bullet fly over her head. Her right hand came up to craft a Bending, the colours stretching until Isara and the fountain were completely unrecognizable to her.

When the next bullet came at her, it hit a patch of warped space-time and looped around in a tight U-turn. She sent it flying back toward its master.

The Bending vanished, and Melissa found herself looking at a shocked Isara who couldn't stop staring into her own empty hand. One of Jena's old tricks. Reflect the bullet so that it strikes the shooter's gun.

Isara's weapon was now lying in the grass near the fountain.

The other two Keepers raised their weapons.

"No!" Isara growled, snarling as she shook her head. The

woman strode forward with determination. "The girl is mine! Guard my back in case any of her little friends show up, and be ready to make a tactical retreat."

Melissa stood up straight and tall and began the slow, steady walk toward the battle she would have preferred to have avoided. Maybe other Keepers found a thrill in the fight – Jena had, though she would never have admitted that – but Melissa didn't. This was just duty. That and nothing more.

"Come, girl," Isara said. "Let's have a little fun."

Tarell backed away as he watched the Justice Keeper – a young woman from Earth unless he missed his guess – advance upon Isara. Melissa Carlson passed between two of the concrete lampposts that formed a ring around the fountain.

Her face was grim, her eyes focused upon Isara. "Normally, this would be the part where I ask you why," Melissa said. "Where I ponder what would make somebody like you use your power for evil, but I already know-"

Tarell ignored the exchange; it wasn't about him. He had no intention of fighting *anyone* who carried a symbiont, even if she was young.

Scanning the perimeter of the park, he looked for signs of other Keepers and saw nothing of consequence. Just a bunch of people who ran across the road and took refuge in nearby apartment buildings. It had only been a few minutes since the shooting started. The Keepers weren't here yet, but they would come. They always came.

Tarell knew.

Not because he had been a Keeper, mind you – Slade had had less success than he would have liked at turning them – but he had spent most of his adult life running from Keepers, dealing Euphoria and Diamond Snow. He'd even dabbled in Amps a few times.

Only *some* of Slade's converts had been Keepers that he had brought around to the right way of thinking. Many were people who would never have been allowed to take a Nassai in the first place, people that Slade had recruited and then slowly introduced into the ranks of the Justice Keepers over the course of a decade.

It was-

Tarell touched his fingers to his temples. A screech that he barely recognized as his own voice came from his throat. "What...Who's doing..." There was a pressure on his mind; his symbiont was writhing.

He turned to his right and found a man walking between two trees with branches that intersected, forming an arch of green foliage. A tall and slender man in black pants and a purple coat moving with a kind of serpentine grace. His face with high cheekbones and tilted eyes looked like it belonged on a statue, and long, silky black hair fell over his shoulders.

Tarell closed his eyes, bowing his head to the other man. "Lord Slade," he said. "I am honoured by your presence."

Grecken Slade drew himself up to full height and then turned his head to survey the field. "What are you doing, fool?" he snapped. "The Justice Keepers will be upon you in seconds! Why would you expose yourself like this?"

"Lady Isara-"

A sneer pulled Slade's lips back from immaculate white teeth. "Isara!" he bellowed, fixing his attention on the woman. Tarell could perceive her as a wispy silhouette in his mind. "Once again, you have threatened the success of our mission!"

Strangely, Isara seemed not to notice.

Dropping to one knee in the grass, Tarell kept his head down. No need to offend his master. "We were told this was your will, my Lord," he whispered. "That you sent us to serve the Inzari-"

"Stop babbling, fool!"

"Yes, my Lord-"

"When I want-"

Out of the corner of his eye, Tarell noticed something that he had not seen before. A young woman in shorts and a tank-top stood off to his left with her arm extended, aiming a gun at him. "Idiot," she said. The image of Grecken Slade vanished from his mind just before a bullet pierced his skull.

Ben was running at full speed, tracing a circle around the park, huffing and puffing with every step. Sweat rolled over his face, and he shook his head in disgust. "Sooner or later," he whispered. "This lifestyle is gonna get you killed."

When he was a quarter way around the circle, he stopped.

Ben threw his shoulder against the trunk of a tree, gulping down air as fast as he could. "Come on, Tanaben," he said in a rasping voice. "A few months out of action did not dull your skills *that* much."

He peeked around the trunk of the tree.

In the distance, he saw the bubbling fountain and a distracted Calissa Narim who was staring up at the sky for some reason. She would have noticed him, of course – even if only with her spatial awareness – but there had been dozens of people running in all directions. If she didn't consider him a threat...

Behind Calissa, young Melissa fought with the woman who wore Jena's face. *That* couldn't be easy. Ben didn't know Jena that well, but he wouldn't have liked to have been the one to pull the trigger on her doppelganger.

The other one – some man that Ben didn't recognize – just stood there with his back turned, focused on something on the other side of the park. Was that Keli's doing? There was no way to know for sure, and he didn't have time to wonder. He just hoped that Keli had planted his multi-tool in a convenient spot.

Lifting his right forearm, Ben tapped at the touchscreen on

his gauntlet, readying a program that might save his life. He still had a few tricks up his sleeve.

He drew aside his jacket and took a pistol from the holster on his left hip. Gripping the weapon in both hands, he stepped around the tree trunk and pointed it at Calissa.

The woman noticed immediately, her head turning to fix green eyes upon him. In the instant when he fired, Calissa's body stretched into a blur of colours, the bullet that would have killed her swerving off to his left.

The fallen Keeper resolidified and strode toward him. "Tanaben!" she exclaimed, shaking her head. "I was wondering if I would ever see you again. I owe you for putting me in that cell!"

She lifted her own weapon.

Ben ducked behind the tree, grunting as a bullet zipped past on his right. Nothing hit the tree trunk; he suspected that it would be thick enough to provide adequate cover, but Calissa was precise. She wasn't going to waste ammunition.

"You're not gonna win this!" Ben called out. "We've got people everywhere!"

Something hit the tree trunk with a loud *THWACK,* and he knew that Calissa had fired off a shot just to intimidate him. Companion have mercy, couldn't they have let him keep his force-field generators? Those weren't even illegal! Well, not for an agent of the LIS, they weren't. But he was a private citizen now.

"Last chance!" he called out.

Without looking to see – he would die if he poked his head out from behind this tree – he tapped his multi-tool and activated the program that he had prepared. One, two, three, *now!*

He stepped into the open.

Calissa spun to face something on his left, her hand coming up to create a patch of rippling air in front of herself. The threat she was responding to was a stream of white tracers that flew across the open field and somehow winked out before getting within a hundred paces of her. Not real bullets.

Holograms.

Ben took aim with his pistol.

In a fraction of a heartbeat, Calissa became a streak of gray and blue that reformed into a person several steps to the right of where she had been. Her hand came up to point that damn gun at him.

Ben spun around, pressing his back to the tree trunk in the instant before a bullet flew close enough to scrape off some of the bark and send chunks of wood flying. Damn! That was his last resort! He had nothing left.

"You're a tricky one, Tanaben!" Calissa shouted. By the sound of her voice, she was getting closer. "I must admit, I would never have anticipated that one!"

Ben shivered.

A high-pitched squeal from Calissa made him jump back. Had the woman been hit from behind? Hard to imagine with a Justice Keeper, but not impossible. Should he take a peek? Or would that get him killed?

Cautiously, oh so cautiously, he peered around the tree trunk. Calissa was there, in the field, with the heels of her hands pressed to the sides of her head. Her face was red, and there were tears on her cheeks. It was as if she had developed a sudden headache.

Ben noticed Keli coming toward him.

The telepath moved at a slow, steady pace, her face grim as she stalked through the grass. "Kill her!" she snapped. "I can't hold her forever!"

Calissa dropped to a crouch, and the sound that came out of her mouth made Ben imagine a dying pig. The woman was suffering, but he could see that she was already fighting through the pain.

"Kill her!" Keli insisted.

Ben looked at the pistol in his hand.

He closed his eyes, taking a deep breath, and then made a decision. "Stun-rounds," he said, listening for the beep that confirmed the change in settings. He could kill another human being if he had to, if his life was threatened, but not if they were helpless.

Lifting the weapon in both hands, Ben squinted at his opponent. Then he pulled the trigger.

A charged bullet hit Calissa in the chest and sent a jolt through her body that made her arms flail about. The woman fell face-first into the grass and then suddenly went still. They would take her back to her cell.

"Come on!" Ben said. "We need to help Melissa."

Melissa stepped through the space between two lampposts, standing with her arms hanging limp. Her mouth tightened as she stared down the other woman. "Normally, this would be the part where I ask you why," she said. "Where I ponder what would make somebody like you use your power for evil, but I already know why."

Grinning maliciously, Isara closed her eyes and bowed her head. "The usual bland, sanctimonious moralizing I've come to expect from a Keeper." The woman took one step forward, the fountain spraying water into the air behind her. "You've learned your lessons well, girl."

"You killed those people."

"And many others!"

Melissa felt her lips peel away from clenched teeth, her face suddenly burning with intense heat. "You're a mockery of everything that Jena stood for," she said. "It's about time somebody put you down."

Cold dread welled up inside her as she watched the other woman close the distance between them in three quick strides. "Think you can?" Isara asked in a sweet voice. The kind of voice a mother would use to soothe a crying infant. Melissa found herself backing up toward one of the lampposts. "I'm not so sure. The only Justice Keeper who had any chance of besting me is dead."

Isara turned her body for a high roundhouse kick.

Melissa ducked and felt a black boot pass over her head. She came up in time to watch Isara bring her leg down. The woman stood so that Melissa saw her in profile.

She kicked out to the side, driving a foot into Melissa's stomach. Pain flared up, and it was so very hard to breathe, so very hard to concentrate. Tears blurred her vision, but she saw her opponent closing in on her.

Isara threw a punch.

Melissa ducked, evading the blow by inches. She slammed a fist into Isara's belly, then rose to back-hand her opponent across the face. The other woman stumbled away, blood leaking from the corner of her mouth.

Melissa charged in, punching.

Bending over backward as if she were made of rubber, Isara reached up to seize Melissa's wrist with one hand. She snapped herself upright and then drove her open palm into Melissa's chest. Keeper strength did the rest.

The other woman released her grip, and Melissa went stumbling backward. Her back hit the concrete lamppost as the air fled her lungs. So much pain. She was barely even aware of the other woman's approach.

Isara spun for a back-kick.

Melissa stepped aside.

Isara's foot hit the lamppost instead, and cracks spider-webbed over the concrete. Chunks of it fell away, dropping to the ground. God have mercy! The woman was just so strong! There was no way she could win this.

As she backed away through the grass with her fists raised in a defensive posture, Melissa tried to catch her breath. "You're nothing like her, you know." It came out as little more than a whisper. "Your daughter was better than you in every way."

Isara pulled a small throwing knife from a sheath on her belt, and then flung it with all her might, augmenting its velocity with a touch of Bent Gravity. By instinct, Melissa threw up a Time Bubble.

The sphere of warped space-time expanded, the world beyond its surface fuzzy and blurred to her vision. A short way off, Isara stood with her arm extended, a knife hanging in mid-air before her.

Several paces away, the man who had come here with Isara was down on one knee with his back turned, staring at two trees. Keli was next to him with a gun pointed at the man's head.

The knife continued its slow approach.

Melissa turned her body sideways.

When she let the bubble vanish, the knife flew past behind her, close enough that she could feel the whoosh of air on her back. Not far off, Isara blinked and then smiled with a burst of laughter. "Not bad, girl!"

Isara ran at her.

The woman leaped and kicked out. At the very last second, Melissa leaned back. Her hands came up to grab Isara's foot, and Bent Gravity did the rest.

Isara was thrown backward, propelled by an unseen force. Her back slammed into the concrete lamppost, and then the woman fell to land on shaky legs. It was hard not to feel a little pride after that.

Melissa charged forward.

She jumped and curled her legs as she soared through the air, intending to flatten her opponent against the post. Rage and fury. This was going to end in-

Isara moved out of the way.

Melissa landed.

A hand clamped onto the back of her collar and then shoved her face-first into the lamppost. Hard concrete against soft skin. She had a bloody nose, and everything went dark for a moment.

Melissa turned to find Isara standing there, right in front of her. Four hard knuckles collided with her face, and then another fist slammed into her stomach. It was so hard to breathe, so hard to think.

A hand seized her hair and pulled her head down, forcing her to double over. Isara leaped and brought her elbow down between Melissa's shoulder-blades, forcing her to the ground. *Oh, God...I can't win this.*

Dimly, Melissa was aware of the other woman's silhouette standing with fists on her hips. "I have to give you credit," Isara said. "You've learned a great deal in such a short amount of time."

Melissa pushed herself up on extended arms.

Her vision cleared in time for her to see the tip of a boot strike her right between the eyes, and then she fell over onto her side, with the lamppost behind her. *She's going to kill me! In Jesus's name, I pray for strength.*

"Did you really think you could win?"

Isara hoofed her in the stomach.

Bent Gravity lifted Melissa off the ground and flung her backwards into the post. She bounced off and landed on all fours, shaking her head to clear away the fog. *Come on, kid,* a voice whispered in her thoughts. *Don't quit on me now.*

Not her own voice...Not Jena's either. Not really. Jena was gone. But somehow, she knew without a moment of doubt that this was exactly what Jena would have said had she been here to say it. *You can do it. Remember what I taught you.*

Isara turned on her heel and stalked away from the pole with her back turned. "You have a strong will, girl," she said with a shrug. "But surely you must understand that you stand against the champion of the gods themselves."

Gods don't need to commit mass murder, the voice whispered. *She's a liar, Melissa. Don't listen to her!*

Turning partway, Isara looked over her shoulder with a solemn expression. "I once offered Lenai the chance to join us," she said. "Sadly, she turned me down, but perhaps you might be wiser."

Melissa, I can't do it for you. It has to come from you.

Isara strode toward her with a smile on her face, laughing softly with satisfaction. "You *have* learned much," she said. "You can be an asset to us; the rewards for faithful service are beyond your imagining."

Melissa, get up!

Rage flared to life inside her, boiling her blood, setting every nerve-ending in her body on fire. It hurt – dear God, it hurt – but somehow the pain didn't matter. She found within herself the strength to rise.

Wiping her bloody mouth with her forearm, Melissa winced and shook her head. "Never gonna happen," she snarled. "You really believe your threats are gonna make me back down? I *knew* Jena Morane, and you, madame, are no Jena."

"She was nothing but a clone, the product of a-"

"Yeah, I've heard," Melissa said. "It doesn't matter. Jena may have been the clone, but you, Isara, *you're* the fake!"

The woman flinched at that.

"Come on!" Melissa said. "Let's end this."

Like the spirit of a banshee swooping low over the tall grass, Isara moved forward for the kill. There was a serpentine grace in the woman's stride, a predatory focus in her eyes. She drew back her arm and punched.

Turning her side toward the other woman, Melissa caught Isara's arm in both hands. She forced Isara to double over with her arm extended. Trying to break a Keeper's bones was a bad idea – it would require quite a bit of strength, and she was tired – so she simply used the opportunity fate had provided.

Melissa whirled her opponent around and ran Isara head-first toward the lamppost. With a shove, she sent the other woman stumbling toward a head-on collision.

Isara leaped, kicking the lamppost and pushing off with a surge of Bent Gravity. She back-flipped through the air. *As expected. It's what Jena would have done.* Melissa only needed a thought to erect a Time Bubble.

The dome of warped space-time formed around her with Isara hanging suspended in mid-air just above its peak. All the time in the world and yet no time at all. Her skin was already beginning to burn.

Melissa turned around, allowing the Bubble to vanish.

Isara landed in front of her.

Melissa kicked her in the chest, driving the air from the woman's lungs. She spun and hook-kicked, one foot whirling around to strike Isara across the cheek with a most satisfying *crunch.*

It all seemed to happen in slow motion; Isara toppled over sideways, blood flying from her open mouth. The woman landed in the grass and bounced once, flopping onto her back.

As she came around, Melissa saw her opponent struggling to sit up, wincing from the pain. "No!" Isara scrambled backward on all fours, gasping and panting. "No, it's not possible!"

The woman stood up on shaky legs, then spat a gob of blood into the grass. "How?" she whispered. "How can you..."

Melissa stood before the post with fists raised in a guarded stance, her gaze focused on the other woman. "You said we had no Jena," she growled. "But you're wrong! I carry Jena's symbiont! She lives on in me!"

She looked up to see Ben and Keli running toward her, both panting as they jerked to a halt several paces behind Isara. Keli doubled over and wheezed. The woman was not used to this much exertion, though Melissa suspected that some of that was the result of pushing her telepathic abilities to their limits.

Shutting her eyes tight, Melissa sucked in a deep breath. "The others?" she asked, nodding to them. "Have they been subdued?"

"Calissa is stunned," Ben answered.

Standing up straight, Keli folded her arms and shook her head. "The other one will never be a problem again," she said in a voice as cold as liquid nitrogen. "Why you insist on keeping your enemies alive is a mystery to me."

Isara threw her head back, laughing softly. "You're on the wrong side, my dear," she said. "Are you sure you wouldn't prefer to use those remarkable talents to serve the true gods of this world?"

"Like hell," Melissa said. "And this-"

Her words were cut off by the soft hum of an anti-gravity drive.

A Class-3 assault shuttle, shaped very much like the head of an arrow, swooped low over the surrounding buildings and settled to a stop over the park. The hatch in its belly opened just long enough to let something drop out.

A SlipGate.

The metal triangle had two thruster modules clamped onto it, and they both spat ignited gas toward the ground, slowing the Gate's descent. It landed on the other side of the fountain with a loud *thud.*

The shuttle pitched its nose upward and flew off toward the upper atmosphere, no doubt trying to get out of here before anyone shot it out of the sky. So, this was Isara's escape plan. Too bad it wasn't going to-

Without warning, Isara shot upward, propelled by Bent Gravity. She curled up into a ball and tumbled sideways over the top of the fountain.

"No!" Melissa screeched.

Instinct kicked in, and she ran around the fountain as fast as her legs could carry her. That vile witch wasn't getting away! Not this time! Someone had to make the woman answer for her crimes.

On the other side of the fountain, Melissa found Isara standing right in front of the SlipGate. "Cheer up, girl," the woman said. "What's a hero without a villain to give her life meaning?"

A warp bubble surrounded Isara's body before Melissa could get close enough to do anything. The other woman was a blurry figure, standing there with a mocking grin, and even though sound could not pass through the barrier, Melissa knew she was laughing.

The bubble collapsed to a point and vanished.

29

The park was silent and still in the aftermath of the attack. No one moved; no one spoke, and the wind that should have been warm and comforting had a distinct chill. Only then did Melissa notice the corpses. Her mind had been too focused on staying alive to really take in the sight of them.

There were several that she noted: a woman in a green dress who was sprawled out on her side, a man in shorts and a t-shirt who stared lifelessly at the sky. If only they had gotten here just a few minutes sooner...

Melissa hugged herself, shivering as a chill raced through her body. She shook her head and let out a squeak. “No,” she mumbled. “It's not fair.”

She sank to her knees.

There were sirens other Keepers moving through the park; she heard them, sensed them as they arrived. Paramedics and emergency response drones as well. All around her people were weeping or praying.

A silhouette came up behind her, quickly resolving into the shape of Anna. “Thank the Companion,” the other woman said. “Melissa, are you okay?”

Closing her eyes, Melissa felt tears on her cheeks. She shook her head so quickly it made her dizzy. "No..." It came out as a hoarse whisper. "No, I don't think that I will ever be okay again."

Anna crouched down beside her, slipping an arm around Melissa's shoulders. Her eyes were full of sadness. "You saved these people's lives," she whispered. "Many more would be dead if you hadn't been here."

"It was just dumb luck..."

Clapping a hand over her mouth, Anna shut her eyes and cleared her throat. "Yeah, I'm not so sure about that," she said. "Be honest with me, Melissa. You went looking for her, didn't you?"

Melissa nodded.

"Why didn't you tell us what you were doing?"

"Because you would have stopped me!" Melissa groaned. "You would have said that a cadet had no business going after someone like Isara, but I was the only one who could beat her. The only one..."

"What do you mean?"

Melissa said nothing.

Anna stood up and took a few steps forward. The woman whirled around, staring down at her with a grimace. "Jena's symbiont," she said. "You've had it accelerate your learning curve."

"Yes."

"Melissa, that's *very* dangerous!"

Craning her neck to fix her gaze on the other woman, Melissa blinked a few times. "Jack did it!" she protested. "So did you, for that matter! When you were stuck on Earth, you learned English in a few days."

"We had no other choice," Anna said.

Melissa wasn't willing to argue. It seemed everyone was making dangerous choices in service to the cause. Jack and

Anna had pushed their Nassai to accelerate the rate at which their brains formed neural pathways; her father had bonded with the N'Jal. Jena and Raynar had given their lives. Why should she be any different?

Melissa stood up with every intention of slipping away quietly. She would have to pay a visit to Larani and endure whatever lecture the woman deemed appropriate. Not to mention her father. When Harry got wind of what she had done, he would be livid. More so after her lecture just a few hours ago.

She turned to go, but the sound of frenzied whispers got her attention. On the other side of the fountain, three people stood side by side, watching her as if she had just come down from heaven. "It's her," one said.

"She saved us."

"How old is she? I know Keepers look young, but-"

Applause rippled through the park, applause from the people who had taken refuge behind trees, from people who were waiting as paramedics loaded their loved ones into white shuttles painted with the red shepherd's crook that indicated a medical vehicle. All around her, people were clapping.

"Looks like you're a star," Anna said.

Melissa felt her cheeks burn, then bowed her head in chagrin. "Yeah, I guess so," she said. "Which was *not* what I wanted."

Late afternoon sunlight came through the window in Larani's office and glinted off the surface of her long, rectangular desk. The Head of the Justice Keepers stood behind that desk with her back turned, one forearm braced against the window pane as she stared out at the buildings across the way.

"Reckless," Larani said. "But...Impressive."

Melissa sat in a soft chair with her knees together, peering into her own lap. "Thank you, ma'am," she said with a curt nod.

"But I only did what any other Keeper would do. I was very lucky."

"Yes, you were," Larani agreed. The woman let her arm drop and stood there with her shoulders slumped, heaving out a deep breath. "You were all very lucky. And in more ways than you realize."

On Melissa's left, Ben sat with his arms folded, his mouth a thin line as he watched Larani's back. "If it means anything to you, I wasn't looking to get involved," he said in a soft voice. "The girl can be very persuasive."

Melissa could see Larani's faint reflection in the window. The woman was smiling. And not just any smile, but one that indicated satisfaction. "I'm beginning to realize that," she said. "Surprising in one so meek."

"Meek?"

That came from Keli, who sat on Melissa's right and gazed into the cup of tea that she cradled in both hands. "Don't confuse quiet with meek," she murmured. "The girl has an iron will."

The *girl* was sitting right here and listening to every word these people said about her. A part of her was miffed, but it was just a mild irritation. Not worth disrupting this meeting, certainly. There were larger concerns.

Larani spun around to face them with her hands clasped behind herself, head held high as if she were about to give a speech. "Mr. Loranai, Ms. Armana," she began. "I've recommended that you be offered the highest symbol of valor among civilians: the Silver Crescent. And as for you, Cadet Carlson..."

Melissa steeled herself for whatever came.

With her eyes shut tightly, she could still perceive the other woman as a silhouette who leaned forward with her hands braced on the desk. "Nicely done," Larani said. "But your decision to allow your symbiont to imbue you with Jena's knowledge-"

"I know, ma'am."

"I sometimes think the lot of you are *trying* to give me a heart attack." Larani fell into her chair, forcing out a deep breath. When Melissa opened her eyes, the other woman was watching her intently. "You've proven yourself to be more than capable. Frankly, we *need* Keepers like you."

"Ma'am?"

A warm smile blossomed on Larani's face, and she shook her head slowly. "No, my dear, I'm not promoting you," she said. "You've got a lot to learn before you're ready for that, but I *am* willing to let you go on certain field missions."

Melissa hopped out of the chair, standing up before she realized just what she was doing. God help her, how did one respond to something like that? Words tumbled through her mind, but she found the courage to open her mouth.

Larani raised a single finger, cutting Melissa off before she could utter one syllable. "Provided, of course, that you are properly supervised."

"Yes, ma'am."

Reclining in her chair with elbows on the armrests, Larani steepled her fingers and ran her gaze over all three of them. "As for the rest of you," she said softly. "I'm willing to overlook certain past mistakes so long as you are willing to play by the rules."

Laughter from Keli left Melissa with the distinct impression that this conversation wasn't going to go well. The telepath lifted her mug and took a sip of tea. "I killed one of Isara's men today," she said. "I could have incapacitated him; I chose not to."

"That isn't what I wanted to-"

"You know my stance, Larani," Keli went on. "This is war. In war, you seek to win. I will gladly work with you because I recognize Grecken Slade's underlings for the threat that they really are, but I will do it my way."

In one smooth motion, the telepath stood and set her empty cup down on the desk. She straightened her back and managed to look very much like a teacher lecturing one of her students. "If you have a problem with that," she said, "I suggest you think deeply on it. Because I'm going after Slade's people with or without you, and you may just want to be in a position where you can keep an eye on me."

Keli turned and walked out of the room with the grace of a woman in the finest ball gown. She paused at the door. "I know what you're thinking, Larani," she said. "And no, I *don't* need my talent to manipulate you."

Melissa shivered when she was gone.

"And you?" Larani asked, turning to Ben.

He stood up with his arms hanging limp, frowning down at himself. "No," he said, shaking his head. "I don't think so. Put me in for whatever citations you like, but this was the last time I put my life on the line."

"Tanaben, you-"

Ben threw his head back, blinking at the ceiling. "Keli's right!" he snapped. "You *won't* let me do things my way. I developed technology to give myself a fighting chance against Keepers, and what did you do?"

Larani's mouth dropped open, and she shuddered as she took in a deep breath. "I understand your frustration, Tanaben."

Red-faced and fuming, Ben stepped forward and glared at her as if he thought he could split her head open by sheer force of will. "You threw me in prison!" he growled. "You took away my weapons."

"Tanaben, please-"

"And it occurs to me," he added. "That the reason is pretty simple. You just cannot handle the thought that an ordinary human being might defeat you through cunning and grit and determination."

What to do? A part of Melissa wanted to play peacemaker, but she had the distinct impression that doing so would only make things worse. Ben was clearly in no mood to be reasonable, and Larani didn't need some first-year cadet fighting her battles for her. But there had to be *something.*

Ben crossed his arms and hunched over, trembling as he let out a sigh. "I worked with you for *months,*" he said in a voice thick with anger. "I risked my life in New York, and you didn't seem to mind me using illegal weapons tech *then.*"

"That was different."

"Why?" he bellowed. "Because you say it was different? It was no less illegal, but you did it then. You are the very picture of hypocrisy, Larani. You're perfectly willing to break the law when *you* deem it necessary, but when *I* deem it necessary – when I deliver weapons to colonists who were being slaughtered, when I choose to get the information we need by any means available – suddenly I become a traitor in your eyes?

"Who made *you* the arbiter of when it's all right to break the law? It's time that we outgrew this idiotic notion that Bonding a symbiont somehow indicates moral superiority. Isara carries a symbiont. Look at her!"

Larani just studied him with wide eyes, and for a moment, it seemed as though she were about to cry. "If that's how you feel..." There was no venom in it, only sadness. "I'm sorry, Tanaben."

He turned away from her, taking a few steps toward the door, and then paused in mid-step. "I'm sorry too," Ben whispered. "I've done everything in my power to protect this planet, and I did it my way."

God, Melissa thought. *This isn't happening.*

"What do I have to show for it?" Ben went on. "A criminal record? A broken heart? My name is anathema to anyone who recognizes me, my chances of finding any kind of respectable career are slim to none...No, I've given enough for my people. They have no right to ask anything more of me."

He stormed out.

A scowl contorted Larani's features, and she let out a breath. "I'm sorry you had to witness that," she said, pressing the heel of one hand to her forehead. "But he has a point, I suppose."

"So what now?" Melissa inquired.

Larani spread her hands over the surface of her desk, bringing up a menu in the SmartGlass. She tapped in a few quick commands, and then the holographic projectors began to hum.

A transparent image of Leyria rippled into existence above the desk: blue oceans and bright green landmasses. It looked very much like Earth, but the continents were all shaped differently. "We tracked Isara's shuttle into orbit," Larani explained.

A single orange dot rose up from the planet's surface and then began to fly around the globe in a tight circle. It traveled only a few inches before it flickered and vanished. "Two phoenix class cruisers converged on the shuttle," Larani said. "They destroyed it."

Squeezing her eyes shut, Melissa nodded once. "So she's dead then." Tension that she hadn't even noticed a few moments ago began to drain from her body. "Well...That's one less thing to worry about."

"I wish it were that simple," Larani said. "The ships that fired upon Isara's shuttle both detected a vibration in SlipSpace mere seconds before the shuttle's destruction. The most likely explanation is the use of a SlipGate."

"The pilot escaped," Melissa murmured.

"And any passengers as well."

Melissa practically fell back into the chair she had vacated, setting elbows on her knees and lacing fingers over the top of her head. "She's alive." The words came out as a breathy whisper. "Of course, she's alive."

"You don't sound surprised."

"Would Jena go down so easily?"

Larani's mouth tightened, and she turned her head to stare at the wall. "No," she answered. "No, I suppose she wouldn't."

No, Jena would not go down so easily; in fact, Jena would have planned on her shuttle being destroyed. She would have used the shuttle as a way to fake her own death while planning to escape by SlipGate the whole time. "Can you track her?" Melissa asked. "Is there any way to find out where she went?"

"I'm afraid not," Larani said. "There are thousands of SlipGates on this planet, and we already know that Slade's people have kept Gates in reserve, activating them only for a few moments when they need to make a quick escape and then deactivating them again. I've asked Anna to run a search algorithm for any Gates that were active at the moment when Isara's shuttle was destroyed; so far, she's found nothing."

"So, after all that, we have nothing."

"It seems that way," Larani mumbled. "Isara could be anywhere on this planet."

The rectangular sheet of SmartGlass on the wall across from the foot of Harry's bed displayed a news report that he didn't really want to watch. Some kid with a pale face and red hair that he wore slicked back stared dead-pan into the camera as he enunciated the latest take on Isara's attack.

Harry wasn't interested; it had been three days of nothing *but* news coverage that analyzed the event from every possible angle, three days of reminders that his daughter had thrown herself into danger and come through it better than he had.

In a green hospital gown that still smelled of laundry detergent, Harry sat against the inclined mattress of his bed. His graying hair was a mess, and there was stubble along his jawline – shaving was no easy task at the moment – but the worst part of it all was the pain in his chest.

The doctors said he was doing well, that he would make a full recovery, but after nearly four days of this, he had redefined his concept of hell. But then, that was what he got for going up against two Keepers.

Two Keepers.

Melissa appeared in his doorway in a yellow dress with short sleeves and a round neckline. Her hair was left loose, falling over her shoulders. "Dad?" she said. "How are you feeling today?"

Harry shut his eyes tight, ignoring the pain. "Surviving," he muttered, trying his best to avoid moving too much. "Still feels like I've got a sword sticking out of my chest, but I'll live."

Melissa stepped aside to reveal Claire standing in the hallway in flip-flops, denim shorts and a white t-shirt. Her hair was done up in twin braids that were tied up with red elastics. The girl looked uneasy, her big eyes glistening when she saw him. "Dad," she said, running into the room.

"Hey, kiddo."

"Are you all right?"

Pressing a hand to his chest, Harry shut his eyes as he tried to sit up. He flopped back down onto the mattress. "I'll be okay," he wheezed. "The doctors say I'll be ready to go home in another week."

"Oh...Good..."

Claire had been to visit him several times, but he had slept through two of those, and the girl was understandably uneasy. She puttered about at the side of his bed, and his heart broke for her. Claire liked to put on a facade of casual indifference to pretty much everything around her, but she was still just a kid. Still hit hard by all the things that kids weren't ready to deal with.

"I thought..." Melissa said, stepping forward with a plastic container in both hands. "Well, I thought we could have some cupcakes and maybe spend some time together."

Harry felt a grin stretch across his face, trembling with soft laughter. That brought him pain, but it was worth it. "Of course we can," he murmured. "Come here. I want to hear everything that happened today."

His eldest sat in the chair next to his bed, lifting the lid of her container to retrieve a chocolate cupcake with green frosting. "There's not much to tell," she replied, setting it on the table next to his bed.

"Has Anna been taking care of you two?"

Melissa blushed as she smiled into her lap, no doubt feeling anxious about the fact that he hadn't yet lectured her on the idiocy of going after one of the most vicious women in the galaxy on her own. He had no intention of doing that. Not after what he had done. "Yeah, she's great," Melissa said. "Like the big sister we never had."

"Or wanted," Claire added.

Glaring at her younger sister, Melissa pursed her lips and shook her head. "Anna thought that we'd want a little time alone with you," she explained. "She's waiting for us in her office."

Turning his head toward Claire, Harry closed his eyes as his cheek sank into the pillow. "Did you tell your sister that you're proud of her?" he choked out. "She was very brave when she saved those people."

Claire stood beside his bed with arms crossed, frowning down at the floor. "It's not that impressive," she muttered. "She just beat up Jena's evil clone. I heard Ben and Keli did most of the work."

"Claire..."

The girl looked up at the ceiling and rolled her eyes. "Okay, okay," she snapped. "I *am* proud of you, Melissa."

On the other side of the bed, Melissa sat primly with her

hands in her lap, her eyes downcast. "That's okay, Claire." It was barely audible. God help him, his daughter was still a little shy. After all the praise and accolades...Well, if fame hadn't cured Jack of his self-loathing, Harry supposed there was no reason it would change Melissa.

"Come here," Harry whispered.

Claire crawled up on the bed on his left side, snuggling up next to him and putting her head on his chest. "I'm sorry," she murmured. "It's just...If you two keep going off to fight the bad guys, one of these days, you're not gonna come back."

Harry pinched Claire's nose, and she squealed, slapping his hand away. "Stop it!" she said, though her giggles made it clear she wasn't all that upset. "That wasn't fair. I'm trying to have a serious discussion."

Well...There it was.

Kids grew up way too fast.

"I will always come back for you," Harry replied in a rasping voice. He kissed his youngest daughter's forehead. "Always."

He stretched a hand out toward Melissa, and the girl rose from her chair, leaning over the bed so that he could wrap her in a hug. "No matter what happens," he went on, "we will *always* be a family."

Harry managed to sit up just long enough to press his lips to his eldest daughter's forehead, and exhaustion took over again. "I'm proud of you," he whispered. "Melissa, you've grown up to become the kind of officer every lieutenant dreams of having in his department."

"Really?"

"Really."

Melissa stood up straight with tears glistening on her cheeks, then turned her head so that he wouldn't see. Too late, but he wasn't going to draw attention to it. "Thanks," she said. "So...Um...Is there anything good on TV?"

"Oh sure, plenty!" Harry exclaimed. "There's Denabrian

World News's exclusive interview with Melissa Carlson, HistoryLink's profile of Melissa Carlson, the Unedited Biography of-"

"Okay, okay!" Melissa said. "There must be something else."

"Something *interesting*," Claire added.

"Well," Harry suggested, "I've been in here a few days, and I've had plenty of time to peruse the options. Ever heard of Vaylia? They're a media company that specializes in family-friendly entertainment."

Claire propped herself up on her elbow and leaned her cheek against the palm of her hand. "Like Leyria's version of Disney," she said. "Ralita's seen pretty much every one of their movies."

"Yeah," Harry said. "I was thinking *Elephant House*. What do you think?"

The girls agreed, and pretty soon, Claire was snuggled up with him again. Melissa sat next to the bed, holding his hand as they settled in for a film about an adorable big-eyed elephant who sets out on an adventure. It was a moment of happiness, a break from all the pain they had endured lately. It wouldn't last, of course; new problems would arise, new struggles that pushed them to their limits, but for the moment, they were a family, and everything was right with the world.

30

A blue sky with thin, wispy clouds stretched on over a fountain that sprayed water into the air. People had gathered in the grass that surrounded that fountain: reporters with camera drones that floated over their shoulders, political aides who shuffled about and, of course, the odd spectator.

A man in gray pants and a blue jacket with silver trim along its high collar stood before them all, the centre of attention. Square-jawed and stern, Jeral Dusep surveyed the crowd before speaking. “Please...Please,” he said to quiet the hum of voices. “I know that we are all grieving.”

Turning slightly, he gestured to the fountain behind him while keeping his eyes fixed upon his audience. “Five days ago, this place was the site of a tragedy.” Murmurs rose up in response to that. “A tragedy perpetrated by those in whom we had placed our deepest trust, those who should have protected us.”

At the back of the crowd, Larani stood in black clothing despite the hot sun. Pants, shirt and a jacket with a high collar: all black. It seemed appropriate in light of what had happened here.

She was nervous.

Jack was next to her in his usual ensemble of Earth clothing, standing with arms folded and a frown on his face. “Big with the pandering, isn't he?” the young man asked. Larani said nothing.

Dusep faced the crowd with hands clasped in front of himself, his face as smooth as the finest porcelain. “It must have raised questions for you,” he said. “It certainly raised a few questions for me.”

One of the reporters started speaking.

Dusep shut his eyes, bowing his head to the man. “Please,” he said with one arm outstretched to forestall any interruptions. “I will be happy to answer any questions, but let me share my concerns.”

The man looked up, and his dark eyes were like augers, seemingly fixed directly on Larani. “For centuries, we have placed our trust in the Justice Keepers,” he said. “Under the belief that the Nassai choose only the best and brightest among us.”

Already, Larani could feel her stomach turning. Sooner or later, something like this was bound to happen. There had been incidents of Slade's cronies misusing the powers granted by their corrupted symbionts before, but most of those had taken place on Earth. Earth was lightyears away, barely a blip in the local news. If Earthers distrusted the Justice Keepers, well... Earthers distrusted a lot of things that were in their best interests.

Even the incident at the university – while noteworthy – was still vague enough for people to be unsure of exactly what had gone on. One of the Sons of Savard had attacked the student body: that much was certain. But Isara's role. Did people really see her Bend bullets away from her body? Could she have simply been a woman who had enhanced her physical abilities with

Amps? The pundits had been debating that one for the better part of two weeks, and Larani had been content to let them. But this...There was simply no denying what had happened here.

"Deadly violence unleashed by three Justice Keepers," Dusep said. "A massacre, the likes of which have not been seen in our fair city – on our *planet* – for decades at the very least. And who was the ring-leader of this little band of terrorists? None other than Director Jena Morane, one of our world's most decorated Keepers."

Anxiety turned to rage, turned to cold venom in Larani's veins. The man was lying through his teeth, and he knew it!

"Oh, Larani Tal will tell you that this was not the *real* Jena Morane." The wolfish grin on Dusep's face made several people laugh and several more step back instinctively. "She's a clone. Or, wait, no...Apparently, the Jena we knew was the clone. It's all so very convoluted. Tell me something: are we prone to such conspiracy theories?"

"No!" several people shouted.

He had them eating out of the palm of his hand. It wasn't hard to sense the mood of the crowd, and people were getting restless. What was Dusep's game in this? Larani tried without success to guess at his motive. Why was the man who consistently spoke out on the need for stronger security measures suddenly turning against the Keepers?

The naive part of her wanted to believe that he was simply outraged and directing his fury at the nearest available target. A *reasonable* target, if she was honest with herself. But that sort of emotional reaction wasn't in Dusep's nature. The man was a pragmatist, first and foremost.

So, what did he gain from this?

Stepping forward, Dusep thrust out his chin and ran his gaze across the assembled spectators. "I think it's time we asked ourselves some hard questions," he said. "I think it's time we challenged the false belief that Nassai choose only the best and brightest among us."

Bleakness take him...

"The Justice Keepers need to be held to a higher standard of accountability," Dusep went on. "It's clear that we need greater oversight. For that reason and many others, I am officially declaring my candidacy for the office of Prime Council."

Applause from the spectators was accompanied by a few whistles.

Crossing her arms, Larani let her head droop. "It's beginning," she said, shifting uncomfortably on the spot. "I knew that he would make a grab for power sooner or later, but I never expected this."

Jack was at her side with his hands gripping the fabric of his t-shirt, biting his lip as he stared down at the ground. "Classic fascism playbook," he said. "Make your audience angry and then give them a target."

"Every time someone says 'it could never happen here...' "

"You think it's gonna escalate?"

"I think that it's a good thing Grecken Slade is dead," Larani replied. "Because if he were here, this would be *exactly* what he wanted."

Isara stepped out of the bedroom in her small cabin to find fat raindrops pelting the living room window. Water cascaded over the glass in sheets, making it nearly impossible to see the thick forest of pine trees beyond.

A crackling fire filled the room with the scent of wood smoke and offered enough warmth to drive away the chill such a deluge would inevitably bring. This far north, even late spring could bring unpleasant weather.

Two chairs were positioned side by side at the window with their backs to her, and somehow, she knew that one was occupied. The half-finished glass of water on the table between them was *one* clue, but really, she could have sensed this man's presence even if she were deaf and blind.

Isara wrinkled her nose, then shook her head in irritation. “Come to check on me?” she asked, striding across the room. “You should know I have the situation well in hand. The Inzari will be pleased.”

As she rounded his chair, she found Grecken Slade sitting with a blank expression on his face, staring vacantly through the window. The man looked just as handsome as he always did with smooth skin, tilted eyes and black hair that fell past the small of his back. “I am aware of your progress.”

“And your assessment?”

A cruel, mocking smile was Slade's response, but he never took his eyes off the storm outside. “You've done surprisingly well with limited resources,” he said. “I admit, the incident in the park was...quite inspired.”

“You wanted discord.”

“I did indeed.”

Isara stood next to his chair with arms folded, unable to find the will to look up. Of course, the heat in her face wasn't helping matters. “The seed has been planted,” she said, defending herself despite the fact that Slade had offered praise. “It won't be long before everyone is wondering if they can trust the Justice Keepers.”

“Yes.”

“Which begs the question...What happens next?”

Grecken Slade sat with his elbows on the armrests of his chair, peering through steepled fingers at the window. “Why, I should think that would be obvious,” he replied. “We begin the next phase of our plan.”

The End of the Sixth Book of the Justice Keepers Saga.

Dear reader,

We hope you enjoyed reading *Dirty Mirror*. Please take a moment to leave a review, even if it's a short one. Your opinion is important to us.

The story continues in *Severed Bonds*. Read the first chapter for free at https://www.nextchapter.pub/books/severed-bonds

Discover more books by R.S. Penney at https://www.nextchapter.pub/authors/ontario-author-rs-penney.

Can't get enough of the Justice Keepers Saga? Visit Rich's Patreon for more exclusive content at https://www.patreon.com/richpenney.

Want to know when one of our books is free or discounted? Join the newsletter at http://eepurl.com/bqqB3H.

Best regards,

R.S. Penney and the Next Chapter Team

ABOUT THE AUTHOR

Richard S. Penney is a science-fiction author and futurist from Southern Ontario. He graduated from McMaster University with a degree in mathematics and statistics. Rich knew that he wanted to be a writer ever since he was a child, when he would act out complex stories with his action figures.

He has worked in a number of different fields, including banking, teaching and software QA.

In 2014, Rich published his first novel, *Symbiosis,* the first volume of the Justice Keepers Saga. The story was one that he had been planning to write ever since he was a teenager. The Desa Kincaid novels grew out of a tandem story that Rich started on Theoryland.com, a Wheel of Time discussion site.

Rich has been an environmental activist since his early twenties, and he has given talks on sustainability in Greece and Australia.

CONTACT THE AUTHOR

Follow me on Twitter @Rich_Penney
E-mail me at keeperssaga@gmail.com
You can check out my blog at rspenney.com
You can also visit the Justice Keepers Facebook page
https://www.facebook.com/keeperssaga
Questions, comments and theories are welcome.

BOOKS BY R.S. PENNEY

Symbiosis (Justice Keepers Saga I)

Friction (Justice Keepers Saga II)

Entanglement (Justice Keepers Saga III)

Relativity (Justice Keepers Saga IV)

Evolution (Justice Keepers Saga V)

Dirty Mirror (Justice Keepers Saga VI)

Severed Bonds (Justice Keepers Saga VII)

Dark Designs

Desa Kincaid: Bounty Hunter

Dirty Mirror
ISBN: 978-4-86750-426-0

Published by
Next Chapter
1-60-20 Minami-Otsuka
170-0005 Toshima-Ku, Tokyo
+818035793528

20th June 2021